CW01432047

Stuck with Tuck

Crave & Cure Productions
Book 1

Daisy Jane

Copyright © 2023 by Daisy Jane

All rights reserved.

No part of this book may be reproduced in any form or by any electronic or mechanical means, including information storage and retrieval systems, without written permission from the author, except for the use of brief quotations in a book review.

The story, all names, characters, and incidents portrayed in this book are fictitious. No identification with actual persons (living or deceased), places, buildings, and products is intended or should be inferred.

Cover Photo | Wander Aguilar

Editing | Laura Davies

❀ Created with Vellum

Author's Note

Stuck with Tuck is a story about a male adult film star who is actively working. This book has multiple scenes where the hero, Tucker, is having sexual relations and/or intercourse with women and men who are NOT the heroine.

There are no emotional attachments between Tucker and the other film actors, men or women. It is purely intercourse as a job. With that said, if reading a story where the hero is with another partner is something you can't stomach, please carefully consider whether you read this book. It may not work for you, and that's okay.

Again, your hero only has **feelings** for the heroine, and there is no other man (OM) or other woman (OW) drama at all. But **he does have intercourse with other people in this book**, while pursuing the heroine.

Please consider this information before reading.

Dedication

For the people with open minds.
For those who never yuck others' yums.
For everyone who says "I'll give it a try" instead of "ehh, no thanks."
For the lovers, not the haters.
This one's for you.

Foreword

At the end of your life, you'll never say
"I wish I would have tried less things."

Prologue

Vienna

The most delicious dick I've ever seen.

...TWO AND A HALF YEARS AGO
"That's some *Gilmore Girls* fantasy you're living in," Darren teases through a nasal snort. I glare at him. I'm mad at myself, but projecting is my specialty.

"Oh, *excuse me* for hoping my roommate could be my friend!" I dramatically flop across my bed, draping my arm over my eyes. "It's not like I expected us to be best friends or anything. I mean, no one can compete with you," I say, a cross between teasing and honesty. He'll always be my bestie, but I'd love to not be frenemies with my roomie, too. "I just, I don't know, wasn't expecting her to be–"

"A complete and total bitch?" My best friend deadpans and it's the straight-laced infusion of reality I need to crack the tension. I can't help but laugh.

"Yeah," I agree, "kinda."

Darren takes a seat next to me and my body slides toward him on the mattress, so I sit up. He claps a hand over my back.

"Listen, you know how people like Madeline are. Everyone is their competition. And if you're not someone she's competing against, you're a stepping stone. It's a *her* thing, not a *you* thing," he declares, surprising me with reassurance. Darren only tries to assuage my hurt feelings if it's dire, so when he doesn't come in hot with a speech, I know I'm probably overreacting. He always says, 'Sympathetic Darren is for special occasions only, when it's a real problem.'

"If anything," he continues. "Take it as a compliment. She's this way because she's threatened by literally everything and everyone. Which includes *you*."

I arch a skeptical brow. "You're so sure?"

He shrugs. "Don't overthink it. It's her. It's how she is. I saw it in the first thirty seconds."

I shrug and reach for my Diet Coke, taking a long drink, the searing burn of carbonation making my eyes fill. "Still. Starting a postgrad degree without my parents' support *and* having a shitty new roommate. I'm just getting *this was a mistake* vibes." I give a little *woe is me* sigh.

Darren knocks his shoulder to mine and with his most sarcastic tone asks, "Thought she was gonna be Monica Gellar and you were gonna bumble in here as Rachel Green and strike up the world's bestiest best friendship?"

My cheeks burn. "No," I quip, despite the fact that *yes*, I did kind of envision that. So what? Doesn't every woman long for that in a roommate? The Monica and Rachel relationship? "And *bestiest* isn't a word. And quit mixing references. You should stick with *Friends*, you know I couldn't get into *Gilmore Girls*."

I hear the front door close. Now that my evil roommate has

left, we move from my bedroom to the living space, both of us sinking down into the lush new couch. I don't know that it's new, not for sure, but it's suspiciously clean and smells like something that just got plastic torn off of it.

"You should try rewatching it now, you know, with the ability to recognize it's not supposed to be real but... entertaining." He grabs the soda from me and takes a sip. "Then we can watch the reboot together." He wiggles his brows, but I'm not sold.

"Because Samson doesn't want to watch it with you, not because you *want* to watch it with me." I fold my arms over my chest and blink at him accusingly. "We've been friends long enough for me to know I'm being manipulated."

But if I had a boyfriend as gorgeous as Samson I likely wouldn't spend a second of our time together watching reruns either. Equally, I'd probably ditch my bestie the way Darren does to me. I can't really blame him, Samson is older, established, and traditionally handsome.

I'd ditch Darren's ass as often as I could, too. No blame.

Darren rolls his eyes. "Back to *Matilda*."

"*Madeline*," I correct, meeting Darren's smug smirk with one of my own.

"Like the cool little French girl in the children's books." I shake my head, my body being pleasantly engulfed by the glorious new, overstuffed couch. "God, she even has a better name than me. I always wanted to be Madeline as a little girl."

Darren looks at me as if I've suddenly spoken in a foreign language. "Get a grip, Vienna. Who cares if she's named after some stupid kids book. You've wandered off from justifiable annoyance into petty whining. Wind your neck in."

"It's not a stupid kids book. It's a complete series and every little girl wanted to have Madeline's hat at some point." I smack the couch. "And look, her parents not only support her in staying in art school, but probably furnished this entire apartment."

Darren gets to his feet, grabs my wrists, and pulls me to my feet. "Listen, you may have shitty parents who only care about appearances, and you're not getting the fun TV roommate, sorry, but you need to get a grip," he declares, eyes wide. "You don't care about Madeline. You're nervous about the Institute, and you're worrying in advance about life after graduation in three years. You're utterly terrified your parents will get their glorious, juicy 'I told you so' and you're tripping. For Christ's sake, leave queen bitch Madeline out of it." He glances at the couch, then back to me. "And be happy her parents love and spoil her. Reap the benefits, get through your masters, and enjoy it, okay? Because snarky and sulky is *not* your vibe." He winks and cocks his hip at me. "Quite frankly you just can't pull it off like I can."

I don't like what he said but he knows me and he's absolutely right. Both of us fall easily into the cloud of a couch again and proceed to stare at the wall stretched before us. I run my hand along the lush fabric.

I hate that this apartment feels like hers because she's been living here for a few weeks already. How she got the key early, I'm not sure, but rather than waiting to see what her roomie wanted, the woman decorated. Like, ceiling to floor.

Yes I'm being petty, but it's hard not feeling at ease in your own home. I've spent over two decades being an inconvenient disappointment to my parents and now I'm in for another three years of co-habitual contempt. *Joy.*

I narrow my eyes at the thick white slab of molding tracing the perimeter of the apartment. "I'm pretty sure she had that crown molding installed."

Darren smooths a palm over the luxury we're flopped on. "The Carnegie's would actually approve of that," he quips.

"Right. They'd rather have me live in a place with crown molding and a chandelier,"—I wave my hand up at the literal chandelier hanging from a popcorn ceiling where I'm sure a crappy thirty-dollar mounted light once was—"than be living with someone who actually likes me."

Darren blinks down at me. "I gotta say, I think I'd choose a nice apartment over being buddies with my roommate, too."

I smack him in the chest playfully, and he rubs the spot as if I've actually caused him pain. So dramatic.

"First, ease off the protein drinks because... oww." More dramatic rubbing. "Second, did you hear me? Don't fixate on Madeline. I'm telling you, you're worried about school and post-grad life. That's all it is. Stress and nerves."

I roll my eyes because *of course I know that's why I'm freaking out*. As if this hasn't been on my mind since the first day of art school. It has. It's all I've thought of. And I kept reassuring myself that *'by post grad, I'll definitely know what I want to do'* and yet, here I am, no clue what I'm going to use this masters for.

Because of that, and because my debt is now reaching unfathomable depths, I choose to focus on rude, snotty Madeline and her pretentious storybook name.

Her name that I love, dammit.

"Is it too much to ask that after Bitchy McBitchface ignored me, gave me the small room and didn't even ask me what appliances I was bringing with me, that you back me up? Just once?"

I motion to the Rubbermaid tub on the floor, with my sad pink toaster and matching single-serve blender peeking out. "What am I supposed to do with this stuff now? If she'd responded to my email or texts and given me more than thirty seconds of side eye, I'd know what to do. But I don't know what to do, Darren, and I just wanted you to make me feel better! Not tell me the truth!"

He leans forward, bracing his palms on his knees then rises. "Don't melt down over a box of shitty appliances, Vienna. This isn't freshman year. Just toss them. Fuck," he kicks the box, and the slider button from the toaster pops off, skittering across the laminate floor. "See? Trash."

"I got that toaster at Target when I moved! It was the first house item I ever bought." I blink, and hate that my eyes are getting misty.

I can always count on Darren not to let me look like an asshole. Even when no one's watching.

"Jesus Christ, Vienna. Do not cry over a twelve dollar Room Essentials toaster." He dips to meet my eyes. "Are you okay? I mean, what's going on?"

Ugly sobs wrack my chest, seemingly out of nowhere, but fuel to the fire is obviously being asked if I'm okay. Everyone knows, if there's even so much as one single tear in your eyeball, being asked if you're okay will make it multiply immediately. That's fact.

"Is it your parents? They'll get over it, Vienna. And one day, I'm sure they'll cut you a fat check for all the shit they were wrong about."

I shake my head. My post-grad degree is three years, and while I'm only starting my first, most students go into this with something already lined up. An internship or something but because I have no connections and went to a state school, I'm starting my masters without any idea of where I want to end up and it makes me beyond nervous. Because my parents expect me to fail, and I have to prove them wrong. I've come to terms with the fact that they think pursuing art is a waste of time. I got through undergrad believing with my whole heart that they were wrong.

But at age twenty-three, with three long years ahead of me, a bitchy roommate and no clue what I want to specialize in or pursue as a career, I'm beginning to think they may've been right.

"I'm never going to get a job with the art degree I have let alone crippling myself financially with another one!" I sob, grabbing a chenille throw blanket from the corner of the sofa. It's new, too, and still smells like department store shelves. I wipe my nose with it.

"So I *was* right," Darren says with a fatigued sigh. "You'll find something. You have three years to find something, V, so quit spinning," he says, but again, Darren doesn't bullshit me. And the fact he's not saying it with more certainty makes the permanent boulder in my gut sink just a bit lower.

Still wiping away my tears, I say, "I just... I thought by now I'd have an idea, some connections, a lead on a potential job. You know? Only, all I have is more debt, and I'm not even sure where to start!"

Darren rubs my back. "You could always teach art, you know. My mother–"

"No," I say, angered by the thought of pursuing my love, my craft, my everything... only to teach it to students that are taking it to meet a graduation requirement.

Frustration and fear consume me at the mere thought of it.

He sighs, but doesn't let me linger in my self-loathing. Retrieving my phone from the brand new coffee table, he holds it out for me to see. "You have Free Form Sketch in thirty, and you most definitely need to... *get fixed up a little.*" After wrinkling his nose to let me know I am apparently a swamp monster, he hooks a thumb over his shoulder. "I'm going to go. Get it together woman, strap on a set of ovaries, you're going to crush your courses and get a cool job and your awful parents will choke on their shitty words."

I smile. "Thank you."

He winks. "Whatever, text me later."

A fter spilling coffee down my blouse then snapping my graphite, I get stuck sitting next to *Madeline* in Free Form Sketch.

I'm *really* over this day.

The professor gives a QR code for the syllabus and all other information we may need, saving us the wasted fifteen minutes of him reading it off.

We dive right into our first in-class assignment about line and discovery. I think the professor has said the words "line and discovery" so many times that they've truly lost all meaning.

Seriously.

I'm on the cusp of feeling insulted at how basic this class is starting off when a sea of murmurs wash through the small space consisting of only 15 easels.

Even Madeline is intrigued, her spine elongates as she peers around her easel to the front of the room. She looks like a cat feigning indifference at a treat they secretly want to devour.

I'm more a dog girl, myself.

"What is it?" I ask, but of course she ignores me. I glare at the back of her overly coiffured head, with her perfect honey colored chignon, staring daggers at her shitty manners when my attention is grabbed by the professor, who begins speaking.

"The life model is going to stay masked. Don't humanize him. Focus on the lines of his physique."

Oh, the model is here. Maybe some of these people have changed their focus mid-term, and they're new to seeing nude models. I've seen tons. Probably over fifty by now, honestly. It's nothing to me anymore. Truly just an object to model lines after.

Madeline adjusts her easel, and *he* comes into focus.

The figure model who, even with a mask covering his face, is awe-inspiring. He steps onto the makeshift stage in a white robe and part of me wonders if he comes to campus in a white robe? How weird would that be? Who is he, Hugh Hefner? But then I spot a small duffle bag on the ground, blue jeans poking out from the unzipped top.

The thud of thick cotton hitting the floor makes heads swivel from our easels, and another wave of hums ripple through the room.

This model is like The Vitruvian Man. Rippled, muscled, chiseled... shit, I'm insta-wet. From behind me, someone whispers, "Did he hop out of the window of an Abercrombie and Fitch store or what?" and I nod along with that because yeah, that's exactly what he looks like. I close my mouth and wipe my lips in a discreet drool check, and wonder what he's thinking about. Then I catch his eyes and *holy shit*— he's looking *at me.*

"*Ohh-kay,*" I breathe aloud. His mask torques, and the corner of his eyes lift and I realize hot Abercrombie guy is smiling... at me.

Then, before I can catch myself, my eyes drop and my gaze is halted by his dick. His naked, soft, thick, long dick, might I add.

Realizing I just took a dick-check glance for zero artistic purpose, I look back into his eyes to find him watching me, crows feet telling me he's still grinning.

"Oh god," I murmur, ducking behind my easel in complete embarrassment. I'm acting like this is my first sketch class with a figure model and it's not. I've done an entire four years of undergraduate art, damnit. I shake my head, trying to ditch my humiliation even though my skin feels like the surface of the freaking sun.

Taking a deep breath, I shake it off, and hold my graphite to the paper. *You gotta pull yourself together. Day one of class cannot be a failure.*

I peer around the canvas and—*fuck.* My belly flutters something fierce and I'm rendered motionless and overwhelmed by a heady need in my core. The hot faceless model with the huge dick is *still* looking at me.

I smile a tiny bit and begin my sketch.

And while I'm sketching his pecs, I'm thinking of that thing between his thighs.

And while I'm shading his hair, I'm thinking of... *that thing between his thighs.*

And while I'm detailing the shape of his thick quads, I'm thinking of—you get the picture.

Oh, and I'm thinking of his balls. They're so... they are a *healthy* size. Whatever that means. Out of nowhere, there's a cough lodged in my throat.

I swallow thickly, pretending that I'm not insanely fucking wet and bothered.

"We will be using Mr. Eliot for the duration of the semester," the professor begins and my arm stiffens. I'm completely thrown by this information.

This guy? The entire semester? I'll never fucking pass this class with this thirst trap *king* five feet away. I've been single for too long. I'm too emotionally vulnerable. I'll do something stupid like try to have sex with him. Or worse, *fall in love.*

A smile curls my lips as my hand skims the length of my white paper. A sinful idea stirs and moves through me, compels me, and pretty soon, I'm done and everyone else is still sketching. I lean back, and enjoy my masterpiece. Because—make no mistake—it *is* a masterpiece.

Just a *very* inappropriate masterpiece. One that doesn't scream "*getting my masters and starting my respectable art career next*" but rather, "*fuck me with that third leg of yours, mister perfect specimen.*" Yeah, not the vibe I'm going for as I edge into the most stressful few years of school.

I pick up my pencil, sign my name to the bottom corner, then promptly crush the paper between my hands, making sure it's more crumpled than my bean burrito wrapper after a Taco Bell bender. I toss it in the trash, grab my pencils from the trough of the easel, stuff them in my bag, and slip out like the guilty, dirty little artist that I am, apparently.

Because I *cannot* last another minute around that man without spontaneously orgasming, much less sketch him for an *entire* semester.

Walking through the hall, I dig my phone from my pocket and pull open the student user dashboard and promptly click "add/drop class."

A moment later, it's done.

And I can focus on school and not worry about being distracted by the most delicious dick I've ever seen.

1

Tucker

The archangel of porn.

"That's my good girl. Now open a little wider for me, baby," I rasp, knowing the words so well they've nearly lost meaning. It's common dialogue we run in many scripts, but I'd like to think I deliver it a little differently each time.

Today, I'm with Uma. Uma Ryder, one of the leading film stars at Crave & Cure. *One of.* Not the top.

Because the top actor at C&C Productions is *yours truly.*

Tucker Deep.

But Uma is great, and when I work with her, I play to her strengths, tapering my dialogue or altering my dominance to compliment her. She's the star, after all. I may be the top in the industry, and what I do is *absolutely* work, but the women in this business work so much fucking harder and always have to give so much more. They deserve to shine in every scene.

Uma makes a beautiful submissive. She glows when she's on her knees serving. It's truly a role I believe she is meant to play or fill in some capacity in her life. To compliment her natural strengths, in scenes I act as a soft dominant, nurturing her desire and—her limit—not getting too rough.

I thrust my hips into her face and spear her throat. She can't take all of me. Only a few of the women here can and a couple of the guys.

Even without taking every inch, she's still fucking phenomenal. Knowing I've reached her limit, I slow, and trace the corner of her mouth with my thumb. Catching her eyes, I give a tiny nod. Imperceptible to the future viewers, but everyone in this room knows what I'm doing.

I'm *making sure.*

Of what?

Of fucking everything. That she wants to keep going, that she's okay, that this position is comfortable, that she isn't nearing her limit, that she's happy, that she's feeling sane, *everything.*

It's how we make movies here. Based on consent and realness, championing the important things versus fetishizing the sensational. Trying to make everyday sex a thing to be proud of, to set the standard, while also making kinky sex a normal thing to take part in.

Honoring the mental and emotional headspace of your partner is a must.

When we're in a scene, Crave & Cure urges us to treat our co-star (or *co-stars*) with the same respect and care you'd give someone you're in a relationship with. It's the only time in our work that we're more than co-workers. We're a sliver beyond co-stars and co-workers, in the name of creating responsible art.

I nod again letting her know that I'm okay too, then Uma nods, eyes welling. I loop my hand around her neck. In and out,

I pump my hips, my eyes heavy and my mind weightless at the tight clutch of her throat all around me.

She lets me fuck her like that for a few minutes maybe, and then I flip her onto all fours. I drag her mouth to mine, leaning over her shoulder, and whisper, "Tell me."

She understands the meaning. "Yes, I'm ready to be a good girl for you."

From behind me, I grab the gold foil package and tear it open. Quickly, I roll it on and slip inside of her swollen pussy, groaning at her heat. Uma uses lube warmer and fills herself with heated lube before each scene. It's her preference for comfort, but also depending how many takes are needed - it's just convenient.

At first it felt weird and made me feel like I needed to pee, but now, I'm comfortable. It reminds me of her. And I like Uma. She's fucking awesome and a good friend.

And it's super fucking sleazy to comment on someone's need to use lubricant. I saw someone get punched in the lip over that once.

He deserved it.

Unless you're the one getting dicked down then you get zero input on preferred lubrication. Heated lubricant isn't my personal preference though; I'm a fan of the cooling ones, especially when I'm getting pegged.

"Ah, can feel how ready you are for me," I breathe, finding a comfortable grip on her hips as I rut into her faster, my strokes gaining momentum. My orgasm is building. "I want you. I've wanted you all night," I groan out, following as close to the script as I normally do. If I get the gist, we're good.

The entire ethos with Crave & Cure Productions is making films that make people feel good about having sex. With that in mind, the dialogue is typically very rudimentary. It's what we *do* with the words that makes the films so powerful. The way

15

we breathe them. How our co-stars lap them up. The way sometimes they're uttered on choked breaths, or in nearly unrecognizable mumbles. The words are written, but they're not performed. They're *felt, experienced* and *lived.*

And that's why Crave & Cure is the top adult film company in America. I flip her back over, loving how easy it is to look into her eyes this way.

"I've wanted you all night, too," Uma moans, peering up at me, her cheeks the color of maraschino cherries. She's so fair, fucking always makes her flush a cocktail of pinks and reds.

Today's scene is... a daddy/babygirl thing.

We were at a holiday party, eyeing each other across the room. Before filming started rolling, Uma argued that *Love Actually* is the best Christmas movie. And does it even matter what my pick is? *Anything* is a better movie than a romance that features a man trying to steal his best friend's wife. I said to Uma, "I love you, but you can get the fuck out of here with that utter trash. No epic Christmas movie features a shady friend like *The Walking Dead* guy."

She stuck her tongue out at me, and I didn't even bring up the fact that Snape's character is a cheat, too. Great Christmas movie, *my ass.* Then she proceeded to tell me that in our scene where we're longing for each other across the crowded living room, her glare will reflect the fact that my taste in movies is trash.

I teased her that my glare will reflect my utter disappointment in not only her movie taste, but that she sets the bar for men so low.

I wink, and give her the tiniest smirk as I grab her wrists and pin them above her head.

"I wanted to cross the room and get to you all night. Every time I caught a glance of you, I got hard. Because you make daddy want bad things, babygirl, *things I can't ignore.*"

I lower my mouth to her ear and make a show of taking a nibble. *"Love Actually* sucks," I whisper so quietly that I'm not even sure she heard me. I pull away and continue fucking her, picking up the pace as the set designer, Cohen, waves an *actual* flag in my peripheral.

The flag is purple with three black letters printed across. VIN. When I came to Crave & Cure and they told me VIN was short for vinegar, and I knew immediately I'd made the right choice. Everything else was so new and intimidating but vinegar—I knew what that meant.

Vinegar strokes are the final tugs before orgasm. The strokes that, no matter what you do or how hard you try to dig your heels in, are without a doubt going to push you over the edge. The flag, then, means *wrap it up.* When they wave the purple VIN flag, I know what to do; *get to the cum-shot already.*

Scenes here are often scheduled down to the minute and they aren't artificially prolonged like at other studios. They pause scenes to reset cameras, re-fluff, or re-lube. Still, our aim is to continuously film from start to finish to retain the realism. In my opinion we end up with a more relatable result.

When I catch her eyes, I see the biting glare and chew the inside of my cheek to keep from laughing.

"I wanted you to look at me, I wanted you to come take me," she whimpers, and though she fully sells those lines with a throaty little moan that makes my dick twitch, her eyes still say *fuck you.*

"I've thought about this too many times. I shouldn't be saying this, but I've always wanted to know what it would be like to fuck you." I increase my speed as the flag waves again. She pulses around me, doing a Kegel to urge me to orgasm. See what I mean? Women work so much harder than men. Doing a Kegel to simulate her orgasm for my cock's benefit is actually written into contracts at some production companies. Seriously.

"I've come in my hand and all over my sheets too many times to the fantasy of filling and fucking you until you can't walk." She tightens around me, panting, slapping at my chest like a woman on the edge.

Her tongue sweeps her top lip, and that's her tell that she *really is* on the edge. She's going to come if I take her there.

Another few pumps between her spread legs and I'm teetering too, lowering my mouth to her throat to leave her flesh pink and marked. After sucking her skin and making her moan, I bring my lips to her ear and tell her again, "If I'm going to watch Alan Rickman be an asshole, I'm going to watch *Die Hard* and bask in him being thrown off a building."

Viewers will think I've said something sweet or hot, because Uma moans in response, her spine rolling. I take her nipple in my mouth and suck as I rut into her again, hard and fast.

She comes, her pussy choking me in rhythmic waves. I topple over, too, driving all the way inside before stilling. My hips jerk as my cock twitches and unloads into the condom.

As my release comes to an end, I crumple and collect Uma against my chest, stroking my fingers through her hair. When Augustus, our fearless and faithful director, shouts cut, Uma pushes against my chest, trying to wriggle away from me.

I hold her tight, grinning down at her. We're both glistening with sweat under these huge lights, and she blinks up at me, panting.

"It just takes place during Christmas time, nothing else gives a Christmas vibe. A bunch of failing relationships that make love look hard is not a warm Christmas vibe, I'm sorry."

"Tucker, I'm not debating this! It's my *opinion!*" Uma

gruffs, and I release her right as she shoves me off, sending me toppling off the tiny bed.

From the floor, I stare up until she peers over, grinning. "Sorry."

I push to my elbows, my eyebrows in my hairline. "Oh I'm sure you are. Do you treat William this way? Push him around when he disagrees?" I cup my elbow in my palm and attempt to scrub away the pain, wincing dramatically as I do. "Poor William."

Uma glares at me. "I don't push William around because he knows *Love Actually* is an amazing movie."

"Tuck," Augustus calls, appearing at the foot of the bed, his hands braced on his hips. His silvering hair looks white under these harsh lights, and with his white button up shirt, he looks almost angelic.

The archangel of porn.

"What's up, Aug?" I get to my feet, and begin rolling down the fully loaded condom. Snatching a tissue from the bedside box, I roll it up and take another to clean myself up. I peer up at Augustus periodically as I do. "Need another take?"

He looks at Uma, hooking his thumb over his shoulder. "Uma, great job. No retakes. We got what we needed. You can head out."

She beams. "No voice over work?"

Sometimes, if we're too muffled in our opening dialogue, Augustus sticks us in the sound booth with the engineer, and makes us redo our lines. For whatever reason, we all hate doing it. In the moment, those lines feel good. Afterward, when you don't have a raging erection and a beautiful naked human being stretched before you and you're in a tiny padded room with a thirty year old guy who you've heard say a total of seven sentences in two years, it's a little weird.

Something about saying *spread your legs and let daddy see*

how he makes you feel while looking into the eyes of a disinterested engineer is just... *not the vibe.*

Augustus shakes his head. He doesn't smile back because Aug rarely smiles. He's very serious and focused and at first I wondered why. I mean, it's porn. Enjoy yourself, you know? Once we started working together, it made sense why Aug is so reserved. Being respected in an industry like ours can be hard (no pun intended), but through his extensive care for every detail and his vision for each film, he's managed to become one of the most respected film makers.

"Not today." He turns to me, done with her. "We have a meeting. Get dressed. Lance will grab you a plate. Come to the conference room when you're ready."

I don't recall seeing a meeting on my schedule today. I think I'd remember that considering we don't have many conference room meetings here at Crave & Cure. Monthly team night is usually at a restaurant, or someone's house, so the conference room meeting for today has me... curious.

With my sweats hanging low on my hips, I toe into some slides and grab a t-shirt from the neatly folded stack in the dressing room. Glancing at my reflection, I feed my hands through my hair, trying to tame some of the post-fuck frizz. A spritz of cologne on my neck so I don't smell like sex, and I'm out the door, heading toward the conference room. The door is shut, which isn't unusual, but what is different is the light is on. Noise is coming from the inside. For some reason, as I'm about to enter, I get a little nervous.

What in the hell is this meeting about?

I tap with my knuckles then push inside, peering at the glass table and the unfamiliar faces settled around it.

A middle-aged man, maybe late forties, wearing what appears to be a very fucking expensive suit. I know what a nice suit looks like now that I own several. His is tailored, making him look that much more important. A well-fitted suit is like the quintessential little black dress for women, I think. He rises, and the younger man at his side rises, too, smiling awkwardly as his eyes drop to the table top.

"There he is! Tucker Deep. Just the man we're here to see," the man in the nice suit says, extending his arm over the table to usher me into my seat.

Augustus and his assistant Lance look up at me. They're sitting next to an open seat and a plate of food sits in front of it. Lance tips his head toward the chair so I step inside and have a seat.

Before my ass is even fully in the leather, Suitman extends a tanned hand to me. "Tucker, so good to finally meet you. I'm here with an opportunity you can't refuse."

Despite the expensive tailoring, Suitman is giving me used car salesmen vibes with this level of ass kissing. He needs to work on his pitch... but he *has* piqued my interest.

21

2

Vienna

Shoulders squared off like Blanche Devereux on a mission.

"Yes, absolutely," Madeline sings into the phone, her overly animated conversation making my skin crawl. Seriously. I recognize that my parents would likely rather perform a synchronized lobotomy on themselves than call and give me moral support on a hard day, but still, this cheery conversation is bordering on creepy.

"Sounds great, Daddy." Her bright blue eyes flick to mine, narrowing with irritation. She's annoyed that I can hear her conversation and will likely accuse me of listening in, despite the fact that we are in our shared kitchen space and I'm simply existing. We've been living together and going to many of the same classes but despite the fact it's been two and a half years, I had her figured out in a month.

Turns out, as painful as it is for me to admit, Darren was

right. Madeline is pretty miserable, which always confuses me because her parents are so supportive—financially and emotionally. She earns great grades, she alleges she's got a job lined up after our last year, and all of our professors dote on her.

It's annoying. It's annoying because she has it all and is still a royal cunt.

I snort to myself, causing my coffee to bubble in my mug. A Royal Cunt. Maybe that should be the theme of my next piece for sculpting. I glance down at the counter where my actual piece for submission is resting in an open Kraft box. Yeah, A Royal Cunt would've probably earned me a better grade than what I did sculpt.

Another sip of coffee and Madeline's ending her phone call, predictably turning to face me the moment her phone is in her bag.

"Next time, I'll put it on speaker, so you can hear *every* detail." She rolls her eyes and steps into my personal space, hooking her finger on the box to peer inside. She laughs, and my stomach bitters at the noise. "This is your first piece? Seriously?"

In sculpting, we have two major submissions. Our entire grade for the class isn't solely based on just these two projects, but this first piece is to earn a grant. The grant is awarded to the most symbolic piece, and I could really use that money to pay down my student debt.

I will never understand why art school costs so much if most artists earn so little.

"Yeah," I say, pretending to be unfazed by her cruelty. She judges everything, but that doesn't make it any easier to swallow when it's directed right at me. "I'm sure yours is much better, Madeline, so just show me."

I'm being sarcastic. Or maybe I'm just tired and resort to

conceding straight out the gate so that I don't have to argue with her. There really is no arguing with Madeline. Perfect Madeline with the shiny blonde hair and bleached smile and her beautiful paintings and perfect sculptures and free art school can *kiss my ass.*

I smile. And the Cheshire grin that spreads her thin lips sends a shiver rolling through my shoulders. Her grin slides down my back like ice water.

Turning her back to me, she rustles around a bit before producing her sculpture. I blink down at it, unsure if what I'm seeing is... *what I'm seeing.* Palms to kneecaps, I crouch and blink at it, then meet her eyes.

"Madeline, is this a... *vagina?*" I blink at it again then jump to standing when I realize... This is likely modeled after *her* vagina.

She squints her eyes at me in what must feel, to her, like a deathly glare. On my end, I worry her forehead vein is going to blow and am not, in fact, intimidated. I'm too tired to be intimidated.

I fretted over this damn sculpture all night. I completed it three weeks ago with all the confidence of Britney Spears in 2002 but now? The morning it's due? I'm in complete spiral mode, believing I'm undeserving of it all. Imposter Syndrome has me pinned to the bed and is fucking me deep.

Seeing Madeline's vagina sculpture helps.

It's... "It's pretty small," I say, mentally measuring to see if it will even fit the criteria for the assignment. Our professor gave us minimum and maximum dimension specs for the first and the second is up to us.

"Some women are petite," she retorts, shoulders squared off like Blanche Devereux on a mission. "I guess you wouldn't know that."

I roll my eyes. I knew it. This is *so* sculpted after her own vagina. Who does that? Who makes a mold of their private parts to show a class full of people? So fucking weird. And yet, the way her chin juts out and her lips are pursed, it seems like she knows something I don't.

And once again, I'm completely insecure of everything.

I lean in, sweat sliding down my spine, my heart hammering. "Were we all supposed to do vaginas?" She's so fucking sure of herself, she has me genuinely confused.

She rolls her eyes, snatches her little vagina to her chest and turns away from me, storing it in whatever little vagina travel contraption she's devised. "No, *Sausage*," she sneers, and I die a little inside every time she calls me Sausage. It's just so gross and offensive and rude.

And easy.

If you're going to be a jerk, at least get creative.

The second time we met, after I'd met her with Darren, she couldn't remember my name. I reminded her it was Vienna, and she said, "What, like those sausages?" And I made the mistake of saying yes, because my name *is* spelled the same way.

But she's called me Sausage ever since.

"But I chose to make my first piece about something beautiful, something that really represents life."

I lift a finger and her face sours. "Technically, you sculpted labia. And labia do not represent life. They are just a manhole cover."

After the words leave my mouth, I realize they're more crude than necessary but still true. Madeline really thinks her pussy lip sculpture is representing something other than her own ego and it gets under my skin. She always worms under my skin that way.

25

"Stop saying labia."

I smile. "You just said it."

She rolls her eyes. "Good luck with your shopping cart sculpture, *Sausage*."

I glare at her but it's wasted because she collects her things and storms out, slamming the apartment door with unnecessary force. I look into my box, my skin clammy from my panicked sweat.

It's not a shopping cart. I mean. It *is* a shopping cart but... it's decrepit, wheels falling off, contents spilling out into a shattered looking pavement. It's spilling and dying all at once and the moment is chaos.

It's the disintegration of greedy bankers.

I sigh, but force my spine to straighten with confidence I don't truly feel. This is good. It is meaningful. The professor will not give a tiny pussy a better grade than a piece that really tells a story.

I walk out of the apartment with my head high and my insides churning.

If I'm defeated by Madeline and her tiny pussy, I'm going to get so drunk.

*F*OUR HOURS LATER
"It meant something! It mea—" I hiccup again, and roll right back into my point. "Meant something!"

Darren nods, his focus on the bartender across the room. He motions for the tab, then looks at me with irritation written all over his smooth-shaven, gorgeous face.

"You're so handsome," I tell him, hiccuping again. God,

hiccups make you want to pee, don't they? "Your boyfriend is so handsome, too," I remark, picturing Samson in one of the fancy suits he wears. I love fancy suits, they're so sexy.

Darren folds his arms across his broad chest, and blinks at me, expression unimpressed. "Don't get sloppy drunk alone. It's dangerous and stupid, and that also makes you selfish."

"Shellfish?" I question, immediately realizing my slurred snafu but a bit too tipsy to care. I roll my hand forward, nodding, telling him to carry on as I hiccup again... and again. "How am I selfish?" I add after he sits silent, blinking at me for more than a minute.

"I don't want you to get murdered because you went out alone and got drunk. Then I'll feel bad. That makes you selfish."

I cup my hands to my heart and tip my head to the side. "Awww."

He rolls his eyes as the bartender approaches. Darren rises off the stool and reaches for his wallet, slipping a black card across the bar. "Her tab, then tip yourself," he says.

When the bartender thanks him and walks to the register, I lean into Darren and waggle my brows at him. He plops back down as I ask, "Got Dad's card tonight?"

He places his palm smack dab in the center of my forehead and pushes me back onto my stool. "I told you not to call Samson my Dad. It's weird. And he's not that much older than me."

He is, but I'm too drunk to argue. "Like you've never called him *Daddy*." I giggle but then my shoulders drop as my failure hits me again. "I got a C- and she got an A, Darren. It's just not fair."

He gets his card back and leads me out of the bar, into the passenger seat of his car. Once he's inside and buckled up he turns to me and says, "Sex sells. Your piece meant something to you, but not everyone wants art to remind them of what's wrong with the world." He shrugs as he throws the car into reverse, peering over his shoulder as he does.

"Sex sells," he repeats.

And I'm annoyed that he's likely right.

3

Tucker

Being excited without a hard-on isn't something I'm used to.

"Debauchery, as you're aware, is the leading brand in the industry. It makes sense that as we branch out to create more personalized, licensed products that we approached you first, Tucker. The leading brand, the leading man," he shakes his head, as if us not working together is ridiculous. "It just makes sense."

In a way, it does. Pairing the best with the best will likely yield the optimal product for the consumer. But I also know that this is business, and if I get too geeked out on the idea of my dick being a sex toy around the world – because that's what they're pitching – I may not make the best choices. Taking a deep breath, I temper my immediate excitement, wearing my best poker face.

I glance at Aug, whose brows are knitted together so tightly, I genuinely don't know if he's just thinking or pissed off.

"The plan would be a gradual roll out this summer, with the first design being the only available at launch. Then, assuming sales meet our expected forecasts–" the man in the suit looks at me with serious eyes. "Even our most conservative estimates have sales skyrocketing from the initial launch, Tucker, I promise you that. Your dick will be in one out of five bedside drawers all across America by this time next year." He grins then adds, "then we roll out the other three designs."

He raises his hands in the air, making a show, and the man next to him follows the movement with his head. Suitman makes a marquee with his palms. "Picture it," he starts, nodding to me and Aug. "Four separate models of Deep dicks, a dick for every Tucker fan," he says, spreading his hands wide to accentuate the announcement, as if the words are painted in the sky.

It's showy, but it is show business and he is making a pitch. I glance at Aug, who still looks unimpressed and annoyed, then over at Lance, who is coincidently rising from his seat.

"Gentleman, if you'd give us a few minutes to speak privately," Lance smiles, pointedly.

Suitman—whom I've learned is named Dalton Fitzgerald—stands, his hand working the button of his jacket near his waist. "Of course, of course," he waves down the air, assuring us all is well. Shimmying behind the chairs, Mr. Fitzgerald and the other guy step into the hallway, leaving the door open behind them.

Lance makes his way to the door, nodding to Aug. "I'll make sure they have refreshments at the craft services table," he says, stepping outside, tugging the door closed behind him. Likely, Lance is going to make sure the men don't bother anyone on set, namely, the female actresses.

We may be a progressive film company, but that doesn't

mean we've been able to impart our behavioral standards on companies and vendors we work with. Lance will watch over Mr. Fitzgerald until we're done here.

Uma's gone, but I've got another scene in thirty minutes, so Isla is likely here getting ready. I need to wrap this up so I have time to prepare. How do I prepare for scenes? Triple S: shit, shower, and shave, a sensible daily routine but particularly smart if you're about to be pegged. I'm not today, but still, not a bad habit in this industry anyway.

"I can't tell what you're thinking," I say to Aug when Lance has closed us in the conference room in privacy. "Is this a good deal?"

Slowly, Aug runs a hand through his formerly jet black hair, strands of silver shining beneath the conference room lights. "Well," he says, staring down at the paperwork they'd passed out to us. It's a spec sheet with business plans and projections, all just a loose idea until I agree. "I think it's a killer deal, and that's what has me a little... skeptical."

Arching a brow, I tear into the fruit plate placed in front of me. Dunking a strawberry into some yogurt, I chew around the large, juicy bite as I ask, "Too good to be true?"

Augustus nods slowly. "I don't see anything off-putting in the contracts, but we'll have legal take a look." He reaches forward, collecting his copies of the contract and his cell phone from the table. A few taps and swipes and he's telling Crave & Cure legal all about the deal, in the most concise terms.

He ends the call, and turns to me. "If you'd like, you can tell them yes tentatively. Legal will go through everything tonight and have a solid answer in the morning along with any suggestions as to how the contract can change."

I nod. "I can't believe they want to give me two hundred and fifty thousand dollars to make a mold of my guy," I say, shaking my head. I tap the contract in front of me. "Did you see that? As long as the first one is a success, they want three more designs made, all with a signing bonus of two hundred fifty per." I look down at my lap, mostly to annoy an easily irritated Augustus, and pat where my cock rests sleepily against my leg. "You're a million-dollar dick, buddy," I tell him.

Augustus shakes his head, running a hand through his hair. "Anyway," he says, refusing to acknowledge me talking to my cock because that's Augustus. Smart as fuck, loyal as hell, talented as all get out. But he doesn't play around. Ever.

"And the percentage you'd earn on each sale. I'm not sure you realize how good half of the profits are in terms of a deal. Normal deals sit closer to fifteen percent, not fifty."

I scratch my sternum. "I'm just that good."

Augustus blinks at me then lets his phone and the papers slide back onto the table. "Get Lance. Tell them we're ready."

I blink at him with false confusion knitting my brows. "Me get him? Um, I'm the star. I think you should get him."

I'm out of my chair and opening the door before I have to look into his cold, angry eyes. He loves me, he does. We love each other really, which I'm not sure a boss and employee always have. But he discovered me, and has taught me so fucking much already.

"Lance," I shout into the hallway, earning me a gruff sigh from Augustus. A moment later, Lance, Suitman and mini Suitman are back, and the meeting is on.

I strap-on my poker face. "My lawyers," I start, because Crave & Cure offers free legal to all employees. Just one of the many perks. It also just makes me feel kinda cool that I have a lawyer to cover my ass when things like this come up. "They need to look over everything. They'll report back to me tomorrow. But until then," I say, finding Suitman's eyes, "it's looking like a yes, tentatively of course."

He leaps up from his chair, sending it careening into the

wall behind him. But it goes unnoticed as he claps his hand against mine in the most aggressive handshake I've ever shook. Seriously. This guy is pretty fucking stoked about this deal.

"Great to hear, Tucker, great to hear it," Suitman says, turning to face his assistant and smiling with either relief or smugness, I can't tell which.

Next to me, Augustus thumbs through his contract. Nudging me, he guides the tip of his finger below a passage and I quickly read.

The sex toy shall be molded with medical grade silicone. The sex toy shall be molded by the in house sculpture artist nominated by Debauchery, and maintain the position through all pieces. Tucker Deep, care of Crave & Cure Productions, will have four molds done. One prior to phase one launch, three done sequentially after. All four molds and sculpted mock ups shall be created by Devin Tomlinson.

There is a line beneath the artist's name, and the number of sex toys, leading me to believe those are likely negotiable options.

"Devin Tomlinson?" I question aloud as I stare at his name on the dotted line. From beside me, Aug nudges me with his elbow.

"You know," he starts, keeping his voice low. "There is an artist who's made an impression on you." His brows lift as he attempts to impart a name on me non-verbally, eyes widening.

I shrug and shake my head. "I don't know any artists."

His jaw flexes as he curls his fingers around the top of the contract, lifting it from the table. "Tucker," he sighs. "You do know an artist. One that has impacted you greatly, actually."

I blink.

He rolls his eyes. "The sketch."

And those two words grab me by the shoulders and shake the sheer oblivion from me. Holy shit.

The sketch.

The gorgeous brunette who sketched it appears behind my eyes as detailed as that night. Over two years have gone by but I can still recall her face as well as I can recall her sketch, which is very fucking well.

"Oh shit," I breathe, my hand unexpectedly catching my exhale.

Aug nods. "There you go," he says of my late arrival at the point.

I face Suitman and his sidekick. "Can I use someone else? Someone besides this Tomlinson guy?"

I realize this is a long shot, but literally it's the only time I've had the opportunity to even try for the shot, so I take it.

"Like I said, my lawyers will take a look but there is something." I swallow and hold the gaze of Mr. Fitzgerald. "I have an artist I'd like to use."

I scrub a hand down my face. "I'm sorry if this means the contracts need to be reworked but," I start, "I'd really like to locate my artist first, and offer this job to them."

"Are they capable? We'd have to vet them. They've got to be able to do the job, Tucker. Devin finished at the Art Institute last year. He's got an impeccable resume."

I nod. "That's awesome, man," I say of Devin because fuck yes, working in your field one year after graduating is awesome. But I hope he wasn't banking on this gig, because he's definitely not getting it. Not if I get my way.

"I'm only doing this deal if I get to offer it to my artist. It's a deal breaker for me."

Fitzgerald smiles uncomfortably, but as soon as I outstretch my hand, he claps his into it. A wide grin stretches his face, and I can practically see dollar signs in his pupils.

"Sounds great."

Lance ushers them out, leaving Augustus and myself alone in the gleaming conference room.

My eyes widen. "Help me find her?"

He nods.

Despite being the number one adult film star who is *excited* basically all the time, the prospect of finding her after two long years... it makes me truly excited.

And being excited without a hard-on isn't something I'm used to.

4

Vienna

I think I'd risk dismemberment for this amount of money.

Calmly, I drag the broom along the stamped concrete, collecting invisible dust. "She doesn't even fucking need the grant, Darren," I sigh, my face heavy and swollen. I've cried off and on all day for the last few days. I look like shit warmed over and to make matters worse, I think I'm getting a cold, too.

A cold in the summer is one of the worst things ever. Having boob sweat *and* a runny nose at the same time? No. No fucking way. It's too terrible to even think about.

I push hair off my face, already feeling dampness on the back of my neck. I hate this stupid job. *Work at a museum,* they said. *Get your foot in the door early,* they said.

I sweep floors and answer phones.

They don't even *allow* me to discuss the art with patrons.

Seriously. I did it once and my boss made it quite clear it was the last time. The *or else* didn't need to be spoken.

"It's just such bullshit. I need it. I need it and she needs nothing! *Madeline*," I hiss, saying her name as snarkily as I possibly can. Seriously, I'm rivaling the mean girl in the high school sitcoms. But I can't help myself. She just... gets under my fucking skin.

"*Madeline* has everything," I finish, hating how jealous I sound. I may envy how easily everything comes to her, but I'm not jealous of her. I will have everything I want... in time. And when I get it, it will taste that much sweeter because I did it on my fucking own.

Without my parents' help. Or support.

Or love, seemingly.

Darren appears in front of me, and stands slowly, rubbing his hand down my back. I don't actually think I'm getting sick, I think I'm on the brink of an anxiety attack.

"Vienna Carnegie, I love you and you know I would only say those disgusting three words to you under two circumstances, right?" he asks, but it's rhetorical, and he rolls on. "If I were dying," he drags out, pressing his lean fingers into his chest. "Which I'm not."

I nod.

He continues. "Or if I'm absolutely certain that what I'm going to say is going to knock you off your fucking rocker, and I don't want you to hate the messenger."

I practically gasp as he claps a hand over my shoulder, ducking to meet my gaze and hold it. "If you needed it, you'd have it."

I blink at him, mouth open, tongue sticking to the roof of my mouth, uncomfortably. I swallow so hard one of my ears pops. But I stare at him, my mind running a million miles a minute.

If you needed it, you'd have it.

"I could really use the money. She just... doesn't need it." I blink and for whatever reason, my stomach sours and I have the strongest desire to sit. But I don't. I stay on my feet and collect my punishment, as he seems to be framing it up as such.

"If it was really that crucial to your life, you'd have it. And just because she doesn't need it, doesn't mean you do."

I take a step back, my stomach dropping, a hollow sensation running through me. My eyes burn with frustration, but I refuse to let tears fall.

"Are you calling me melodramatic or insulting me as an artist?" I poise my hands on my hips.

He keeps one hand on my shoulder, but no longer crouches to hold my gaze as he says plainly, "Ever since you met Madeline, you wanted what she wanted. I think mostly because it gave you something outside of your control to focus on. But you didn't need that grant, Vienna. What you need is to do what you truly want to do." He licks his lips, taking in a breath that makes me fear there's more to come.

"If that means your parents are right, and art school isn't the thing, then that's okay. Don't prove them wrong and be miserable." His gaze is unrelenting, and as much as I want to look away, I don't. My chin trembles as I suck in a steadying breath, finding my words amidst the chaos in my soul. I don't like what he's implying.

"Do you think that I'm not a good enough artist to be at the Institute? Do you think they were right? I'm not talented?" I place a trembling hand to my sternum and blink at him, my fury drumming like a pulse.

He shakes his head slowly, and it aggravates me how calm he is while he stands there picking me apart piece by piece. I'm so outraged I could scream, but my body aches and my mind... is tired. I can't bring myself to argue with him. Not with the strength it would require going up against an unyielding jerk like Darren.

A jerk I love, I might add.

"I did not say that. You're willfully misunderstanding me, woman." His eyes look like whiskey when he's angry, chestnut and smooth. "What I mean is, if you want to quit because you're miserable, then do it. Compounding your misery by comparing yourself to Madeline and hating Madeline does not fucking serve! You have enough obstacles in your way, martyring yourself on another is fucking pointless!"

I watch him and grow sicker by the second as he pants and gasps, as if the truth he's just told has been weighing on him so heavily. Now that he's free, he can finally breathe.

That's how much I've annoyed him apparently.

I think about the grant briefly while blinking at him, my mind suddenly a bit hazy. Character assassinations will do that to you.

Did I want the grant money or did I just not want debt? Because the grant money comes with its own problems. Yes it comes with the recognition of my talent, a commitment to create, the freedom to work on my craft. But it also brings obligations, demands and deadlines.

I don't know that I wanted that, even though I do want to be a working artist. I honestly do but… doing it at the beck and call of someone that essentially just loaned me money and gave me a grant-winner title doesn't really seem glorious at all.

Winning the grant isn't the achievement I was even chasing but more so, the money.

I'm in so much debt already. Nearly ninety-thousand. That grant, though small in comparison to what I already owe, would have helped. It would have knocked a brick or two from my back, because recently, it's felt incredibly heavy and I honestly needed the break.

A break I won't get because Madeline won and I'm spinning out about it but... fuck. Darren's right. It's not about Madeline and it never has been. It's about loving what I'm doing while also not knowing at all what I want to do. It's incredibly frustrating to have a passion and a talent but not know how to turn that into anything. And Madeline always knows just what she wants to do. *Shit, I am jealous.*

I'm frustrated with myself. I feel like I'm not progressing.

"Fuck." What else can I say? I chew my bottom lip a moment and find his eyes, my hands sweaty around the broomstick I picked back up after dramatically dropping it in favor of my hips a moment ago. "I'm sorry if I've been drama," I say softly, a little embarrassed. "You're right. I'm just... lost right now."

He nods. "And you know I think you belong in art school, so don't start shit with me, Vienna," he says, casting a serious glare that warms my chest. Then, more softly than he's ever spoken to me, he says, "It's okay to be lost."

A crooked smile curls his lips, and I return the sentiment, grinning at him. I love when friendship is both messy and beautiful, and I believe we embody that to a tee. As he readies to wrap an arm around me and pull me into a pacifying post-argument hug, the gallery door swings open.

We usually don't get a lot of walk-ins at this location. We're more of a hosted and scheduled type of event museum, but we are open to the general public several hours daily, should they want to experience the gallery.

A fit but slim man walks in, smoothing a tan hand along his icy blonde hair. With his wide jaw and cool blue eyes, I blink at him for a few seconds, hypnotized. He nods, noticing my blatant staring but boldly ignoring it with a sterile gaze.

"I'm looking for Vienna Carnegie."

The broom slips from my sweaty hands and crashes to the

floor, the rattling noise ping-ponging in my sore brain, making me wince.

This insanely good looking man is looking for *me*?

I lift a palm and open my parched mouth, saying dryly, "That's me."

His tongue peeks out, wetting his lips. He offers an envelope to me, my name typed out on the front, clear as day.

"Can I get a few hours of your time this afternoon so I can explain that?" he nods toward the envelope which I immediately open.

My eyes scan the letter so fast, I don't really comprehend anything at all.

But I saw a number.

I look at Darren. "I'm taking the afternoon off."

He nods, sizing up the handsome man in the suit. "What's your name? In case she doesn't come back. Who do I tell the cops dismembered her?"

"Lance Davis," he says, completely unaffected by Darren's insinuation.

I think I'd risk dismemberment for this amount of money.

My head spins. I was just moaning about how much I've been stressing over money and this young Chris Evans walks in with a mysterious meeting and a paper with my name and big numbers on it? What in the actual fuck?

I step toward him, leaning in while keeping my eyes on an annoyed Darren. "I just want you to know, Lance," I say, trying out his name. "That I want really healthy long hair, smaller ankles and a cuter laugh."

He blinks at me, completely confused. I'm sure he thinks I'm a nut job but hey, he did stroll in here mere moments after I was crying about being broke. If he's some kind of fucking genie or my fairy godmother or something, I can't miss my chance.

But he blinks a few times before saying, "Okay, well... are

you available to discuss this further or not?" And I realize he's not a magician. He's an annoyed businessman who is now also sufficiently annoyed with me personally.

I snatch the broom from the ground and press it to Darren's chest. "Here you go, see ya loser," I tease, sticking out my tongue.

He smirks, but waves me off all the same. "Okay, bye I guess. Call me later."

A few paces outside the museum, I catch up with Lance.

"They won't need you back today?" he asks, tipping his head back in the direction of the museum.

I shake my head. "They never really need me."

We stop next to a black Tesla with black windows, and he opens the back door to me. Before I get in he says, "*We* need you."

And god, I really want to believe him.

5

Tucker

I found her. She's here.

Dallas drags a hand through his hair, his nostrils flitting violently like a flag in heavy winds. He's barely hanging on, I know because I've seen him on the edge many times. I've brought him to the edge many times, too.

He groans, and his grip in Maya's hair loosens, hips slowing to a cautious pace. "Here it comes," he grinds out, his teeth clenched, jaw set. I look down at Maya, on her knees between us.

She holds still as he scrambles to get one hand on his cock, the other still nestled in her hair, keeping her head upright. He strokes, featherlight moans drifting around me as he orgasms, abundant ropes of cum streaking Maya's breasts and belly.

When he's nothing but a heaving chest and shuddering

spine, Maya brings her focus to me. Off camera, I see the familiar purple of the VIN flag being held up. My turn.

With one hand wrapped around my base, the other still on Dallas's cock, she brings her mouth to the glistening head of my cock and slips me past her lips.

She sucks me in, and when her throat constricts around me, I know she's tasting what's left of him while sucking me.

It's hot.

On the first suck, my eyes fall closed and a guttural moan rises from my belly and booms through the small space. Something about her mouth on me after bringing him to orgasm always puts me over the edge. It's so fucking beautiful how easily she brings us to our knees, while she's the one *actually* on her knees.

I catch her gaze as she removes her hand, taking me as far back as she can. I give her the subtle blink, letting her know it's close, giving her the subtextual warning to pull off it a little to avoid a water hose down her throat.

This isn't a swallow scene—very few performers at Crave & Cure participate in "consumption" and only the ones who are comfortable are approached for those roles. In this scene, she's supposed to play with the cum. I step back, and Dallas clamps a hand along the curve of my neck and shoulder, rasping, "Give her what she needs, *brother*."

This is a step-siblings shoot, and our parents are away. The storyline isn't groundbreaking, but the tenderness in which we enacted the scene is what I'm proud of.

Maya wasn't squeaking and moaning... not unless she had the urge to do that. She wasn't calling us *bro* and we weren't dressed in ridiculous children's clothing to make the viewer understand the dynamic set forth. Instead, Crave & Cure offers a short story with each movie they make, setting the tone through succinct yet thoughtful prose & dialogue, as to what the viewer can expect.

It's edited before the film starts, so viewers have the option to fast forward. But if they read it first the way it's intended, our movies go from porn to something *real*. We're fucking but we're also feeling. It's a lot. And I don't know that everyone really appreciates what we do, and how much of us this job takes. How we want more for adult movies than fake moans and facials. We want emotion, depth, connection. Understanding that our job is fucking hard. Yes, it is also amazing, but it's not without challenges.

I add my cum to Maya's chest in thick, hot ropes as the intensity of the scene washes over me. I think of how Maya slowly edged us on the couch, how we trailed our fingers up her bare pussy just to tease her, how we laid her in bed and grinded into her from both sides just to make her wild. How we each slipped a finger into her eager pussy, fucking her till she stretched enough to take another digit from each of us, pummeling her deliciously until she shattered for us.

Now, as Dallas and I stroke our softening dicks, we blissfully stare down at Maya, who is leaning back on her elbows, the canvas of her body on full display.

"Our secret," she whispers, big brown eyes moving between the two of us.

The sharp smack of Augustus's slates our heads twisting backward, to the open, cannibalized portion of the set where the crew stands.

"Solid?" I ask, reaching for a towel off-camera nearby. I crouch in front of Maya and bring the terry to her shoulder, slowly wiping her off.

Aug nods. "We're good. Maya, you're on deck for the lead-in in the booth."

At my side, Dallas reappears, bringing another damp cloth

down on Maya. She nods past us to Aug. "Sounds good. I liked the little story this time."

Dallas swings his head back, getting some of his long hair off his face. "Me too. I liked how we protected you when our parents first got married. Made it feel authentic. Like I can understand how we'd love you more than a stepsister."

Though Maya will read it for the voice over, all of us always read the little story. I think it helps us reconcile what we're doing, especially if a scene is extra taboo or aggressive. Having a story put it all into perspective makes what we do really feel like art and not exploitation.

Agreeing with them, I finish wiping her chest as Dallas carefully tackles her belly. When we're clean and have all agreed that this was a successful scene, we help Maya to her feet. Normally, we'd retreat to our separate dressing areas, Maya in the back where there's access to the wigs and makeup, and Dallas and I hitting the locker room for a quick shower, then food.

Except today, Maya stops us. "Hang on, guys," she says, as Augustus approaches from his chair where he'd been rewatching the last scene in private. Sometimes as we clean up, he'll approach us for a retake or voice work.

Collecting our shorts from the ground, Dallas and I redress as Maya clears her throat, her dark eyes bouncing nervously between us, bypassing Aug all together.

"So...." she draws out. "I don't want anyone to feel bad," she starts, and immediately a smile curls my lips. Maya is always so careful and sweet when she has a suggestion or complaint, so much so that it makes her uncomfortable. I don't like her being uncomfortable, but the fact that she's so empathetic always makes me smile.

It's a trait you don't see in this business too often. Fortunately at Crave & Cure, we're all down to earth, respectful people. It's mostly the reason we were chosen. We were selected in various ways, but thoroughly vetted and given a psychological test. So while this industry is full of self-serving, cruel assholes, fortunately C&C isn't.

But even for us, Maya is so damn sweet.

"What's up, Maya?" Hoping to make whatever's on her mind a bit easier for her, I ask, "Is everything okay?"

I look back at Aug, who is still standing quietly at our sides. He jumps right in, and it's then that I realize Maya has asked him to be here. For... whatever this is.

"Drink pineapple juice. Maya is scheduled for a few more scenes this week and they are all cum-heavy swallow scenes. She's having a hard time stomaching the flavor of one of you, so fix it." He digs into his pocket, thumbs through his phone a second then shoves it back in his pants. "There. I text you both the list. You should know by now, but in case you don't, now you do. Consume everything you can on that list."

"Consumption" scenes are rare, but Maya is one of the actresses comfortable doing it. The male actors are screened for STD's before hand, so everything is safe.

I reach down, cupping my dick as if he has ears and will be horribly devastated by the aspersions being thrown at us. "My cum tastes bad?" I ask, eyebrows sliding into my hairline. I can't hide my shock because this is something I've never heard. In fact, I've always been told the opposite. Then I try to recall the last time Maya even tasted it... it's been years.

Maya eyes dart between us, and I remember how she opened this entire conversation. *I don't want anyone to feel bad.* I turn to Dallas, and give him a short but potent titty twister. "Dude, you have funky spunk."

He reaches out to seek revenge, but I'm too fast. Plus, I hate titty twisters. My nipples are so fucking sensitive. Seriously, it's written in my contract that other actors cannot touch my nipples unless we've been purple-flagged to end the scene.

I'll shoot right away if they do.

I slap his hand away several times before Aug clears his throat, the universal sign for *knock it the fuck off.*

"Is it me?" Dallas whispers to Maya, leaning away as if we won't hear her response despite the fact we're all a foot apart.

Maya bites her bottom lip, eyes fixed on Aug, waiting for answers. He sighs, and claps a hand on Dallas's shoulder. "Yes, it's you, okay? Maya didn't want to make you feel bad," he says, rolling his eyes at that.

We know where Aug stands. He isn't one to protect our feelings when it comes to underperforming, funky spunk or inability to bring partners across the finish line, or any other truth for that matter. He always says, *if everyone is real about what they're feeling and how they're doing, we can make a helluva film. We can even work off some emotions, too, and knead them into the scene. But if we are forced to stomach things we don't like, it all crumbles. Then we're just hypocrites making normal porn pretending it's better.*

I agree with him and grin at Dallas. "It's your Matcha lattes, man," I tease.

He shakes his head, running a hand up the back of his neck, dark eyes wrinkled with confusion. "Fuck, I guess it must be." He looks at Maya, sticking out his lip in a forced, playful pout. "I'm sorry My," he says, "I'll figure it out." He looks at Augustus, making the promise to him, too. "I'll grab some pineapple juice on the way home. Don't worry, I'll be good to go for tomorrow's shoot."

Augustus nods, and finds his way back to his chair where his assistant Lance waits, his iPad unlocked, vivid screen glaring up at him.

Maya slips away after reassuring Dallas that she's not upset but that she can't take anymore, and I quote, "ammonia cleaner cum", or else she will definitely vomit.

When it's just the two of us walking back to our dressing room, I ask Dallas about his new girlfriend. Because she loves Matcha lattes, and she is the reason that he's been drinking so many lately.

Dallas is one of those guys who wants to be in love so damn badly that he goes full Power Ranger. At least, that's what Aug and I call him, kindly, behind his back. As soon as he meets a girl that checks even a few criteria boxes of his, he goes full mighty morphin' and turns into whatever it is he thinks she wants.

I get it. I get not wanting to be alone, and feeling like you can make some changes if it makes the relationship fit a bit better. The place where I lose him is *fundamental* changes.

Pretending to like things that don't actually mean anything to you.

Like Matcha lattes that make your cum taste like window cleaner.

I sincerely hope one day the guy realizes that he's solid as himself, and he shouldn't have to pretend to like things he doesn't in order to find "the one".

I've told him as much, I know the therapist we all see once a month has told him a variation of that, too.

But when you're lost and love hungry, sometimes you're deaf to the truth. Been there, done that. My last and only serious girlfriend told me she wanted me to quit making movies. Well, I say quit making movies but what she really said was *you better stop fucking other women on camera, or else we're done.*

I loved and trusted her, and I pretended to understand her desire for me to quit. I mean, on some level I guess I did. If I were a different sort of person, maybe watching the person I'm with fuck another person would bother me. But I think I'm cut from a different cloth, because I've never felt jealous at the idea of watching. Granted, I've never done it because it's always been my girlfriend having to watch me (I've never dated anyone in the industry before), but still, I think I could be comfortable with it.

I can separate work from personal, but she couldn't. And no amount of me trying to appease her frustration when I'd come home after a long day on set would put her at ease.

So when I tell Dallas he cannot fake it until he makes it, I know from experience. "We want what we want. And unless it feels real and organic to change for someone, don't force it. Because it's not the recipe to your forever. It's a recipe for funky spunk and a break up."

He laughs, but it's humorless. "I don't mind the Matcha," he says as I plop down on the couch in the dressing room. Tugging on a shirt from the folded stack, he smooths the sleeves out as he thinks aloud. "I mean, I don't love the music she likes and she does watch a ton of stuff on TV that I'm not into..." He trails off and before I can jump in and nudge him toward the obvious, which is that maybe they aren't soulmates, the door swings open.

Lance, iPad tucked under one arm, a coffee in his hand, appears. "Meeting in the conference room in ten minutes. Shower now and meet me there."

I look up at the wall, where a round clock hangs, black hand ticking silently. "I have forty minutes until the next scene," I say, sipping the water at my side. "This better be quick—"

"She's here," Lance interjects, his eyes widening briefly. "Your artist. I found her. She's here."

My mouth goes dry as I blink at him, and from my peripheral I see Dallas's gaze ping-pong between me and Lance. I grab my towel and jump in the shower and I think I break some kind of world record. I'm out and toweling myself off, snatching my heather gray sweats and a long-sleeved shirt from my stash nearby.

"Where's the fire? Who is this mysterious *She?*" he asks, but I can't respond, because my mind is fucking spinning.

Lance's smile is slow and small, and sweat beads along my spine in reaction. "She watched the last scene, you just... didn't notice."

I grab my dick over my shorts as my eyes widen. Then I realize that I am absolutely fucking stupid because... she's seen me naked before. She sketched me two and half years ago.

Still, watching me fuck without knowing she's there... I snort, realizing the irony of the moment. Millions of people watch me fuck online and I'm clueless as to who those individuals actually are. But somehow knowing she's watched me orgasm... my stomach fills with flutters, some so large, the water in my gut lurches and I feel queasy for a moment.

"Let's go," Lance demands, this time irritation seeping into his tone. "I pulled her from her job, Tuck. Don't make her wait even longer."

I'm on my feet, ignoring Dallas's barrage of questions, and trailing behind Lance like an excited puppy all the way to the conference room.

And when the door opens, and I lay eyes on her, I swear to fuck I can't breathe. It's really fucking her. He found her.

She's wearing a frown, and her tawny eyes are pinched on me with irritation. I don't miss the way she takes me in, head to toe, and I also don't miss how her expression softens just slightly. Like she wants to be mad, but wasn't expecting me. And just maybe she likes what she sees.

I know *I like what I see.*

Even more than I did when I first laid eyes on her.

My heart flutters as I slide into my seat, giving her my best, most suave grin. Offering my hand, I introduce myself.

"Hi, I'm Tucker Deep."

She stares at my hand like I just fisted the devil, and her stubborn nose wrinkles. With her hands still twined together in her lap she says, "Tucker Deep? Seriously?"

I grin, loving that she's going to make me work for her. Even if it's just friendship, she won't concede easily, I can see that. But I like a challenge.

Especially challenges with long, gorgeous legs, curves that make my hands ache to touch them and dark eyes that steal my breath. Those are my favorite kinds of challenges.

"Nice to meet you, Miss..." I trail off, knowing very well what her name is. But I want to hear her say it. I need to hear her say it.

"Vienna," she offers quietly. "Carnegie." She glances at Lance, then Aug before her eyes veer back to me for a split second. Refocused on our leader, she asks, "Why am I here?"

I resist the urge to say *because I need you* even though it's the truth in more ways than one. Instead, I sit quietly and watch her intently as Augustus and Lance make the pitch.

6

Vienna

Don't be sucked in by the charms of a porn star.

Just because I'm an artist doesn't mean I take on the entire stereotypical persona of one.

I wash my hair regularly, thank you very much. I do own Birkenstocks, but not just those. I've been known to have some paint stains on my clothing, but not all of my clothing. I haven't listened to Jack Johnson in years and when I grocery shop, I don't buy organic. I can't afford it.

So yeah, I don't fit the bill of the stereotypical struggling artist. Besides, I'm not struggling, I'm fucking drowning.

Somehow knowing that I'm not the cliche stereotype makes it a lot easier for me to indulge in this idea of fate.

Kismet, destiny, karma, call it whatever you want. But it's really fucking hard for me to not feel fate slithering up the back of my shirt and wrapping herself around my neck as I stare at this handsome, older man while he spews gobs of information at me.

I was just feeling bad about not winning the grant money, and I was literally mid-complaint about whether or not I'm following the right dream when a man in a suit walked in off the street with a business opportunity for me.

If I needed it, I would have it.

I mean, if that isn't fate deep throating me to get my attention, I don't know what is.

My focus returns to the silvering fox before me. "My name is Augustus Moore," he says, reaching out his hand. We shake and immediately, the small gesture gives me an inch of confidence.

To him, it's just an introduction. But to me? It's respect, and that's not something you get as the dust particle sweeper in a stuffy museum. Not often, at least.

He extends an arm, indicating he wants me to sit. A moment after I do, the other man who came and retrieved me from the museum appears. He gives the smallest of controlled smiles paired with a head nod, then takes a seat across from me, next to Augustus.

"This is Lance Davis, my assistant." Augustus peers at Lance then back at me. "Though it's insulting that he bears the word *assistant*."

I arch a brow, and really resist the urge to fold my arms across my chest for fear of coming off like a bitch but *come on.* Just being a hot old guy who apparently directs porn is not reason enough to belittle this man.

"Because being an assistant is an insult?"

His eyes narrow, and the beautiful man whom I'm going out of my way to ignore makes a snorting nose, a cross between laughter and... fear. Augustus leans over the table just slightly.

"You are twisting my words," he says slowly as he studies

me. The crows feet add wisdom versus age, and though he's intense as hell, this man is attractive.

"Are you purposely misinterpreting my meaning?" He leans back, drumming his fingers on the tabletop as he stares at me. My pulse spikes, and the silent pressure of being the only woman in a room with three men starts to infiltrate my veins, making me anxious.

"As opposed to?" I ask, both curious and annoyed.

Augustus ignores my question, and I hate that I somehow already feel like I'm on his bad side. "I'll give you the benefit of the doubt, it's an insult to call him an assistant because *he is everything.*"

My eyes dart to Lance, the man in question. He sits stiff and upright, eyes focused on me, letting the compliment ping right off of him. Though to be fair, he's been quite cool and robotic in the thirty whole minutes I've known him so maybe that's just his vibe. Stiff. And not the fun kind.

"Anyway, back to the purpose of this meeting. We brought you here to discuss the role of principal creative for a project Crave & Cure is collaborating on with another company. A lot of money is going into this, but even more money to be made. And I bring up finances because I know what it's like to be a struggling art student. And I believe your talent and skill will be put to great use. The payday on this will dwarf what any painting or sculpture would sell for at this point in your career." Finally, Augustus looks at Tucker, which makes me feel safe to finally look at him.

He's grinning at me, wide eyes shiny, the rich emerald hue one of the most gorgeous shades of green I've ever seen. Like vibrant moss feeding off the sun, stretching across stones under a crisp current. His chestnut hair is thick and messy, like he's been running his hands through it. Well, *someone* has been running their hands through it.

Because Tucker Deep—God, what a ridiculous name—is a fucking porn star. He does sexy times for money... on camera. His adorable haphazard hair quickly morphs into just been fucked hair and that fact sits less pleasantly in my stomach. But also, maybe it sits well a little further south of my stomach.

I look at Augustus again, trying to keep my chin high and my spine straight. The voice inside me is absolutely screaming *whatever it is, the answer is yes* because I need the money.

But I've sat in the backseat for eighteen years listening to my dad's business calls. I'd never tell him, but I learned a lot of things. Mostly that my dad is a jerk. But also... some business things.

I keep my poker face on, and follow a bit of dad's advice. Instead of champing at the bit, I play it cool, sitting back in my chair as if I'm the richest woman in the world and this gig is something I could easily take or leave.

"What kind of project? And what company are you partnering with?"

I can't imagine why a porn production company wants an art school student for any reason. My eyes crawl up and down the conference room walls, discovering them to be bare. Not even a shitty inspirational poster or one with the company's values. Just bare walls.

"Debauchery," he states simply. "Have you heard of it?"

I'm hit with a memory from a few nights back. Me sprawled across my bed, blankets piled up around me like a bunker, my hand death-gripping my toy. I tasted blood from how hard I bit my lip when I came.

"I think I've heard of them," I reply coolly, hoping my cheeks aren't flush from my total bullshit. Heard of them? I've been single for a while. I own several Debauchery toys.

"Debauchery, as the leading adult toy company, came to us, the leading erotic film company, seeking a partnership. More specifically, seeking an alliance with both C&C and Tucker, our top performing male actor."

From next to him, Tucker clears his throat, and even the way he does that sends a flutter through my core. I really want to roll my eyes at myself because *don't do that Vienna.* Don't be sucked in by the charms of a porn star.

"Tucker has selected you specifically," he adds, and my eyes veer to the handsome, sinewy man with a smile on his full pink lips and a twinkle in his eyes. God. I fucking hate that his smarmy charm is working on me. My mind is angry, but my pussy... she is not.

"He can't speak for himself?" I ask, forcing my gaze back to Augustus.

Holding back a sneer, Augustus slides me a pile of paperwork before rising to his feet, letting his hands smooth over his thighs. "Before you think you're above making sex toys, take a look at this contract."

Then Lance and Tucker get to their feet too and suddenly I feel like I've fumbled the ball, like I've fucked up somehow. But I can't just be brought to a business meeting off cuff with no one to advise me or anyone to talk to and agree. And of course I'd ask questions. It would be a red flag if I didn't!

Panic seizes me, which is ridiculous because I don't even know if I want to do this. Why am I worried that they'll change their mind? I snatch the papers off the table and stand. Following a few paces behind them, I stop when Augustus halts, half in and half out of the room. The others are gone.

"Miss Carnegie, a true artist can respect and see value in all art forms." He tips his head to me in the coolest and shortest goodbye I've ever received.

When I step into the hallway, two women in white bathrobes are walking by, arms linked at the elbow. "I thought so too," one says to the other, clearly mid conversation. Both of them, wearing ear to ear smiles, look up at me, stopping in their tracks.

First they both glance at the papers clutched to my chest, then up at my face again. They smile warmly and it's so strange because I don't know them and I've never met them but their immediate kindness is... intoxicating.

I guess I expected actresses—even for adult films—to be... different. Unkind maybe? Stupid assumption, I realize.

"Hey sweetie," one of them says, tucking a piece of honeyed hair behind her ear. "You looking for someone?" She briefly glances back down to the papers then adds, "You lookin' for Aug?"

I shake my head. "I was actually just leaving," I reply as my cheeks pinken.

From around the corner, Lance appears. "I'm walking you out," he says flatly, and I wonder if this guy is ever happy. Shit, his boss gave him an incredible compliment and he looked like someone pissed in his Cornflakes.

The other girl, this one with shiny dark hair and bright green eyes, beams at Lance. Both of them are so... beautiful. And nearly naked. And Lance seems... unphased. I guess that happens working here. Nudity and sex must be... commonplace.

"Lance, we won't tell anyone. Is she the new girl you guys have been whispering about for months?"

The blonde clasps her hands together, jutting her fingertips into the underside of her chin, biting into her bottom lip impatiently.

Lance says nothing but turns to face me, sticking one arm out. "It's this way," he says, ignoring them.

I smile at the two women, then follow him outside into the chilly yet sunny San Francisco day.

"Well," I say awkwardly as Lance pulls open the door on a

silver Prius, a bright WHEEL GET YOU rideshare sticker splayed across the back window. "Thank you."

Lance says nothing but closes the door, rests his hand on the top of the car before leaning in the passenger side window. "Charge it to C&C." He glances over the seat, back at me. "It's on us."

"Thanks," I say quietly, and then I'm being driven back to the museum, a stack of papers in my lap.

I look again at the figure in big block numbers.

That is a big freaking number.

The idea of accepting a job just for the money makes my skin crawl. But I need it. I lost the grant to Madeline, the museum is never going to feature me, and all other career trajectories at this point are so far fetched, a job in my field seems impossible.

This literally hunted me down and fell into my lap, right as I was feeling desperate. The word from earlier in the day rolls around my mouth again.

Fate.

I can't help but let a snort escape me as I push through the museum doors, frigid air encircling me the moment my heels click against the tile.

I am not fated to be a dildo maker.

Stopping in my tracks, I survey the museum walls. My gaze catches on a canvas, illuminated by a picture light above. Centering the piece is a woman, her skin pale and lips baby pink. She wears a gauzy gown, flowing wildly around her ankles. Woven through her strawberry hair are strings of gold beads, flowers and leaves tied throughout. She rests in a large halo, exotic flowers and sharp edged shapes filling the space behind her. Setting the stage for her beauty.

The art nouveau piece was painted by Alphonse Mucha,

and though art nouveau isn't one of the styles I'm inspired by, the piece is breathtaking. Absolutely gorgeous. It's... timeless.

I step back, my eyes growing warm as they wander to a small column centering the room. Waist-high, on it rests a sculpture. Bronze with a black base, the piece is of two women, their bodies curving away from each other, forming an open circle. Above them, arms out and linked, they cling to each other. They're faceless, and their bodies are devoid of shape and form. But somehow, the piece speaks to me emotionally. It resonates with me. I myself am devoid of structure. I'm lost, floating with no purpose.

Warm tears slide down my cheeks.

I lost the grant because my piece had too much to say, too much integrity. Madeline won because sex sells.

Augustus's words interrupt my thoughts, *a true artist can respect and see value in all art forms.* What if Madeline didn't win because sex sells? What if I judged her piece simply on the fact it was hers and never considered the art in it?

Darren appears, hands on hips, unknowingly catching me from an emotional freefall. "Back already? What was that about?" he leans in. "Did they flip you?"

I snort. We've been binge watching The Sopranos when his boyfriend is at the office late.

"Actually," I start. "Maybe they did." I hand him the papers and say, "Dinner tonight. I need Samson."

His eyes widen as he scans the top paper, locking on the number at the bottom. "Uh, yeah, we clearly do."

7

Tucker

She and I are meant for more than making dildos together.

"Thanks so much, my man." I slap four twenties in the driver's palm, and slide out of the seat, dragging my rolling suitcase out behind me. I close the door and watch the rideshare driver disappear down the darkening residential street.

Then I feast my eyes on one of my favorite places in the world.

The aged and worn red lacquer front door swings open, and the smile that takes over my face is huge and immediate.

"There he is! Come on, loverboy, get in here!"

I practically leap up the short walkway to the front porch, where my dad envelopes me in a massive bear hug. The familiarity of his embrace makes my chest tight and my cheeks burn with how big my fucking grin is.

"Missed you, Dad," I tell him, though my last visit was only

61

five weeks ago. Still, I wish I saw my family every damn day. If commuting was even remotely possible from Oakcreek to San Francisco, I'd do it. But six hours in the car each day after a twelve hour call schedule isn't possible.

Stepping inside, my entire body softens at the smell of home.

Everything about my parents house is exactly the same as when I grew up here. Same gnarly avocado colored carpet, exact same couch and even the pictures lining the halls have yet to be updated.

I love it.

Dad presses a finger to his lips, and makes a show of tiptoeing. He always does that when Mom's working. We make our way down the hall quietly and find ourselves in the doorframe, staring into the guest bedroom.

Mom looks up, two huge pieces of romaine lettuce hanging from her hands. She mimes squealing, shaking in her stance before pumping her fists in the air, mouthing *Tuck!*

Then she holds a piece of salad up, giving me her pointer finger. Dad leans in as if I've never been told one minute with the finger and whispers, "She needs another minute."

I nod at my Dad with a smile. "Got it."

Then Tessa Eliot, Oakcreek's leading newborn photographer, turns back to the sleeping infant, salad ingredients surrounding them. Mom's infant photography centers around turning babies into adorable inanimate objects or items.

I've seen her turn babies' faces into a sunflower's pistil, peas in a pod, the scoop of ice cream among a sea of cones... you name it, and my mom has likely put a baby in a photograph doing it. Seriously.

She positions a tomato around the sleeping infant's face, adding a carrot from the table of supplies nearby. Dad grabs my shoulder and leads me to the kitchen, the nucleus of our family.

"Let's let her finish up," he says, clapping me on the back as I settle into a chair at the table. He pops open the fridge, snagging two beers out.

I twist the top off after he hands it over, taking a seat across from him.

"This was unexpected," he says before he savors his first long drink. I take mine, too, and the beer burns behind my eyes, and my nose tingles. But immediately, I feel the small presence of it in my veins, and my body lightens.

God, being home just feels so good.

"I missed you guys," I tell him, setting the bottle down, my fingers already playing at the loose edge of the label. I'm not nervous to tell him my news, but I'm nervous that my news won't turn out the way I want. "And I've got something to tell you guys."

Dad arches a brow, rubbing his hands together. "Ohh," he says, eyes shining. "I'm all ears."

I take another drink of my beer, itemizing the things I want to tell him in order of importance. The least important first.

"Debauchery set up a meeting with Aug. And as it turns out, I guess they want to partner with Crave & Cure for a new line of products."

Dad sips his beer, smoothing a thick hand through his salt and pepper hair. I look just like my dad, same as my brothers Theo and Tripp. Even Tegan, my sister, looks like dad. The running joke is that mom's DNA couldn't stand up to Dad's and that he married her to have mini-Tim's.

"Wow," he breaths out, a proud smile beginning to sweep his face. "And let me guess, they want to give you a toy of your own."

I smile before sipping my beer, and after I polish it off, I say, "The entire line." Then I wait as the information seeps into him. A moment later he extends a curled fist over the table.

"That's amazing, kid." He rises and it's my cue to rise, too, because Dad's a hugger. He pulls me against him, his hands firmly against my back as he pats. "I'm proud of you, Tucker."

"Thanks, Dad," I offer, swallowing around the tight knot in my throat. Being respected and loved, appreciated and adored by your parents no matter what– I know what I've got, and I know it's rare.

Not sure all families would be cool with their son becoming a porn star, but when my life changed trajectories majorly two years ago and I came to my dad, confusion in my heart and pain in my eyes, he sat with me. He listened to me. And then, from the kindest and most selfless disposition, he advised me.

Telling him now that a sex toy company wants to make a line of toys celebrating my cock, well, isn't awkward. Because he's made it that way. Even my mom and siblings, too. They recognize that while different than being a mail carrier like dad or a photographer like mom, work is work. And to me, porn is my career.

A job I happen to really fucking like and be very good at, yes, but in an ideal world that should be true of most jobs. Why spend my life doing something I loathe to make someone else rich? I like this job. I'm making enough money to help my family and I stay secure for a very long time. Those are all good things.

And the fact that my family was able to see the good things versus the stigma and societal judgment, well, it's why I feel like I'm always swallowing down emotion and staving off one, big healthy ugly cry.

The doorbell rings and Mom passes the baby to its mother, who was apparently making a phone call in her car outside. When she's locked the door, she saunters in, her blonde hair shoved off her face with a big pink headband. She peels us apart and takes dad's spot, embracing me like it's been years, not just over a month. But I get it, and hug her back deeply, too.

"What's dad congratulating you about?" she asks, smoothing her hand over my cheek as she studies me, love and adoration in her tired blue eyes.

"Crave & Cure is partnering with Debauchery," I start, knowing full well that my entire family is well-versed in the hierarchy of adult film company names, adult actors, and toys. "And they're launching a Tucker Deep line. The entire line is just me."

She looks at dad, grinning, then back to me. "Oh honey, I'm so proud of you," she coos, yanking me back into another hug, this one much tighter, the pride and love surging through her giving her Hulk-like strength.

"Where's Tegan?" I ask about my younger sister as my mom gently guides me to a seat at the kitchen table, collecting her apron off the hook nearby.

Reaching behind, her shoulders move as she ties the apron at her tailbone. A moment later, she's got the cutting board out and all of the ingredients for a summer salad at the table.

As she chops romaine, she fills me in. Dad grabs us another pair of beers.

"The American Kennel Club Agility Invitationals are coming up, she's logging extra hours with Freddie the Cavalier King Charles Spaniel this week. You know, to make sure he's show-ready." Collecting the romaine, she tosses it into a stainless bowl, moving on to the tomatoes. The blade glides through effortlessly, leaving a perfect ring of tomato along the board. "Theo's coming for dinner tonight. He'll be so happy to see you," Mom says with a smile as she plucks a juicy slice of tomato from the board and plunks it into her mouth.

"Theo's heading up? No way! I'm glad. I'm still annoyed I didn't see him last time I was here."

My older brother, who is really the spitting image of my dad, sans the graying hair, is incredibly busy. He owns several pawn shops, all quite successful, and recently, he's had a camera crew following him around for a new reality show they're filming. I haven't seen him in over two and a half months.

And he's a bad texter. Like the type of guy who has a flip phone still and no apps that can connect to the internet. It's beyond frustrating. But totally his style.

"He needs a break from filming," Dad offers, looking at me with knowing eyes.

"I get that," I say, remembering how much I wanted to drive to Oakcreek and sit on the couch with my family and play SkipBo just six months ago when I was inadvertently contracted to do nine days of shooting back to back. I was in nearly four scenes a day.

Let me tell you something.

Blowing my load is great. Epic, sometimes, even. But thirty-six loads in nine days does something to your brain. Maybe it's because it was work and not love driving me to come like a train on a non-stop cross country passage, but whatever it was, I'd never disliked porn until that week.

"So did the lawyers go over it all?" Dad asks, reverting back to the reason I came. To deliver the news.

"They did. They told Aug all is well."

Crave & Cure is unlike most adult film production companies, and one of the ways they stand out is how well they take care of their employees. Each actor has access to a full legal team, even if it's a personal matter that occurred before you came to Crave.

Augustus, who is the only director at the company, is also the CEO. However, only a select few are privy to that information. I'm one of those few, with a non disclosure agreement promising I keep it to myself.

I signed, because it's standard for the legal department to protect Aug. But I wouldn't have betrayed him by sharing that, anyway. Not ever. I would not be here without Aug.

I grin at mom as she pinches my cheek, now chopping English cucumbers. I haven't even told them the best part. Nabbing my dad's gaze, which can be tricky when mom's in the room, I can't fight the Cheshire-grin pulling at the corner of my mouth.

"There's something else," I tell them, still staring at Dad. Because Dad—well, and my entire family—knows how I met her. But we're moments away from them knowing how far I've gone to see her again. Once I tell them, the whole family will find out. And I'm okay with that.

Because I'm also here for advice.

From both of them. Who better to ask relationship advice than the couple that has been married since they were nineteen?

"They brought in an artist," I tell him, sucking down a nervous pull of stout. "One Debauchery sourced to create the molds for dil—" I clear my throat. My parents are definitely cool with it, but I still try to be respectful in front of my mom. I mean, she's my fuckin' mom. "Toys," I correct. "Some guy who apparently is a great sculptor or something. Anyway, he's going to work with me to create the designs, then use the molds to create the toys. That's, I guess, how these toys are made."

Dad nods. "Like bone clones, only real professionals." He sips his beer as if he didn't just casually mention the clone your own cock at home kit that was hugely popular a few years back thanks to Go Girl magazine.

Mom smacks him in the arm. "Tim!"

"Are we on the cusp of a like-father, like-son moment? Dad

clones his dick, then I clone mine? Aww," I tease dad, which is really aimed at mom, since she's the one with rosy cheeks. "Dad," I drag out, a grin so big I could pass for the Joker. I drape a hand over my heart. "Oh my god."

Moms steadies her knife on the side of the cutting bowl then rubs her palms together, reaching into a reusable bag to retrieve a bright red bell pepper. She grabs her knife and begins slicing and deseeding. I look back to Dad, and wiggle my eyebrows.

"There's more. I started with the least exciting thing first."

Dad drains his beer. "Oh yeah?"

"Remember that sketch class that I was in when Aug found me? Remember the–"

Dad interrupts me with uproarious laughter. "Remember?" he questions, his tone laced with teasing. "Of course I remember."

"Well," I clear my throat, pulse hammering at the base of it, the next part is so ridiculous I'm having trouble getting it out. I swallow, and my ears pound. "I got Aug to tell Debauchery yes under the condition we use her. I said, this guy is out and she's in. That is, if you can find her."

I knew practically nothing about her. I didn't know what year she was that night two and half years ago. I didn't know if she dropped out of school that very night or transferred.

But I did know her first name. I could never make out the scrawl representing her surname.

Dad leans in, ignoring how one of the beer bottles clank into the other. "Did they find her?" He swallows, the anxious anticipation thrumming through him too.

I nod. "Yeah, yeah they did. She's in her last year at the Art Institute."

Dad leans back in his chair and from the peripheral, mom's

head volleys between us, trying to sort out who and what we are talking about.

"What's this? What are we so surprised about?" she asks finally after Dad takes another long minute of silence, just blinking at me.

"That's incredible."

He says it like he feels just how I do: like finding Vienna again after two years feels like fate.

But I balance my giddy emotion with a reality check, accentuated with a careless shrug. "Well, I mean maybe it's not so far-fetched, she was in an art class and school is usually a couple of years. It makes sense that she was still there."

I ignore the statistics of students who drop out of graduate or specialty programs, and lean heavily into the idea that it isn't fate. That it's actually logical and simply a thing that happened. She was still there, Lance found her. That's it.

Dad doesn't buy it, but before he calls me on it, he looks up at mom. "Just a girl Tuck was crushing on at the Institute, that's all."

She arches her brow. "When you were life modeling?"

I nod. "Yeah. I never even met her. Just... yeah." I lift my beer to my lips, but it's empty. Dad chuckles and grabs me another without leaving his chair. The perks of a small kitchen.

"That seems pretty serendipitous," Dad says as I'm taking a drink. "I mean, she's kind of what made you say yes to Aug that night. She changed the course of your life, and now you could potentially change hers."

I swallow the sudden rush of giddiness that sweeps over me. It's just from drinking two plus beers so quickly. It's not because I agree with him and feel like Vienna and I are predestined.

No, it's not that. Because thinking someone is your fated mate is fucking silly. Crazy, even.

Isn't it?

I shrug. "Whatever it is, I'm not sure she's convinced. I don't think she wants to be an artist who makes fake dicks." I wince and look up at mom, who's onto slicing mushrooms. "Sorry."

She shrugs. "Sex is part of life. Honoring sexual health is important. If your son's appendage makes a great toy for women to...*facilitate their needs* with—That's fantastic. I'm proud of you."

Dad hijacks the sentimental moment, saying, "So she's got the offer, but that doesn't explain the worried face son."

"Yeah," I nod, "she's got the contract. But I don't think she's convinced."

My parents are both quiet a minute, because we're all thinking the same thing. It's not the first time any of us have been hurt by the stigma of being in the sex industry. My parents and siblings have experienced a fair amount of shaming in the last two years. And I've had a healthy dose of guilt, judgment, and all the other sprinkles on the "you're a disgusting monster" sundae.

And though I didn't say those words, I think we all know what I mean when I say Vienna has yet to be convinced.

I am worried she doesn't know if she can work in this industry, because she thinks it's less than everything else.

Most people start there.

But if she sees how C&C operates for herself, there's no way she could think that. She'll see what a great person Aug is to have on your side. And what a great industry this is when you're working for and with the right people.

"Well," Dad says, "convince her. I'm sure whatever generous offer Aug made her may have enticed her initially, but it's down to you to close the deal and make her see that what you do is important. That you take your job seriously and by extension, making a toy with your name on it is just as important."

My mom nods along and their honest and unending support of their son being a sex worker is what keeps my head from spinning off right now.

Because I need Vienna to say yes to this job. I need time with her to get to know the woman with the devilish smile that captured my attention so completely in that class. Everything in me is telling me she and I are meant for more than making dildos together.

Wow, that would be a very abstract greeting card.

8

Vienna

I guess I'm stuck with Tuck

"Don't drink it fast like that. It's meant to be savored," Darren says, dragging out the last word as he stirs a pot of red sauce. Sauce I'm sure he claims is homemade but I know it comes from a jar from Trader Joe's on 9th street.

"I don't want to savor it." I empty my glass in one swallow.

"You don't want to get hammered again, you want Dutch courage," he corrects, and he's right. I don't. I just want a tiny buzz. For my nerves to settle just enough to finally breathe.

All of this has been so much to process. So much to digest.

I still have room for wine, though.

"Ugh I know." I pinch shredded mozzarella from the plate and drop it into my mouth, earning me a disgusted groan from Darren. I glance at Samson, but he is unaware of what a bad dinner guest I am because his nose is still buried deep in the contract.

Perks of being best friends with a guy dating a lawyer. Free legal advice. But judging by the scowl on his face, this may be my first and last free session.

"How's it looking?" I question, my shoulders perking up as I peer over the pot of sauce, to my papers spread between his large hands.

He tips them toward his chest. "I'll let you know," he says, giving me a pointed look that says *don't push your fucking luck.* I smile.

"You look amazing in that suit."

He returns his focus to the papers, trying not to bask in the compliment.

"Explain to me what the biggest problem with it is?" Darren asks, his question wriggling beneath my skin like barbed wire. But as we lock gazes, I see true confusion etched in a ridge between his brows, deep creases striking in length across his forehead.

"I'm an artist, Darren!" I sigh with exasperation, my shoulders giving away my internal defeat. "I'm not enduring years of perfecting my craft and amassing crippling debt to be a cock maker!" My temples pound, and ironically that's probably the first time *cock* has made any part of me pound.

Darren lifts the wooden spoon from the stainless pot, placing it down gently in the porcelain trivet. His head tips to the side, the flat expression on his face making my stomach knot.

Before he can lay into me, Samson closes the file of my documents and slaps it onto the table. He gets to his feet and grabs his drink from the counter. Propping his back to the sink, he glares at me. Sweat slides down my back because something about a lawyer with a cruel gaze is intimidating. Makes you feel guilty or exposed, or both.

A shiver whips through me when he clears his throat, almost patronizingly. "You do realize that Crave & Cure is the biggest, most sought after adult film company in all of the United States. They could get anyone. They're asking *you.*" That final *you.* The way it lifted at the end, felt like a slap in the face.

"Jesus," I breathe, my chest heavy with shame and feeling smaller than I have. I'm a strong woman but I'm not sure I'm prepared to hear the home truths I can feel headed my way. "Tell me you don't like me without telling me you don't like me. Is that the game we're playing, Samson?" My stomach coils as dread creeps in at what he's about to say.

He snorts. "I don't dislike you, Vienna. But that's my point." He takes a sip of his drink and I glance at Darren, knowing my mouth is boundlessly agape. But I can't close it. I feel so vulnerable and... they are my safe space.

He catches my eyes. "You are coming off as... *entitled.*"

"Entitled?" I lurch forward, disbelief curling my shoulders and neck.

"Yes." Samson lowers his empty glass to the counter and levels with me. "Why are you under the impression that you are too good for this job? Seriously? Give me one reason."

I lick my lips, and my tongue sticks to the roof of my mouth. Fuck. "I'm graduating from the Art Institute," I retort, rather half-heartedly. My pulse beats in my throat like a panic-inducing traitor, and suddenly I'm mad at myself.

Mad I can't just come here and vent and be heard and safe. Mad that I'm not feeling worse, and at the moment, very fucking angry.

I don't want to defend this because the truth is? He's right.

"You're acting like you're too fucking good for creative

work in the adult industry. And quite frankly, I question if you're good enough. Because the person that's right for this job is a person who realizes what an opportunity it is. That person would not be sitting in front of me with a sanctimonious look of horror at being offered said opportunity." He licks his lips, and I wonder why he's so passionately angry with me about this.

Am I the asshole?

"If the top of any other industry offered you a role as prin-ciple creative, you'd piss yourself and tweet to all of your 103 followers about it." He has a big vein in his forehead that pulses to the beat of his anger.

Anger toward me, no less.

"Take it easy," Darren limps in on my behalf, and I roll my eyes at him. He's already torn the flesh and meat from my bones; Darren's timing is lame.

But I'm so hurt because... he is right. I am only turning my nose up at this because it's porn. And I associate people who work in the porn industry as... *lesser*. No porn star went on to become a traditional film actor and win an Oscar. No one working on the set of a porn shoot got the gig of designing a Broadway set. And no one who makes cocks for a living has a spotlight in Vanity Fair.

"You're right," I tell Samson, getting to my feet. "You're right. I'm judging it because it's porn and I don't feel like anyone super successful comes from porn. And I want success." I shake my head, snatching my purse off the counter.

He doesn't intimidate me, but I don't have any desire to stay here. This day has been overwhelming enough without being Samson's personal punching bag, too.

"Your success may look differently than you envisioned." His voice drops an octave, and his shoulders soften. I hate that his singular demeanor shift changes the energy of the whole room. I hate that he has that power. But he does. "Let me rephrase that. Your success may look different from what your parents envisioned."

I breathe deeply, the corners of my mind darkening.

"You could make good money at this, Vienna. And be proud of it, too. You're deciding already that you couldn't be proud of this, but you could." He steps closer and I hate that my eyes grow warm. I analyze my hands where they're wrapped around my purse.

"I'm angry that you don't let yourself be happy. You're always sabotaging yourself, and I hate to see you waste opportunity because of judgments someone else instilled in you."

"Samson," I say carefully, very cautiously to tiptoe around the huge boulder of emotion wedged in my throat.

"We've known each other for five years, Vienna. I don't hate you. I hate that you can be closed-minded. To your own detriment."

I gasp, and my eyes sting with unshed tears. "I am not closed minded." I think about the words. About how Samson was right before. Could he be right now, too?

"You're so focused on trying to prove your parents wrong that you are losing sight of why you went it alone. Your success cannot be measured based on *their* narrow view of the world. Whatever you do with this degree, you will never be a success in their eyes. Whether you have a critically acclaimed show at the museum or you sculpt cocks. So why are you so concerned about what other people think? What does success look like to you?"

"Fuck," I say, bringing my hand to my mouth. I look up at him, and his gaze nearly brings me to my knees. Dark and serious, but full of care. He's right. I feel like a continual let down. Maybe I do push away opportunities because in the back of my mind, I'm afraid of what people will think. What my parents will think.

Oh god. I feel sick.

"You are right yet again," I sigh, wishing I could just collapse right there, and melt into a pile of liquid humiliation, and slither down the drain. But before I can do that, I have to at least get home so I can be a puddle in my own house. "I'm going to go."

Darren races around the counter and gathers me in his arms, looking down at me with pursed lips. I look past him to Samson, standing where he was, his features soft.

"Don't go. He's not trying to be mean, but he's right."

"And," Samson offers, "I haven't told you my thoughts on the contract."

I slide back into my seat and set my purse on top of the counter. By the stem, I slide the glass toward Darren, who has returned to his pot of sauce.

"Fine. More wine. And no more forced epiphanies. I get it, I've been a snob."

"You are a product of your environment," Darren says carefully. "But just because your parents are awful and Madeline is a snot doesn't mean you have to live your life to someone else's standards. Run your own damn race, Vienna."

Samson is the one to refill my wine, and to my surprise, he does this before he refills his glass. "Ever ask Darren how many years he swept floors at the museum?"

I assault the countertop and slap my palms down flat, whipping my head to face my best friend. "You said you started at the desk right away," I shout. "You little liar."

He gives Samson a look of warning before returning to me. Taking a moment to collect his thoughts, he calmly says, "I swept the floor for three years before Dahlia even spoke my first name."

"Jesus Christ." And with that, I take a big drink of wine. "And that's what I'm working for? Respect from a woman who treats us like..." I trail off, unsure what's comparable. My parents have a cat and I swear to God, they talk to her more than Dahlia's spoken to me. In over two fucking years.

The museum is looking more like a prison now than a place to weep at soul-altering art.

"What did you do to finally get the desk?" I ask, swirling my wine and taking a breath to calm my nerves. But the way his lips twist nervously for a second, rolling together then popping to stall time, I have a bad feeling.

"Have you heard Dahlia reference Chaz?" From behind him, Samson snorts. "Don't laugh, Sam," he scolds, returning to me battling a smirk of his own.

"Chaz the great," I say easily, because in my head, I always call the unknown man by that moniker. Because, when Darren isn't around, she's always huffing about how *Chaz would know much better* and other unsavory things.

I've never mentioned the name to Darren to fish around because I didn't want to share the context in which I'd learned it. "What about him?"

"He worked the desk before me." Darren lifts his chin, attempting to compose himself but now the ghost of a smirk is manifesting in a laugh wracking his chest.

"Oh. So... what? He quit? Or you like, what, went behind his back and stole it out from him or something?"

Samson lets out a low whistle, shaking his head as he turns his focus to his feet.

"I didn't mean it like that," I say, "I just mean, what? Why are you guys twitching over this Chaz person?"

Darren settles his shoulders, holding them square with mine, chin high. He collects a breath, pushing it out hard, and then, "He died. We are not laughing because he died, because we really liked him."

Samson is suddenly slightly solemn when he adds quietly, "He was a cool guy."

"You've never talked about him," I say, because Darren and I have known each other for the better part of five years.

"We weren't close. And I didn't work with him hardly ever." Darren shrugs. "Really, we weren't close but we did like him. He came over a few times for dinner. Always well-mannered."

I take pause, trying to sort out the problem. Or the obvious clue I'm so clearly missing. Because they're eyeing me.

"What?"

"He passed on a Saturday. Dahlia came to the apartment. I opened the door and she said 'Chaz is dead. You have the desk. Don't embarrass the gallery.' And that was it."

I still don't understand what's funny. "I don't get it," I say, tracing the rim of my glass with my fingertip. Using my other hand, I nudge my glasses up my nose, blinking at him. I want to understand.

"I closed the door and turned to Samson, and I think I was in shock but... I just started crying and saying, 'I finally got the promotion.'" He smiles but instantly, it falls, leaving his face sharp and pointed. "It was the first time I realized the entire system had made me a worse person. Because I liked Chaz, but I can't deny part of me was glad to take the job. To have the opportunity." His serious eyes find my wet ones. "How fucked up is that?"

My voice is quiet, reassuring. "I think that's human nature. You still had to go on. And you wanted that job."

We're quiet a moment before Darren says, "You wouldn't have thought that, though, would you?"

"The whole point of the Chaz story is to show you that your perfect dream of being an artist who showcases her main-stream-popular art in the museum she used to work at," Samson adds, diverting the conversation, "Is complete fucking bullshit."

I blink at him, studying his passionate eyes and the way they bunch slightly at the corners, his few years on Darren evident.

"No one makes it because they followed some set of idealized notions of the proper way to do things, not really. Sure, some people manage to truly make it by people discovering that they are the best. The gifted, talented, honored, special one. But not often. Because now it's all about who's dick you're sucking, how much money you're paying to have your shit plastered over every square inch of the internet, and who you know. Who knows the person that gets you there. What favor you can curry, what trick you can perform." He shakes his head. "Art, entertainment, sports, life. It's all that way, now. The successful don't make it because they did it the right way. They have to be willing to toss their proverbial tie over their shoulder and get on their knees. Still, they have to beg. It's never enough. Once you're up there at the top. I don't think you'd like the view; the carnage behind you of what it took to get there."

My chest heaves as his words spin through me, leaving me dizzy and critically off balance. "And... porn's not that way?" I ask, genuinely asking. Desperate for the answer to be no. Because I believe that speech. I've seen it first hand.

Madeline's pussy won a grant.

Madeline's aunt plays golf with the dean.

"Crave & Cure is not only the leading porn film production company in the United States but they have the highest retention rate. All around. Actors, set hands, assistants, etc." He taps the closed file on the counter, the one I would've stormed out with had I left. "They get full benefits. Even the fluffers."

"You can stay at the museum. You know I love you being there. But he's right. Until I die, you could be sweeping floors unless you're willing to fuck some rich senator and get some cash to buy your place on the floor."

I gasp and run my fingers along the gold necklace looping my neck. I'll pretend they're pearls. "Is that how Dahlia selects artists to be showcased? Who pays her the most?"

Darren nods slowly. "Duh."

"Oh my god," I drawl.

"That's business. And if you want to be successful, then you need to realize that being an artist is also being a business. And from a business standpoint, you should absolutely take this job with Crave & Cure."

Tucker's face flashes in my mind.

Who am I kidding? I've thought about his face about a thousand times in the last hour alone. God he was so hot. His eyes, holy mother of god. They were so gorgeous. So fucking green and at the risk of sounding like a WB show from the 2000s, sparkly, too. The kind of eyes that make you stare. Make you forget what you were doing.

"I'd be working one on one with Tucker Deep," I say, ready to amend my statement with his title as their top male lead, but I don't get the chance.

"Tucker Deep," Samson nods approvingly, a smile lifting his eyes. "We like him."

"You guys *know* him?"

"Oh my god *Little House on the Prairie*, we're a gay couple. We watch porn. Of fucking course we know who Tucker Deep is." He shakes his head, and Samson slides a hand along the back of Darren's shoulders, bringing their sides together.

"Grow up, Vienna." He says, dropping a peck on Darren's cheek. "And Tucker Deep always seems so fucking into every scene. It's acting, but at some points it feels so real, so genuine, I don't know. You forget it's porn and you feel like you're part of this private thing. It's... unique and hot."

Darren beams up at him. "That was hot listening to you describe it," he balks softly.

I take a drink of my wine, and consider the evening.

Tucker is... good at his job. Not to mention, gorgeous as hell. And *I'd get to touch his penis.*

Oh my god. Hot and cold shivers wrack my body, somehow all at once, making me flush. Low in my belly, everything grows achy and tight. And suddenly, I wish I were home. Locked in my room. Debauchery toy at my side.

I'd have a good income, at least for a year. That's the length of my contract, despite the fact that I'd be paid a lump sum and only do a few months of work at a time for each casting. I'd be obligated to stay on hand between launches, almost on retainer. Then after that, free.

I'd be working for a company that Samson claims would not only value my work but also me.

Free and *much richer*. One hundred thousand dollars richer, plus the possibility of being on retainer with Debauchery, if their sales projections are met the first week.

It would give me some breathing space to look for a position in the art space, outside the museum. I've always liked the idea of working at a small, roadside tiny little art outpost, where I feature pieces I've created from my in-home studio.

But I've never had money to travel, never had the means to really create the pieces I had planned, etched in my heart.

My parents would hate it.

"Well, when you lay it all out like this" I sigh, putting on an air of indifference. "I guess I'm stuck with Tuck. At least for a year." I take a drink of my wine and internally scream at the top of my lungs because yeah I'm making dildos but I get to touch Tucker Deep's dick and I am not mad.

9

Tucker

My personal mission is to change her mind.

"Ahhh," I exhale loudly, and it bounces back into my empty bed. My apartment is a penthouse and it overlooks a busy city, one that rarely sleeps. But still, the lack of noise in my home deafens me sometimes.

Morning is the worst.

You have to pull yourself out of the warm covers, exposing comfortable flesh to the sting of daylight. Ugh. Mornings should start with your arms wrapped around someone you love.

I dream of the day where I wake and bury my nose in her hair. Whoever she is. Kiss the top of her head, down to her temple, then steal her mouth and suddenly I'm sliding inside of her, and she's moaning before she's even said good morning.

Instead, I let my toes search for the undiscovered, cool

pockets in the sheets, because that is my greatest morning pleasure.

My morning wood almost depresses me at this point.

I sit up in bed, glancing at my phone on the nightstand. It's 7:04 in the morning. I have to be on set at nine, so I have plenty of time for my workout and a shower. But not before I jerk off.

My morning wood might depress me, but I have three scenes to do today and I like to start out with one round already out of the chamber before I arrive. Earn me a little more tease time, give me a little extra.

As I reach into my briefs, I think of Vienna, and the way she wrinkles her nose to get her glasses to slide back up. How she studies people with those gorgeous hazelnut eyes of hers. She intimidates the fuck out of me and makes me hard, and god, her sketch.

I have to know if she's taking the job. I abandon my dick and reach for my phone, swiping to our text message thread.

> Did Vienna Carnegie accept the job?

Lance seems to never sleep, or if he does, very little. He's animalistic in some ways. His response bounces my way in under thirty seconds.

LANCE

She's coming in today. A secondary meeting. Hasn't given us an answer yet.

My thumbs are moving the moment I see the word today.

> What time is she coming in?

Ten.

84

The grin that stretches across my face is so big I actually feel a bit creepy for a second. But she *is* being hired to touch my cock.

It may, however, be a little creepy how I'm grinning about looking forward to it. But it's not *her* seeing *me*, it's just the goddamn idea of seeing her. Getting another few precious minutes to admire her. Absorb her. Paint an indelible image of her in my brain. Know every slope and plump detail of her so well that I can mold her from memory, by hand. I look down and find my cock long, thick and so very fucking hard.

I walk toward my closet and push the clothes aside, exposing the thin black frame fused to the wall. I shove my hand down my briefs and fill my palm, my dick throbbing.

Stroking, her name sticky between my lips, my knees attempting to buckle, and I come in less than a minute.

Seeing Vienna today has me wondering if a round two won't be needed. Those cute little fucking glasses and those damn eyelashes. Makes me hard again just thinking of them, cum still sticky on my hand.

Jesus, time for a cold shower. I have to prepare for my scenes.

I turn the knob to C, and push Vienna out of my head, for the next hour in the name of good porn.

You're welcome.

"So you think he's lying?" I ask, popping a green grape into my mouth, my other hand holding my naked dick.

She volleys her head, the ends of her blonde ponytail swishing along her back. "I don't know. I mean, does he really not want the watch because he doesn't wanna seem flashy or does he not want *me* to pay for the watch?" She dusts a piece of graham cracker off her nipple then looks back up at me. "Why are men so moody?"

Plucking a strawberry from my bowl, I take a bite, attempting to put myself in Chanel's boyfriend's shoes. If I had a partner who made more money than me, would I feel weird accepting gifts?

Um, no because gifts that come from the heart give me a fucking heart-on and that's awesome.

Yes, giving and receiving emotional care and support to someone you're head over heels for gets me chubbed up. I can't help it. I think it's because all I've ever really known for sure that I wanted from life was love. And I know guys don't openly admit that, but I'd bet they feel it. There's no way I'm the only one. I want someone to hold my face in their hands as they kiss me. I want someone to slip their hands up my shirt and pull their nails down my back. I want heels in my ass. I want long hairs from her head caught around my balls. I want arguments and passionate sex. I want it all.

"Maybe it's the money thing, but for me, I wouldn't give a fuck. If that watch made you think of me, then I would wear it loud and fuckin' proud on my wrist."

She inhales another graham cracker, putting toddlers around the world to shame. "I'm not asking him to announce it to the world that I bought it. I don't care about that." She finishes the snack and takes a sip of water through a metal straw. She doesn't want to mess up her lipstick, but she's about to suck me off in the next scene. A bit ironic. "I just wanted to get him something he's always dreamed of having. That's all."

I wipe my fruit sticky hand down my thigh and clap my hand to her upper arm, smiling. Chanel and I have always had a relationship that's honestly more close to friends that have grown up together and aren't at all into one another.

We haven't grown up together but we have been working together for the last two years. Chanel helped me learn the lingo and ropes when I came to Crave, and for that I'll always be grateful. It's not to say that others didn't help, because they did, but she pulled me aside and gave me pointers in a way that didn't completely overwhelm and intimidate me.

If Aug is the archangel, she is my guardian angel. *Of porn.*

Hard to believe Tucker two years ago was unsure and slightly nervous. But Chanel was one of the actresses that helped me come out of my shell. And no, that's not a euphemism for foreskin.

"I know that's your intention. Because I know all you want to do is make him happy." I curl my arm, bringing her to me, placing a chaste kiss at her temple. Her nipple grazes my chest and my dick, still in hand, stiffens at the contact. He's reacting —it's kind of his job.

She ignores my dick between us, growing fat and happy in my hand, and grins at me. "Thanks, Tuck."

"You deserve someone who appreciates who you are, Chanel."

"Tucker," Lance calls as he approaches, an iPad tucked under his arm. I swear if he didn't have an iPad under his arm and a grouchy look on his face, I may mistake him for someone happy.

Blonde hair always styled perfectly, his fade always sharp and impeccable, the coiffure of silken hair toppling effortlessly to the side, Lance stands in front of me. His dark eyes narrow on Chanel, then come to me. "Are you both ready?" he asks, glancing at his watch before peeking at the schedule on the iPad. "Three minutes. Do you need Russ or Cam?"

Playfully, I wince and look down at my half-hard cock. I

start stroking, grinning at Lance. "Russ and Cam can fluff Dean and Drake. I can stroke."

He rolls his eyes and turns on his heel, beelining for Aug who stands huddled over his Canon R6 Mark II, the camera he maintains is the best after all his years in the business.

"You really never use Russ or Cam?" Chanel asks, sliding a tube of mocha colored lipstick along her supple lips. Rolling them together, she blots using a tissue, moving her fingers through her hair next.

My shoulder burns as I continue to jerk, watching her. I'm not jerking *to* watching her, and both of us know that. Porn sets can be weird, and it's about the only place in the world where you can have a conversation about fancy watches and relationships while jerking off and talking to a woman, all while not feeling anything for her.

"I always want to be able to excite myself," I reply. When I started this job, I was worried I'd be ridden hard and put away wet so often that by the time I got into a relationship, sex would be challenging. That I'd need so much extra stimulation, bells and whistles, whips and partners—I made myself the promise that I'd aim never to use a fluffer to get me hard before scenes. Even though Crave has both traditional and completely non-traditional fluffing on hand.

Still, I have stayed true to my word.

She smiles after dropping a small comb back into the makeup bag on the table. "That's good, Tuck. I like that."

I shrug my shoulders. "I keep thinking once I meet someone, it'll all pay off. But I can't seem to meet anyone who wants to really date me, you know? I'm a novelty. The prize in a Cracker Jack box. Having a porn star boyfriend. Once that wears off, I'm just a guy who fucks a lot and women don't seem to vibe with that."

While I had no plans of wallowing in the fact that being a

male porn star actually *doesn't* open you up to a world of relationship options, today, it surfaces. And I know why.

Vienna is coming in.

And soon. Within the next few minutes, even. And I know I don't know her, not really. But she feels like such a big part of my story; a reason why I am where I am today.

And the fact that Lance found her. I don't care that he seemed to think it wasn't a big deal. It meant something to me.

She means something to me. Even if it's ridiculous and completely mirroring the plot of a movie my mom and sister would watch on cable TV, I don't care.

With her on the way, whether her answer is yes or no, I'm still in my head. Nervous and talking about shit I normally reserve for Dad, Theo and Tripp. Sometimes even Mom.

Fortunately, Chanel is cool and I trust her.

She tucks hair behind her ear, fiddling with the split ends as she strokes her fingers through. "I know. Kinda why I want it to work with my boyfriend so much, you know? That's one place we're solid. He knows work is work, and he never shows me off like a... well, a porn star."

This topic finds its way into my therapy from time to time. The way people want to date porn stars just to have sex with them, like we're a crazy box on the bucket list they never expected to check. *Fuck a porn star!* Then we're just a novelty left on the side of the road, someone's used as a shocking anecdote at parties after a few too many glasses of wine.

Feelings and wants are rarely considered. It's usually sex, more sex, maybe meet my friends and be asked a thousand questions about porn, then dumped.

It's brutal.

But I hold out hope there is someone out there for me, someone who doesn't see me as a novelty. As a brag. As a thing.

Because I want that deep connection, that home space that

engulfs you in security and love the moment your toes curl the threshold. I want arms around me, kisses on my throat, whispers of love and giggles of secrets in my ear. I don't want a one time fuck. And I don't want to be introduced, before my name, as "the guy, you know, the one who does *movies*."

Lance reappears, nodding toward the set, directing me to my mark.

"Get positioned, we're testing lights. Then it's go time." He swipes along his screen, nodding easily. "And the scene today is Chanel's first time."

He passes the script to me, and I thumb through for less than ten seconds, my eyes taking in the key words and refreshing my memory. In our usual *Curb Your Enthusiasm* style, we'll absorb the key details of the script and interpret them as freely and naturally as possible.

With Chanel on her back centering the twin bed, I stand above her, my fingers curled around the end of her robe's tie. Her dark hair is splayed against the pillow beneath her, bright eyes wide. She pinches her nipples, getting them looking wanton and needy for the scene.

I roll a condom on, prepared to impale Chanel as soon as the camera starts rolling.

"You'll find a good one, one that loves you for you, not for this," Chanel whispers up at me from the bed, as we wait for Lance and the crew, who amble on set to test the lighting. Extreme warmth sears my back, and that's how I know that we're that much closer to starting the scene. The light they shine on me to make my eight inch dick look like ten inches (thanks, shadows) is on and ready, and like Pavlov's dog, *I'm* ready.

"Thanks, C," I whisper, and then–

"And we're rolling," Augustus states loudly, bluntly, followed by the metallic slap of his slates.

One knee on the mattress, I blink down at Chanel. My virtuous virgin, the object of my affection, the girl whom I've waited for years to claim. I've loved her, according to the script for this movie, *for years*.

I'm her brother's best friend, and right now, she's giving herself to me in the hopes that I will offer more.

And I do. The scene we're filming after lunch today is our wedding night.

Yeah, a fair amount of Crave & Cure films are like romance novels brought to life. Complete with a meet cute and epilogue where viewers get to see how happily the couple is still fucking, even after the main story is over. Blending the unique trait of complete storytelling and full romance with porn is... amazing. This is what porn should be. Not the cold, calculated, fake moans and artificially enhanced cocks pounding for an unrealistic amount of time, making people feel like trash about their sex lives.

"My little dove," I whisper, my thumb making slow circles on the pink satin between my fingers. With a short, strong tug, her robe opens, pooling around her bare body on the mattress. "Spread your legs and let me show you all of the things I've wanted to do for years."

She whimpers, and my cock, nearly completely hard, closes the gap between semi and hard-on at the noise. Chanel is so good at innocent whimpers. I think it's a big reason why they continually cast her as the good girl. She plays the role well.

With my hands now on her knees, I give her legs a gentle shove, exposing her bare pussy to me.

"Freeze," Aug shouts, causing us to literally freeze the moment. The makeup girl runs on set, pressing a fluffy pad to the tip of my nose, and then my chin. She moves to Chanel, doing the same. While she does, I glance over at Aug, to see if I can gauge his expression on how we're doing so far. But instead, I see Vienna.

Two paces behind Aug and Lance, Vienna stands, her long, dark hair twisted into a bun on the top of her head, arms wrapped around her torso. In overalls and crocs, her face free of makeup, glasses already sliding down her nose, I smile.

She doesn't return the smile but instead begins glancing around, as if she thinks the smile was misguided. Before I can reassure her, the makeup girl is jogging off set, claiming to have gotten rid of all the shine. Then Aug is resuming the scene.

And when I look back down at Chanel, I see Vienna.

I know it's wrong to act out this scene with her in mind, and I know it's pretty strange to feel so infatuated with a perfect stranger but knowing her eyes are on me... drives me wild.

"You have no idea how many times I've envisioned this, sweet girl," I groan, sliding my thumb up the split of her pussy, Chanel squirming to the sensitive stroke.

Finding her clit, I make lazy circles on it with the pad of my thumb, getting high from the way Chanel's eyelids flutter. Would Vienna take her glasses off during sex? Would she melt for me this way?

Reaching down, I grab my sheathed cock and bring the shiny head to Chanel's groin, resting it as I continue to edge her.

"Touch me," she whimpers, bringing her hands to her breasts, pushing them together as her head swings back, exposing a runway of creamy skin along her throat.

Leaning over, I abandon her clit and bump her hands from her breasts, replacing them with mine. My lips come to hers but not in a kiss. I whisper against her as I knead her tits softly, thumbs grazing the stiff peaks, "I've pictured this so long. Nothing I imagined does you justice." I swallow, dropping my mouth to her neck, sucking in her skin. She squeals at the gesture, making her turn her face to find mine. "The way you melt at my touch, the way you taste."

We kiss. She moans into my mouth as I rub and squeeze her tits. Beneath me, her hips lift, desperate for contact, desperate for my cock.

I reach down and position my crown at her opening, surging my hips forward to give her the head, plus another inch or two.

She mewls at my thick cock spreading her, giving the cry a little more energy and voice than usual. After all, she's putting on that I'm tearing her hymen in two. Which I am not.

"I've imagined this, too," she sighs dreamily as I serve her another few inches. "I've wanted you forever."

It takes all of me to not look over at Vienna like an absolute crazy person so instead, I give Chanel my most intense, intimate eye contact, using her as a safe place to get lost in. Using the scene, too.

"Me too, little dove," I groan, the familiar pressure building between my legs, and urgent ache rumbling through my balls.

In and out, I fuck Chanel in slow, gentle strokes, my hands lost in her hair as I sway above her. Her eyes hold mine, and I see Vienna in the moment, beneath me, trembling, anxious, but so fucking ready to be *mine*.

"Tell me," she whispers from beneath me, all tight and hot around my dick as I fuck her slowly, rhythmically. The type of sex meant to draw out long, core-shaking orgasms. The type of sex I want to have with *her*. "Tell me how I compare to your fantasy of me."

"My fantasies are nothing compared to actually having you," I tell her, then I drop my mouth down her body as I find her breast, and suck it into my mouth. She writhes beneath me, nails dragging up my back, mewls of desperate pleasure enveloping me.

"Yes," she pants as I slowly thrust my cock in and out of her. I lick my way up her chest, to her neck, and find her mouth again. In the peripheral, the VIN flag waves. As the scene features a virgin, it's not meant to last as long as "regular" sex. A virgin would need to be fucked carefully and gently, and unless she wanted a UTI and an aching cervix, she couldn't go forever.

Chanel, who reads me, clenches her cunt around me, pushing me to reach the finish line for the scene. I move my hips a tiny bit faster, sinking into her a bit deeper with each stroke.

Her lips are on my jaw, fingers in my hair as she moans, "Give me your orgasm. I want to know what it's like to feel you come inside me."

One more glance down into her wide dark eyes, another moment where I envision Vienna, her eyes closed, cheeks pink, expression one of a sated, loved woman. It's all it takes for me to still inside Chanel, my cock throbbing as I flood the condom with my hot, greedy orgasm.

Around my length, Chanel succumbs to her own release. She's one of the women at C&C who can't help but topple to the feeling of a man coming inside of her. And I love knowing that with her, we'll have a good time together.

As I'm peppering kisses to her rosy skin, telling her what a good job she did taking all of me, how well she accepted my cock, Aug calls cut. His slates slap, and it's the cue needed to bring me out of the moment, back to reality.

I slide out, grabbing the heavy tipped condom in one hand, outstretching my other arm to Chanel. She takes it, grinning, still catching her breath.

"Does anyone have a first time that good?" she asks. "And by the way," she adds, facing Aug who now stands next to us, Lance's iPad in his hands. "I came but didn't say it because virgin's do not have vaginal orgasms their first time. I'm sorry. That's just not a real thing."

Aug nods. "It was just what I envisioned," he says to her before turning to me. "We have a meeting with Vienna Carnegie," he tells me, and I'm surprised that Lance hasn't told him that he's already spoken with me about it. Lance isn't just an assistant, as Augustus mentioned before. I don't know that Aug could run this company without Lance, and I don't know that this company could run without him either. They're tight, thick as thieves, despite the fact they're both guarded as shit.

Still, Lance having not shared with Aug is rare. "I know," I say. "Lance told me this morning. He didn't tell you?"

Aug's face flashes with concern, but it's tempered within a moment. He glances at the iPad then up at me. "Conference room in five minutes. Catch a shower. After the meeting we'll take lunch and film the wedding and epilogue scene. Chanel, head over to make up. They're starting to work on your prosthetic."

She jumps in place, eager to have a big, fake pregnant belly strapped to her. Then, he turns and heads straight for Vienna, whom I've been forcing myself not to stare at since the scene ended.

Did she enjoy it? Did she even watch?

I watch as Augustus says something to her, then ushers her toward the conference room hiding in the hallway off the main set. If she doesn't take this job, I want to believe I'll be fine. Truthfully, she's a stranger. A stranger turning down a job shouldn't affect me.

But I know if she says no, I'll be wrecked. Because she's part of the reason I'm here, and if it's not fate that brought us together, nothing fucking makes sense.

I head to the locker room, immediately hopping under the shower spray, desperate for cool water to temper my burning skin. The heat flares, even through the chilly downfall, and I know that feeling won't go away until I see her.

After drying off and securing sweats around my waist, slipping into a t-shirt, I saunter into the conference room. Debauchery isn't here today; this meeting is solely for Vienna. To find out if she wants this job.

My pulse knows why we're having this meeting, and it's hammering like crazy as I slip into a seat across from her, trying my best to not act the way I feel.

Desperate.

I get comfortable in the plastic chair—as comfortable as a 6'3" man could ever be in a chair that collapses to fit under your bed—whisper something of zero importance to Lance, then let my gaze drift over the table.

Her cheeks are flushed, and for that matter, her neck and collarbone bear the same rosy hue. My lips twitch, battling a more than satisfied smile at the idea that she's flush from watching my scene.

I extend a hand over the table, half of a handshake, and say, "Hi, nice to see you again."

She peers at my hand like I may have wiped my bare ass with it, and wrinkles her nose. Her freckles are darker when she scrunches her face like that, and those goddamn frames she pushes up with one fingertip... between my legs, my cock plumps.

"I washed my hands," I say teasingly, but still, she doesn't shake it. I take it back, but my feelings aren't hurt.

Because I don't think she's *actually* grossed out by me or my hand that has been all over Chanel's pussy. The flush of her skin and the swelling in her bottom lip—the one that is a result of her biting it—tell me what I need to know.

She's turned on, and I can work with that. I can knead that into more, I know I can.

"Well, not sure if you remember me from the other day but I'm Tucker Deep. I'm the cock you're casting."

"If I say yes," she retorts, and though the words could be pointed, they're more hesitant than anything. She came here unsure, and I really hope that Lance has worked whatever magic he works to get her to agree. And this feels like my only chance with her.

"You'll say yes," I boldly state, much more hopeful than confident. "I think you like being here more than you're ready to admit." I sit back, the conference room chair squeaking as I get comfortable in a partial recline.

Augustus rereads some of the terms, and she asks a few questions, more to clarify that she did indeed understand. Then she tells Aug that her lawyer reviewed the contracts.

If she showed this to a lawyer, that means she's actually considering it. I pull myself closer, putting my entire lap under the cover of the table. Because hope has me bricked up.

After a few more details are worked out, Vienna looks at me then brings her pen to the paper, scrawling her signature on the lines tabbed just for her. My heart seizes, and I have to press my curled fist to my lips to stifle that pleased grin that holds my face utterly hostage.

Lance says something to Aug and the two of them rise. Lance drops a hand to my shoulder, indicating that they're leaving, but I'm not. I don't know if it's because they have some-where else to be and I don't, but they leave after collecting the signed contracts and exchanging hand shakes.

Vienna rises, ready to follow them out, but I can't squander the gift of privacy that Lance has given us. She doesn't realize it's a gift, and maybe it's just for me, but still, I won't waste it.

"Can I take you out to celebrate your new job?" I ask, closing the distance between us. We're just a few feet apart, and if her eyes dropped to my sweats, she'd see how much I liked watching her sign her signature. How much I like having her here.

Quickly, I drop into a seat at the table, leaving her looking puzzled above me. Barely above me, I might add, because Vienna is so petite.

But I don't want to be sporting an erection when it's just her and I together. Not yet, at least. Not until I have her consent that my erection is something she personally wants.

I'm not a goddamn creep.

"I don't think so," she says after a moment. The way her eyes roam over me critically, a tiny wrinkle in her nose, seems to say *I don't date porn stars.*

Then she ducks her head in a nod of acknowledgment, hands me a tight lipped smile, and exits the conference room.

She said no to a date. And she may have an idea in her head about who I am. But she's here. She's working at Crave & Cure.

My personal mission is to change her mind.

10

Vienna

Disrobe and apply the coconut oil.

"We use silicone because it's an elastomer. That means it's able to stretch but also regain its shape. Perfect for a toy we want to have *give*, but to ultimately retain its form," Dalton says, wearing a smile like we're not discussing what comprises fake dick.

Inhaling a deep breath through my nose, I exhale discreetly, keeping myself focused on the materials lesson. I have to get used to being so free and open with sex. Because I am officially an employee of Crave & Cure.

The last time I was around a beautiful, naked man, I ran out of a class then promptly dropped it because I was so... *unfocused*. This is really going to be a test of my discipline. And to top it off, when it comes time to do the official casting and final sculpting, I'll be touching *Tucker*.

Dalton speaks about the temperature-resistant benefits of silicone rubber as I imagine Tucker last week.

Watching him in that scene with that actress, the one pretending to be a virgin... Jesus. I've never been into porn because all the fake whimpers and staged groans always gave me *big cringe energy*.

But this scene they were filming. It was... incredibly hot. Nothing like any of the porn I've ever watched before.

Tucker's sex and sinew on full display, glistening with perspiration brought on by controlled, sensual lovemaking. Well, that and maybe those big ass bright lights, too.

I never knew porn was so close to an actual movie set. I always envisioned a guy with a camcorder, and a few women in club dresses, on their knees, waiting to keep the male actors warm between takes.

But this is not that.

Crave & Cure is everything Samson told me about and somehow, already much more.

Unprofessionally, but thank god in secret, my pussy clenches at the memory of Tucker making love to that beautiful woman. The filthy utterances, the gentle groans he let free as he slid home, making her come as he filled his condom.

I know it wasn't lovemaking, but the way he made it feel so intimate and real. I shake my head, confusing Dalton, who has no clue I've been privately fantasizing and romanticizing.

"Following so far?" he asks, brows quirked.

I nod. "Biocompatible and water-resistant," I parrot back to him, fortunate that my brain clung to a few of his words while it was also daydreaming of Tucker.

"For the first few weeks, I want you to practice the casting portion. The silicone molding and final added details will come after we perfect casting." He grins, ruddy cheeks pink. "I'm getting ahead of myself. I'm just excited to be working with

Crave & Cure, and this new medical grade silicone. Add Tucker in the mix and," he stops, head shaking reverently as he dreams. "It's going to be a huge line," he says finally.

"I'm excited too," I force a smile, and get to my feet as he does.

"It may take fifty times for you to get the casting clay to water ratio just right, because his body temperature will come into play."

"Wait," I stutter, stopping us both in our tracks. "I thought I'd be working with the clay and the setup process. On my own."

Dalton smiles. "With Tucker, too. If you perfect the mix and it doesn't work for him, you're at square one. It will be trial and error with Tucker as your muse. This kind of lengthy process is pretty typical as we need what will ultimately become the phase one master mold to be free of any imperfections. There's only so much you can correct post cast and Silicone is an unforgiving medium."

Failing in front of other people is not something I like to do. Years of being denigrated by my parents each time I even struggled at something has my stomach in knots. But failing in front of Tuck? A man who's eyes I could quite happily get lost in. That's not on today's list of things to do.

"I can really test and get the formula ready on my own," I offer with my palms outstretched, eyebrows high, my voice hitting Mariah levels of high. "I know he's busy, it may make more sense for me to try it for a few days alone."

Dalton raises a finger to interject, but my mind is racing. I can't do something for the very first time—something I should be good at because it is in my field, it is the reason I've been hired—in front of Tucker. "Maybe we use another actor to sit in, until the formula is just right?"

Smiling, Dalton lifts a Debauchery canvas bag from the

ground, and passes it to me. It sinks to the floor when it's in my possession, and I grunt to hoist it up. This bag is heavy. Peering inside, I see it's all the supplies I'll be needing for this phase of the project.

"Tucker's already altered his shooting schedule to make time for this." He leans down, serious. "This is a big project for him, too, Ms. Carnegie."

It's a warning cloaked as fact. What he's saying is *quit being squeamish and amateur and get in the fucking work room and start making casts of cocks.*

Because for however much Tucker is likely earning from this deal, something tells me Mr. Fitzgerald stands to make much more. Keeping him pleased is likely crucial to keeping my contract.

So I put on the largest smile I can muster and slide the canvas straps onto my shoulder, clinging at them with both hands. "Lead the way."

After removing all of the supplies from the bag and setting them along the table, I grab my bowl and begin measuring water at the small sink. As I'm adding enough water for two batches, the door opens behind me. I think it's going to be actors, coming in to grab a drink or use the microwave, because I'm fairly certain this is some sort of makeshift break-room. But when I turn, there's Tucker, standing in his basket-ball shorts and t-shirt, his feet bare, sandy blonde hair a chaotic, windblown mess.

"Hi," he says, lifting a hand. And suddenly I realize I'm not just going to see his dick (again) but I'm going to touch it. A lot. For many days.

"Hi," I reply, turning my back to him to hide the flush that comes over me at just the sight of him. God he's hot. So hot that the insides of my thighs tingle and my nipples, my stupid freaking nipples, get hard. Note to self, wear a padded t-shirt bra to hide traitorous nipples next time.

I pop the bowl into the microwave and set the timer, needing the water to be exactly ninety degrees for the compound to set up.

"I just wanted to say," he says, his voice deep and even keel, somehow both soothing and sexy. "I heard what you said to D. Fitz out there."

D. Fitz– Dalton. Ah. So Tucker's a nickname guy. As a woman who is referred to as *sausage* because I happen to share a name with a weiner company, I'm not a fan of people who feel the need to impress nicknames on everyone. It's kind of annoying.

My annoyance has nothing to do with the fact no one has ever given me a *nice* nickname. Nope. I'm not bitter.

Him being a nickname-giving douche helps. Anything that tears him down from the *I'm hot and you're going to touch my cock* pedestal that I have him on works great for me.

"Everyone starts somewhere. And even if it takes time to perfect the recipe or whatever, when it comes to this stuff,"—I turn to see he's sitting atop a table, ankles locked, legs swinging. He lifts the compound mix bag with a finger before letting it fall back to the table—"It takes how long it takes. But don't worry about wasting my time. I'm here for you."

I'm here for you. I know he means in the context of my fake dick making, but the way those four words are softer than the rest, a little quieter too. Then he smiles and it's not a corny grin or a cocky smirk but a private, personal, meaningful smile. Genuine and sweet.

Well, fuck.

"Th-thanks," I reply, returning to the table where I've laid out the supplies. Using the food scale, I set the bowl of water on it and reach for the bag of compound. Tucker scoops it up, handing it to me. "Thanks," I say again, this time more sure.

I grab a pencil from the spine of my spiral notebook and begin jotting down the first batch's numbers. Tucker's shadow falls across my paper, and just knowing he's there, watching and waiting, stunts my focus. And even with the chemical and dirt smell of this mixture, I can still smell the clean notes of shampoo and deodorant, a touch of aftershave and a hint of hair product coming off Tuck.

My clit pulses at the faint masculine scent of him, and in a feeble attempt to steer my brain away from Tuck, I stir the mixture aggressively. I stir hard, trying not to imagine how warm and slick his erect cock will feel in my hands. The big, hard thing he slid into that actress before... my mouth waters at the memory.

I take a discreet and steadying breath, then turn to face him, so glad I wore my overalls again. I'm holding the bowl so close to my stomach, the gray mixture smearing against the denim. I turn and face him. The most gorgeous man I've ever laid eyes on.

I hate that the thought even exists somewhere in my head. I hate that it's real enough in my subconscious that it bubbles to the surface. Whether I want it to or not.

He's way too hot for me.

And I know I'm perfect just as I am. I like to call myself petite instead of short. I'd described my tits as plump versus small, and my hips as grabbable versus wide. I love myself, and how I take care of my body and health.

Even so, I'm insanely insecure. Something about him almost drives me mad and as I slowly advance toward him, clutching the bowl to my belly, I find it hard to breathe. The edges of my vision and the corners of my mind grow fuzzy as my heart pumps in overdrive. I swallow hard, and force my pulse to steady.

"I have no idea if this is going to work. It could take me one hundred tries. The water temperature has to be just right, and your body temperature could affect the mixture if I haven't mixed it well enough and–" I stop one foot in front of him, lowering the bowl to the table. "It's going to be messy and uncomfortable and take a lot of tries. And then after, it will be a lot of me staring at your–" I clear my throat, suddenly a twelve year old girl, unable to say *penis. Say it, Vienna. Just say penis!* I swallow through a desert-dry mouth. "I will be closely analyzing the subject in order to get the details right on the silicone, once we're past casting."

My face is a furnace as I slowly look up to find his eyes.

The grin he wears as he shoves a hand through his tousled hair sends everything in my belly aflight, toppling weightlessly. Holy crap. I swallow again. I know why they call them thirst traps. I'm actually thirsty.

"Okay so... you'll need to disrobe and apply the coconut oil."

The sound of his thumbs hooking the waistband of his shorts is something I'll be thinking about with my eyes squeezed shut later tonight.

11

Tucker

A little star struck by Tucker Deep

It's fortunate I need to be hard for this.

Because whether I want to or not, I'm going to be hard very soon. There is no way I can be this close to Vienna when she's so flush and nervous and not turn to steel.

She wore those overalls again today. I was hoping she would. She looks fucking cute as hell in those, and all that silky dark hair in that messy, *I'm too busy* type of bun. Goddamn it gets me going. All the dark clay smeared up her forearms, the look of determination in her eyes as she attacks a clump of casting compound with her wooden spoon. I love how her nose wrinkles and her tongue pokes out as she concentrates.

"How's that first mix looking?" I ask her as I get comfortable on the table. There was one topped in plastic and I assumed that was for me to lie on, in case the compound gets messy. I strip completely, including my shirt, just so nothing is in the way. Definitely not because I saw Vienna eyeing my pecs and shoulders during the scene she watched.

Using her knuckle, she nudges her frames up her nose as she looks at me. "I think it's okay." She looks back down to the compound as an air bubble releases, sending droplets of sludge spattering against her overalls.

"Those your sculpting overalls?" I ask, taking in the various stains along the straps. Almost like, she had filthy hands and was desperate to get out of them and struggled with the hook. I envision her clay-stained hands grasping at the straps in a panic as my lips press into her neck from behind, begging her to let me in.

She looks down at her outfit then up at me just as I begin stroking. I'm already half hard just being with her. Talking to her. Learning about the girl who, unbeknownst to her, was part of why I decided to take the offer to work for Crave & Cure.

"They're my work"—she lifts her head after a feeble attempt at wiping away the spatter, losing track of her thoughts as her gaze catches on my shoulder. My flexing, pumping, torquing shoulder. Because I'm—"oh my god!" she shrieks, spinning to give me her back. It's now that I notice the small red heart tattoo on the back of her neck. So high up in her hair-line that she'd have to be wearing the top knot like today, and you'd have to be just a foot away, like I am, to see it.

This private discovery has my skin burning and I grip myself a little tighter, tug myself a little faster. "I have to be hard, Vienna, you said it yourself."

With her back still to me, I can't help but grin. She's here to make a cast of my cock, yet, she's struggling to look at me naked.

I make a quick assessment of the situation. She's either

really religious or... flustered by me because she's attracted to me. I'm not an egomaniac, but I work in adult entertainment. I've dealt with a handful of newbies who come onto set, wet behind the ears, a little star struck by Tucker Deep.

This is how they behave.

But this is also Vienna, so I want to know for sure. "Are you... religious?" I ask her, and the question diffuses her embarrassment. She turns slowly, her eyes darting between my hand wrapped around my hard-on and my face.

She licks her lips, her chest rising and falling noticeably quick. "I'm—" she narrows her eyes, and in this light, I can see all the colors in them. Not just one shade of brown but many. An ombre of chestnuts with swirls of honey and a fleck of gold, she quite possibly has the most breathtaking eyes I've never seen.

The fact my cock gets harder in my palm while I study her eyes is telling. This girl is meant for me. Every single part of me feels that, from my pinky toe to the very last hair on my head.

I've never jerked off to eyes. I've never had to go out of my way to make someone comfortable before.

I mean, I'm not being selfish or egotistical. I put my co-stars at ease. And I make them come, for real. None of that fake porn moany bullshit orgasm stuff here.

But outside of work. Off the set. I've honestly never met a woman that I thought about so much. That I've felt so goddamn drawn to. That I want to care for.

"I'm not really religious, no."

Relief courses through me at her reply. That only leaves one reason why she'd be jumpy and nervous.

Picking up a plastic tube resting on the table near her supplies, she holds it up. "I'm going to pour the mix in the tube and then we're going to put you—we're going to stick your—"

her cheeks flood with color, and I have to stifle an actual groan right on my lips because groaning right now would be weird. Yes, I'm jacking off. But *still*. We're having a conversation and I'm a professional.

"Stick my hard cock in there when you pour the mix in, got it."

She blinks at me, lips parted, an expression of shock on her face.

I grin. "Vienna, this job is going to be hard to do if we can't talk openly about my cock."

Eyes still on me, her hands move chaotically until she finds the bowl. Nodding, a strand of her silky hair slips from her bun, falling across her face. She drives her hands in the mix, scooping palmfuls into the tube, clumps of compound going everywhere.

"I know," she says, using the top of her wrist to nudge her glasses up her nose. "Are you ready?" she asks, smearing her palm along the tube's lip to deposit the rest of the mixture inside.

I nod and we both look down and watch her lower the tube down over my dick. The mixture is surprisingly warm and "ooh," she breathes, a pink flush creeping up her neck as she watches my cock disappear into the tube.

I can't help it. Her little sigh and the warm mix, I moan, too.

"*Fuuuck.*" The moan that leaves me is honest and vulnerable, and an octave lower than what I give on set. When her dark eyes find mine, wide and shiny, I almost think she knows it, too. She knows that the moan she just heard was real, and private. She licks her lips, and if my dick weren't in a mix of clay and grit right now, she'd see how much I like her licking those plump lips of hers.

"How's it, uh, how's it feeling?" she asks, peering down at the tube.

"It feels like warm cement," I reply honestly. The part I leave out is that it feels more than good to have her watching me. Knowing I'm thick and fat inside that tube, aching and pulsing under her care. It's not the same high I get when I'm on set. It's better. A more exclusive, singular high that throttles in my chest, spewing energy and excitement through my limbs, making my lips tingle and my fingertips ache.

With her clay-messed hands, she twists the dial on an egg-timer. "Four minutes. Can you stay erect in there for four minutes?"

Reaching out, I nudge her glasses back up her nose, loving the ittiest sigh that puffs from her lips as I do. "Since your hands were messy," I add, my voice quiet. "And yeah, I can stay hard for four minutes."

"Without... friction?"

The truth is, four minutes would be a hard time to stay this hard without any stimulation. Another truth? I can do it with her this close.

But if that isn't the creepiest thing I could possibly say, I don't know what is. So instead, I stack my hands behind my head, elbows out, and smile down at Vienna, holding the tube of mixture over my dick.

"Easy."

The timer ticking away our time together makes my nerves go wild, my heartrate kicking up a notch. "So are you going to turn your back to me when I get naked and get ready for the tube every time?"

She twists her hand, readjusting, but careful to not move the tube. I don't know anything about this process but it feels very much like she's being as cautious and careful as possible.

And I like that she cares about her work and this job, even if she doesn't want it.

Looking at me a beat, she rolls her eyes, then refocuses her gaze on the timer. I'm sure she feels like it's the only safe place to look, but I don't want the image of Vienna Carnegie counting down our sessions together to be what's emblazoned in my mind after this venture.

I chuckle, and she looks at me, smirking. "Fine," I say, not wanting to force her to watch me. Who am I, Louis CK? No way.

But I saw her watching me on set before. The heady expression melting her normally attentive demeanor, the way her shoulders sloped and her lips parted, how her cheeks stayed flush with need until long after the scene was over.

I think she *likes* watching. And if I can get her to enjoy this job, then maybe she'll start to enjoy spending time with me. See me as more than porn star dude with his cock in a tube.

"You don't have to watch. How about this, you keep your back to me at the beginning of each session and I won't give you grief about it. But in exchange, you come out and watch some of the scenes every day."

Her eyes narrow to a sharp point, and I feel prodded by them when they flick between mine. "Or I just do my job and leave, and don't trade promises with you."

I pushed too hard too fast. And in our roles, I can very easily seem predatorial. After all, a man in a position of authority, however temporary, should never be the sexual aggressor. Because that would make him, aptly so, a predator.

And that's not me.

"That works, too," I smile, playing off my disappointment. The timer sounds, and a moment later she's wiggling the tube from my dick. A slurp and pop, then I'm free, hard cock slapping against my belly.

And when it does, she makes a noise.

A tiny, sexy little gasp.

And because the timer has sounded, the room is so fucking quiet that her tiny gasp floods the space like an uproarious cry of pleasure. Along my belly, my cock stiffens.

And she sees.

"You know, you can come out on set," I say, pretending to not have noticed the effect my dick had on her, "You don't have to make any promises or agree to anything." I glance over at her, still staring at my dick. Pride makes my face hot, but I continue because I know it will take having more than an enticing cock to win Vienna Carnegie. "If you ever want to watch, feel free."

Smiling at me, she wets a white terry rag and hands it to me. "You can sit up and... clean up."

"Are we going to do another one? Gotta do more than one of these a day, right?" I smooth the cool rag over my groin, collecting dry bits of gray compound. And despite its attempts, the cool rag doesn't soothe my hard-on. Because every time I think he's going to stand down, I look at Vienna and lose all hope.

She busies herself with cleaning up the mess she made. That one strand of dark hair swaying in front of her face, making my fingers itch to pluck it up and tuck it back. "Just one today," she replies, dropping the muddy bowl into the sink basin, flicking the sink water on.

"So you're done with me?"

Finally she meets my gaze. "For today, yes."

I slide off the table and collect my clothes, taking my time to put them on. I don't want to leave this space with her, not yet. If everyday goes like this, before I know it, she'll be out of contract and we'll just be buddies.

But fuck, I also don't wanna go too hard too soon.

"Thanks, then. And I'll see you tomorrow. And like I said, you're welcome to come out to the set and observe."

"I don't like watching," she retorts defensively.

I smile. "It's okay if you do." And before I let her deny it, I step out of the room, my clothed dick in my hand.

I know who I'll be thinking about in my next scene today.

12

Vienna

Watching, period.

"Sausage, you can't be serious. Dahlia will fire you on the spot if you show up wearing that," Madeline hisses over the top of her glass of fresh squeezed grapefruit juice.

Madeline, with her miles of shapely legs and her perfect complexion, her flat belly and perky ass and tits. Perfect, blonde-haired, *my makeup never melts off my face* Madeline. I have neither the time nor the patience for her bullshit attitude this morning.

"I'm not working at the museum right now," I tell her, despite the fact that I haven't even told Dahlia yet. I can't miss an opportunity to shock Madeline. And as much as she acts like speaking with me is a charity, she wants the tea. "But it's nice to know you're concerned."

I slide my glasses on and twist my hair, securing it at the back of my head with a claw clip.

"A claw clip and overalls," she comments, eyes crawling over me like I'm wearing a suit made of maggots and garbage, I swear.

"It's comfortable," I defend, annoyed that I feel the need to defend myself. I don't have to, so why do I? "I like these clothes," I say again, more confidently this time, for my own sake.

"Yes, I know how comfort is your main goal in life. I've seen your sweats drawer. Overflowing." She finishes her juice, and if it's tart, it's not as bitter as her normal flavor because she hardly even puckers her lips as the last of the citrus slides down. "Where are you going dressed like that? Are you making a garden somewhere? Perhaps painting a home?"

I know she knows I'm doing neither of those things.

"I'm actually working on the back of a garbage truck," I reply, sarcasm dripping from my tone.

Not missing a beat, she smiles, flipping her beachy white waves over her shoulder. "You'll fit right in. Have a good day, Sausage."

With that, she slings her Dior purse over her shoulder and slips out of the apartment, leaving me to breathe comfortably in my place for the first time all morning.

I'm grabbing a yogurt and spoon for a quick breakfast when my phone rings. I see my dad's name on the screen and really don't want to answer but knowing it's always less than two minutes, I am the bigger person and take the call.

"Hello," I greet coolly, yet with as much warmth as I can muster.

"Vienna, hello."

Ah. the warm and effusive greeting every daughter wants from her father. *Vienna, hello.*

I peel the foil off the yogurt and drive my spoon in, waiting for him to speak.

"Your mother and I would like to come to your final showcase. The one before you graduate."

I nearly choke on strawberry banana 'gurt. "Why?" They made it crystal clear that they think art and being an artist is an absolute joke, and for years they've maintained that stance. No support, emotional or financial, and I could've used both. To have family in my corner.

I'm so used to not having their attention, this vague interest now is unnerving.

"To support you."

I laugh. Really laugh. Head back, double chin in effect, belly tight, pee slipping out type of laugh. And then my father ruins that, too.

"Vienna," he barks.

I say nothing because there is nothing to be said.

But not according to William Carnegie. "Send us the date. Your mother and I will both be in attendance."

"It's not for months," I tell him.

"We need time to plan."

That statement is funny to me, too. No shit they will, I'm assuming a buttload of golf tournaments and board meetings will need to be rescheduled, perhaps a ball or charity event missed. Their assistant will probably die of shock when they're told to arrange travel here. Assuming they remember which school I'm attending. The Institute is prestigious and though they don't know it, getting in wasn't easy.

I am secondary to every other commitment they have. Everything comes before me and what I love.

I'm not trying to write a country song. It's the truth.

"I'll send the dates once I have them. Nothing's been finalized yet. We're trying to secure the on-campus museum for the show."

"That's probably the only opportunity many students have to be showcased in a museum. That's a nice idea." He clears his throat, completely bypassing the fact that he just insulted an entire graduating class of artists who have been working at their craft at elite institutions for years. That I'd be one of those students who would only ever be showcased in a museum if it's under the guise of an art student project. "I have a meeting. Be well, Vienna."

Be well?

"Love you too," I say to thin air as I slide my phone into my purse and finish the rest of my yogurt. This morning is off to a shitty start.

Strawberry banana is my least favorite flavor, too.

I'm completely set up in the Crave & Cure work room—that's what I've labeled it—with my first bowl of water heating in the microwave when Tucker Deep appears.

For a moment, I imagine myself sweeping floors at the museum while simultaneously being ignored by Dahlia—and every other patron.

Tucker beams at me. Literally, beams. All white teeth and dimples, hair looking beachy, like it's been picked up and tossed around in the wind, the sun at his back and ocean around his feet. God, he really just looks like heaven on vacation. And I know he's just being kind to me, as the artist hired to cast his cock and make him a sex toy legend, but *still.*

I'm temporary here but he makes me feel like I belong. I was at the museum two and a half years and I'm not sure Dahlia even knew I was there most of the time.

"Vienna," he says, his voice loud but also light. Bumps rise up and spread over my skin, and I find the smile I return is so big, my cheeks burn a little. I temper it, not wanting to seem like I'm crushing or unprofessional.

As he saunters in—because the way Tucker walks can only be described as a saunter—I think about my behavior.

I *did* think I was too good for this job until Samson handed me my ass that night. And now with a man who looks like he was chiseled from granite and dipped in a pool of sex appeal standing before me, wearing a grin just for me, I feel... *almost* not good enough. Like he deserves someone who wanted this job... just the way Samson said.

"Hi," I say finally, realizing I was awkwardly silent for way too long.

"Deep in thought?" he asks, hopping up onto the table, making the plastic sheeting bunch. I smooth it out around him, desperate to be unaffected by his cedary, soapy scent.

After taking the warm water from the microwave, I pop a thermometer in, waiting for the gauge to rise. The first cast I made was too soft for silicone and therefore, garbage. I realized I'd probably under heated the water, and the compound never fully set.

I smile at him, controlled and kind. *Professional.*

Tucker might be more kind to me than Dahlia, that's true, but still. I don't want to work in the adult film industry. I want to be an artist. A *paid* artist. And after this contract is up, there will be nothing for me here. So instead of falling for the literal shining star, I need to stay focused. Cast that cock and get the hell out with my heart intact.

"Just thinking about the ratio of compound to water, and the water temperature. And if altering the water temperature doesn't yield different results, I'm thinking of parsing out the compound ingredients, and building one from scratch."

He blinks a few times, not so much confused but more like he's considering me. Finally, still wearing the traces of a sexy smirk, he says, "You sound like a scientist, not an artist."

"There's some science to art," I tell him, feathering the mixture over the surface of the water. Add a little, stir a little, that's my method. "In this case, the mixture recipe has to be just right in order for the compound to set. Without it, we can't pour the silicone. So there's that."

I add a little more, my forearm wrapped tightly to the bowl, holding it securely to my belly. I stir as I go on, soothing my nerves with rambling. Because if I'm talking about things that definitely do not matter to him, then I'm not catching feelings or thinking about that forearm between his legs.

"And if you think about it," I muse, going to town on a thick clump that reminds me how much I don't like oatmeal. "Science and art are really striving to do the same thing in the world, aren't they? They both attempt to serve people up with an idea about the world, and then take that idea and think about it on their own. Draw their own conclusions."

Once the liquid is mixed consistently, I reach for the tube but find Tucker is grabbing the open end of it, his eyes waiting for me.

"I've never thought about art and science both having the same goal," he says, "but now that you put it out there like that... I think you're right."

I know it's supremely shallow of me but I'm surprised. I didn't expect Tucker to have a deep side, no puns. I thought he'd be egotistical and vapid.

"And you know what's interesting?" he adds, sliding to his feet from the edge of the table, only to begin disrobing. Immediately I turn my back to him, heart in my throat, pulse in my ears.

"What's that?" I reply, picking dry chunks of compound from the denim bib of my overalls, stalling, trying to act like I didn't just hide my face from a penis.

"How similar they are in nature, but how vastly different the people in those fields are from one another," he says. There are a few quiet moments and then I'm met with the sound of his palm frisking his cock, getting hard for me. *No, Vienna, not for you. For the job.* My cheeks flare at the self-imposed cringe then he says "You can turn around. I'm done."

I swallow and take a breath, making myself picture his penis in my mind before I actually come eye to eye with it. That way, it will be old news when I turn around and look at literally the biggest, most perfect mouth watering cock I've ever laid eyes on.

Granted, my experience is limited but still, he's impressive. The perfect blend of pinks when he's completely aroused, his defined crown giving way to a wide, sleek head. The shaft, while fucking and stroking, has a few thick veins surfacing, marking him with his unabashed strain. He's long enough to stack his own fists on his length, and then some, and thick enough to make the woman in that scene I watched moan with slight discomfort as he slid inside. And his balls. Big, full, resting beneath his shaft with little sag. It's not just a good dick, it's a fucking total package, and I want it. I wonder if I'll get to keep one of the toys? Hell if not, I may buy one.

"Yeah," I say, reaching again for the tube. I begin scooping mixture in, this time directly from the wooden spoon versus using my hands. "I mean, that's a generalization but definitely, I see what you mean."

"But most artists I know don't look like you either, though," he says, and my breath catches in my throat because... is he complimenting me? Or?...

"So," I say, finally on the cusp of looking at *it*. I get the mixture ready, my spoon is loaded, the tube is out. "Are you ready? Did you, you know, get ready?"

You could just look down and find out, Vienna.

He smiles. "Yeah, and I used the coconut oil." Lying back against the plastic, fists stacked beneath his head, his swollen biceps on full display, my mouth goes dry. I look away from his arms, but am met with his thick chest bubbling with muscle.

Nope, can't look there.

My eyes veer down, finding his knotted abs and an Adonis belt.

Okay, not safe.

My pussy pulses. My eyes veer lower, not because I think I'm going to find something safe to look at but because I can't stop myself.

My eyes go to his very thick, hard cock, and at the very same, most unfortunate moment, my stomach growls.

Loudly.

Like one of those really loud, desperate growls you get only when you're around people. Those mortifying howls that have people wondering if you're medically OK. Yeah, my stomach really went for it.

Fucking strawberry banana yogurt.

My eyes dart to his face, and I can see he's going to war with the smile that is begging to swallow him. Kinda like me.

Wait, what?

"That was an unfortunate coincidence," I tell him, unable to hide my own smirk. Filling the tube, I slide it down over him, and I don't know if I need to move as slowly as I do, but I definitely pretend it's necessary. I even crouch a little, peering at the edge of the tube as if I'm monitoring how I slide it on.

The truth is, watching Tucker's cock slide into the tube full of compound brings me the hottest of chills, makes my cunt squeeze with need, and my belly twist, my entire body on the brink of implosion from how aroused I am.

Watching him sink into... a woman. This tube. His hand. Anything.

"Looks like it's on. How's it feel? It's not touching the tube in there?" I ask, aiming to keep it very professional. All the while I'm realizing... I like watching him.

A smirk touches his lips but he fights it. "What's not touching the tube?"

"Your *member* can't touch the side of the tube, or else the silicone will leak out when I pour it in," I reply.

"Member?" He isn't able to keep the teasing from his face. And his smile makes me smile.

"I'm going with *member* for now, yes. When and if I decide to call it by its legal, Christian name, you'll know."

At that, he laughs and I laugh too, not minding the embarrassment in my cheeks and neck. "Okay, Vienna," he says on the heels of laughter. "And my *member* feels good. Not touching the tube," he says. I feel him watching me as I twist the egg timer, setting it a minute longer than before.

"Okay, well, the timer's running."

Moving around the space, I grab my bowl and wooden spoon, then wipe the surface, collecting the small amounts of extra compound, making sure it doesn't go down the drain.

When doctors are moving around the exam room, they make small talk. That's how they get around the awkwardness of having a person with all or some of themselves exposed in the same room. Small talk. I try it on, seeing how it works in this vastly different but also largely similar situation.

"So Tucker, how did you get started in the adult film industry?" I ask, just to keep things polite in the workroom. So it's not awkward. Swiping a paper towel over the counter, I gather stray mess and toss it into the wastebasket.

"It's actually kind of a cool story, I think so at least."

I glance his way, showing him I'm listening, nudging my glasses up my nose with the back of my hand. Understanding the cue, he jumps in.

"I had taken this gig as a life model," he responds, slow and thoughtful, like this is the beginning of a very long and interesting story. I nod with indifference, but inside, I'm screaming for every flipping detail.

"Oh yeah? I've done that. I mean, not been a model but taken a life class, where a live model comes in for the entire semester."

His face morphs into something I've never seen on him before. Then again. I've only seen him in a handful of very limited situations, I have no reason to know his confused face. If that even is what it is.

Brows pinched, expression muddled, the corner of his mouth partially lifts.

"Yeah? You took just one?" he asks and Jesus, I definitely need to keep my distance from this man. The way interest takes over his features is dangerous. Makes me believe that I am special to him, that he really cares how many sketch classes I've taken.

"Yeah, just the one. I dropped the class and ended up taking a sculpting for realism class instead." I drag the food scale near me, and rest a second bowl on top, ready to measure out the second mix. Sculpting for realism led me, paired with my desire to lash out on my parents, to the piece I just created. The piece that lost to Madeline's coochie. So yeah. Great choice there, Vienna. I probably should've stayed in the figure drawing class.

"Why just the one?"

I glance down at him. The way his eyes are holding mine makes my ovaries do a little leap, a leap I am not proud to admit. I'm usually stronger than this. Too smart to fall for the guy out of my league.

"Uhh," I hum, remembering that first and only class those years back. I was in a mood having dealt with Madeline's shit and Darren was giving me zero sympathy. It could have been my mood that day.

Could have. But totally, most definitely wasn't.

I remember why, five minutes before class ended, I crumpled up my sketch, tossed it and snuck out.

The life model, despite the fact he wore a beanie and medical mask—for anonymity—*turned me on*. But there was more to it than that.

Staring at his sculpted physique and massive soft cock made me... both turned on and sad. Turned on because, yeah, obviously and sad because seeing a gorgeous man naked and soft made me yearn for intimacy. The type of intimacy that exists between lovers who expose all their vulnerabilities to one another. It made me ache for a man that could walk around soft and exposed, who could simply be himself nude. That's a relationship I want.

And not only at the time did I not have a boyfriend but it had been a long time since I'd slept with anyone.

Not much has changed.

"Tell the truth," Tucker says softly, and when I find his gaze, he's smiling. Green eyes shining, big smooth balls peeking out from beneath the tube. Wow Vienna, you went from being spellbound by his *gorgeous eyes* to staring at his *ballsack*.

"What makes you think I wasn't going to tell the truth?" I

question, hoping my tongue is in my mouth and not on the floor. I drop some of the empty bags in the wastebasket.

"The pause. Anytime anyone pauses, it's to formulate their response. Or if you repeat the question back, that's also a stall." He lifts his head from his stacked hands a little, staring at me over the landscape of his perfect body. "Tell me I'm wrong."

I sigh. "You're not wrong." I face him. "I got... turned on and... it made me lonely. So those two things made me spiral and that kicked my fight or flight in gear. I left and never went back." I shrug, my explanation sounding self-involved and pathetic as I say it aloud. He's a freaking Adonis. There's no way he can relate to feelings of loneliness.

"Anyway," I brush off my answer, not letting him step into it and pull it apart. I don't need that much analysis right now. "I completely hijacked that conversation. Tell me how your modeling got you into porn."

"Augustus was in the class. He sat right up front. He kept looking at me, like, really analytically. And in my head I was like, okay, either this guy is like, the fucking sketch artist of all time and staring at me in this hugely critical way is his process or... he's going to ask me out after." He winks. "He didn't ask me out but he did give me his business card. I turned it over and there was a date and time on the back. It was all very secretive and... well, kinda cool honestly."

"Did the card self-destruct after you read it?"

Tucker laughs, letting his head rest against his fists again, the strain in his neck disappearing. "Now that would've been cool."

"What happened with the card?" I ask, after our mutual laughter has dissipated. The timer goes off and I reach for the tube, but Tucker grabs the base of it first.

"Let me sit up first," he says quietly, his green eyes capturing mine. How does he do that? How does he just look at me and capture my focus and energy? Ugh. This is a dangerous man, I just know it.

Once sitting, he steadies the tube as I smooth a gloved finger around the base, releasing the natural seal, trying to focus on what I'm doing and not on the fact that I'm touching his package.

A whoosh sounds and the tube unseals from his groin. Gently, I slide it off and the sound of his wet cock slapping his belly has my heart racing as I turn, focusing all my energy on the form inside the tube.

Staring into the cylinder, my belly pulses at the indentation he's left behind. A deep groove, darkness filling it, giving the illusion of vast depth and width. Only... it's not really an illusion, and that's what has me swallowing hard, pretending to study the tube to make sure it's usable, all while enjoying the slow clench in my lower half.

As I place the tube in a large plastic bag, taking extra care to preserve it as I transfer it, the door opens. Part of me wants to shout that someone is naked in here, but I realize that opening the door to a self-appointed workroom at a porn production company is not like walking in on someone in a dressing room. No one is surprised and nudity is normal. Instead, I spin and give a smile to Lance.

He blinks at me with a solemn nod, and I wonder how someone as handsome as him, working at a place like this, is so... unfun.

"You have three minutes before your first scene," Lance says, his focus on Tucker.

Tuck grabs the cold cloth from the basin adjacent to him, and smooths it over his bare groin. "Guess it's good I'm still hard, huh?" he asks, but when I look at Lance, he's looking at me. Turning, I see Tucker smiling at me.

I shrug, nonchalant and unbothered. "I guess so. Thanks

for your work, Tuck. See you tomorrow," I say, putting on my very best air of professionalism despite the fact that my panties are drenched, I'm holding a hollow cock in a bag and the hottest man I've ever seen is going to be orgasming one hundred feet away from me in like, five minutes.

Lance back peddles to the door, knocking the frame with a curled fist. "Tucker, now, you still need a shower," he says, all stony and irritable.

Tuck is still focused on me, his lopsided grin, messy hair and raging erection wrapping around me like a damn spell. Because when I realize my cheeks are burning, it's because I'm smiling. Grinning. Like a fool.

"Have a good scene," I say, using my words to push him from the room. To keep Lance only medium irritated, and to not be the reason he gets big irritated, if he does.

"While your silicone is setting—and I know it needs seven minutes to set, I read in that instruction manual the other day—come watch. Just... take a peek."

"I'm here to cast you, Tucker, not be a creepy watcher from the sidelines." I use his discarded groin rag to wipe loose bits of crap from my overalls, because if I don't get it unusably dirty right now, I most definitely would have smelled it once he left the room. And I am not going to be the woman who smells something that touches a hot guy's dick. Because that's creepy.

Even if no one knows.

I use the rag to wipe the side of the bowl, making sure to get *allll* the mess. When the rag is officially disgusting, I toss it in the hamper. And it occurs to me, they have a basket for dirty rags not because of my project but... those are likely... sex rags.

When I look up, to tell Tucker to go, that I'm not going to watch, and thanks for everything again today, he's gone. And something drops in my stomach. Maybe my hopes? Foolish wants? Whatever it is leaves me empty and sour, but what did I expect? Him to stand here and beg me to watch him?

He offered twice, and I said no.

He respected "no." And I'm disappointed.

Annoyed with myself, which we have already established is the worst kind of annoyed. I get the silicone mixture going, forcing myself to focus on the reason I'm here. Work.

I'm here for this limited contract and I'll make great money to pay off my loans and work from there. I won't have to worry about a job as much as before because I won't have the loans breathing down my neck.

I should be happy.

And I pissed off Madeline this morning which is an immature victory that I sadly enjoy.

So why am I disappointed? "He doesn't care," I tell myself as I place a glass container atop the food scale, measuring off the list of ingredients one by one. "He was probably just offering so you didn't feel weird walking out," I add, because that makes sense.

It is more logical to me that he was just being kind. Not that he really cared or wanted me to watch.

As I twist the timer, waiting for my ingredients to cure, Lance reappears in the doorframe, knocking to gather my attention.

"I'll be out of here in five. Once I pour it, I'll pop it in the cupboard to rest overnight," I tell him, motioning the clean counter spaces, indicating that I'm almost done. Almost out of their space.

Lance's brow wrinkles, and he smooths a hand down his clean-shaved jaw, sharp and powerful. A man as controlled as he is... there's gotta be a time where he gives it all up and enjoys himself, right? Where he laughs, smiles, cries, moans. Right?

"This is your space," he says, drawing the words out, as if I need to see them clearly. "I'm not here to ask when you're leaving. I'm here to remind you Tucker is in-scene."

"Okay..." I say, drawing my response out as much. "Do I need to um, watch him for any reason?" I try to think of a way that watching him work will help me create a better toy for Crave & Cure and Debauchery. "I guess seeing him in different lighting would help me understand any expectations consumers might have," I think aloud, recalling that Augustus had mentioned various lighting techniques they employ to enhance the performers. I wonder if they could be imitated with shading techniques in silicone. He also mentioned that after the first release, each subsequent model will be themed to align with the most popular selling toys.

Lance's brow stays cinched, his eyes arresting my gaze with such intensity that my stomach twists. This man is incredibly intimidating. God speed to whoever his partner is. Being trapped under that glare must be frightening.

Or insanely hot, who knows.

"He's never asked anyone to come on set and watch," Lance says, his eyes flitting between mine, the action imparting the importance of his words.

Feeling flutters rise up my throat from my belly, I smile. "Technically," I reply, "I'm already on set. He just invited me to stop on my journey out the door for the day."

Lance's lips fall to a thin line, and I'm pretty sure his nostrils flared a time or two. "He's never asked anyone to stop walking before they walk out the door." He glances at his watch. "Come an hour earlier tomorrow. We have an early shoot and I want him done with casting beforehand."

"Oka–" He's gone before I can respond.

Lance doesn't seem like he's the type to lie for someone else. He seems way too uptight for that. But why does Tucker want me to watch him? Me, the cock casting art school student?

I watched him have sex with one of the most beautiful women I've ever seen the other day.

And I'm beautiful, too. I'm not doing that "she's prettier than me and I'm so jealous" Olivia Rodrigo head trip stuff. No way. I may be insecure about my skills as an artist, and I may wish some elements of my life were different, and sure, who hasn't wished a few times their legs were longer or their tits perkier. I've had those moments.

But I love me. I love being petite, I love the idea of being wrapped around my man, once I have one, and curled into his chest. I like wearing glasses and having hips. I like who I am.

With that said, I like who *she* is, too. She was mouth watering, to any gender or orientation.

Glancing at the timer, I chew the inside of my mouth, wondering what I should do. Should I go watch? He did ask me. I have exactly two minutes to make this choice. Does it matter if he was just being kind? Shouldn't I be polite?

Quickly, I clean up the remainder of the workspace before catching my reflection in the microwave glass. My hair, in another messy topknot with a claw clip because getting dolled up to work with clay doesn't make sense, looks unusually messy. I push some of the dark strands back with my nails, trying to force them into the unkempt mess. I roll my lips together and then clean my glasses and slide them back on.

The timer sounds, and I pour the silicone into the mold, replace the plastic and slide it into the cupboard. With my bag of supplies put away, and the space cleaned up, I grab my mini-backpack purse, feed my arms through and head out.

Once the door is open, I'm met with an overwhelming quiet. On my toes, careful not to be the person who disrupts a movie being filmed, I pad down the small, dark hallway, toward the burst of light. As I reach the end, I'm stopped in my tracks by one of the most erotic, beautiful, intoxicating sounds.

"Ohh. Mmm. *Yeeaaaahh*," the noises begin again, dark and silky, a masculine rasp wrapped in smoke. My stomach clenches up and my cunt seizes, pulsing in rhythmic waves, almost like a mini orgasm. My fingers curl into the wall as I soak in the feeling between my legs, my nipples growing hard as *he* moans again.

"Ohh, ohhh, *ohhhh*." Each iteration is more explosive than the last, yet still breathy enough to sound intimate. With my face burning, I continue around the corner, my vision falling to the scene being filmed, fluorescent lights illuminating the three people from all angles.

Oh. My. God.

Tucker is on all fours, a blonde woman on her knees behind him, her hands gripping his plump ass, spreading him open. She mewls into him as she rolls her tongue around his ass, tracing the tight hole before dipping inside. His spine goes concave as he releases another beautiful, breathy moan into the space, causing bumps to rise up on my arms and belly. It's then I notice the woman on her back, between his legs. She's upside down, aligning her bare pussy with his mouth. If he leaned down, he'd fill his mouth with her.

But he's not leaning. His back is arched, head up, and his eyes are closed. He moans, and I'm entranced. The girl on her back sucks his dick, and my focus darts between watching his thick cock disappear into her open mouth, and to his face, twisted and torqued in complete ecstasy.

The blonde woman behind him continues to feast on his ass while the one positioned on her back beneath him arches off the bed to feed herself more of his cock.

He moans. He rocks. And he moans some more.

His hands curl, balling the bedsheet up between his knuckles. His bicep flexes, lines of strain bulge from the strong column of his neck, and his thigh grows rigid. He moans again, and I swear his moans are the sexiest thing I've ever heard in my life.

Arousal slips from my lips, and I've been so wet for so long that all my lower half begins to feel cool and damp. I bring my feet together to clench my pussy and flex my thighs, desperate to release pressure without anyone around me being aware.

Then again. Are they hearing him? Are they watching this? How is everyone not clenching their thighs and secretly trying to sate their burning loins? Because my loins are *so* burning.

I take my eyes off Tucker long enough to survey the room. Lance is eating grapes, scrolling on his iPad, not at all interested in the scene. Augustus, who is equally as terrifying as Lance, if not more so, is watching the scene from the camera screen, nodding quietly. The other actors standing around are on their phones, or flipping through their own iPads.

No one seems to be achy and hot like me.

Tucker moans again, and I grip the wall more tightly, feeling his moan between my legs.

God, what would *he* feel like between my legs?

I don't even get to envision it because Tucker's head falls. "Fuck that's good," he moans.

Cecile, who I've met briefly and is currently the one sucking his cock, blinks up at him, her dark lashes flitting as they strain to see one another. Looking down at her with those full lips wrapped around him, thick lashes fluttering... I'd probably come too if I were him.

With a lift of his hips, he's out of her mouth, his pink, hard cock twitching above her naked body. The woman behind him moves with him, her mouth sealed to his ass, savoring him like a delicacy.

Below him, Cecile wraps her palm around his shaft and strokes. His back arches, his eyes close and he explodes, his orgasm spitting across her face and chest, leaving streaks of white-hot release everywhere.

Watching him orgasm. Watching them make him orgasm. Watching, period.

I come. I stand there, hand gripping the wall, sweat pasty on my forehead, coming. My cunt spasms, clenching and releasing over and over as my core tightens and my breathing hitches.

My chest heaves and my nipples ache as I watch her stroke his cum out, all over her flesh, until there's nothing but a single, thick drop at the slit, slowly threading their bodies together as it drips.

As my orgasm tears through me, Tucker reaches the end of his, lifting off one hand to cup the face of the gorgeous woman acting as his canvas.

"Thank you," he whispers, his voice still as soft as his moans. Over his shoulder, he turns, peering down the length of his back at the other woman. She's smoothing her hands over the round globes of his ass, smiling happily, like being part of his orgasm was a bucket list item.

"Thank you," he repeats. And the snap of Augustus's slates tears me from the hypnotic, beautiful moment.

Quickly, I turn and lose myself in the handful of people loitering by the exit, and slip outside. The sunlight bathes me in a stark dose of reality, and I tip my chin to the sun, desperate to snap out of this Tucker induced trance.

Getting in my car, I clip my seatbelt at the hip, promising myself that I will never watch him again.

Because I like watching him. A lot. And the last thing I need to do is like Tucker Deep even more than I already do.

And I drive out of the Marina District, toward Pacific Heights, the small area in San Francisco where our quaint, rent-controlled apartment stands near the Institute.

Even though I'm going home to Madeline and I'm ninety-percent sure that the mold we cast today won't work, I'm still wearing a smile.

Because I'm thinking of him. I wish I could have heard the rest of his story about Aug discovering him but still... I never left the museum wearing a grin.

Just sayin'.

13

Vienna

I've seen his penis

After our latest casting session is complete, Tucker lingers at the door frame, and I do my best not to get lost in the way his thick fingers curl around the wood. I can't even look for more than a second, because often that's all it takes. A couple of lust-filled seconds of looking at the way he does something mundane—like grip a door frame—and I am envisioning those hands all over my body, taking me from starving artist to insatiable lover with a stroke of his thumb along my bottom lip, a graze of his palm against my bare breast.

He's just that damn good.

"Vienna?" he calls from his spot, I know because I feel him hanging there from the peripheral of my vision.

"Yeah?" I offer, pushing a stray dark strand of hair from my forehead with the back of my hand, cleaning supplies strewn before me as I wipe down the scale.

"Would you be interested in getting coffee? Later today?" He drums his fingers along the wood of the door frame as I glance up, just in time to catch a smile that inflates things behind my ribs. He shoves a hand through his hair, and my stomach clenches, wondering what his hair feels like. Is it as soft as it looks? Would I fill my fingers with it if he went down on me?

Why did I ever give in and agree to watch his scene? He's been the star of all of my fantasies every day for a week. I can't escape Tucker's... penis. It's everywhere. And both he and it are wearing my resistance down with their charms.

"Uhh," I stumble, tipping my head to the side, trying to dislodge the terrible, dirty, delightful thoughts. "Sure," I agree casually, despite the fact that the Vienna inside me is currently pulling on her cheerleader uniform and putting her hair into pigtails as she prepares to jump up and down and scream victory. "Where at?"

"The place down the street, on the corner. I know it looks like hell on the outside, but they make some of the best drinks." He studies me for a moment, his eyes lingering on mine. "We have to drink it there, though. Glass mugs and stuff."

"I like that," I say, imagining a quaint place with dim lights, no loud music and foam designs costing me $8 like most of the places in the city.

"Me too," he says with a smile, a smile that makes me smile, and before I can stop myself from being the cheesiest human ever, he knocks the door frame with a closed fist. "Meet you there at two. It's called Rise & Grind."

"See you then."

He winks. "Can't wait."

He's gone and I'm left doing math—do I have time to run

home and then back to our coffee date? I look down at the work I have left and survey the bib of my very worn, very filthy overalls. Between the put-away for the casts, the noting of sizes and weights of casted cocks pre-cooling, and the entire cleanup, I have at least another hour of work.

Fuck. There's no time.

I pace to the microwave in the workroom and peer at my hazy reflection, smoothing flyaways back as I roll my lips together, trying to bring traces of my lipstick back to life.

Lance pops his head in, presumably looking for Tuck, but startling me as he does. "What are you doing?" He narrows his icy blue eyes and a chill climbs my back. God, he is intimidating. And yet from what I've observed since I started, Aug seems to command him with just a glance.

"Debating if I have time to run home after work before I meet Tucker for coffee at two," I spill, because Lance is hugely intimidating and being less than candid with him just feels like an unwise decision. Even if just over a coffee date.

"Has he seen you outside of this space?" Lance asks, speaking to me now more than he ever has, and maybe ever will. After all, this is a man who wears a suit every single day and looks like he hasn't missed a workout in twenty years. Something tells me he doesn't banter or make a habit of small talk.

I shake my head. "No, just here. Makin' dicks," I smile nervously.

His expression doesn't shift from uninterested as he says, "Then what makes you think you need to change now?"

I realize the question is rhetorical as he walks out, leaving me staring down at my overalls and all the work I have left to do. His words help me make up my mind. That and the fact that I likely don't have enough time to change, anyway.

I get on and finish up my work, stealing moments to clean

as I go because multitasking fills my cup in a way nothing else does. When I'm all done, I glance at my phone to see it's a quarter to two.

Checking my teeth, fixing my hair, and giving myself a little spritz from my travel perfume I keep in my purse (because non-date or date, smelling like cock plaster is not a vibe), I sling my backpack over my shoulder and head out. I don't pay attention to the set for fear of losing focus—even if it's not Tuck. Seeing these people make adult films in real life is... hard to walk away from.

The outside bathes my face in warm sunlight, and bumps break out on my arms in response. It feels so good that I stand there on the steps of Crave, just basking in it for a minute.

Definitely not stalling because I'm nervous to have coffee with Tucker.

Nope, that's not it. Because I've seen his penis. And watched him orgasm. Why should I be nervous? Perhaps because cocks and cum out of the equation—I like him. And butterflies come as a package deal with new crushes. Everyone knows that.

Striding down the sidewalk, I take in each person that passes me, people watching as a way to distract my mind from him. He asked me to coffee, so all those feelings that maybe Tucker likes me too—I wasn't wrong. But what business does an art school student have dating a porn star with a big life like Tucker's?

Doesn't matter that I can't see the path for us. I'm walking to this coffee shop like it's my job, because Tucker, I want him. Every moment I can get, even if it ends up being nothing more than a friendship. I want him in any form.

Anyway, just the excitement of being around him is fun. And fun is good, even if it's not forever. Or so I tell myself as the coffee shop on the corner comes into view, a flickering neon OPEN light glowing from the bottom of the push door.

Turning to scope my reflection in the antique shop next door to the coffee shop, I stop in my tracks to see... Tucker inside.

In one hand, he's holding an old camera. The other hand holds his phone to his ear, a broad smile sweeping his full lips. He studies the camera for a moment, speaking to someone on the line. A moment passes and he slides his phone into his pocket, and retrieves the old camera with both hands. He turns it over, dragging the blunt tip of his finger along the instrument, tracing the f-stop knob before cleaning the viewfinder. A small, weathered woman in lavender pants and a green sweater tottles over, motioning to the camera with her head.

He greets her with a warm smile and handshake, and they converse a moment.

And I, ever the voyeur that I am, stand and soak up the casual, private moment.

It doesn't surprise me to confirm that Tucker is sweet and gentle with people. He's sweet and gentle on-set, and not one ounce of me ever thought that was just a work persona.

The woman walks with him toward the register, and he leans over the old wooden desk, talking to her, both of them chuckling over something he's said. I find myself smiling as I watch, and this soft, private side of him is something I want more of.

Though to be fair, I'm starting to think I want more of all sides of Tucker.

I don't stand and watch him finish the purchase for fear of being noticed lurking outside the shop like some sort of stalker. Instead, I pop into the corner shop and stand at the counter where I order an espresso and biscotti, then take a seat at a small two-person table in the shop's corner.

This is everything I thought it would be. Sort of dark, the smell of ground coffee beans and frothed milk heavy in the air, light jazz wafting from somewhere in the near distance. Cool air clings to my arms, but the first sip of espresso keeps my body at the perfect temperature, and I'd have to think this little shop planned that.

No one else is here, and I study the ecosystem of greenery hanging in ceramic pots from lines of jute, giving the shop a quaint, personal kitchen feel. I love it.

Then the little rusty bell hanging from the handle jingles Tucker's arrival, and my eyes immediately lock to his. From his wrist, a plastic bag dangles, presumably with the camera inside. He says hello to the barista by name and orders a coffee before coming to sit across from me, his cologne slicing through the coffee-infused air, sending a wave of heat to my core.

"Sorry I'm a few minutes late," he breathes, like he rushed the three steps from the antique shop to here, and something about that makes me smile.

"No worries," I tell him, trying to control my twitchy grin in reaction to him. "What's in the bag?" I ask, feeling a bit snakey for lying but saying *show me the camera I watched you buy* feels a little red flaggy, so I play dumb. Probably the only time in my life, ever.

His eyebrows lift happily as he sails a large hand into plastic, returning with the camera.

"Into photography?" I ask of the old camera that now, up close, I can see is a treasured old Leica. I dabbled in photography during undergraduate long enough to know that what he's got is of value to photographers and collectors.

He volleys his head, tugging his shirt away from his body. I can't help but steal a glance at the flash of flesh that appears at his neckline when he does, my heart gaining momentum at the tan sliver. I've seen him naked but somehow, peeks at his body still drive me wild. Beneath the table, I cross my legs and focus on him as I sip my espresso.

"I don't want to say no because I am. But... I didn't buy the Leica for myself, and I'm not into it enough to buy a relic either." He sips the coffee when it's delivered to the table, saying a polite thank you to the older barista. With his green eyes back on me, I've never felt so... important. "It's for my mom, actually. She collects cameras." He turns the old device right side up, pointing to the inscription running the length. "This is where you find out what year it was made, and I don't know if this one is super rare or anything. But I figure if she doesn't want it, she can give it to my brother."

"Brother a photographer?" I ask as he takes another sip of his coffee, his full pink lips curling the white porcelain mug in a way that makes me think non-coffee date things.

He laughs as he wipes the foam from his lip. "I was going to say, but you didn't give me a chance to sip." He winks, and drops his voice. "Eager Vienna."

My cheeks flood with embarrassment, but his hand comes to mine atop the table.

"Kidding." He takes his hand back, returning to the camera to put it back in the bag. "My older brother actually owns a chain of pawn shops, and at one of the locations, he has a bunch of photography gear."

"Only at one location?" I ask, interested as I dunk my biscotti into my dark roast espresso. My parents always hated when I dipped stuff in espresso. My dad always said that dunking things into drinks was for five year olds, and honestly, just the memory of those words have me double-dunking the thick slab of biscotti.

"Well," he starts, following the long cookie as I push it into my mouth, biting with a soft crunch. "Well," he tries again. "I think his shop in Los Angeles gets a lot of movie gear from hopefuls that just couldn't get there, you know?"

"Abandoned dreams," I say, nodding my head. "That makes sense."

"My brother finds some aspects of owning a pawn shop quite sad, so why he owns several locations is beyond me," Tuck adds, sipping from his mug. His hands are so large, it almost looks like a doll's cup with him holding it.

"Sad? Why does it make him sad?" I question as I drag the final piece of biscotti through the dark drink.

"People giving up on their dreams," he says easily, like this is something he and his brother have discussed at length. As an only child, deep conversations about life with a sibling almost seem dreamy at this point in my life. A twinge of jealousy sparks between my ribs. "He hates to see people come and pawn things with promises to return, because over ninety-five percent of the time, they never do."

"Geez," I breathe, processing those stats. That's a lot of lost love and hope. "I get why that'd make him sad," I admit, thinking I'd likely feel the same way. "But I'm sure there are other things that are cool, right? Does he ever see super unique antiques or anything?"

Tucker nods as he sips his coffee, stretching his legs adjacent to the table, stacking his feet at the ankle. The way he casually moves has me wanting more of this Tucker. This average Joe. Only there's nothing average about him. "Oh yeah, all the time. I mean, it's not like on TV where something ends up being worth thousands, but still, monetary value hasn't stopped him from sending me pics of some super cool stuff."

With my espresso and biscotti downed, I have nothing else to focus on but Tuck.

"What's the coolest thing he's sent you a picture of?" I ask him as I chance a glance behind the counter, finding the barista gone. This place is very private, and I wonder if he likes it as a getaway from the bright lights and chaos of Crave.

He pulls one of those delicious mits down his clean-shaven jaw as a contemplative rumble moves past his lips. "Hmm, I'd have to say getting the original Atari was pretty cool. I mean, we never had the Atari growing up because we were a little young, and neither of my parents have one either." He leans forward, steepling his hands together. "We're a video game family. So scoring an old console was cool for all of us, but especially my brothers and sister and me. We're..." he bites his lip, green eyes holding me captive as he chooses the right word. "Competitive."

Again, competition with siblings sounds like fun. Tucker's life seems...full. Bursting at the seams, and the twinge of jealousy I felt mere moments ago is no longer there. Replacing it seems to be a smile, and a flexing in my heart. I want to experience Tucker's siblings playing video games, I want to see the pawn shop and meet his mother.

"Anyway," he says, finishing his coffee, "how do you like this place?" He looks around, and the flex of his neck has my pulse increasing. "It's cool, right?"

I swallow, nodding. "Yeah, I love it, actually."

"Me too," he agrees.

"Do you come here often?" I ask.

"Isn't that my line?" His grin is so wide that it stretches over the table and dips into my overalls, touching me in places that smiles usually don't touch. "I come here a few times a week, at least I try. It's not like I think they need the business, but, I really do just like it here. It's so calm." He glances out the window to the unusually quiet city street, a trace of drizzle on the sidewalks. Back to me he says, "It's a nice contrast to the studio."

"I shared that thought," I admit. Tracing the rim of the white porcelain, I say, "If you weren't doing what you do now, what do you think you'd be doing?"

He lets out a low whistle, leaning back in the small wooden chair. "Man, great question, and it's definitely one I've thought about a lot, Vienna."

Vienna, the way he casually slips my name in, making the conversation feel personal... I like that.

"I really don't know, but I'd like to think it would be something just as cool."

I can't imagine Tucker doing anything that isn't cool, because he's just one of those guys that's effortlessly suave in every situation. I'm about to pay him that complement when my phone rings.

I narrow my eyes on the phone screen as soon as I tug it from my purse. Pursing my lips, I debate answering. Looking up, I see Tucker watching me. "It's my dad," I tell him, and because he and I have been getting to know one another every single day he comes in for casting, I've already given him some insight on my relationship with my folks. "He's been asking me about final show dates for my sculpting piece. I should take this," I say, making a choice that immediately feels wrong.

Tucker rises. "I'll give you privacy. Can I wait outside and walk you back to your car?"

My chest swells. "Sure. Thanks."

I answer the phone and listen to my dad bark hellos at me as my eyes follow Tucker out the front of the small shop. He peers into the bag, enjoying his find, and I can't look away.

"Hey Dad."

"Vienna, hello."

So warm.

"What's up?" I ask, noticing I sound distant, but I'm the only one who notices.

"You never got back to us with the date for your final art show." He clears his throat. "The end of this ridiculous self indulgence you call art school is approaching. You're finally done and can focus on a real career. We'd like to come celebrate that."

Real career? My dad's best quality is always having a scathing burn on the tip of his tongue, I swear.

"I don't have the date yet," I lie, because I don't want him there. Or my mom. And isn't that the best gift I could give them? Letting them off the hook? "I'll let you know when I do but I gotta go."

He doesn't ask how school is going, he doesn't even question why I have to go. He simply says, "Okay then," and our call ends.

But my eyes are on Tucker who is now dropping bills into a man's coffee cup, wearing a smile as he does. I take my time walking out of that coffee shop, because the walk back to my car is less than five minutes and then I won't see Tucker again until tomorrow.

"That was quick," he says when he turns away from the man to face me, the bell on the door giving me away. "Take care of yourself, man," he says to the homeless gentleman right before he loops his arm through mine and steers us back down the street toward Crave.

We walk back, Tucker questioning how the biscotti was while telling me nothing could be better than his mom's baking. Once we're at my car, my body hums for him to lean in and kiss me, and disappointment silently courses through me when he doesn't.

But it was just a friendly coffee date, and a kiss wouldn't be appropriate.

"See you tomorrow Vienna. And thanks for having coffee with me. I had a wonderful time."

"Me too," I say, tempering my excitement at that fact.

I drive home wearing a smile, one put there by Tucker Deep.

14

Tucker

My signature style is just been fucked

DAD

How's it been with Vienna?

How's the casting going?

I lower the dumbbells to the ground and slide my hands along my thighs to dry them. "Siri, stop." Immediately she stops reading my text messages and my music starts back up just in time for me to pause it. I get my phone out and start writing my dad back.

I think it's going well? She's casting me daily. It's a process. As soon as she has a prototype completed, she said she'd show me.

> How are you liking spending time with her?

I smile at the question. Dad knows just how I feel about Vienna. And he also knows that I'm great at playing things off. That's the defense mechanism I built up when I first started making films.

Shrug it off like you don't care and their words lose meaning. If you don't react to them, eventually they won't say anything to you. That trait carries over nicely to romantic feelings, too. Pretend it's casual and all good and no one will press you.

Except, that doesn't work with my dad. Because he's my best friend, and he knows me as well as he knows himself.

> I like it. I wish we had more time together.

> Maybe she'll struggle with her job and they'll extend her contract?

> This woman doesn't struggle. She just buckles down and figures stuff out.

> You write that as I sit here sipping coffee, watching your mother turn her strawberry baby into a full fruit salad because the berries weren't ripe enough.

> Seems like the Eliot men have a type!

> Smart, resourceful women.

My mom is definitely smart and resourceful. I picture her, in my mind, pacing around her photography room, a sleeping infant tucked into a tiny basket, fruit splayed out all around her. Mom is rubbing her palms together saying, *this works too. Heck this may work even better* and then she's snapping photos with a grin on her face.

Did you ask her out yet?

> We had coffee and I asked her to come watch a scene but I don't know if she will. She doesn't seem wholly comfortable with the job she took, or with what I do.

Not sex positive?

> I don't think it's that

Remember how culture shocked you were at first. She may just need some more time.

> You're right

As I usually am

Are we still good for our visit next month?

Tripp could be portside in two weeks, and may be able to come with us

> We're all good for the visit

> Gotta go. Casting starts in a few and I wanna eat first.

> Talk to you soon. Love you Dad. Tell Mom I love her.

Love you too son. I'll tell her.

Moving around the craft service table, abandoning my workout, and pouring a cup of coffee. I spend five solid minutes, grabbing a plate and stacking it with all the accouterments. Slowly, I walk with full hands down the hall, excited when I see the light on in the workroom, and the door propped open.

With hot coffee scalding my hand through the flimsy cardboard cup and a paper plate way too overloaded given its tensile strength balancing on my palm, I rush in. Set my stuff down so I don't spill or slip and create an epic mess.

But I'm stuck in my tracks, my heartbeat growing erratic, my neck getting hot.

Vienna, dressed in those same cute as fuck overalls, her hair in two thick braids wrapping the crown of her head, glasses teetering on the tip of her stubborn, adorable nose. Her hands are stacked as she pumps and strokes my cock. My silicone cock. When she gets to the base, she twists her wrists, a small hum rumbling off her lips. I watch as she grabs the bottle of coconut oil and wets her palms some more, returning to my cock.

And that's all it takes. Less than thirty seconds of watching her play with the test toy version of me and I'm bricked up. Hard and thick, but the most present of aches isn't in my cock.

"Good morning," I announce, unable to hide my erection. I came for cock casting so I wore basketball shorts.

Adorably, she startles, eyes going wide, mouth falling open. But she doesn't take her hands off the cock. And I fucking like that.

I slide the plate onto the counter and nod to it as I pop the lid off the coffee. "I brought you coffee. And since I don't know how you take it, I brought some sugar packets, a few of those little creamers and also some breakfast."

Her jaw wobbles, like she wants to speak but isn't sure what to say. I nod toward the thick dick between her hands. "You got a successful one from the last casting?"

She looks at my cock in her hands, and the cock between my legs throbs as I sit at a stool across from her, my lower half tucked under the table.

"Veins," she says, wrinkling her nose strategically to send

her glasses back up her face. "I'm checking to see how detailed the veins are. If the cast isn't picking up all the details that Debauchery wants, I'll go in and add them."

I arch a brow as I hold a packet of Splenda up. She shakes her head to the sweetener. "How can you add them?"

Her eyes veer to the black bag resting on the counter next to her. "Debauchery had this delivered to my apartment this morning," she says, her hands moving slower on my cock now, and for some reason, even though she's ending her vein hunt, I'm getting more and more turned on by the second. "It's a fancy camera. They said they want you in detail, down to the bump. So I'm tasked with taking up close high resolution photos and then I'll be manually going back to add to the prototype."

I look at my dick between her hands, then she follows my gaze to it, too. Cheeks flush, she tilts her head to the side, and the way she studies my cock has me almost losing my mind. *Almost* knocking the fake cock from her hands and tossing her across the plastic, tearing those overalls off and giving her the real fucking thing.

She removes her hands from my dick, then turns to face the sink. After washing and drying her hands, Vienna faces me with a smile. "Thank you for the coffee. And I take it black," she says, picking it up from the table next to me. I watch her lips curl the edge of the cup, steam clouding her glasses as she takes the first sip.

My balls ache in response to the small sip.

"Do you like bagels?" I ask, not because I care if she eats the bagel that I brought her but because I want to know what she likes.

She nods, snapping one purple glove on at the wrist, then the next. "I do but I'm not hungry." Using a pair of metal scissors, she cuts open the mixture and begins mixing. "Two minutes. Will you be ready in two minutes?"

She pushes wisps of hair from her head with the back of her wrist, and I get a vision of her sweaty and naked, hairs clinging to her forehead as I fuck her hard in the center of my bed.

"I'm ready now," I tell her, not wanting to come off as a complete perv by telling her I'm sporting a hard-on, but the truth is, that's why we're both here—for me to be hard.

"Oh,y-you,yeah? You're ready?" she stumbles, nodding for affirmation.

I can't help but smile. I love how genuine her energy is. She doesn't spend time crafting careful responses or putting on airs. Vienna is always herself, right at the surface, and in the entertainment industry, that's a relief. A much needed, much desired relief.

Hooking my thumbs in my shorts, I'm about to yank them down when she spins around.

"I'm sorry, I know it's crazy for me to feel so uncomfortable watching you but god, I don't know. Watching someone undress this close together and then not having sex feels weird. Like... I feel totally creepy if I watch you take your shorts off."

I laugh at that, because it's exactly how I felt when I had to get naked in front of the production team the first time. Augustus had seen me in class and vouched, but before they signed a contract with me, I had to show them what I was made of. I felt so strange stripping down and being watched, and having it not end in orgasm or sex.

"I know what you mean. When I started, it felt weird getting naked for people that I wasn't going to have sex with. But now, I don't know, I guess I just view nudity and sex as common place while I'm here. On the outside of this building, it's different. But inside here, a hard cock is as normal as a cup of coffee."

I position myself at the table, and turn to watch her. She grabs the tube after placing the bowl by my side. This part, where she removes all the clumps in the mixture, can take a few minutes. And I don't ever want to waste a single minute with her.

She fumbles with the first cast, spilling large clumps on the floor while cursing under her breath. Actually, they aren't real curse words but cute little softened swears, like *freaking a* and *crap balls*.

The next one at least goes into the tube more smoothly after I knock her hand away and make her promise to let me hold it. She works more slowly this round, putting the compound over my hard cock in small portions, a cup at a time. Though the mix is warm and feels absolutely heavenly, the reason I stay hard in that tube is her.

We sit in silence a few minutes as she works more gray sludge into the tube, and then, absolutely unable to waste one more moment with her where I'm not getting to know her better, I launch into small talk.

"Where did you grow up?" I ask, clenching my ass together as the compound begins stiffening around my base. As it hardens, it gets tighter, and it feels good. I don't think good enough to orgasm, but I also know with Vienna in the room, I'm not taking any chances. Clenching my asshole is my last minute move to stave off blowing my load.

"Brisbane," she says, huffing out a sharp breath to toss a loose strand of hair from her face.

"Can I?" I ask, wiggling my fingers in hopes she'll let me tuck the hair back.

She nods, and goes back to her work, but I catch a glimpse of the smile on her lips. I smile, too, and tuck her hair back as she moves her gloved hands around the base of my cock, checking the tube seal.

I'm a porn star. I fuck in front of roomfuls of people. I show my orgasm face, cock and butthole to millions of porn viewers.

Not much in my life is private.

But this moment of pushing hair from her face as we work together, as we talk about our lives, it feels more private and sacred to me than anything on set. And that realization makes my heart jump into my throat because I want more of Vienna. In a way I've never experienced. And huge cock or not, I can admit... I'm scared.

Still, I continue talking to her because I want to use every moment we have to get to know her.

"Brisbane?! Holy shit—"

She looks up at me, hands still on my groin. "Not Australia. Everyone thinks that. Brisbane is south of San Francisco." She pauses, wrinkling her nose a little. "You've really never ventured south of the city? It's not far. If you head to Palo Alto, you pass right through."

Though she hasn't reciprocated the question, I tell her where I'm from. "I actually haven't ventured out too much in the two years I've been here. Especially south, even for small day trips. My parents live up north, in Oakcreek, so I usually just go between home and here."

Her brows pull together, and lines of confusion carve her forehead. "Isn't here home?"

I volley my head. "I mean, yes and no. The house I grew up in, the place where my parents still live, will always be home to me. No matter what. It's just... the feeling I get when I see it, when I walk through the front door..." I trail off, envisioning the 1800-square-feet that's brought me so much happiness, love and security over the years. "It's home."

I meet her eyes, and find sadness in them. "What did I say?"

154

With a sad, small smile, she shrugs, twisting the egg timer to add another minute. Since the last tube failed, she's changing things up. She glances at her notebook, times, formulas, notes filling the lined pages. I love how smart she is, and how serious she takes getting this right. And something tells me, it's not just about earning money. It's about proving herself.

"Well," she starts, after a heavy-sigh. "That just sounds... like everything I've always wanted, actually."

"Tell me about your family," I say as her eyes lift to mine, timer set.

She sighs again, and I feel the pain in that release of breath, the stress she feels. I almost want to stop her and tell her that if this is too hard of a topic, not to share with me.

But I'm selfish. I'm a glutton for all things Vienna Carnegie, and I need to know more.

"My parents are very... gosh, I don't know. I was going to say traditional but that doesn't really feel right." With her gloved finger, she traces the top of the tube mindlessly, likely searching for a non-disparaging way to describe her folks.

She braces her shoulders and huffs out a defeated breath. "They're judgmental and pretentious and they care more about what people perceive than anything else. They hate art. They think it's indulgent and wasteful, and have never, ever been supportive of me. In fact, they haven't paid a dime towards my schooling—not that I expect them to at this point—and they've never been to a single art show or anything of mine."

"Have you had your work in a lot of shows?" I ask, wanting to temper the emotion of the conversation so I can get more from her.

She wrinkles her nose. "No, but I've had a lot of shows at the Institute, you know, for graded assignments, finals, stuff like that. And they've never once come."

"I'm sorry," I apologize. That's some fucking bullshit. I can't imagine my parents not being there, and how I'd feel if they weren't. It would devastate me.

"It's okay, I'm used to it by now. They did say they were coming to my final show in a few months." She crosses her fingers playfully.

"I take it they wish you'd gone into a different profession?"

She snorts, but embarrassment colors her cheeks. She brings the back of her wrist beneath her nose, shaking her head. With flush creeping down her neck, she checks the tube again as she says, "I don't think they care what I do as long as it's 'respectable'. And art is definitely not respectable in their eyes. My dad is a corporate banker. My mom is the woman who shouldn't have become a mother but did it to soften her icy image."

"Jesus," I breathe, because I can't imagine saying that about my mother, but more than that, I can't imagine believing my mother didn't want me. I want to pull Vienna into a hug, to rub her back and hold her and make her feel wanted and special. Because she is. Only, it's way too fucking soon for me to do any of that, so I sit there, wearing a neutral expression with my hard dick in a tube of mush and listen.

"So they wanted me to be anything corporate. Make a ton of money, own shit, have my name on buildings, just... highly unrealistic materialistic stuff."

"First Bank of Vienna does kind of have a ring to it," I tease gently. She grins, and the sadness from the conversation melts off her face as our gazes hold for a long moment.

"Where's Oakcreek?" she asks, before adding, "and what's your family like?"

Just the mention of Oakcreek and my family has me grinning. "It's in central California, only about six hours north from here. A small town that has the absolute best small town vibes."

"Please tell me there's a downtown that has Edison lights

strung over the streets with Wednesday night farmers' markets and windows painted with sales and all that cute stuff." She clasps her gloved hands together in prayer. "Please, because I absolutely love that shit and have been dying, my whole life, to find a town that resembles the towns in Hallmark movies."

Everything she's describing is absolutely Oakcreek. My heart beats heavily in reaction to her loving my hometown already. "It's exactly like that."

Her eyes flutter closed. "I am so jealous."

"You don't have to be. Come see it with me sometime. I'd give you the Oakcreek tour and take you to the best, most small town places." I wiggle my eyebrows. "We have a bakery that has an old wooden cash register with a hand crank to open the drawer. They don't even take credit cards."

"Shut up." Her eyes are wide with excitement.

"Swear." I say, flashing the scouts honor sign. Which, I realize, is just plain odd when your cock is hard and in a tube of goo.

Our conversation switches gears as the egg timer sounds, and we refocus on sliding the tube off my dick more easily. After some *gosh dangits* and *freaking a's*, the tube is off and Vienna has her back to me as I towel my cock to rid myself of debris.

"How's it look?" I ask as I watch her elbows move, working to dislodge the mold from the tube.

I slide off the table and pull up my shorts, because unless we're casting my dick, having my hard dick out is just weird. And I'm trying to get her comfortable with Crave & Cure, and me, and my kickstand gunning her down while we converse about how we take our coffee isn't helpful.

"Good," she nods. "Good enough for me to try the silicone with, I think." She spins, aiming the hollow cast my way for me to see. I peer inside and nod my head.

"Cool. So what made you want to be an artist?"

The end of one of her braids swings over the bowl of compound as she mixes, and all I want to do is wrap it around my palm and tug. Tug her down hard and fast, feel her take my cock in her mouth, stare down at her glasses fogging with desire as she sucks me dry.

Thank god I'm still supposed to be hard.

She pushes the end of the braid over her shoulder. "It's pretty cliche but basically, from the time I was old enough, I've been making things. Cutting up all of my mom's Glamour magazines and making collages, asking my parents for wind and click cameras to take photos, painting, spending my allowance on modeling clay to create. Whatever it was, I wanted to make something. It's always been where my heart is. Creation."

"I know what you mean," I reply, somewhat in awe of her response. To know what you want to do from such an early age has to feel fucking incredible. All you have to do is chase your purpose. Probably saves a lot of freshman year soul-searching while listening to Dave Matthews and pondering life.

She snorts, and I don't think I've ever called a grown woman adorable until now. But that little choked giggle has me smiling. "What?"

"I just... I just pictured you as a little kid, running up to your parents and being all, dad, mom, I know what I want to do!" She scrapes the wooden spoon along the bowl's edge, sending a clump of gray mixture to the bottom with a thunk. "Time for round two, grab the tube," she says, collecting some of the smooth mix with a gloved hand.

I place the tube over my cock and am disappointed that she doesn't watch. I know that in this strange job, she's trying desperately to maintain professionalism. And I just wish desperately that she wouldn't.

"I guess what I meant was, I know what you mean because that's how my sister is. Her whole life she wanted to be a dog trainer and that's exactly what she is."

Vienna slows her scooping and looks at me. "A dog trainer? Really? That sounds really cool. And fun."

I shrug, positioning my hands behind my head. "She loves it. Owns her own business and everything." Inside the tube, my dick pulses. She smells like the coffee I brought her, and mixed berries and... I squeeze my eyes closed, focusing instead on... my sister. I don't want to think about her but I don't want to come in this tube, either.

"But I think work is work, no matter the job, you know? She has rough days, rough weeks," I say, remembering when there was the whole worm incident at her facility a year ago. Imagine a kindergarten class where one kid gets lice then all of them do. This was like that but worms and dogs.

"I get that," she says, and then she starts backfilling the tube with mixture, and my spine stiffens. But even the cold putty doesn't thwart my needy erection.

"Have you been home to visit your parents lately? Back in Brisbane?"

Her head swivels to face me, eyes wide, brows pinned to her hairline. "Not even once, actually. I never go home. I never visit."

"No?" I can't imagine not visiting my parents. Not wanting to go home. Home is truly what keeps me centered. Home and the people that live there. Though with what she's told me, I'm less surprised at her response. I'm sad for her, and for her parents.

She shakes her head, grabbing what seems to be the final scoop of mixture. "I should be clear. I go back to Brisbane sometimes. But I don't go to the home where I was raised. I don't visit my parents. They don't visit me. It's fine how it is."

Her sigh bears so much weight, I'm surprised she doesn't topple over or fold in on herself. My body tenses at her response because I hate the idea that her family isn't her support system. Hell, I hate that for anyone.

Family *should* be your everything, the only reliable thing.

"Like I said, they aren't supportive of my dream to be an artist."

I'm locked and loaded with a handful of exploratory questions, like *what did they say about you pursuing art* and *when is that last time you saw them* but she surprises me by going into detail.

"I think if I'd chosen one thing, like photography or painting, they'd maybe have supported me. But I don't know. The truth is, after I was accepted to the Art Institute, I wanted to explore. I mean, life makes you feel like if you don't have a job and 2.5 kids by the time you're in your late twenties that you're failing. I wanted to use these years to explore where I'd really like to be in the art community. Which form of expression speaks to me the most and enriches me the most. But they didn't see it that way." She takes a breath, and the shine in her eyes hurts between my ribs. "They didn't want me to go to art school in the first place. But then to come to art school unsure of my future, with no plan? That really pissed them off."

There are a lot of things I want to ask but her mood has morphed to something slightly more somber, and it feels like my fault. Instead I say, "I'm sorry. That's shitty and I'm sorry, Vienna. Being an artist is a vulnerable, unique thing and I respect you for it."

She rolls her lips together. "You mean that?"

I nod. "Without a fucking doubt." And then, because her face is still so unsure I add, "Not everyone has that artistic capability in them. So those that do, deserve to shine. Make the world a more beautiful place."

160

Her face drains of expression, rendering me both worried and confused. I don't want her thinking I'm just saying that. "My mom is a photographer," I add. "So yeah, I really mean that."

She goes silent for a moment as she twists the dial on the egg timer but when she's done, places both hands on the tube to help me keep it steady. I can't stop seeing her stroking my dick when I walked in, and I feel myself twitch in the tube. Time to keep talking. "What's your dream job?"

Studying where her hands hold the tube, she chews the inside of her cheek a minute, and I can spot the reflection of my groin in her glasses. "I've always known I wanted to create art and make that my job. But now that I'm months away from graduating from the Institute, I don't know anymore. I mean, for so long just going to art school was the dream. I guess I didn't dream beyond my initial dream. And now I'm making dildos and abandoned my museum job with nothing lined up for work."

"This gig will give you a little nest egg, right? So you don't have to rush into a job you don't really feel passionate about?" It's funny. My dick is out, yet toeing into a conversation about money and finances feels a lot more personal. When she tips her head from side to side, worry begins to build in my gut.

"So part of my parents not being big fans of the arts meant that they didn't pay for my classes. Nearly everything I make from this job will go towards my student loans." She brushes her hands along her thighs, pretending to check the timer but we both know she just set it. That tells me all I need to know about her folks and the way they make her feel. "That's okay though. I mean, I should never have felt entitled to an education just because they're wealthy. In a way, it's been my first good but really tough life lesson. I'm grown, so I need to figure out my life on my own."

"It's nice to have people to help you plan, though," I say, imagining my folks when I came home the night Augustus approached me. "Or a partner," I add, because I can easily see myself with Vienna nestled in my lap, my fingers stroking through her silky hair, lips at her throat, telling her anything and everything she needs and wants to hear. And it would be genuine because I'd do anything to support her.

The more we talk, the more I feel like I've found my person. The person meant for me, but also the person *I* was made for. I long to be her person.

She dodges that comment, digging her phone from her bag on the counter. She holds it out to me, and I get excited that she's sharing something personal. A moment later her phone screen displays the image of an unfinished clay sculpture.

It takes me a moment to understand the image, but when I do, I lean in, eager to analyze every curve and detail.

"I like sculpting," she says quietly while my focus remains on her phone. "Which kind of made this whole thing feel like..." she sucks in a breath, holding it with puffed up cheeks before huffing it out in a laugh. "A sign." She laughs at herself, shaking her head, crimson smearing up her neck.

"Why are you laughing?" I ask as the timer sounds.

Handing me the phone, she grabs a pair of purple gloves and feeds her fingers into each. "It sounds so cringey to think it's my fate to sculpt but right as I'm on the cusp of thinking maybe sculpting is where I want to steer my efforts. I submitted that piece," she nods toward the photo as she wets a handful of small cloths in the sink basin. "And I got a C- so then I thought I had it all wrong. Maybe sculpting isn't for me. Maybe I was wrong about what I'm meant to do." The phone screen times out so I set it down next to me as she eases her fingers inside the tube at the base. "Then Lance found me and asked me to sculpt your dick. And some part of that felt like fate."

My mind races with unspoken words, sentiments so powerful to me that I don't feel ready to say them. I don't feel like I can possibly say, I feel the same way about you, that fate brought you to me, me to this job and brought you back again.

My lips part, and I'm worried I'm going to say it. I'm worried my self-control only works on not coming in-scene and that I'm going to open my heart like a bag of Skittles and scatter them out everywhere for her to see.

She turns back to her station, wrapping the second mold to refrigerate. And as I'm on the cusp of asking her another question, Lance peeks his head inside.

"We're moving the male-male shoot up an hour because Fox has to drive his mom to the doctor. So after Fox it's Maxi, then another casting."

"Alright. I'll be out in a minute."

Lance glances at Vienna, then back to me before ducking out, an irritated look on his face.

"I think he hates me," she says quietly after the door closes. I reach for my shirt, and feed my arms through. Before hooking it over my head I say, "He doesn't hate you. He's just very grouchy."

She nods, then looks at me suddenly, gnawing on her bottom lip. "I'm sorry if I'm not supposed to ask this, or if there's an etiquette to this but..." she swallows, the question getting stuck in her throat.

"Ask. I promise, you can't offend me." I lift a finger and playfully amend my statement. "Unless you say The Office is stupid, or that Reese's are gross."

Her lips flatten into a line. "Don't talk crazy."

We both laugh, and then she says, "The male-male scenes..." She trails off, and starts again. "Are you..." she stumbles again, so I pick up where she falls.

"I am bisexual, Vienna, so I'm good to go in nearly any

scene. I mean, I have hard limits, which are written into my contract, but those are not gender-related."

She blinks, her mouth falls open, she nods, she swallows. And as much as I want to dive into that reaction, Lance opens the door again and says, "Now, Tucker."

I shoot a wink to Vienna, and head out, hoping that every casting session goes this way. A step in the right direction with the Debauchery project, and learning more about her.

"She's a sub, but not any sub. Your sub," Augustus says, mindlessly circling the tip of his finger around the rim of his coffee cup. "She submits to you willingly and calmly, as passively as possible. The best sub is perfectly receptive to their dom's commands, so give her a few things to work with, and she'll carry much of the scene." He sips the coffee and smacks his lips, earning a salty side eye from Lance.

"Your time to own this film are the aftercare scenes, and the shower scenes. And I counted. You're both equal billing on screen time so this is a great one for both you and Maxi." Aug finishes his coffee and drops it into the wastebasket nearby.

I look back to the set where Maxi stands, strappy black high heels on her feet and nothing else.

"Sounds good. So you want her to do oral first? You want me to come?" I reach down and grip my cock beneath the thin 'throw on' shorts which are essentially a cheap pair of boxers we wear while Aug is directing us.

He nods, glancing down at the tablet cradled to his chest. "Yeah. Then we're cutting for your refractory and for a set change." He curls a fist and reaches it for me to bump, so I do. "Ready?"

I nod. "You know it."

I just came out of a male-male scene with Otis half an hour ago. It was such a good one, too—one of my favorite kinds. We played friends since childhood, developing into lovers as we explore and gain understanding of our sexualities together. I love scenes that explore what people actually go through—I remember having some exploration with a buddy of mine when realizing I was likely bisexual that wasn't far from the scene we filmed.

Otis and I took our time—well, eleven minutes—exploring each other. He dragged his heavy, calloused palms over my chest, teased me by grazing my inner thighs with his unshaven jaw, kissed me behind my ear and all down my spine. His soft words of care and tenderness swept through me as he laid me on my back and entered me, slow and careful. Missionary with a man is one of the most intimate ways to orgasm, and Otis is great at bringing me to the edge. I finished on cue, as always, and the scene turned out fucking great, if I may say so myself.

We went from that to this with a shower in between, but I'm ready as ever. You have to be in this business.

Striding on set, I pull Maxi into a hug and press a kiss to her forehead. "Maxi, it's been a hot minute," I smile, taking in her gray eyes. She's the only one I've ever met with eyes like that, and the silvery color now makes me think exclusively of her.

"Tucker Deep!" she squeals in my arms, playful and sweet. "It *has* been a while. What's the last thing we did together anyway?" she asks, lifting to the balls of her feet to stroke her fingers through my hair. My signature style is *just been fucked*, and women playing with my hair while I fuck them is how I get it.

Though men have been known to pull my hair, too.

"I think Darcy in Dallas," I muse aloud, trying to remember if we've done anything together since. Though it's hard to recall because Crave & Cure's updated take on the porn classic *Debbie Does Dallas* was so good, we talked about it for ages after.

She nods, outstretching her hand for her assistant, who squeezes a bit of oil into her palm. "You know what, I think you're right. Well that was last year, Tucker. How are we not getting cast more together?"

I reach into my boxers and clutch my dick as Lance strides through, telling us to take position while they check lights. I moved to the spot marked on the floor, and Maxi follows, dropping to her knees.

She looks nothing like Vienna. She has height where Vienna is the perfect height for me to drop my arm along her shoulders while walking side by side. Maxi has hair extensions, the ends of them grazing the top of her butt. Her hair is white and Vienna's dark. Hell, everything about them is different.

But when I look down at Maxi, Vienna is all I see. Only I don't see her as I saw her this morning. She, like Maxi, is naked. Perfect handfuls of tits out, nipples stiff, lips swollen. Her palms wrap my thighs, fingers plunging deep into my flesh to steady herself.

Augustus's slates clap, and on cue, Maxi tips her head up, facing me. "Use me," she whispers, following the scripted line.

I feed my fingers through her hair on the side of her not facing the camera, as not to block the best angle. Though I heard Maxi's voice and recognized the words, still, I feel Vienna. *I see Vienna.*

"You are not in control here... you will take everything I have to give you."

Maxi sinks down on my cock, sucking me to the back of her throat. Responsively, my head falls back.

"Fuck, just like that. You take me so well. Good girl."

From a few feet away, I hear Aug give the signal for the second camera to take over, focusing on the way Maxi's lips seal around me. My eyes open, going off set for a moment, but a crucial moment.

Vienna is standing there, her arms wrapped around herself, the ends of her braids resting on her chest. Those braids rise and fall, alerting me to her sluggish breathing. Maxi moans, my shaft shuddering down to my balls.

I see Vienna. I trap her gaze and I say these words, words etched by her hand that have bewitched me for so long.

"You control me."

She gasps, and I come and by the time the slates are slammed and when the scene is over, I look over, but Vienna is gone.

15

Vienna

And who is Tuck?

He reaches over the table, and my eyes get caught on the way his bicep flexes as he does. He snatches the papers, then sends them sliding along the shiny surface of the conference room table.

"Aug, Lance, Dalton, get the fuck out. Now." His eyes stay on me as he commands the room to do as he says.

The three men, more powerful than Tuck in many ways, obey, standing and sifting out the door single file. The power left in the room belongs solely to Tuck, and I feel his control over me vibrate through my veins as he rises, stalking toward me.

"Get on the table."

I open my mouth to say no. To say we only just met. To say get out of here, I'm not doing that. But I can't speak. I can't argue. And in my gut, somewhere, I think obeying him is exactly what I want.

A moment later, I'm on the table on my back, Tucker Deep positioned over me, cradling my jaw in his hand.

"I'm gonna fuck you until you can't do anything but cry and mumble my fucking name," he whispers, his tone soft, words harsh.

I like harsh.

My pants are off now and so are his, and before I lay eyes on the pipe between his thighs, he's surging forward, entering me with force.

It doesn't hurt, and I don't feel the burn of his generous size spreading me open. Instead, my body goes achy and needy, writhing beneath him on the desk. His eyes bore into mine from above, promises of more rough sex lingering in them as he begins pounding into me relentlessly.

He fills me, not just between my thighs but everywhere. My belly, my chest, my brain—all of me is wrapped up in this man who thrusts above me, the most beautiful green eyes holding mine.

"This is what you need, this is what you've been missing," he crows, dropping his mouth to my throat for a quick bite.

"Ah," I moan in response to his teeth exploring the slope of my neck. Above me again, lips swollen from his exploration, hips still moving.

"This pussy is gonna be mine one day," he says, still taking me in long, powerful strokes that have my eyes fluttering and my pulse pounding. "You're gonna be mine to fuck forever," he keens, his pumping picking up the pace.

Looping the back of my neck with one hand, he balances his weight on his other arm as he holds our mouths together. Against my lips he says, "Come now, Vienna."

And like my body takes cues from Tucker Deep and only him, my cunt spasms and my belly twists, as electric chemistry rushes through my veins as my orgasm seizes me.

Tucker stills, his green eyes boring into me as I spasm all around him.

"Here," he offers and a moment later, his cock is pumping into me, flooding me with hot release. And when he's pulsed and given me everything, he lowers my head to the table slowly, whispering, "you control me."

I jerk awake in bed, sweat soaking my t-shirt, clinging to my back and chest. Wisps of dark hair stick to my neck, as sweat beads atop my eyebrows and upper lip.

Holy fuck.

What was that? That was... a very delicious dream about... Tucker.

Before I can talk myself out of it, my hand is in my panties and I'm lying back against the damp pillows, stroking my fingertips over my wet, swollen clit.

I squeeze shut, trying to find the Tucker from my dreams again. It feels less sinister to masturbate to a fictional Tucker, so I dip back into the sleepy fantasy, hearing his words over again as I touch myself.

"I control you," he breathes, and I can't help but feel like he really does. Like I'd do anything to feel him slide into me as he tells me how good I feel, his lips at my ear.

I picture him commanding the room, taking me on the table, owning my body like he knows it better than I do.

My shoulder and arm ache as I stroke my clit faster and faster, my orgasm already at the surface.

I tip my head back, imagining his lips along my throat all over again and it's all I need to come in hard, violent waves all around my fingertips. Panting, moaning his name, after a moment my body shudders as the last of my orgasm leaves me, and I'm left a slick, sweaty heap in my bed.

Despite the fact I should be opening the can of worms labeled "dreaming about and masturbating to Tucker", I drift off easily, not waking until the sudden beep of my alarm the next morning.

Annoyingly, Madeline found out today that I am currently not working at the museum. Not that I just wasn't going there the other day, but that I'm officially not going for a while. I am definitely curious how she knows but talking to Madeline for one moment longer than required is as fun as getting a tooth pulled. The difference being at the dentist, they at least give you some happy gas or numbing agent.

I have to endure Madeline sober, and it's painful as hell. So knowing just how she found out—and giving her the satisfaction of my curiosity—is just not going to happen.

We've been in the art lab for several hours together. Yes, *hours*. And I know we live together but somehow I see her less at home than on campus and this lab is literally just the two of us left.

I try to focus on the lump of modeling compound in front of me, my notes spread open adjacent. I had so many ideas for this final piece. The big piece for the end of the semester, and year. So many.

But after my last piece received a subpar C-, I feel all sorts of insecure.

From beside me, because somehow in a large lab meant to hold fifteen actively working artists we are side by side, Madeline makes her classic noise of disapproval.

"A piece to represent something larger than itself," she parrots the instructions of our final assignment from memory while peering at my sketches from her spot next to me. "What are you gonna make, Sausage?" She giggles, and my skin crawls. "Ohh, you should totally make a sausage and say it represents you!"

The way she laughs at her own terrible joke is literally one of the cringiest things ever but I don't tell her. Because being that cringe is punishment enough.

Mostly.

For the first time all day, I glance in her direction. We were given the option of medium, though the end result needed to be a hand-sculpted piece. I went with modeling compound and since I've been using it so much lately at Crave & Cure for Tucker's line with Debauchery, I've grown much more comfortable and capable with it. Peering over at the large creation centering Madeline's workspace, I see she went with traditional clay.

It's challenging and far more time consuming to add detail to clay than compound, and though I have no proof, I can't help but feel like Madeline chose her medium after I chose mine, making sure whatever she did was just a touch more complex.

"Is that..." I roll closer to her, for the first time ever, and tip my glasses up as I near her piece. "Is this another vagina?" Then I look at her, waiting for her offense or claim that it's actually a flower. But she folds her arms over her chest, her blonde hair curling beneath her arms, expression unimpressed.

"Yes, Vienna," she says my name like it's some sort of sarcastic joke. "It is the female reproductive system."

I snort. "You're sculpting another vagina. Hell, maybe I should sculpt a dick."

"Don't be crude, Sausage. A woman's genitalia is symbolic of human life. I've taken a singular body part and sculpted the entire reason for the human population." Gum I had no idea she was chewing slides in front of her teeth, and I watch her cheeks puff as she blows a small pink bubble. I'm never chewing pink gum again. "Symbolically a dick simply cannot compare."

I realize the point she's trying to make here. I do. Yes, life begins inside the womb and yes, a woman is what brings forth life. But she didn't sculpt a womb. And labia are not symbolic of human life, and neither is a swollen clit.

Hate to split hairs but... no I don't. This is Madeline who calls me Sausage. Let's split some fucking hairs.

I raise a single pointed finger to the air after slipping my glasses back on.

"Actually, labia aren't representative of life. Labia are to the reproductive system what curtains are to windows, decoration." I fight the smug smirk tugging at my lips. I cup my chin in my hand as I thoughtfully study her massive pussy creation.

Turning, I grab my modeling compound and begin tossing it from palm to palm. "Why wouldn't you sculpt the actual organ responsible for growing life? Although having said that you could rename the piece "Ego" since this will be the second time you've presented *yourself* for appraisal. I'm assuming this is another self portrait?" Obnoxiously, I grin at her, pleased with how her face contorts with disgust.

When I brought it up, sculpting a penis was a joke. But the more she goads me, the more she talks shit, the more I think of Tucker and his dick. Then I think of his moans and how beautiful they are. And what is he doing when he's letting loose the most beautiful of those moans? He's coming. And his face when he comes is... truly a work of art. Somewhere between relinquishing power and taking what he needs, his expression is a blend of both pained and liberated. It's breathtaking.

From the other side of the desk, my phone lights up and Darren's name, complete with a headshot spans the screen of him wearing a beret and a black mustache from our matching mime Halloween costumes last year —Samson doesn't do costumes.

Rolling over, I snatch it from the desk and answer.

"Hey," I say to my best friend who, at half past two in the afternoon, is likely at work. I don't think he's ever called from work. "Everything okay?" I ask, feeling a bit jittery at the timing of his call.

"Hi," he whispers, and that's how I know that Dahlia is there.

"What's up? Is everything okay?"

There's rustling on his end and then the heavy closing of a door. His voice is no longer private when he returns to our conversation. "Fine. But Dahlia came in today."

I sift through pages in my notebook until I come to a clean space for sketching. Pinching the phone to my shoulder with my head, I grab my pencil and start the bare bones sketch of... an image I can't shift from last night's dream. "Yeah... it's her museum," I say slowly, trying to understand why he's telling me that Dahlia is there. Uh, no shit.

"She's here right now Vienna," Darren says, pointed and bitchy. I hate when he calls me already impatient. It's as if I've messed up before I even messed up. "She's still here."

"Okay..." I say, stretching the word like a piece of chewing gum between my finger and tongue.

"You know who else is supposed to be here today?"

I stop sketching, excitement coursing through me. Despite the fact Dahlia is moderately corrupt and so very rude, she has been known to host a variety of up and coming artists local to San Francisco. "Oooh, who?" I ask eagerly, feeling Madeline's attention.

"You," Darren shout-whispers, and I can almost envision the veins in his neck and temples popping with anger. "She hasn't asked yet but you need to decide, Vienna. Are you quitting or bullshitting her until you can come back?"

A couple of weeks ago, my museum job was one of my highest priorities, but ever since Darren told me how he got his job, I can't bring myself to prioritize the museum. How can I? Not when it's blatantly obvious that without either money or influence or both, I will not only never be promoted, but likely never be shown there.

But my contract with Crave & Cure is temporary.

My degree in art and my drive to be a paid, successful artist in San Francisco is not temporary. It's forever. I can't burn a bridge before I've even started.

"I'm hoping to stay there, I'll talk to her. It's just been difficult managing my time and the museum was an obvious sacrifice."

"When the contract is up, maybe they'll decide to task you with something else and extend it," he offers, and I don't know if he really believes that's possible or if he thinks it's what I need to hear.

"Did she say anything about me being gone?" I'd raced out that day without so much as a note to her when she wasn't there and honestly, I knew I'd likely get away with it.

There's a pause and in that silence, I find my answer. "So that's a no," I laugh humorlessly, shaking my head as I peer at my open notebook, ideas swirling. "Why am I entirely unsurprised?"

"Just, talk to her before you don't have the chance. And Vienna, I can't lie for you. Okay? I *want* to be here." It's the softest he's ever been with me, and I hear the subtext. Darren wants to be at the museum, so lying for me if I get caught not being there to sweep dust would put his job at risk. And I'd never want to do that.

"I will," I reply quickly, guilt shrinking my voice.

He sighs. "Thanks. And who knows, maybe this gig will really bring you bigger and better." I detect a hint of hope in his voice, like he believes it may actually happen.

Surprise surprise. Darren, the Emperor of Indifference, is secretly a closet optimist. Who knew?

"Oh wait, you're already onto something bigger," he teases.

"I forgot you watched Tuck's stuff!" I whisper-scream, cupping a hand to the phone now because I don't want Madeline to know Tucker's name. I don't want her to even know he exists. She'd probably try to take him from me.

Wait.

He's not mine to take. I meant she'd try to lift this gig from me. She'd probably send Augustus a bunch of hand-crafted cocks with a note that says "Better sausage than Sausage's sausages" or something equally witless.

Ugh.

Jealousy burns in my chest despite the fact I'm not entitled to it. I peer back and see Madeline rolling a thin strip of clay on a piece of granite, likely making yet another mini clay pube.

"I have to know," he says, his voice low, too. "Is he big when he's soft too?"

"Hmmm," I muse, knowing the answer but again, feeling protective of it. "I signed an NDA, Darren. You should know this."

"Damnit." he breathes. "Worth a try."

"Well, I'll talk to Dahlia this week. I promise."

"I really hope you don't have to come back here," he says softly. I know exactly what he means, and I hope the same thing. But like my loving father always says, hope in one hand and shit in the other and see which fills up faster.

"Oh I'll be back. Don't get too excited. I'm only stuck with Tuck until we finish his *likenesses* and then I'm back to making sure rich people aren't bothered by dust as they stare at a wall in a dark commercial space in silence."

"Don't get catty," Darren snarks.

"Have a good day," I beam before ending the call and putting my cell down as a weight to keep my notebook spread open.

Returning my focus to my lump of modeling compound, I know exactly what I'm going to make.

"Why are you smirking, Sausage?" Madeline butts her face into my space, eyes narrowed suspiciously. "And who is Tuck?"

Ugh.

My dad did have another saying that was a little more eloquent. He said, if *you don't have anything nice to say, ignore them.*

Digging my fingers into the compound, I take his advice and get to work.

16

Tucker

I'm just shoving my cock in a tube

...A FEW WEEKS LATER

"And for those of you who have yet to check your email or calendar," Augustus says, his eyes scanning the full room of actors, "Tonight is the monthly Crave & Cure party and Tucker will be hosting."

From beside me, Uma ruffles my hair and from behind, Otis pinches my elbow. I turn to eye him, winking at Uma on the way.

"And don't worry, I have gluten free snacks ready for you this time," I whisper back to O, who has grown to be a close friend of mine over the last two years.

"Good, man, I had the shits for three days after you hosted last time." He shakes his head, blonde hair swinging around him. He's the only male here with longer hair, and I fucking dig it. If my mother wouldn't hate it so much, I'd grow mine out too. He looks majestical and godly when he fucks. I get hard just watching how his hair clings to his sweaty shoulders and throat as he's pounding one out in a scene.

At other adult film companies, actors are usually contractually obligated to maintain their physical appearance to always closely resemble when they sign. Augustus, striving to merge reality and fantasy while maintaining classic elements of pornography, made sure our contracts didn't have any of that shit.

"You will change. Your tastes and needs should always be adapting, evolving and growing. That means your appearance will, too. I set no limits and no parameters. Your appearance is yours and I'll never comment on it. Because we're here to make people fall in love with sex and romance, and physically that needs no bounds."

Still, O is the long hair guy.

He's also gluten-free but refuses to adhere to it unless it's easily available and ends up having digestion issues much of the time.

"No one made you eat an entire charcuterie board, man," I grin, remembering the *kid on Christmas* expression he wore when seeing his first ever adult snack board.

"You know I can't resist treats and snacks," he banters. Augustus's gaze stabs us and we cease conversation.

"Tucker," he adds, still glaring. He barks but he doesn't bite. At least, I've never seen his teeth. Subtly he lifts his eyes to a place behind me and it's then I realize that Vienna is here. The workroom door, which is usually opened by Lance, is likely closed and locked since he was setting up for the staff meeting.

"Can I be excused too Daddy?" Otis teases as I slip out of my chair to make my way toward the back of the room.

Holy fuck. I take two steps toward her, Aug's voice picking up and droning on at my back, when I stop.

She isn't wearing her overalls today. Instead, she's got on these sexy as fuck baggy jeans that are all ripped up and kinda short. Her bare ankles peek out, leading into black Converse, the laces gray with age and wear. With those jeans that make me think of the gorgeous women who danced in music videos when I was a kid and a loose Clueless t-shirt, complete with the words *As If* at the top, I can hardly move.

Her hair is down and straight, long and shiny, and her glasses are different today. She's swapped her normal frames for clear ones, and I have never been so fucking attracted to a woman before.

That's saying a lot since I fuck for a living.

I continue toward her, my heart thudding, a grin on my face. When I reach the back of the room I take a second to catch my breath, and in that moment, we study one another.

I wondered off and on for a long time about who Vienna really was. What was important to her. And why she never came back to that class. The only thing I really knew was her name and what a fucking talented artist she was.

Staring past her thick eyelashes as she blinks ruefully, bottom lip pinched in her teeth, it slaps me across the face right then and there.

I'm learning who she is, and she's more than who I envisioned myself being with. And I'm also learning that pursuing art is less about making a name for herself as an artist, it isn't ego, but more so, about exploring her talents and creating something she's proud of, something she feels something about. Her goals are the antithesis to her parents'.

And now the only thing I'm really left wondering is... how does she feel about me?

"Hi," I whisper, Aug still going on about the shoot tomorrow.

She smiles, and for whatever reason, that small smile in the partial darkness at ten past eight in the morning with Crave as the backdrop and Aug as the soundtrack, reality takes me down.

I don't just want Vienna. I need her, I crave her.

Happiness, excitement, hope, nerves, jitters... electricity. I've never felt all of these things rolled together with one person until her. I've been fascinated with the idea of her since we met but now I'm consumed by all of her.

I open my mouth to say something—I'm not sure what—but she beats me to it.

"Hi." Her amber eyes roll around the room a little uncomfortably. I study her for another moment, trying to understand what's going on. Quickly, I replay the first ten minutes of the meeting in my mind. Mention of the party tonight could be what has her feeling awkward.

Lance approaches from behind, pushing between us to enter the small hallway. We watch as he unlocks the door and props it open with his foot, his face impatient and scowly.

"Come on, let's get to work," I whisper so Aug doesn't get distracted, but when I do, wisps of her hair dance in my breath and tickle my lips. I fantasize about having that hair wrapped in my fist, seeing it draped across my pillow in the morning, and casually stroking my fingers through it while her head rests on my chest. Hair dusting me has me fantasizing about romance and domesticity and how much I want those things with *her*.

"Your first scene has been pushed two hours," Lance comments as I usher Vienna inside, mostly so I can get a smell of her and check out her ass.

Yup. I said what I said. Under the guise of being a gentleman, I'm really just perving on her. And I'm okay with that.

Lance eyes me, knowing exactly what I'm doing, and stops me with a palm to my chest. "I want you to be the first to know, since you'll share top billing , that Augustus is trying to get Lucy in on a contract at Crave. Her deal with Jizzabelle Studios is ending soon. He's been wooing her for half a year. And she's very close. She's coming in for a meeting and contract negotiations very soon."

"Wow," I breathe out, letting the word linger. I can hardly compute. Lucy Lovegood has been the top earning female adult film star for as long as I can remember. I used to jerk off to her magazines as a teenager. "Lucy Lovegood," I repeat her name, which is met with annoyance from Lance.

"Yes, Lucy Lovegood. Anyway, I wanted to let you know. And we'd like to keep it under wraps until things are locked in place but Aug wanted you to know."

I stroke my knuckles down my chest, picturing the leggy, curvy brunette. Jizzabelle is so different than Crave. After my first film appearance was a commercial success, Jizz reached out to me. Tried to woo me away with offers of a company car (on lease, which I'd have to pick up payments on after the first year) and as many male-female scenes I'd like. The studio execs gave me *lying under oath is fine as long as no one knows* vibes, and I never took the meeting.

I learned after that they run things in the most outdated ways. They don't feature any same-sex scenes and that's just a no.

Lucy being at Crave & Cure, under a contract where she can explore the type of roles and scenes she's truly passionate about makes me so fucking excited. Because she's superb under bad conditions. But led by Aug? Fuck. She'll be unstoppable.

"I'm just... in shock. Excited. Nervous. That's... incredible. I've always loved Lucy," I tell Lance, who is already edging away from me, iPad in his hands, eyes veering between me and it.

"I'll be back in one hour and fifty four minutes," he says, not acknowledging my little fanboy moment. "Don't forget, if you still want to make those contract changes, you have an appointment with legal after your shoot. They'll be in the conference room at four." He is down the hall, calling out orders to a set hand, onto his next task.

I stand there one moment longer, lost in a daze that not only am I working this cool as shit job with dope human beings, but now I'm going to be working with someone I watched since I was eighteen.

When the microwave timer sounds, I close the door behind me and face Vienna, who now wears an apron over her torso, the long black fabric tied at her neck draped over her shoulder. Her expression is no longer soft and sweet but now stoic, her focus on the bowl where she feathers in the compound as she stirs.

I drop my pants and reach over my head to yank off my shirt, then hop up onto the table, plastic sticking to my bare ass. "Vienna," I say, piercing the shifted mood. The closeness, the smile we shared, the eye contact from minutes ago—it's like it never happened.

But it did.

I'm on the cusp of asking her if everything is okay, but stop myself. I remember my mom telling my dad once that if he suspected something was wrong, he was likely right, and instead of asking her what's wrong, why doesn't he try and solve the issue on his own. *Don't piss me off then force me to hold your hand to understand why,* she'd said.

I've always looked up to my parents, and wanted a relationship like theirs. Sure, they get angry and sometimes raise their voices. But it's always followed with copious amounts of love and conversation, leaving them better off than before, and therefore, leaving our family stronger than ever.

I clear my throat to earn her attention, but she doesn't look up. Only nudges her glasses with the back of her plaster coated hand.

"Vienna, can I have your phone number so I can text you directions to the C&C party tonight?"

She looks up at me, bypassing my naked body and hardening cock, to study my eyes. "You don't have to pity invite me," she says, her voice weak from insecurity.

I narrow my gaze, almost angrily, and shake my head. "You work here. It's mandatory," I say, then I just smile. And she blinks at me a few times, still stirring mindlessly, before finally smiling, too.

"Get your phone out," she says, her cheeks flooding with color.

Once I do, she tells me her number and I program it into my phone, immediately sending her a text so she'll have my number, too.

"There," I state as her phone dings a second time. "I sent you a location pin to my apartment."

She peels off her first set of purple latex gloves and wipes the traces of moisture off on her apron, picking up her phone. She taps a few times and I watch the exact moment she sees where my apartment is.

Eyes wide, jaw slack, her voice rattles when she says, "You live in Presidio Heights? Those are like penthouses, Tucker."

She blinks down at the phone, then up at me again, then down at the phone. When she finally looks back up at me again, she smiles, but it's so artificial that it's nearly insulting.

"That's incredible," she says softly. "Your parents must be incredibly proud."

I arch a brow and grin at her. "You know, if you'd have said that when you started here, I'd think you were insulting me."

"Probably," she says, speaking softly, locking her phone then reaching for a new pair of gloves. "But really, they must be so proud of you."

"They are," I reply, leaning back to reach the liquid coconut oil. Squeezing it into my palms, I begin to coat my dick, eyes on Vienna, attempting to decode her, trying to understand what's got her hesitant and stand-offish. I'm using these sessions to get to know her, and right now, we feel miles apart despite there being less than two feet between us. "They're great. They've always been supportive. And they're stoked for the toy line."

She wrinkles her nose but can't fight the giggle that erupts, despite the fact she wants to. "Isn't that strange? Knowing your parents will see the toy and know what you look like, you know, down there?"

I smirk at her. "Naa, I mean, I definitely don't want to be in a room with a sex toy replica of my cock and my mom or my sister. But all in all, I don't care if they see the toys. It's just part of my job."

"They don't—" she starts but stops herself, then tries again, and the struggle with whatever is on her mind twists her features adorably. Etches in her forehead, lip pinned beneath her teeth, she hedges, "—they don't watch *your* movies, do they?"

"They're cool. But they're not weirdos."

She laughs, light and airy, feminine and sweet. And my cock is ready to be cast. "Touché."

Vienna scoops handfuls of mix into the tube which I have positioned on my erect cock. She peers inside as she fills the tube, and I don't miss the tiniest little hitch in her breath at the sight of me.

"So... I didn't mean to eavesdrop but I heard what Lance said to you earlier," she starts, speaking slowly, like she has to pace herself in order to maintain her indifferent persona. Which tells me everything I need to know, and that information makes my heart race.

"Lucy," I breathe, realizing it was likely the information of the highest paid and most popular female porn actress coming to Crave that has Vienna feeling strange. "Is that why you've been quiet?"

"No!" she asserts, laughing the fakest and most unconvincing of laughs. A laugh that has me so fucking happy that my grin actually makes my cheeks ache its so big. "I'm not– I haven't been quiet."

With Vienna's gloved hand at the base of my cock, her pinky casually grazing my balls, I take a chance. It feels like I'm trying to jump from mountaintop to mountaintop. But the risk of falling is worth it. Because if I make it, I'll be in goddamn heaven.

"I'm very eager to work with her, Vienna, because she's a force to be reckoned with in this industry. And every person I've worked with has taught me something invaluable and made me a better performer and a better person."

Her eyes veer between the full tube and my gaze. "That's—"

"I'm not done," I tell her commandingly, wanting her to be fully aware that I feel nothing for co-workers. "I'm excited to work with Lucy, but it's still work. And she's still only a co-worker. Lucy, Otis, Uma, any of them. They're all great people. But they're just co-workers and friends. Nothing more." I hold her gaze to impart the important subtext. "Whereas how I feel about the woman I want to date? The woman I want to be in a relationship with? Those feelings share no common ground with how I feel for co-workers."

"No?" Her breath is bated, like she knows what I'm getting at but won't let herself make the assumption.

She places her other hand on top of the tube, freeing my hands from holding it. Her glasses begin to slide so I reach out and push them up, earning me a shy smile.

"Nope," I shake my head staunchly then curl a strand of hair around her ear, and take her face in my palm. Here it goes. "I like you, Vienna. And I think you may like me, too. And because of that, I want you to understand in no uncertain terms that what I do here is work. And only work."

She doesn't reply, but I'm okay with that. I understand years of hesitancy in her choices and feelings from being unsupported and second-guessed by her parents weigh heavily on her. If she gives me the chance, I'll work to undo that. Time for a change of subject to reduce the tension I can see bubbling under the surface in her nervous gaze.

"Last week we were talking about favorites. We got through ice cream, chocolate chip cookie dough; soda, Diet Coke; comedy movie, 21 Jump Street; and meal, a Strawberry poptart which I still maintain is not a meal but," I raise my hands, "to each their own."

She laughs, draping a damp towel around the base of the tube. Last week the casting was sticking to my groin, pulling the compound, therefore, stretching it inaccurately. When she'd filled it with silicone, she'd found that it was a little longer than the real me, and her contract has her promising to get all the toys as close to my actual dick as possible. Down to stray hairs, veins and bumps. Seriously.

"I can't believe you remember all my favorites," she replies, popping the tube off my dick as soon as it releases its suction. Immediately, she hands me the oil. "I need to do at least four more, so oil up."

"You know," I say, filling my palms with the fragrant oil. "If you think a Strawberry PopTart is bomb, you'd love my mom's strawberry popovers. They're so fire," I say with a slight groan, recalling the tiny little pastries mom makes for special occasions. I haven't had them since Easter last year, but fuck me sideways, I had to have eaten at least fifty of those little calorie bombs.

Worth it.

No sooner is my pink cock glistening with fresh oil does she have the tube on me. She takes my hand and rests it on top of the tube. "Hold it until the mix is ready," she orders, reaching for the second bowl of prepared mix. Now that we're a month into this, she's established a more efficient routine. We're doing more and more casts each time, and even different angles now, too, so before she leaves, she gets it all set up for the next day.

She makes me want to be more organized, but she also makes me want to eat strawberries out of her pussy while she screams my name.

"Mm," she says, popping another bowl in the microwave. "Those do sound good."

"My family is actually coming to visit pretty soon," I say slowly, waiting for the realization to take hold of her.

But she mixes, oblivious of what I'm trying to get at. How can I have my cock out and hard, stroke in front of her, and yet, asking her out and asking her to meet my parents feels insurmountably difficult.

"That sounds nice," she says, looking up to smile at me.

"You should come to my place when they visit. They'd really like to meet you." A knot rises up my throat, and my pulse beats erratically as I await her reaction. Her response.

"They can't possibly want to meet me," she snorts, which I find adorable but she apparently doesn't, because she goes flush and cups a gloved hand to her face. "Oh god, I snorted."

"I heard," I grin at her.

When she pulls her hand away, cock mix is smeared on her face.

"You have-" I motion to my face, making her spin and use the reflection in the microwave. She reaches for paper towels and wipes at her face, turning back to me once it's cleaned off.

"And they do want to meet you, you know," I say again, this time my voice unwavering and even keel.

"Okay," she says finally. "That could be cool."

We continue talking, swapping stories about everything from our first kisses—both of us experiencing this while playing the tweenage favorite 'seven minutes in heaven'—to our very favorite places in the city. Before I know it, our time is up and Lance is in the doorway, tapping his foot.

I have the strongest urge to pull Vienna into my arms before I leave, drop a kiss on the top of her head, and whisper to her that I can't wait to see her later.

But she's more Crave & Cure's than she is mine, so instead, I smile, raise a palm and say goodbye.

Because for now, it's all I can do.

"And you're sure about this, Mr. Eliot?" Dante, the head of Crave & Cure's legal team asks me.

It's strange to be called by my legal name while under this roof, but when it comes to financial and contractual obligations, legally they have to use my real name.

Still strange to be anyone but Tucker Deep while I'm here.

"I'm sure," I say, nodding my head vehemently as I pop green grapes into my mouth. After my last scene, I yanked a plate of snacks from craft services and made my way into the conference room.

Aug doesn't have a clue I'm doing this. He'd probably have a lot of opinions if he knew. But I'm doing it, because not only do I want to but it feels like the right thing to do.

"You cannot revise this again, not so close to the first launch date. So if you sign the revision today, it's final. I want to make sure you're aware it's final," he says slowly, the way dumb people speak more loudly at people who speak a foreign tongue, or are hard of hearing.

"I'm aware. Let's do it."

"Okay," he says, fingers skittering across the keyboard on his laptop. "To verify, you want Miss Carnegie to receive half of all royalties out of your end, in addition to her contracted stipend of one hundred thousand."

I nod. "Yep."

Dante smooths his hand down his tie, adjusting what needs no adjustment. "Tucker, I can't stop you from doing this but I want you to realize, what you're doing, it's life changing for her. And if you're doing it out of the kindness of your heart, great. But if you're doing it in hopes of getting in her pants-"

I stop him there. "Stop right there Dante, I'm doing it because it's right. She's making all of these toys, she's spending hours analyzing high resolution pictures of my dick skin so that the toys have every single beauty mark and vein. She has earned half of whatever these toys earn, and she's worth it."

"Okay," he says with a singular nod.

I can tell he thinks this is a pussy chase. An extreme effort to get a girl to fall for me. But it's not.

She needs the money more than I do but the truth is, she's doing the work. I'm just shoving my cock in a tube. She deserves it.

17

Vienna

Have fun with Deep Dick

I've always wondered what it felt like to have so much to do that you have to take your work home with you. To be so indispensable to a company or integral to a project that your downtime disappears and you're consumed by your work.

I just never imagined that would mean a desk littered with various versions of a very well endowed man's penis.

Over the last month or so, I've figured out a lot about the compound I'm using, and how it best works with the medical grade silicone Debauchery wants me to use. Still, I don't have a singular toy that's perfect or ready yet. But the first prototype is *very* close. One more pass to add this monster vein Tucker has running down the top of his fat shaft, and it'll be ready to present.

I twist the lock on my bedroom door, and much like a child

trying to keep out a bullying older sibling, I push my desk chair to the door, under the handle.

Madeline isn't even home but... this feels salacious. I've been touching Tucker's cock for weeks. I've been analyzing photos, holding the toy of him in my hands, feeling the jagged timbre of his laugh in my cunt as I stroke away bits of casting compound.

I've been torturously edged for over a month. And today, Tucker said he likes me. And I'm going to his house. The place where he sleeps and goes to the bathroom and jerks off and laughs and talks to his parents and—Jesus. The most intimate thing for normal couples is seeing each other naked for the first time and sex, too.

But I see him naked daily. I've watched him come. I've watched him come while a woman ate his ass and another sucked that beautiful dick of his.

Whatever we are, we aren't normal.

The idea of being in his personal and private space has me burning up with nervous energy. I envision wandering around his place and stumbling into his room, finding a huge bed with messy sheets and signs of lovemaking everywhere. Condom wrappers, empty water bottles, lube. I imagine him coming up behind me and looping those stalwart arms around my waist, tugging me back so my ass feels how much he likes me in his room.

"Oh god," I moan, taking a seat on the edge of my bed, conjuring a complete fantasy. One I've been suppressing for weeks.

But today, with several Tucker cocks spread over my desk, with his sultry words on loop in my mind, I can't fight it.

I don't even want to.

Rising, I push off my jeans and my panties, catching my reflection in the mirror near my bed. Naked lower half, arousal glistening on my pussy. The sight of me being horny for him only heightens the pressure in my belly and the throbbing in my clit.

Stepping toward my desk, I reach for the prototype that's nearly finished.

"God," I breathe, suddenly aware that my nipples are painfully erect. I set the cock down next to me, and peel off my shirt and bra. In the mirror, I see myself in a way I never have.

Flushed with hunger and desperation.

All for him.

I know he said he likes me, and I believe him. But I also know that for a man like Tucker Deep, he probably doesn't mean it in the way I hope. In fact, he's likely looking for a little fling until my contract is up. And I won't do that.

Because I'll fall in love with him. I know I would.

Therefore, nothing can happen. I'm not going to return to the soul-sucking museum *and* have a broken heart. That's too much depression for one girl.

I cup my breast in my hand, remembering the way Tucker touched that beautiful woman the first time I watched him. They were in a daddy kink scene, and fuck me upside down, it was so hot.

But also... beautiful. Can I say daddy kink is beautiful? Because it was. I understood right then what the vision for Crave & Cure was really about. Real sex, real passion, real bodies moving together while loosely following a concept.

It's so hot.

He was so hot. The way he sealed his full lips around her areola and suckled at her breast like he needed nourishment. Add having my tits tongued and sucked to the very long list of things I want Tucker Deep to do to me.

Lowering my head while pushing my cupped breast as high as I can, I trace my nipple with the tip of my tongue, imagining his tongue. My neck hurts in this position, so I only do it a few times, but a few times is enough.

I reach for the cock next to me, but skip the lube because I'm so wet my thighs are sticky. Bracing my feet on the mattress, leaning back on one elbow, I position Tucker's plump head at my opening. Instead of pushing him in, I bob my hips, slowly fucking it inside of me.

Inch by inch, I writhe over the dildo until he's fully inside of me, and my walls are spasming, my core clenched. Then I go to town, gripping the silicone base, my nails digging deep into it as I fuck myself—hard.

Sweat slides down the valley of flesh between my breasts, and as I fuck myself with Tucker's cock, I don't picture him fucking me. Not anymore.

I picture him fucking *her*. Lucy Lovegood. Uma. The girl from the virgin daddy scene a few weeks ago. I picture him taking Otis, I picture him coming on the back of a faceless person.

I fuck myself harder, his immense girth creating burning waves of fire through my core, sending jolts of pleasure from my g-spot through my pussy and all the way to my taint. Letting my head fall back, I twist my gaze to grab an eyeful of my reflection.

Sweating, knees up, back arched, nipples tight knots of need, monster cock in my hand, my pussy lips bright pink and swollen from getting pounded.

It's the first time in a long time I've let go of worry and just... enjoyed.

"*Yes, yes, yes,*" I moan uncontrollably, not bothering to stifle my volume or temper my excitement. It feels good to feel good, and to finally feel in my cunt what I've been feeling with my hands.

This toy is *so* going to sell.

"Come for her," I breathe out, pinching my eyes shut, imagining Tucker sliding in and out of a beautiful co-star, the room filled with his masculine, beautiful, heady grunts. I love those grunts. His sex noises make me wet and needy, they make me want to serve myself to him on a platter and beg him to take me and feast. "Come inside her, fill her up," I pant, fucking myself, still seeing his body, ropy with muscle, knots of discipline and dedication taking the form of abdominals and thighs that flex with power.

I push *him* inside me again, harder, loving how every part of my lower half both burns and throbs from his sheer size, from the feel of him inside of me.

Beneath my eyelids, I see him. I see him stop, the pert globes of his ass tighten, narrow hips jot forward, and his head falls back. Silky strands of sandy hair plastered to his sweaty forehead, his release takes hold, and as he grunts and moans his pleasure, his eyes open.

And they find me across the room.

"You," he breathes, his voice husky and raspy all at once.

My eyes open, going to the Tucker replica pushed deep inside me. I watch myself in the mirror as my body spasms around him, desperate to milk him, eager for his cum, for my own release, for everything.

He looks so good inside me. I've never felt so full, so stretched, so sated. I fall off my elbow, my sweaty back connecting with my bedspread as my orgasm sears down my spine, landing low in my gut. In waves more tumultuous than a stormy sea, my orgasm rocks me over and over until I'm literally out of breath, a sheen of sweat sparkling on my flesh.

When I take the toy out, my stomach hollows and instead of relief, I feel emptiness. I miss the sting and burn of him. The pleasure of him.

Yeah, these dildos are going to make this man rich. And I

completely, without a shadow of a doubt understand all the hype around Tucker.

Because he fucks women way better than I just fucked myself with him, and that was the best orgasm of my entire life.

Right as I'm slipping into my robe, ready to take a shower before the party, my phone dings in my purse, so I dig around until I find it.

There's a number on the screen, not a name, so I know it's not someone I have programmed. Piquing my interest, I open the message.

I see several messages, all sent earlier in the day, with a new one at the bottom. I read the most recent message first.

TUCKER

> I'm looking forward to seeing you tonight, outside of work.

A smile sweeps my face as I go back and read the others.

> It's Tucker and now you have my phone number, too.

> By the way, my real name is Tucker Eliot, in case you want to program me as that.

"Tucker Eliot," I test it aloud and find myself smiling. I like that name.

After a long shower where I shave extra good for no reason in particular, I blow dry my hair, and stand in my towel in front of my closet.

I've worn overalls around Tucker mostly, with the exception of today. If I overdress for this party, I'll look like I'm trying to get his attention. I mean, I do want his attention, I just don't want to appear that way.

Ultimately, black leggings and an oversized Fleetwood Mac t-shirt, paired with an open flannel and my tried and true Converse is where I end up. Sliding on my clear frames, I smooth my fingers through my hair and call it good.

Darren calls as I'm double-checking that my hair straightener is off.

"Hey," I say, glancing at the clock on the wall. "What's up?"

"Have you talked to Dahlia yet?" he asks, bypassing any opening greeting. That makes me nervous. Jumping straight into a question about our boss? Yeah, my stomach twists itself into knots.

"Not yet," I reply. "But, before you bite my head off, I did email her. But she hasn't responded."

"Good," he says, his relief evident in the heavy breath he unloads. "Good. Because she was in rare form today, and I don't want you to completely lose this job unless it's your choice."

"What's up her butt?" I ask, snatching my water bottle from the counter, sliding it under the faucet to refill it. I check out my outfit while I wait for it to fill.

"Life. Me. Art. A butt plug."

I snort at that, twisting on the lid to my water as I keep the phone pinched at my shoulder. "A butt plug. Yeah right. She's such a tight ass I don't think she could fit a pencil up there."

"Eww, Vienna, I do not want to think about Dahlia with a pencil in her ass," Darren groans.

"You brought it up." I remind him, glancing at my watch. I have exactly forty five minutes to run by the store and pick up something and head over. Never show up anywhere empty-handed. "Hey, there's a Crave & Cure party tonight. I guess they have them every month for staff and actor bonding or something. I don't know. Either way, I'm invited and I have to go. Like, right now."

"Oh a party full of porn actors. That sounds exciting," he coos, his obvious daydreaming thick in his voice. "How's it going with Deep Dick anyway?"

Sometime last week, Darren begged me to show him the progress on the Debauchery line and so I gave in. Except, Lance is the only one with a key so Darren settled for a photo.

He's been referring to Tucker as Deep Dick ever since. People have no imagination when it comes to nicknames.

"Good," I nod, smiling. "But I'm trying to stay realistic. After this gig is up, I'll be unemployed with little acclaim to my name. So also falling in love with some dude way out of my league is a *really dumb* move. One mini crisis at a time."

"Falling in love with some dude out of your league *is* really dumb?" The judgmental *you've only known him a few months* is right there, unsaid but vibrating on the line.

"Would be, I mean," I correct with what feels a little dishonesty. "And anyway, I want to show my parents they were wrong, you know? I want an exhibit in a museum where people can't wait to hear me talk about my piece, my process. I'm not going to get that at Crave & Cure. They want me to make a good dildo, that's it."

Darren mulls over my comment, letting a little throaty 'hmm' into the phone. "I know you still kinda think what you're doing is tacky-licious, but if you stop thinking you're above making dildos, it could be an open door to more. And also, if you take the Carnegie stick out of your ass, you may see that what you're doing is art. Creation is art, even if it doesn't look how you imagined."

"It looks like an eight and a half inch dick."

"Oh you don't need to remind me," he rasps, likely replaying a memory of Tuck in his mind.

"Take it easy over there," I laugh, then glance at the time again. "I gotta go. I'll text you later."

"Have fun with Deep Dick."

I end the call, feeling a little guilty.

I *did* just have a lot of fun with Deep Dick.

18

Tucker

Mine and only mine

"What's up, Lancelot?" I slap my hand along his shoulders, guiding him into my place. He's been here before, a few times, but still always enters like it's a medical facility trying to traffic him for secret testing. He shirks out of my grip and passes me a bottle of red wine that likely cost more than all the food and drinks at this party combined.

I don't like wine. It burns my nose and makes my head hurt the next day.

"Thanks, man," I say, setting it down on the counter. "Aug with you?"

Lance licks his lips. "He's right behind me, yeah."

As much as I love working with almost everyone at Crave & Cure, I don't hang out with them outside of work except for these functions. I visit my family a lot, and do a lot of things on my own. But Augustus and Lance, who work together side by side day in and day out, seem to spend a lot of time together outside of work too.

I've always been intrigued by that. Are they working? Do they do nothing but work? Or are they just best buddies? I stroke my hand through my hair as I watch Lance cross the apartment, pressing a palm to the window frame. He looks out thoughtfully, taking in the bustling city below, like he's centering himself.

"Tucker," Augustus approaches me from behind, and I watch him follow the trajectory of my gaze all the way to Lance at the window.

"Hey, can I ask you something?" I ask, my gaze flicking between the two men. Lance may be Aug's assistant but I definitely respect his role and think of him as a boss. He deserves to be thought of that way, too, for all he does.

"What?" Aug responds, his eyes roaming slowly over Lance's back. It's a party and Lance still came dressed in a white dress shirt, slate fitted dress pants, and coffee colored dress shoes. His hair is sleek and stylish, jaw clean shaven, and nothing about his stiff shoulders and tight brows say he's in *party* mode.

Aug, who is at least wearing a casual t-shirt and jeans, seems only slightly more relaxed. And when I really study him, I'm not even sure that's true. Worry and fatigue are etched on his face, crows feet pinching the corners of his eyes, stubble coating his jaw.

"You and Lance spend a lot of time together," I start, and notice that Aug shifts on his feet, letting his eyes come to me. Dark and narrowed, his expression morphs from inquisitive to almost serious.

"And?"

"Well," I start, feeling like I've waded into unexpectedly

deep water. And also kinda scary. "Do you guys ever take time off? I mean, I assume you're together all the time because you're working but damn"—I look back to Lance, who is no longer holding the window frame but now speaking tightly to Otis—"You guys ever take a day off?"

Augustus, who I know to be extremely private, swallows. He surveys Lance, his gaze softening for a split second, before returning to me with stoic indifference. "Don't assume," is all he says before changing the subject, motioning across the large loft toward my bedroom. "Show me the piece. I've been curious to see it again."

He follows me to my room after I knock fists with Otis and give Uma a hello kiss on the cheek. We stand in front of my closet doors as I slide it open and push back all of my clothes to reveal the back wall with a piece of art hung in private. Above is a small spotlight lamp used in art galleries, and I reach out to flick it on, casting a soft glow over the framed sketch.

In silence, we both take it in. I look at it often, but Aug has only seen it once. He tips his head, studying the sketch. We both know it's not just the sketch, what's written, or the signature. It's the timing of it, what it meant to me. What it *still* means to me.

As harsh as Aug's no nonsense demeanor can be, he never gives me grief about the significance this sketch holds with me. He knows it's part of my journey, and in a strange way his. The night I met him and found her is pivotal to me, to my destiny.

"You going to ask her out?" he asks, still looking at the framed art.

With my focus on it, too, I shrug. "I don't know. I want to but I'm afraid that she won't be able to see past what I do."

He sighs, stuffing his hands in his pockets. "You never know until you try."

"Augustus, is this your way of telling me you're a hopeless romantic and a total optimist?"

He faces me, and I see that no part of him thinks my joke was funny. "I'm saying she likes you and you like her and if it can be as simple as that, let it be. Life is hard enough."

I nod, wanting to believe him. But the truth is, dating a person who has sex with other people is challenging, and liking someone may not be enough. It isn't that simple. Not to me. And likely, not to Vienna, either.

But I don't tell him that, and instead say, "Yeah, maybe." Massaging my chest to rid myself of the numbing ache, I slide the clothes back with my other hand after flicking off the light. I know Vienna likes me, but I recognize it may not be enough. Aug claps his hand to my arm.

"Talk to her. Figure things out before you've fallen."

The smile I give him is somewhere between the Joker and a wince. "Catch me? I'm already falling."

He nods as if he knows what it's like to love someone you may not be able to have, and yet, I can't recall seeing Aug with a partner, or even mentioning one. But Otis appears in the doorway of my room, ending our conversation. I slide the closet door shut.

"O, did you see the spread? The entire second charcuterie is all gluten free." I say, directing everyone back out of my room.

He strides over, blonde hair wavy around his shoulders like Thor or Fabio. I pick a piece up by the end and wiggle it. "You good? How are ya? What've you been filming lately?"

Aug walks away, and I watch as he takes Lance by the elbow and guides him onto my wraparound balcony, both of them looking aggravated.

"Ahh, I've been getting a lot of male-male stuff lately. It's been fun as hell," Otis says, taking a pull from his mixed drink that looks like cranberry juice and something else.

"Yeah?" I nod. "I haven't had many of those lately, just a few. Kinda miss it."

He winks, and I can't deny that gesture paired with his handsome face gives me a little burst of heat in my groin. It's physical, though, because as much as I like Otis, it's only physical.

My heart is with Vienna.

"Did you hear?" his eyes widen as he steps toward me, glancing over his shoulder to verify Aug and Lance are still preoccupied on the balcony. "Aug's trying to get Lucy Lovegood!" He rubs his chest, shaking his head, fantasies rolling behind his eyes as he grins. "Now that'll be cool as shit. She's so good. I've heard such good shit about her, too."

"I did hear, yeah," I say, wondering how Otis knows because it was told to me as discrete information. Either way, it won't be a secret for much longer because she's coming in next week. Everyone will see her, and they'll connect the dots. "I'm pretty stoked, too. I know Fox said he worked with her a few times before he came to Crave and said she was a lot of fun, and super cool."

Even though we're porn stars, being a cool, fun person isn't a given. A lot of people at other production companies are using drugs to perform or to deal with the emotional wear *of performing* for little compensation under animal-like conditions. Finding actors that come to Crave that have been in the industry a long time that *aren't* broken? It's rare. Hearing Lucy has a resilient heart and personality after years on the scene is rare. And it doesn't surprise me that Aug is reeling her in.

It truly sounds like she belongs at Crave.

"Oh shit," Otis turns, spotting the actor in question. "Fox is here and you just reminded me I have to pay him for our fantasy league." He grins, finishing his drink. "Thanks for all the gluten free snacks, man. It's gonna make my scenes in the next few days a lot easier."

I wince. "TMI, man."

He grins, then drifts through my apartment to Fox, and they embrace with a hearty laugh and back-slapping hug.

I love that Crave nurtures kindness and comradery, versus competitiveness and hate.

I love Crave.

If Vienna had a problem with me doing this job, could I quit?

Would I choose Vienna over Crave, and this life I've carved out of a random, haphazard opportunity?

The lump in my throat and fire behind my eyes tells me I know what choice I'd make if I had to choose. But right now, there is no choice to be made. Because I don't know what she wants.

The door swings open, and there she is. Leggings and a band tee with a flannel wrapping her waist, a gorgeous smile on her face as she says hello to Cohen, the set designer and a director too. The crotch of my jeans seems to shrink.

The question volleys back to me, louder in my brain than ever. If Vienna had a problem with me doing this job, *could I quit?*

And I know, without a doubt, I'll get to the bottom of that question tonight.

I have to.

"He didn't just love it, he's obsessed," Maxi gushes, holding her phone out for me to see the bazillion photos of her son on his birthday. "You have no idea, Tuck, seriously. Thank you."

I tap a photo of the four-year-old, and it enlarges. He's got Maxi's same golden hair, wide blue eyes, and a partially toothless grin that makes me smile. He's perched on top of a blue bicycle, no training wheels in sight.

Maxi only works for Crave part time, because she takes care of her ailing father. He's battled his insurance company for ages, and because of that, Maxi is paying his way out of medical debt. He's now on Crave's insurance because Aug fought for it, but she still has hundreds of thousands to pay back.

Which means despite her hefty income, things are tight.

It's why I bought her son the bike. And if the roles were reversed, and I was in need of anything—happiness or money— I know she'd do the same.

Any of us at Crave would. Because we're family.

I swipe through other photos, loving how happy this kid is. All for a bike. Simple and nothing to me, but everything to him. And to Maxi, too, for that matter.

"I'm glad he likes it, Maxi. That's awesome."

"I'll pay you back once I'm above water, I swear," she says sheepishly, with a tone that tells me people in her life have not been understanding of her circumstances. And caring for an aging parent is a huge job, and it sucks that people have made her feel like shit.

I smile as she puts her phone away, gratitude lingering on her face. "You are not paying me back. That's insane."

Her eyes warm and I tip my head toward the large marble bar in my kitchen, where various charcuterie assortments, refreshments and other treats are spread. That's another great thing about living in the city, outside of Crave and all the culture, is the fact you can get anything delivered to your house within a couple of hours.

"Get yourself a drink or something to eat, I got the snacks from Board & Bite downtown."

She rubs her palms together, eyes going wide. We all love Board & Bite. They have the best spreads.

"Did you get the dessert board?"

I grin. "You know it."

She pats my shoulder as she breezes past me. "Good man, you're a good man Tucker."

A moment later, she's got honeycomb candy and chocolate covered apricots piled high on a small plate, chatting with a friend that Otis brought with him.

Surveying the space, I find Vienna tucked into the corner with Dean, another actor from Crave. His real name is Arlo, but his screen personality is kind of this weird, James Dean knock-off, but it works. And the guy can rock a leather jacket like no one's business.

I like Dean.

But right now, he's got my blood boiling. With his arm over Vienna's head with his palm to the wall, he's talking to her, and her focus is really on him, a smile resting on her lips. He surges forward, getting to the punchline of whatever he's saying, and she erupts in wild laughter, her dark hair going everywhere.

She laughs so hard her glasses slide down, and she knocks them back with her hand that cradles an imported beer, then takes a sip. The way her full rosy lips press against the bottle has my mind spinning, and the raucous laughter that continues between them in the next few seconds has me fuming.

Sweat breaks out along my back and forehead and my pulse bounces in my throat as I settle deeply into jealousy's ugly hold.

As if she can sense my energy, her eyes come to mine, and every single nerve ending that was lit with fiery anger a moment ago, is doused and extinguished when she smiles at me, toothy and wide. Air rushes from my lungs as I raise my hand, smiling.

She holds a finger up to Dean, and my cock thickens at the idea that she's choosing me over him. It's stupid and territorial and alpha—all things I am not. But she brings it out of me.

She makes me want to stake claim to her as if she were property, because all I can think about is making her mine.

Mine and only mine.

Yes, I see the irony.

I adjust my dick as she approaches.

"Tucker, your place is so beautiful." She beams, her gaze moving around the room to acknowledge the penthouse.

"I'm really glad you're here," I tell her, even if she didn't have much of a choice. Aug is pretty serious about all of us being together once a month to unwind and take sex out of the equation. He says, in addition to us having monthly therapy appointments on Crave's dime, it's important that we all see one another outside the studio. *Humanizing*, he says.

Since Crave has the lowest turnover rate for any adult film company in America, I'd have to say he's right.

"I'm having a nice time," she says as she hooks hair behind her ear and takes another drink of amber ale.

I'm about to ask her to come to my room, to show her the art and talk to her about how I'm feeling, in no uncertain terms. But Maxi and Uma appear at my side, with Isla and Cecile, two other actresses with C&C.

"Tuck, what the fuck? Why didn't you tell us about Lucy?!"

The women encircle me, and I lose Vienna to their chaos. She backs away, smiling awkwardly, and before I can tell her to stay close, that I want to speak with her, she turns and Maxi claps a hand on my forearm.

"Tell us everything you know about Lucy Lovegood," she demands, eyes glittering with excitement. From her side, Isla clasps her hands together, driving her fingers under her chin eagerly. "Tell us, Tuck. Oh my god, tell us it's true because I've loved Lucy for years!"

I talk about what I know of her coming here in the vaguest of terms, not looking to get on Aug's shit list while also recognizing that he's clearly told someone besides me, since they all know.

Though the porn set is a lot like a hair salon—a lot of gossip. Tons. The only difference is, surprisingly, it's never negative. More so, rumors of exciting things, surprises, and hopes. Yet another reason I love Crave.

Before I know it, twenty minutes have passed. I edge out of the circle of Lucy fandom chatter, and look around my apartment. People are scattered throughout, chatting and snacking, with Otis and his friend loudly playing Mario Kart on my big screen. Lance sips a glass of wine while scrolling his phone when I approach him.

"Hey, have you seen Vienna?" I ask, sifting a hand up the back of my head, trying not to stress. Trying not to focus on the fact that tonight was going to be the night that I talked to her, and now I can't find her and–

"She just left." His focus immediately returns to his phone.

"When?" Panic rises like bile in my throat. I know I can call her and ask her out. I know I can have this talk with her any other time. But to have her at my place, to have that talk at home, it would mean so much more.

"Less than a minute ago," he says, and I swear I'm a bolt of lightning out the front, taking the cement stairs two by two because I don't want to waste a moment waiting for the elevator.

With a nod to my doorman, I slip outside into the always slightly cool San Francisco evening air, pinching my gaze down the sidewalk. Nothing. I turn and immediately spot her, not more than fifty feet away.

"Vienna!" I call out, jogging to catch up. She wraps her flannel around her protectively, but stops and allows me to catch up with her. "Hey, I didn't know you were leaving. You just got here."

She looks down at her Converse, so I do too. And when she looks back up, I find her eyes glassy and her smile lopsided, and a little sad.

"I was feeling... out of place," she says, but her shoulders stay tight and her expression is unwavering. It doesn't feel like the truth.

"Vienna, you work at C&C. You're part of the team. You are not out of place," I assure her, though something tells me it's not what she needs to hear because it isn't why she left.

"I know," she sighs. And if she were mine, I'd slide my hand around her head, lose my fingers to that silky hair, bring her face to mine and show her it's okay to share. Kiss her and make her understand just how much I want to bear her worries, hear her fears, help her work through whatever is bothering her.

But I'm not the guy that takes what isn't his. I'm not the guy that pretends being good looking earns him a free ticket to kissing a person before I have their consent.

She twists her lips to the side. "I felt insecure when you were in that huddle of women." She sighs. "Maybe even a little jealous, though I have no right to be."

"Co-workers," I reason but my chest thumps at her vulnerable honesty.

"I know," she presses her hand to her forehead, eyes

squeezed shut a moment, then shakes her head. "I know. I get that. It's just..." Finally, she gains the courage to find my eyes.

I hold my hand out, fingers splayed, and nod down to it, still holding her gaze with mine. "Come back up with me. Let's talk. In private."

She waffles her fingers with mine, and the feeling of our palms pressed together as we walk back toward my apartment is so soothing and so damn good that it may as well be our bare bodies pressed together.

19

Vienna

I caught something

I really want to make a list of all of the things I've learned about myself in the last few months. I swear I've discovered more recently than all of college *and* art school combined.

Last semester, I tried Boba tea, and was certain I'd be weirded out by the blobs floating around, but the tapioca ended up being delicious. And I was convinced I wouldn't get the value from a Netflix subscription, because I don't watch a lot of TV. But then I discovered Love is Blind, and I've binged four seasons in less than two weeks.

And I suppose the most eye-opening discovery—a bit more important than bubble tea and reality dating shows—I like watching Tuck. I like it to the point of orgasm, which I did not know was possible. In fact, prior to watching Tuck, I'd been massively skeptical and kind of a hater on women who claimed they'd have touchless orgasms just from being so overly aroused. Then I watched Tuck and was served a slice of humble pie as I stood with my eyes locked on his scene as I orgasmed, no touch at all.

Now he's holding my hand and I have a big O on my mind again.

I took this job for money, and I never expected to have feelings for a porn star. But here I am, a goofy grin on my face with my fingers curled around his palm, my heart doing a tapdance behind my ribs.

We move through the apartment, Tuck telling a few people on the way that we'll be back shortly. His kindness and attentiveness is just another wonderful thing about him. The truth is? I'd love to learn some bad, ugly things about him right about now. Because one more good trait and I'll be officially obsessed with this human who is only here for a season of my life.

I am so not ready for heartbreak.

His bedroom is huge, with floor to ceiling windows on one wall. Evening spills across the floor, engulfing the corner of his bed in dreamy purple hue. Tuck hits a switch, and recessed lights come on a moment before he dims them. With his hand still in mine, he slides the large barn-style door shut, and guides me to the side of his bed. Across from the bed are two large rustic doors matching the room doors, hanging on a metal track.

His eyes hold mine as his thumb sweeps over our connected fingers. My breathing slows, or maybe it speeds up. All I know is that together, our hands and eyes bound, I can hardly breathe. I can hardly think.

But I *feel*.

My belly burns with need. Between my legs, everything is wet and hot.

"Tell me how you were feeling before you left," he says softly.

I swallow hard and take a leap of faith that he won't dismiss my feelings. "Honestly? It's hard seeing you with other women. At work, it's one thing. I even like watching you work. But here, just... I don't know, casually I guess? It makes me feel... weird." Low in my throat, my pulse hammers. "It made me insanely jealous."

He studies me, and the trace of a smile that appears on his face gives me hope. Makes my chest tighten. Then his grip on my hand intensifies, and his tongue sweeps the full curve of his bottom lip before he asks, "Can I kiss you, Vienna?"

The words are almost too good to be true. I've seen and held his cock. I've heard him orgasm. I fucked myself with his cock before I came here.

But the question still steals my breath. My response is a stunned half nod. Scared that if I show too much enthusiasm he'll change his mind.

His breath fans my lips and my nose, and my nipples ache in response. My entire chest rises, gravitating toward him as he grins, lowering his mouth painstakingly slow to mine.

Soft and full, his lips feel exactly how I imagined. We give access to one another, opening our mouths as our tongues collide and explore. When he moans into the kiss, making my lips vibrate and my face tingle, I pull back, breathless and dazed.

"How did that make you feel?" He asks while unfairly stroking the back of his hand down my cheek, turning me to putty.

"Good," I manage, mouth dry.

He releases my hand, and moves to the doors, twisting the lock to keep the two closed. My heartbeat thuds in my eardrums because locking the door means something more is happening. *Beyond the kiss.*

With a serious expression, he returns, taking my hand again. We sit on the edge of his bed together as he twists just slightly, better facing me. "I don't kiss any of them off-set and I don't want to. But I want to kiss you, Vienna. And I want to do more."

I lick my lips, my core vibrating from the taste of him left behind. "More?"

Reaching up, he cups the side of my neck, his fingertips dipping into me, sending warmth sliding down my spine. "Do you want more?" He asks, and without any clarification of what it entails, I know my answer. I feel it echoing in my veins.

"Yes."

He brings our mouths close again. "Can I give you more right now?"

I glance at the closed doors, thinking of all of the people on the other side. Leaving his hold, I go to them, checking the lock. I run my fingertips along the latch. If it doesn't hold, they'll be watching us, the same way I've watched them.

I don't know how I feel about that but as if my thoughts are a book, pages spread wide for him to read, Tucker appears at my side. "No one will interrupt us."

With a strong hand, he pushes my hair off my shoulder, running a fingertip under my shirt, tracing my collarbone. "I want to see you. Can I undress you, Vienna?" My name is so delicate and quiet on his lips that I shudder in response. I nod.

He curves his palms around my shoulders, pushing them down my biceps, shedding my flannel. "Raise your arms," he says softly, somewhere between a secret and a private promise. I lift my arms and hold my breath as he peels my shirt off over my head.

With the backs of his fingers pressed to my low belly, an excited chill wracks my chest. He unbuttons and unzips me, and before I know it, Tuck is at my feet peering up at me with mossy green eyes as I step out of my leggings.

Wrapping his hands around my ankles, his thumbs stroking calming circles against me, he says, "I'm so hard, Vienna."

Rising, his words are right there for me to see, a hard ridge visibly fighting his denim. I've seen his cock so many times... But him being hard here, not at Crave, not for the tube or a scene. For me. It hits differently.

My cunt clenches at the sight of his concealed erection, and in an out-of-body experience I hear myself say to him, "Get naked."

His grin makes me dizzy, but he disrobes quickly. And we stand before each other, me in panties and a bra, Tucker in boxer briefs that are currently having their elasticity tested by his straining erection.

My gaze follows but my feet stay put as he walks behind me, letting his hands explore my shoulders and neck. I tip my head to the side as my mind shuts off, the feel of his large hands kneading and massaging causing thought to evaporate. Bringing his mouth to my ear from behind, he whispers, "I'm going to take your bra off now."

I don't speak my permission, but the way I collect my hair to one side to give him a clear shot is my consent. He leaves searing kisses along my neck and spine before unclasping me with ease. My bra falls to my feet, joining the graveyard of our clothes.

Large hands smooth up my ribs, causing goosebumps to break out along my belly and chest.

Tucker is already so different than I imagined. He's unhurried, and careful to make sure I'm comfortable, and eager to tend to every inch of me. He isn't rushing, pinning me down and hammering into me the way I'd expect a casual hook-up to fuck.

He's... *romantic*. And the fact that I'm the recipient of such attentiveness has me spinning to face him. Desperate to find his eyes.

"I'm sorry I said no when you asked me out before," I blurt out, guilt gnawing at me for the way I misread him before. Because he's clearly layered, and not at all what I painted him to be.

His gaze goes hooded as he takes in my breasts for the first time. "It's okay," he says, licking his lips, eyes tracing my areola.

I cup his cheek. He drags his eyes up to mine. "I shouldn't have dismissed you."

His grin is sweet but fleeting, because a moment later he's lowering his face to my breast, kissing before sealing his lips to my nipple. With his hand exploring my other breast, he sucks and kisses, making the back of my head and neck grow fuzzy and hot. Warmth rushes from between my legs as my body prepares for Tucker, and how much I want him inside of me.

His lips are pink and swollen when he stands, and the cool air against my wet breast has my body thrumming for him. "Will you go out with me?" he asks, grinning from ear to ear.

I nod my response as he hooks fingers in my panties, dropping down to the ground again so I can step out of them.

"I'm going to make you come with my mouth, and then I'm going to have you come on my cock," he says quietly, as if the words he's speaking aren't the filthy, delicious promises I've been dying to hear.

Again, I nod, my mouth going dry at his honest intensity. I am lost to him. Hypnotized by his unwavering gaze and feeling like the center of his universe. Nothing exists outside of *us*.

He lies me back on his bed until my head is dangling off. Carefully, he pulls my hair from beneath me, letting it cascade off the edge. The feel of his heavy cock resting against my belly through his briefs has me nearly squirming on the mattress, so aroused that I feel like I'm going a little crazy.

"Tell me if you need to lift your head up, if you get dizzy or anything, okay?"

I nod. He shimmies down my body, kissing my belly, on his way to my pussy. "I masturbated before I came here," I say, the words rushing out of me fast and unexpectedly as I watch Tucker Deep prepare to worship me.

He lifts his head, his expression drunken and hazy, like he's as lost in this as I am. It's an ego boost I didn't know I needed. *I'm* making Tucker Deep crazy. And that is... wild.

"Yeah?" he asks, voice husky.

Craning my neck to hold his gaze, I tell him *exactly* how. "I used my latest casting of you."

The green of his eyes go stormy and dark as his lids droop, a needy rumble erupting from deep in his chest. "Did you think of him?"

Confusion tips my head, and then he rocks to his knees and drops his briefs, keeping them banded around his thighs. Eyes still locked with mine, he grips his cock and strokes, a quiet rumble brewing in his chest. "Him," he says again, as he strokes the *him* in question.

I bite my lip and tell him the truth. "Him and you."

He smiles, leaning forward to tap my elbows, indicating for me to lie back. "Remember, unless you want them to know what we're doing in here," he presses a finger to his lips, miming silence. Kissing my groin, making my cunt seize with need, he adds, "For the record, I don't care if they know. Aug and Lance already know how crazy I am about you."

Wait... what? *Crazy* about me? "They–they do?" I ask,

nearly shaking from the way my pulse surges through my core, centering on my cunt. "You're crazy about me?"

He places his lips on my cunt and kisses, his tongue sweeping through my lips, parting me, discovering all I'm harboring for him.

"Mmmm," he hums in response into my soaked core, his hands coming to grip my hips. Straining up off the edge of the bed, neck fiery, I peer down to see a white-knuckled Tucker feasting on me, his moans driving me too close to the edge.

"I love the noises you make," I tell him as he sucks on my nerve bundle. "On set. And here. Your moans," I admit to him, letting my head fall, taking in the view of the upside down city outside. "God, Tucker, they're so..." Hot doesn't feel like the right word, because they're erotic, addicting, alluring... so many things are bigger and better than *hot*. But with his tongue prodding at my opening, teasing me, I can't be eloquent. "Hot," I say, my breaths coming quicker, shorter, more urgent.

He must hear compliments all the time. In his line of work, I'm sure he could go to any porn website, look himself up, and hit the comments for a spike of confidence and hit of serotonin.

Even so, my words wrap around him, making him devour me more urgently, like my praise directly correlates to how badly he wants me to come.

Then, with my head back, eyes closed, and legs spread, I discover what makes all those women on set lose their minds. Tucker tongues my clit in tight circles before slowly sweeping through my lips, releasing raspy, erotic moans while he does. The more he eats me, the deeper and more desperate his moans grow, the closer I get to the edge.

I must lift my head from the edge to look at him a thousand times if I do it once, because just the mountainous range of his shoulders squared off between my thighs is a sight. Paired with those husky grunts and eager noises, I'm almost a goner after less than five minutes.

With his lips placing a kiss on my clit, he murmurs, "This is my favorite pussy to kiss and lick. You're so tight and wet, it's making me so hard." Then he buries those full lips in me again, prodding his tongue inside of me as he brings his thumb to my clit.

My hips burn as I attempt to spread my legs even wider, giving him even more access. I've never opened myself up so wide and displayed myself so blatantly. I've never had that all consuming urge to be spread open and devoured.

But the way Tucker feasts, letting moans of arousal and approval slip free as he does, I know why I'm spreading myself open for him like a fucking... porn star.

Because I want him, out of this bed, in daylight, for the world to see. And when you want someone so wholly, the chemistry in the bedroom is always on fire. And he was fire without the chemistry. Now? He's a fucking nuclear explosion.

I lift my head again when I hear what sounds like slickness and friction, and discover his bicep and forearm tightly flexed, his shoulder torquing as he jacks his cock crouched over me, lips sealed to my clit.

Watching a man masturbate has always been one of my favorite things. Sometimes when I get my favorite charged friend out to play, I queue up videos of just that—a man in the privacy of his home, pulling down his shorts, freeing his thick cock, stroking himself until he's messy and spent.

Watching Tucker masturbate while he teases my clit, nibbling and sucking intermittently as my body begins to writhe, is a whole new experience.

It's the most powerful vibrator paired with the best libido, it's the perfect friction holding hands with the right speed. It's hot and raw, and the sight proves too much for me to take.

One more glimpse of those strong fingers strangling his thick, long shaft until his head weeps on to the mattress beneath and I'm exploding.

"Tucker," I whimper as my orgasm sears down my spine. My cunt seizes, and Tucker moans into my pussy as he sucks my clit, lapping me through climax.

His sweet moans of accomplishment and silent praise keep my orgasm rippling. He slides the tip of his finger inside me, groaning as he discovers the soaking mess that is my cunt.

"This pretty little pussy came so well for me," he rasps, playing with my wet entrance while still peppering kisses to my clit. "Now, I want you to come again for me, this time, in my lap."

As if I were built to obey—something I've never been good at before—I sit up and we switch positions, Tucker resting his back against the headboard. "Come sink that perfect pussy down on this dick and let me make you feel even better, Vienna," he says, his voice tender, his words filthy.

Something about his briefs still being around his thighs, though now nearing his knees, is also so hot. Like he couldn't even be bothered to completely disrobe because he wanted to taste and please me so bad.

I throw a leg over his lap, hovering over him as we both reach for his cock. My hand curls into his as we guide his wide slick head to my opening. Our eyes find each other, and our expressions mirror one another. Horny, hazy, completely engulfed in the moment.

"How'd you do with him earlier?" he asks, using our hands to stroke him. When our connected hands, holding his cock, brush against my pussy lips on the upstroke, my spine warms and delicious tingles worm their way through my legs. I am so ready for this.

"Good," I breathe, dying to sink down on him and feel the

real Tucker spearing me. "I used the one I'm presenting next week," I add, referencing the first semi-final toy I produced successfully just a day ago.

He continues slow strokes, and jerking a man off with his own hand is a new experience for me. Another thing I'd never thought of doing, but now that I have, realize I've been missing out. Something about feeling his hardened arousal, how I made him that way, how much he wants me to sit on his cock, all of it is... incredibly arousing.

"I want you on top so you can ease me in, take your time, stop when it's too much," he says, removing his hand. Reaching over to his nightstand, he barely manages to hook a finger on the edge of the draw before tugging it open. He snatches a foil package and brings it to his mouth to tear it open. "I'm clean, but I don't have access to those test results right now. They're," he nods, indicating his medical documents are likely in another part of the apartment. A part where people are drinking and making small talk no less. I watch his arms over his belly as he rolls the condom down his cock. Even his arms are a turn on.

Once the rubber is strangling his erection, he places his hands on my hips with possession, nodding. "Okay, beautiful, fuck me until that sweet pussy of yours is screaming for mercy."

I slowly take him, inch by inch, moving up and down as my core adjusts to the thick intrusion. Breathing hard, sweat glistening on my bare breasts, I finally sink all the way down, my groin burning with fullness.

"You look like you were made to take me, Vienna," he croaks, strain filling his neck and jaw. "How do I feel inside of you? Are you full?"

Biting my lip, I nod as I ride, rising to my knees before sinking back down, repeating this motion as the pressure builds. He swipes a thick finger down my sternum, then cups a breast before pinching the nipple, causing a quiet moan to slip free.

"When we're alone, you can ride me all day, and be as loud as you want. Hell, I want you to be loud. I want everyone in a five mile radius to know how good my cock makes you feel."

His words embolden me and I ride him faster, harder, at a pace that's beyond unsustainable. I know I'm close to a second orgasm, and I know I should wait and come with him, but everything he does is fanning the flames. Every sultry word he utters, each time his eyes fall to where his fat cock spears me and he moans to himself, a pinch in his brows as he does, pushes me to the edge.

He presses his hand flat above my mound, the other still holding my hip as I practically bounce on his cock. "I feel myself inside you, Vienna. And it's the best feeling," he groans, applying pressure to my lower belly with his hand as I sink down, taking every inch.

"Tucker," I plead, wanting to hear him tell me he's close, that he's going to topple over this jagged, wild cliff with me.

But his gaze takes mine, and he nods with reassurance. "I want you to," he breathes, nodding, his husky voice doing nothing for my cause. "Come on, you're right there, take it. Take that orgasm, let me feel you come on my cock, come for my cock. Come for me Vienna, please."

Please.

Holy shit.

My head tips back, and as much as I wanted a beautiful orgasm shared between us, this feels pretty fucking insane, too.

I clench and seize all around him, the intensity of my release so overwhelming that I can't speak. I can't even moan. Mouth opened in a silent cry, in a desperate plea, I come on Tucker Deep's cock—the real thing—and nothing has ever felt so good.

"*Gahhhh*," I breathe, my movements slowing as my orgasm tapers, my entire body shuddering. Traces of electricity pop in my spine, rendering me a puddle of exhausted, sated muscles.

Before I know it, Tuckers sliding me off his cock carefully, and hooking his hands under my arms.

I almost squeal as he lifts me off his lap, positioning me on my knees on the floor. But when I see his sheathed cock bobbing over me, I know what he wants.

I reach out to take the condom off, he grabs my wrist. "Don't," he says, both quiet and assertive. "I want you to see my tests before you give me that trust, okay?"

I don't nod. I just blink up at him, my gaze tripping between his beautiful hooded eyes and his erection bobbing in front of me.

He leans down and takes my mouth in a short but hot kiss, loving the way we pass my flavor between us. When he rises, his smile does things to my chest that I force myself to ignore.

"I want you to feel what's going to be inside of you, what's going to paint your bare tits, what's going to rocket over your naked ass and up your back." He strokes his sheathed cock, his belly knotting with muscle. "Open your mouth."

Our eyes stay locked as he edges toward my open mouth, slipping the first few inches of himself onto my tongue. He's hard and heavy, and sweet and salty, too.

"Close your mouth on just the tip," he instructs, and I follow his orders, sliding back on his length until my lips are sealed around his rubber crown.

With his hands now resting on the tops of my shoulders, he holds himself perfectly still as he says, "You drive me crazy, Vienna."

He doesn't stroke his shaft and he doesn't force me down on his cock. Instead, he traps the ends of my hair between his fingers, the other hand still holding my shoulder, as he stares into my eyes. "Just being inside you, I wanted to come the first second. I've wanted to be inside you for way too long."

How long? How long has he wanted me? How long could he have had me if I hadn't been too busy thinking I was too good for a porn star?

His emerald eyes hold mine before his fingertips dip deeper into my flesh, and he tugs my hair just slightly. The condom expands as he holds himself on my tongue, his raspy moans blanketing us.

The rubber expands as he fills it. The sheer weight and warmth of his cum on my tongue driving me wild. "That's all for you, Vienna," he groans, letting his thumb trace the curve of my jaw before coming to my bottom lip. "You look so beautiful."

I start to caress his head with my tongue, playing with his contained orgasm. I suckle the full tip, my nipples hardening. He laughs, growing sensitive post come, and fishes his hands under my arms, lifting me up.

Before we speak, he grips the base of his cock and slips the condom off. Why is watching him take off a full condom like watching him masturbate?

"Earth to Vienna," he laughs, the noise tearing me from my cum trance. Cum trance? Is that a thing? It is when you're with Tucker, I guess.

"That was... hot," I tell him, still staring at the pool of cum in the rubber. "I've never felt anyone come in my mouth... wearing a condom." I roll my lips together and look up at him finally, finding his eyes sparkling and his grin wide.

"Me either. But... I want you to know what's yours once you see my test results."

"You know, I think most guys would've just come in my mouth when I offered," I smirk, sliding my hand around the back of my neck, rocking to my toes.

He leans down to meet me halfway, and we share a sloppy, fiery kiss made that much more hot by the fact his cock, still half hard, presses to my belly.

"When you take me bare, I want your mind to be focused on just one thing: taking every drop of pleasure and cum I have for you." He kisses me, sealing the fiery words with a scorching kiss. "Not worrying about if I'm clean."

"If you say you're clean, I believe you," I tell him, because I know Tucker well enough to know he isn't a liar.

He smiles. "Don't worry, my beautiful girl, there's plenty of time for us. I don't want you *believing* me. I want you to *know* that what I say is true. Okay?"

I nod and follow his hands with my eyes as he ties off the condom and waffles our fingers together with his free hand.

"Come on, let's clean up and go back out to the party."

I stop in my tracks, eyes wide. "Everyone's going to know we just had sex."

He blinks, wearing an adorably charming smirk. "Vienna, I want to be clear. I don't care who in that room knows I just took your pussy with my mouth and cock. Hell, I want them to know. I want them to know who you belong to. If we walk out there and they smirk, it'll be hard not to puff my chest and slam my fists against it, because that's what you do to me. You make me a feral, crazy man who wants you so bad, I wish I could mark you as mine."

Whoa. I lick my lips, and ignore my excited, racing heart. He leads us into his master bathroom and proceeds to, while naked, wipe my body with a cool cloth, ridding me of our sweat and orgasms.

I'm a little sad, if I'm being honest, because the idea of twisting in my sheets, spreading the scent of him, letting the memories of what we just did permeate my bed—that makes me happy.

226

But I don't want a UTI, and fucking like we just did without aftercare would definitely earn me a dose of antibiotic.

Once we're cleaned up and redressed, Tucker takes my mouth in a possessive kiss. Everything is absolutely perfect.

"Would you be my girlfriend? I know we haven't had a date yet and I only asked you on a date like, ten minutes ago, but hell, I think of each casting session as a date, honestly. And I'd love for you to be my girl, Vienna. I really would."

Everything is absolutely perfect. He unlatches the door, and they slide apart, revealing a room full of people, chatting and snacking. I glance around the space of adult film stars and reality rushes back to me.

What we just did was so hot and amazing but... he does that with *them*, too.

Gripping my chin, he forces me to face him. "Please think about this seriously. I want you so badly but I need to know you're ok with it before we go any further."

With that, he's stolen from me as Lance appears, his trusty iPad out, his sights set on Tucker.

"A word?" he says flatly, ignoring me completely. With one last squeeze to our interlocked hands, Tucker smiles at me and goes to Lance.

My head is spinning, and my lower half is pulsing. Tucker just gave me two back to back orgasms then asked me to be his. I want to pinch myself but I feel too silly. Instead, I grab my things, say goodbye to Augustus and the others quietly, and slip out the door.

The urge to run overtakes me as reality hits like an anvil.

I do want to be with Tucker. But can I be with a man who is consistently with others? In times like these, I do what I always do as I walk down the sidewalk toward my car.

I text Darren.

Daisy Jane

I slept with Tuck

I caught something

And I'm confused

Chlamydia?

Worse

FEELINGS.

20

Tucker

I want to watch.

I tap my foot against the hardwood, counting the number of times it smacks the shiny grain. Six.

"Hey son, how are you?" Dad asks cheerfully, despite the fact it's nearing eleven at night and he's likely been sleeping in his recliner for over an hour already. He never misses a call.

"This is your reminder to get up and sleep in bed," I tease, since Dad's been known to catch a few nights in the living room after falling asleep watching murder mysteries.

His chortle makes me happy, but also makes me homesick in equal measure. "I'm headed in there. I got caught up on a case." In the background, the hum of true crime disappears, followed by the metallic snap of the recliner hinges closing. "Well, to what do I owe the pleasure of a night time call from my son? Everything okay?"

"I'm okay yeah but...well, I slept with Vienna."

He drags his hand down his beard, the scrape of stubble clear as day in the receiver. "Gonna need more than that Tuck..." he prods.

"Well... the monthly Crave & Cure mixer was at my place. I offered because you know how close I am to the studio and I have the space. And last time everyone had a really great time playing the double Switches. We had that MarioKart championship."

"I remember you said it was a great time," Dad recalls. "And that's what having a large space is all about. Sharing it for good times."

"Definitely. So I had it here and since she's a part of C&C for the next year, she was obligated to join. You know how Aug is about off-set stuff."

Dad laughs. "Oh I know very well what Augustus is like. But I like that part of him. He wants to keep the team strong, and believe you me, the people working around you being happy is just as important as the job itself."

"I know. Aug's great when he's not being kinda scary," I tell dad, who knows all the sides of Aug because not only has my family met him plenty of times, but I tell dad everything.

"Okay, so Vienna came to the party. Did you show her?" Dad asks. When I found Vienna on the sidewalk trying to leave, I'd asked her to come back up and had every intention of showing her the artwork hidden away in my closet. The piece just for me. It was going to be for her, too.

"I didn't. I got... carried away. It was so different from anyone else I've been with, and I don't just mean different from *my work*. I mean, I've never felt more than... I don't know. More than physical need. It was so much *more* , you know?"

Dad's quiet sigh and careful words bring me peace. "I do. That's the *big deal*."

"What's the *big deal?*"

"That connection." He adjusts in his chair, the infamous squeaky spring giving him away. "That's the thing. The *thing* everyone is looking for."

"I was just going to say," I add, my eardrums ringing a little. "I felt a connection not just physically but mentally. She didn't have to give any cues or tells, I just... felt like I *knew* what she needed.." I scratch the side of my jaw and let my foot tap the floor again, watching it as I think. "I mean, it was an immediate connection." I sigh, raking a hand through my hair. "I don't know, Dad. Being with her is exactly what I hoped."

Dad sighs. "But you're calling me and you're blue." Dad hates the word depressed. It un-ironically makes him depressed.

I tap my other foot now and stare at it as I do. "Well, you know how I feel about Vienna."

"I do. But I can't believe she doesn't feel the same?" Dad's voice lifts, his genuine outrage cloaked in surprise. I love how much he believes in me.

"I think she does feel the same," I start, and then I stop tapping my foot. Gripping the edge of my mattress, I cast a glance at the closed closet door where just a few feet away hangs the piece of art that called me to Vienna two and half years ago. Called me to Crave, too. "But I'm afraid she can't be with me, you know, because of what I do."

"Ahh, now, if she's an artist, she won't be that close minded. It's your job, it's not the same as a real connection," Dad says ruefully. We've had a conversation like this before, though the only difference now is... I really want it to work.

"It's not like how it was with Cate. I *want* to change her mind, Dad," I admit needlessly.

"I know, Tuck. And I won't advise you not to do that, if it's what you feel you need to do. But I've been married a long time, and I've managed to learn a few things." His throat whistles as he sucks down a deep breath, gathering energy to dispense his wise, fatherly advice. Dad's never led me astray. "One of the things I know—and I suppose this spans beyond romantic relationships—but one thing I know is you can't change someone's mind. They have to feel it in their heart, it can't be a switch in the brain from no to yes."

I let out a weighted sigh. He's right. Vienna either likes me enough to give me a chance or she doesn't. And sure, she's not a film star and I don't have to watch her have sex with other guys, but the truth is, if she came home to me, surrendering to my heart and hands, I'd be okay with whatever her career.

"I know. I guess I've felt she was meant for me. I think I was just hoping this wouldn't be an issue."

"That's a bit naive, son," Dad says kindly of my stupid truth, his voice a comforting hum. In the background, familiar depth rumbles as I move the phone to my other ear, sitting up a bit taller.

"Is that Theo?" I question as the rumble starts up again.

"Yeah, that's him. Theo, say hi to your brother," Dad says to his oldest son. In the background, my brother whisper-hisses a tempered hello, which earns a grin from me.

"Put him on a second, dad, alright?" I get to my feet and start taking long strides across the open floor plan of my penthouse.

My penthouse. That always makes me a little happy, because I earned it by making people happy.

The phone passes and a moment later, one of my favorite people is on the line.

"Tucker, The Fucker," he says with a huge grin in his tone. "How are you, brother?"

"Dude, I'm good. What's up? How's the shop? Why are you home?"

Theo's main pawn shop is not far from Oakcreek, but far enough that the drive is a little over an hour. We all moved away to do our own things, but we stayed close enough for weekend pop-ins. Still, we have a group chat. His visit was not in it.

Theo takes a drink, one that I'm forced to listen to. After a belch, he says, "Someone brought in a cool vintage stroller thing. I FaceTimed mom to see if she wanted it and she lost her mind. So here I am, delivering it and mooching home cooked food. Figure I'll drive back after I get a big breakfast and maybe some cookies to take back."

"What kind did she make?" I ask, stopping in front of my industrial fridge. I yank open a stainless door and stare at the tub of partially eaten spinach, a carton of egg whites, and rows of sparkling waters and beers. Homemade cookies sound good.

I put Theo on speaker so I can get access to my phone. While he speaks, I pull up my FoodFly app and search for the nearest cookie shop. They're still open because it's Friday night, so I place an order for a random assortment dozen and hit delivery.

"Chocolate chunk with cherries, and homemade sugar cookie with that thick frosting that makes you feel sick after two but is so fucking worth it," Theo shares. I can practically taste both of them at the mention, and I swear I smell them from here. Sweet, brown sugar and vanilla filling the air. Mom's cookies always made our house smell the absolute best.

"Fuck you're lucky," I sigh.

"Says the porn star," Theo quips. "So what's up, anyway? You're calling dad at nearly midnight on Friday. Something's up?"

"Woman troubles," I admit, loathing how it sounds to be mentioning Vienna to my family under any circumstances but happiness. I *want* to be calling them to say meet my new girl, not that I've fallen for someone who may not be able to stomach what I do for work.

"Shit, man. Is this the artist you've been crushing on forever? I was hoping to finally meet her next week when we come out." He takes another drink, and even though I've been around friends and booze all night, nothing sounds better than a beer at home with my brother.

"Yeah, that's the one, but you're still gonna meet her. She's going to be around Crave for a while. She's contracted through the year," I say, imagining how it will feel knowing she's feet away from me after rejecting my offer to be her boyfriend while I work but have to pretend I'm unaffected. It sounds like torture. And the way I went straight to "be my girlfriend" may have surprised her. Though I didn't plan it, it felt right. All of our casting sessions in the workroom have felt like dates. Being hers does seem like the natural progression.

"What's up? She doesn't feel the same way?" my brother questions.

"I think she does, that's the thing. I mean I know she's at least interested. She may not be in love with me or anything but I know she likes me. The thing is..." I let my sentence stretch until it crashes head on with silence.

Theo steps in. "She doesn't like that you have sex with other people for a living?"

"Potentially, I asked her to really think about it before it goes any further." I sigh. "You know, since I first saw her, I've not dated. I mean, I won't lie. I tried to date Cate, just to see if dating was a thing, but it never made it past one date. I've not fallen for anyone. Never even slept with anyone after a drunk night after work. Not once."

"Not even a peck," Theo adds, because he's already aware of why I'm so nervous. My entire family knows why. The last time I was dumped for this very issue, I spilled my guts to them, because they're my pillars of strength no matter what. Cate didn't believe I could do it—keep it all *work*. She thought I'd inevitably catch feelings for someone on set, because of the sex.

Sex, she argued, always brings feelings, no matter what. Sooner or later, you catch them or you can't promise that you won't.

I argued that a person is as likely to catch feelings for a grocery store clerk who gives them attention, or a guy at a bar who's friendly when you're feeling like shit. People have affairs all the fucking time and they aren't all porn stars. Talk about some fucked up stereotyping.

Then I argued that no matter what she thought, I'd never be able to prove it to her. She'd have to trust me.

And that's where our sunset began. Before we even had a sunrise. We'd only gone on one date. Just one.

Never even kissed.

I don't want to part with Vienna, and we're not even together yet.

"I asked her to be my girlfriend," I admit to my brother, the sound of it making hairs stand up along my spine. My eyes lock on a large cumulus drifting through the darkening sky and I wonder what Vienna is looking at right now.

"She said no, huh?" My brother lets loose a low, pitiful whistle.

"Not quite. We were... interrupted, then she left."

"I'm sorry, man. But the good news is, we'll be there in a few days to see you. We'll go to the crab leg place on the Pier and stuff ourselves 'til we get sick then kick Tegan and Mom's asses in MarioKart."

I laugh. We always beat my mom and sister when we play online together, but there's nothing better than kicking your mom and sister's ass in person.

"I'm looking forward to that. Honestly," I admit, stroking a hand through my hair, a wave of Vienna's scented lotion catching me off guard. I bet my sheets smell like her, but even if they didn't, I think I could conjure up her scent from memory, and hold it with me all night.

Crossing my apartment, I let my brother know what happened. "It's important you know she didn't say no. She didn't really say anything. I asked her out when she came to sign her contract at Crave, but she said no back then. We've been spending so much time together, it felt like the right time." I clear my throat. "And we slept together."

"Is that right?" Theo asks, and then lowering his voice further, "With all the *feelings*... how was it?"

My mouth opens but I can't seem to string together the words to describe how it was. It wasn't good, it was great, but then when I think of other things that are great—chocolate ice cream, taking your jeans off after a long day —sex with her was so much more than that. And if I say beautiful, it makes it sound like it wasn't hot, but it was both hot and beautiful. I sigh and stick to that.

He laughs. "A dreamy sigh, huh? Man, you really like her."

"A lot."

There's silence on both ends of the call, because we both know I'm in quite the predicament. I can't make her like what I do, and I can't force her to endure something that will torture her heart and mind. But I can't walk away. Not yet.

"Well, tell Dad thanks for answering. Don't let him sleep in the recliner, either." I stand at the foot of my bed, staring at the heap of discarded sheets crumpled in the center. "See you in a few days."

"See you. Love you, bud."

"Love you too, Theo."

> Good luck today. I know I only saw the pre-prototype but if I say so myself, it's a great looking cock.

> Never seen one better. HBU?

> Quit fishing for dick compliments, you know it's huge and magnificent.

I can't help but sit a little taller at that, despite the fact that no one can control or take credit for their dick size except genetics. I can still love that she said it.

> I'm glad this conversation is in writing

> I may have to frame it

> Did you have fun last night? I wanted to walk you to your car

> Yeah, sorry I kinda bolted

> I kind of freaked out after we hooked up

> How so?

A snail passes me by as I wait for her response, I swear. Dots appear and disappear, and I picture Vienna's nose wrinkled as she nudges her glasses up and fixates on the perfect response.

> I really liked being with you last night.

Being with you. Translation: *fucking* you. From my spot at my kitchen counter, I push my partially full coffee cup away as my stomach sours. Have I completely misread Vienna? Maybe she doesn't like me, maybe she just wants to fuck me. And I'm the one pushing for something she doesn't want.

I really got a vibe that we were more than physical.

My thumbs start moving, because I'm not the guy who lets miscommunication take anything away from my life. But her text appears first, so I quit.

> Gotta be at Crave soon so I should go. See you soon. And thank you! Presentation day. I'm so nervous!

> You'll be great. Those are beautiful cocks we made.

> See you soon.

While walking to Crave, I devised a plan. And it's a much better plan than when Theo and I were kids and we decided to drop a Mentos into a bottle of pop over mom's rug. This plan has been thought through really well. For the last six blocks, at least.

Her little car is tucked into it's usual spot outside, and just spotting it has me fucking giddy. Heading inside the building, I stop and take a moment to small talk with security, give a nod of acknowledgement to Cohen, our set guy, and head back toward the work room. I give a little knock before pushing inside where I'm met with a sight I'm proud to say is very likely unique to me.

Vienna standing behind a table with four of my dicks standing proudly erect on top, each one slightly different than the other. Looking up, Vienna's arms are out, as if she's performing a magic trick and smoke is about to rise up from the floor. It's dorky and fucking adorable. She's steadying them, likely checking how well they'll stand for her presentation, but she looks so cute doing it.

My chest grows tight as I close the door behind me, making sure to depress the locking center in the handle. Vienna is preoccupied unsticking the sex toys from the table, and misses the sound.

"Wow," I draw out as I close the distance between us, peeling one of the replicas from the table. Skimming the shaft through my hands, I'm surprised at the soft slide of the material through my fingers. "And it feels really good."

She nods fervently. "I know! That one's my favorite. It's done with a special medical grade silicone. It feels the most... well, it doesn't feel *real* exactly but I think it's the most tactile."

I tip my head to the side, wanting to know the differences between all of the toys, but quickly losing the ability to ask those questions. Knowing her delicate hands created all of these, touched and handled me, studied images of me, knowing we discovered one another as she made some of these designs, it only pulls me deeper into the abyss of needing Vienna Carnegie.

"Well, touch is good but consumers won't be buying them just to touch them, you know?" I make my way around the table, standing by her side. She looks like a cold glass of milk after a warm chocolate cookie, and my mouth waters, desperate for a drink.

Heavenly and perfect in a fitted black dress and black high heels that expose just the tips of her toes, nails painted baby blue, my body hums with possessive energy, catching up with my over eager hard-on.

Stirred by my need for her, I rest my hand on her hip. I can't help but fantasize about where we could end up; I envision touching her this way at our wedding, before our first dance.

I'd pull her into me, push her hair off her shoulder and press my lips to her throat. I'd kiss and lick her beating pulse, her excitement fueling my desires. I'd hold her close, and we'd sway to the hushed awws of our friends and family, and I'd tell her how I planned to fuck her until she couldn't walk as soon as we got back to our suite.

"What?" she blinks up at me, confusion arching her brows. "You're staring at your own hand on my hip," she says bluntly. It wasn't the smooth entry I'd planned, but I roll with it and search her eyes for a fleck of reciprocation.

"I was just seeing our future," I admit, the words sounding bold and big as they claim space between us. "But first," I add, sticking to the plan. "Since you've had the real thing," I remind, tugging her near as the cock in her hand falls to the table with a gratifying thud. *Atta boy.*

"Tell me, Vienna, how does the finished prototype compare?" I raise the cock and level it between us, peering around my own replica shaft into her wide eyes.

There's a tremble in her voice when she speaks, but her eyes don't leave mine. "I don't know."

"Didn't you use it before you came to the party?" I invade her space, stepping even closer. Her breath rushes out as a flush claims her, leaving her cheeks in ruddy ombres.

She shakes her head, and my eyes scale the soft curve of her throat, taking in the swell of her breasts, and the way the dress hugs her core. I can't stop my roaming gaze, and as soon as I'm at the baby blue polish on her toes, I start over again, shaking my head. "God, Vienna, you look absolutely gorgeous."

"It's just a black dress," she says, voice hollow.

I ignore her attempt to diffuse my compliment. "You said you used it," I remind her, circling back to the reason why I locked the door in the first place.

"I used the other prototype." She spins the cock in my hands, tracing some of the veins with the tip of her finger. "See these veins? They were the ones I was focusing on after the first casting, to get them right." She swallows and my balls feel it. "I had to stare at photos of your... of *you*," she corrects, "to make sure they were perfect. It's what Debauchery wanted."

She's breathing harder now, so I take the opportunity to step back and toss my thumb over my shoulder, toward the door. "I locked it."

She doesn't even glance at the lock to check, just keeps her eyes locked on mine. "This is the main toy, right? What are the other three? I thought we had to recast for each release?"

Nodding, she says, "Yeah, this one is my preference but I wanted to give them options. Different silicone, and finishes." The focus of the presentation is the first release but I also want to discuss the others. I've seen the outline—phase two is meant to be filled with liquid to simulate a real orgasm, three with a vibrating element stuffed inside a pocket of the silicone, and the finale will have a metal base, meant to attach to a fuck machine. Each of those will need recasting to accommodate the... extras.

I trace the crown of the cock with my fingertip. "I bet it's pretty important that it feels as good as I feel, right?"

At first, she doesn't respond. Only watches my finger journey around the crown between us. Finally she nods.

"Can I touch you?" I ask, my voice unrecognizably husky.

She nods again, quicker, lips parted, eyes flitting between mine.

Slowly, never breaking our heated gaze, I bring the cock to my mouth, and open. She gasps as I slide the head onto my tongue, curling around the underside of it as I feed myself more.

My palm journeys from her hip to her hand, and I replace my hand with hers around the cock. She gives me a bit more, but I'm too big for myself and she pulls it out about halfway.

"I know you're bi," she rasps, chest still heaving. "And I'm not trying to fetishize you but... watching you do that. The idea of you being with a man..." She swallows hard, pinching her eyes closed, her chin pinching to her shoulder.

"Hey," I offer softly, because I don't want her to be embarrassed of anything she wants. That's not how a good relationship works, and if we're going to build, we have to start off right. "Tell me."

Something in my chest flutters when she looks up at me right away, immediately locking eyes. "I want to watch. I want to watch you with a guy and touch myself," she breaths, her secrets flanking me. "But I want to watch you with women, too." She clears her throat. "I like watching you. Period."

She brings the dick to my mouth again so I open for her, and let her watch my mouth work. Her eyelids flutter as I moan around the cock, sealing my lips tight, like I do when I actually give head.

She takes it out, retrieving my hand from my side, and replaces her hand with mine.

And she opens her mouth.

The real cock between my legs thickens, a warm potent ache surging through my lower half. Slowly, I watch her take more of me than even I could, and I can't help but moan needfully in response.

Goddamnit I'm jealous of my own dick, and not the real one.

"That's a good girl, Vienna. You suck my cock much better than I do," I praise, giving her morsels of what I know she's craving. Teasing her, baiting her, and absolutely loving the results.

She forces the cock from her mouth, breathing heavily, nostrils flaring. It's sexy as fuck. "I want to watch you so badly," she pants, her shoulders trembling with her admission.

"Well guess what, beautiful girl, I want to watch you *right now*." I lick my lips and press them to her ear, whispering softly, "Slide your panties down for me."

She moans, hiking up her dress to hook her thumbs in her thong.

"I'd love to slide that down with my teeth." I look down at my painful erection. "Another time. And we don't have much time."

She blinks at me with heavy lids, straightening. "I won't be long."

Fuck. Why does that make me so goddamn hard I want to explode. I want to change the plan and throw her over the table and slam my cock into her so hard her scream shatters the goddamn window.

I suck the dildo into my mouth, and enjoy the crown for her benefit. She moans, she fucking purrs, and I've never felt happier. Never felt more sated, despite the fact I'm nearly burning alive to make love to her.

Looping one hand around the back of her neck, I position my replica between her legs. Goosebumps rise in my wake as my hand grazes her thighs. "Oh my god," she breaths as I position the rounded head at her entrance.

Easing the beast inside of her, she reaches out, clutching my shoulders. My spine floods with heat, and if I didn't want to get drunk on her sighs and binge her little moans, I'd be kissing her.

I also know that right now, she needs my dirty talk. I know she likes it. The proof is dripping down the replica, soaking my fingertips.

"Tell me, Vienna, how did I fuck you?" My voice is low and broken. I've never even used this tone on film. It's private, for her.

"Did I enter you like this?" I ask as I push the head all the way inside causing her to gasp, thrashing a little as she clutches my chest and shoulders. "I was so eager to get inside you last night, I think I went faster than I'd like," I admit, making her head tip drunkenly to the side. The ends of her hair curl beneath her breasts, and I choke on a groan at the movie playing out before my eyes. Better than anything I've ever filmed, easily.

"Did I go fast? Like this?" I sink the cock inside her, and her perfect pussy swallows it eagerly. She whines at the sound of her own arousal, slickness permeating the quiet room.

Stroking out of her slow and into her fast, I pump my arm between her legs several times, telling her how good it's going to feel to come on my dick with this toy up her ass. Telling her how good she'd take my cock in her mouth while riding this one.

How her moans nearly break me.

"I think I slowed down when I felt you tense up around me," I tell her, my voice husky, my cock throbbing. My stomach muscles are clenched as a fucking precaution at this point. She shoots me a glance, and I see her eyes in that sketch class. The girl who found my eyes above my masked face, and sketched me breathlessly as she flushed. I see her in this workroom, taking my cock so well, and I feel it all.

"Let me see," I say, still sawing in and out of her, her pussy getting wetter and wetter, the dildo slippery at the base. "If I slow down, will you come for me, beautiful girl?"

Slowing my strokes, her knees start to wobble and her head swivels slowly to the other side. Eyes still closed she breathes, "Yes Tuck, fuck me. Yes," she pants, her voice as delicate and dangerous as smoke on the water. "Yes, *fuck! Tuck!*"

Her spine squirms as she wilts in my arms, her orgasm getting the best of her. I continue slowly stroking in and out of her, loving the way she sort of rocks against me, bearing down just the slightest as I pull it out. A subtle protest, and I like it.

I place the juicy cock on the table, and take her face in my hands. I can't wait one more second, so I take the kiss I've needed since I laid eyes on her just minutes ago.

She fills me with her gentle sighs, and rubs her groin against mine before pulling her dress down. Releasing her face and looking into her eyes, my chest lightens as I take her in.

"Learned something new," she smiles, cheeks rosy from her labored breathing. "Glasses and orgasms are a dangerous mix."

Reading my confusion she adds, "I've never had one with my glasses on until now. In fact, I've never had one standing with a partner. So, wow. Double cherry pop situation, huh?"

I like that, and I know that's barbaric, but it's the truth.

"I'm happy to be your first." *And last,* I don't say that aloud.

She licks her lips and I take another kiss, this one short. "They almost slid off a few times." Her grin makes my heart pump faster.

"After the presentation, come watch me today. It's a menage shoot." I hold her eyes and speak with sincerity, equating her desire to watch me to the possibility of us. Maybe she'd be open to dating a porn star, if she enjoys watching me work. "I can't make you, but I can withhold my dick from you if you say no."

She grins, toothy and wide and I imagine her with that same smile, but in a wedding dress in the sun. "You can't, actually. And you never can after today, if all goes well. In fact, if they like it, I'll be able to have a houseful of your cock in about six months."

"Please do." I get out my wallet from my back pocket, making a show of getting my credit card. "On my dime. I'd love to fund a house of my dicks for you to live in."

She bats my hand away playfully, so I put my wallet back. "Good luck," I add softly, then take her chin in my fingers, something I didn't think I'd ever do off set. It feels a little *Days of Our Lives*-y but as my thumb smooths along her velvety skin, I don't care how it seems.

It *feels* right.

"It's a great cock, all thanks to you." I mean it, and I want this to go well for her. Only for her. I don't care if it doesn't pan out for me. She needs this, I see it in the way her eyes waver wearily across the line of toys before tipping back to me.

"Thank you."

We stand hip to hip as I wash the cock we used, and she rests her head against my arm as I do. Things have never felt so right.

Vienna's meeting takes place with the Decauchery team in the conference room, leaving me to glance at a closed door every thirty seconds as I prepare for my shoot.

"Filming light on," Aug calls to Cohen, the set director, who flips the switch to the exterior light indicating that filming is taking place. It engages the lock on the external door, so that no one can miss the light and interrupt the scene. "Lighting check," he calls, bringing the lighting coordinator out of the woodwork to sample the light intensity on his device. Once he gives the nod of approval to Aug, he lifts his slates, and we're rolling.

Fuck. I'm in scene. I blink to reality and see Otis, trying desperately to mask his confusion likely as to why I'm out of it. Maxi is already into her lines, and I know my cue is nearing.

As the camera lines me up, I wrap my fingers around the base of her throat. "And I'll mark you here, a collar for you to show your devotion," I say, vaguely remembering the idea of the scripted line.

It's a dual dominant singular submissive flick, requested by the subscribers of Crave & Cure's JustSex x-rated video hub.

I say the line followed by Otis's voice nearly shifting the ground beneath us with its sheer depth and vibrating rasp. My mind beelines for her presentation as Otis holds viewers captive, starting the scene by kissing a trail down Maxi's spine.

She's been in there for nearly thirty minutes. How long does it take to decide on a silicone preference? They can't have any issues with the casting. I know I'm biased but it's beautiful. I'm trying to understand what the hold up is. Why isn't she flying through those doors, beaming with pleased executives on her heels?

I hear my cue, and step in, letting Maxi slide my silk pants down my legs, revealing my erection. Only–

"Oh," Maxi whispers, finding me only a little stiff. I swallow hard, feeling the lasering glare of Augustus's eyes on me. Performance issues can hold up a scene, and while they're normal in the bedroom, on set, we do all that we can to avoid them.

The slates clatter and Lance is shouting my name from the sidelines before I can even face Aug.

"Tucker, a word," he commands. Otis grins at me, throwing a soft punch into my shoulder.

"You alright dude?" Otis flips his hair to one side, using a small towel to blot the sweat from his forehead. He always does fifty push ups before we start filming, so his muscles look swollen, but it always makes him glazed in sweat.

"Yeah," I nod, returning the friendly hit. "I'm cool. Sorry about that, Maxi," I tell her as she adjusts on the chaise lounge between us.

Rubbing her lips together, she flips hair behind her back, unbothered. "No worries, doll."

With my dick in my hand, I head to Aug and Lance, we stand together in a huddle of displeasure. "Give me a second, and I'll be good to roll," I defend, and I don't expect to take much shit for this because of all the guys, this has never happened to me. I always come ready to come.

Aug glances at the iPad in Lance's arms and they exchange a glance, a secret message made up from just a look. I know they're not a couple but the quiet little moment where Aug tells Lance everything he needs to with just a blink of his eyes—I yearn for that. A closeness so deeply rooted in each of us that we transcend trivial conversation.

Lance glances at the screen then up at me. "I had to drop off our suggestions for the future releases. Vienna's doing great in there. They like the toy," he says quietly, turning to face Aug. I follow his gaze, and stare at my fearless leader.

"Put your mind at ease?"

I nod. "Yeah, but why is it taking so long?"

Aug grins as much as a man like Aug ever does. "She pitched a name for the line, so they need a few more minutes."

"What's the name?" I ask, brimming with anxious excitement. But Lance's watch sounds, an alarm buzzing between the three of us.

He nods to my cock without looking. "Get it ready. You've got one minute."

I start pulling on myself as they walk back to Aug's chair

behind the camera. A few tugs and I'm thickening, and that's when I make eye contact with Russ, then Cam. "Need a hand?" Cam questions, nudging Russ. He peels his attention from his phone screen, and smiles up at me.

Crave has options in the profession of fluffers. Since having a job where you use your mouth to keep someone aroused is kind of old school, we also have non-traditional options for actors, like myself, that don't want a "classic fluff."

These two motion down the hall, offering up Crave's response to the fact that, from time to time, actors need some help staying aroused during brief light resets or urgent breaks mid-scene and don't want a suck.

If I were to say yes, knowing I don't like the classic fluff, they'd lead me to a large, comfortable leather chair in a small dark space. They'd give me headphones, loaded with erotic audio, and stand outside the door while I listen, use a stroker or any other toys, and watch myself in the floor to ceiling mirror in front of the chair. It's shadowy and cool, the glimpses you catch of yourself are erotic, paired with searing audio and gadgets. It's Crave's new interpretation of fluffing.

I shake my head. "Na, I'm good."

Closing my eyes for a private moment, I remember the way Vienna writhed on my cock as I drove it up inside of her, her delicate hands clutching my shoulders. She came so fast, just like she promised, and she came twice at my house. She was so fucking hot.

Suddenly I'm not just hard but I'm close. I turn to find Aug and Lance motioned Cohen to step off set. Maxi and Otis are whispering, likely about the recent episode of Ted Lasso, and then I'm being pushed to my mark by a production assistant, my hand being placed against Maxi's neck just as the slates slam together.

Maxi rises to her knees on the chaise and Otis comes to my

side. He slides his fingers through her hair, wraps it around his knuckles before jerking her down to his cock. My hand curls the back of her neck as we guide her open mouth down on his cock.

"Can you make us both happy or will you need to discover pain in order to deliver true pleasure?" Otis rumbles as Maxi's ruby lips seal around his crown.

"Open wider, little bird, and please us both," I tell Maxi, knowing the scene calls for her to blow us both.

We maneuver her between us and I turn, pointing my cock toward his. Our heads collide, smearing together in Maxi's saliva, earning a belly-deep groan from Otis. He drapes his hand along my shoulder as she slides her hands up and down our cocks, pressed together.

"Ahh, yes, make us feel good," I rasp, passing the cue to Otis as my eyes flick up to the door, still closed.

"Not just a pretty thing, but a talented little sub, too," he groans as Maxi opens wide, pulling us onto the fat pad of her tongue. Closing her mouth around us as best as she can, Maxi starts her slow suckling of our cocks, making noises that fill my spine with heat, urgency brewing in my balls.

I love being sucked with another man. Feeling him slide against me, watching the challenge and victory of the person performing the act. Maxi's been here in this scene with us before, and she's so good at it.

Aug calls for the third camera to take a shot of Maxi's mouth, and hold for ten seconds. That's usually the amount of time we get on focus shots before the camera pans to another shot, in order to keep the viewers interested. Adult movies that stay on one shot too long often lose viewers by the thirty percent viewed mark. Aug keeps the shots moving, even showing different angles at orgasm.

I take the opportunity to peer up at the door. Expecting to

find it closed, I'm already looking back down at my cock sealed next to O's when I realize... Vienna is hovering about ten feet behind Lance, arms at her sides, hands clasped in front of her. When she notices my questioning glance—I don't miss that she's intently watching this scene—she raises a hand, and my chest nearly bursts when one thumb pops up, accompanied by the most beautiful, joyful grin.

My heart pumps so hard, my vision blurs. Focusing back on the scene, I stare blankly at my cock next to Otis's, Maxi's hands pumping us into her open, partially full mouth. I swallow hard, and an alarming lump of emotion stuck in my throat.

She did it. It went well. They liked the cock. And she even named the line, from what it sounds.

I'm so fucking proud.

One flash of my hand between her thighs, fucking her with my replica cock as she moaned my name against my lips—"Fuck," I whisper as soon as the camera cuts to a shot of Maxi's lingerie-clad ass—"I'm gonna come," I warn them, my voice as low as it can be, which is hard right now. My veins are full of adrenaline and happiness, knowing that this moment also fulfills her desire to watch.

"Fuck!" I groan out as I start to lose the battle with the orgasm, my vivid memories demanding.

Like the pro she is, Maxi recognizes my cues before my primal war cry, and angles me toward Otis. My orgasm streaks up his shaft in unstoppable, unyielding waves and the moment I'm through, she strokes Otis toward me, gearing him up to do the same, despite the fact it wasn't the scene or the shot we'd set out for.

"You have to please us both to be our sub," Otis says, ad-libbing the shot to make it work. The slates haven't slapped, and the purple flag hasn't been waved, so we roll on.

I risk a glance at Vienna. Hooded eyes and thick lashes keep me from looking into her eyes, but the way she's biting her lip, arms wrapped over her chest now, I know how much she liked that.

Otis orgasms, shooting white streaks against my groin and cock as Maxi holds both of us between her, still on her knees.

"I think you've earned a reward," I tell her, before reaching down to take her by the chin and bring her to her feet between us. I take her mouth and when I'm done, Otis takes his turn.

Then Aug ends the scene. "I know that wasn't what we planned but it's real. Even Doms struggle to keep their composure." He nods at me before dismissing the cast and crew for the day. Lance catches my eyes and pinches his searing gaze on me. He knows that was no artistic move but a desperate man unable to keep his composure. I don't know if he'll keep my secret, but right now, I don't care.

Vienna makes her way toward me as I pull a towel from a chair and wrap it around my waist. With another damp towel, I begin wiping myself up, and glance across the set to find Otis doing the same.

"Messy shoot today," I tell her as she stops in front of me, eyes still a little tired, pupils dilated. My cock attempts to rise beneath the terrycloth.

"Pun intended?" Her smile is contagious.

"Always," I say as Cohen drifts between us toward the set light panel. He flips the switch, turning off the exterior light.

"Do not make me stand here a second longer without knowing how that went," I say sternly, reaching out to rest my hand on her hip. She steps toward me as I give her a gentle tug, letting her know that I always want her nearer.

"I want to kiss you," I admit as she blinks up at me, her breath fanning heavily between her lips.

She rocks to her toes, wraps her hands around my neck and

brings my mouth to hers in a slow, searing kiss. The hairs on my neck rise as that weightless sensation fills my limbs again. The familiar heat of happiness. Real fucking happiness. The thing, my dad called it.

"Too late. I kissed you first," she exhales, a cute grin twisting her lips up on one side. Watching Vienna happy and aroused is better than watching a sunset with your feet sunk into warm sand. Her effervescence is something I need *forever*.

The stage doors swing open with a loud pop, and light floods the studio. I raise a hand to my eyes, trying to blink our visitors into focus. Delivery guys don't typically open both doors.

Vienna presses her hand to my bare chest, pulling my attention away from the disruption. "I named the line Fuck Tuck. I cried that out when you railed me with your own cock before the presentation. I said *fuck, Tuck!*" she moans, mimicking the sultry words she spoke when I stroked in and out of her. And god, the mouth on this girl. The way she dirty talks, how she's borderline vulgar and yet sweet as fuck in the flesh.

"Vienna, you're driving me fucking insane," I rasp, taking her elbow with my hand, tugging her toward me so she can feel what she's doing to me. But I stop in my tracks when I hear the three words that are only spoken by one person.

One person whom I'm related to.

"*Tucker Fucker Deep!*"

Cohen knocks the doors free from the stops, and they swing closed, devouring the brightness.

"Theo?" I call as, yes indeed, my family comes into focus.

"Who's Theo?" Vienna whispers nervously, taking a step away from me.

I wait for her to look my way, and when she does, I hold her gaze.

"He's my brother."

253

21

Vienna

Tucker is a guy you find energy for.

Holy shit. I'm meeting Tucker's entire family while I am massively turned on *and* he's wrapped in a cum covered towel, which is also hot. Fuck my life.

Watching Tucker with Otis *and* Maxi was the sweetest treat I've ever had the pleasure of consuming. I didn't even try to hide my blatant and eager stare, and I nearly sprinted to him as soon as the scene ended.

We were just about to get into the details of my presentation—and maybe even pick up where we left off this morning—and now I'm being introduced to his entire family. I don't think we've ever done anything in the right order. I saw his naked dick before I caught feels, and now I'm meeting his entire family before we've even had a first date. Nothing about us is ever... *typical.*

I fidget with my glasses as I take them in, all of them making these big, happy puppy dog eyes at me, making me feel... amazing.

"Vienna, this is almost the entire crew," Tucker says, after stepping off-set to slip into pants. He returns, feeding his arms into a gray t-shirt he scoops off the back of a cast chair. Roughing his big hands through his sex-slicked hair, my heart pitter patters, wobbly on its axis, beating heavy and quick. He's truly beautiful. And a family guy to boot? *Holy ovary explosion, Batman.*

His family stares adoringly back at him, the fact he's a porn star clearly not a problem. I can't even be an artist without the world ending, and he's making adult films.

And they're here.

On his side.

"Vienna, this is my dad, Tim."

I look into the eyes of an aged Tucker, weathered by a life spent living under the sun. Experience creases the corner of his eyes, and I can tell by the grin on his face that this is a man who has lived kindly. His eyes beam pride as he glances over at Tucker, then back to me. "So nice to meet you, Vienna. I've heard..." He glances up at Tuck for approval, but nervously back at me. "We've heard a lot," he finally says before taking my hand in a sturdy shake. Then he is hugging me and his embrace across my back is heavy and warm. Next I'm facing a petite blonde woman with wide green eyes, mossy and bright.

"Vienna, I'm so happy you're here. We've been wanting to meet you. Tucker has nothing but great things to say." She smiles warmly, as warmth spreads through my chest and shoulders, awareness rattling down my spine. This is what a loving mother is like. Warm and accepting.

"Hi," I say thickly around the knot in my throat. My eyes try to well, but I blink them madly, knowing I will die of humiliation if I randomly start crying right now. Dear god, don't be the mommy issues girl. Don't.

"Tessa," she says, extending her hand to me. I slip my hand in hers and she sandwiches mine with her other. "It's so nice to meet you, I know I just said it but I really want you to know that we mean it." Her eyes brim with sincerity and the kindness does something to me. Makes me envision making cookies at her side, laughing as we shop downtown, text messages between us—I see all the things I wanted with my mom, with this woman. With her, it feels possible. My face goes numb and my knees wobbly, but I maintain my composure and take a deep breath.

I'm overwhelmed with kindness on a day where I proved myself as an artist in the first real opportunity. I fucking delivered.

I nudge my glasses up my nose and stand a bit taller, smiling. "So great to meet you, too. Tucker's..." I step back as we break our handshake, trying to decide how I want to finish that sentence. What definition is both true and fits the parameters of our situationship? We aren't a couple yet, though he asked, so my response needs to be fairly surface. "He's so great," I say finally, shaking my head as a held breath rushes from me.

"Hi," Theo appears at Tessa's side, shoving his hand into mine.

"Hi, Theo," I reply, smiling kindly as my heart races. I feel like one of those cartoons where the heart literally pops out of the chest three feet before dropping back in. I chance a look at Tucker. He's wearing the softest smile, his eyes unfocused on my profile, watching me in dissociated adoration.

A shudder rolls through my chest at the way he watches me. Beneath the black dress, my pussy clenches, still wet from when he fucked me with the toy we made together. Sweat slides between my breasts and I want more than anything to tug at my bra and wipe it away. I hold my smile at Theo as he too tells me how good it is to meet me and how much he's heard.

I kind of want to turn around and look behind me and see if there's another Vienna back there because... Tucker Deep has told his entire family about me? As I think about it, it's Tucker Eliot that has told his entire family about me. Tucker the small town boy, not Tucker the porn star. And that's... amazing.

"Hi Vienna," a soft voice comes from behind me, appearing at my side with a smile on her face. "I'm Tegan, I'm Tuck's only sister."

"The dog trainer, right?" I offer, playing it casually, not wanting Tucker to know I in fact remember every word he's ever uttered.

"Yeah," she says, bobbing her head. "Okay, so... Tuck has been telling *you* about *us*, too." Her allusion is simple, and my flush takes over.

Tucker claps his hands, garnering the focus of everyone in the premises. "Everyone, Waterfront 21, in ten. Gonna catch a quick shower, then lunch is on me." He waves his arms like a flight attendant, and Lance chuckles.

I didn't know he knew how to do that.

We stand around making small talk as Tuck rushes off for a shower, coming back with wet hair and a wide grin. Before I can even acknowledge him, his sister has me.

"Let's go! You can tell us how you and Tucker got together," Tegan says, linking her arm with mine. Then I'm being swept toward the doors with one word echoing in my mind.

Together.

We only just started talking about that. And even then, we haven't really talked about it. Tucker boldly asked me to be his girlfriend last night because he felt our casting sessions were like dates. And I admit, they did feel a lot like dates. We talked the whole time, laughed, toed into serious topics, I always looked forward to seeing him, and we even ate while the cast was setting a few times, too. I guess I just never thought it would turn into more. Until last night, when I realized he indeed feels things for me, the way I do for him. And now I'm spinning because he wants to know how I feel about the fact that he has sex with beautiful people for a living. I judged it when we met, but having seen it, and having gotten to know him, I don't feel the same way any more. It's hot, and he's talented too. But I have questions.

Does his career leave enough room for a relationship?

I can admit to myself I've thought about this before. Late at night, when my mind won't turn off and the sky is dim, I think of what it would be like to be Tucker's girlfriend.

If he asked me again, right now, would I be able to answer?

I believe him when he says it's work.

But would it come up in a fight? Would it add stress when things get rough? Things will get rough. Because that's real. Rough patches that require extra love and care.

And I have to be real with myself. If we argue and he goes to work and makes love to someone else, even if just for the camera, how will it make me feel?

I want to believe I wouldn't mind. I know when things were good, I wouldn't. Right now, I find it sexy and courageous and hot. But if things got bad, could I take it?

Am I strong enough?

Sometimes I feel like I've used all my strength trying to prove my parents wrong about my choice to pursue art.

But Tucker is a guy you find energy for.

And I'd be a total dumbass to let fear take me down now.

"You're coming with us, right Vienna?" Theo asks, nodding toward the SUV he and Tegan are walking backward toward.

"We've got the minivan," Tim declares, a silver van

gleaming in the parking lot behind him. "I wouldn't blame you for riding with them."

Tucker's hand comes down along my back. "I'm riding with my parents."

I smile and find myself saying, "Okay, I'll go with your brother and sister."

"So why'd you want to work at Crave?" Tegan asks after I slide into the backseat of their rental. Damn, starting out with a hard question.

I chew my lip a moment, considering my options but going with the honest truth. "Money. I need to pay off student loans for art school after I graduate. I lost the only grant that had the potential to help, so when they offered me this job and showed me the pay, I just about lost my mind. I couldn't say no."

And now that the presentation's gone well, I don't have to hang onto any silly ideas that somehow I won't earn that money.

I did earn it. I created Fuck Tuck. Sure, it wasn't my idea but I made it, I created what hundreds of thousands of people are going to use to bring themselves to orgasm. And Tucker is the one they're envisioning with their eyes squeezed shut and their legs spread wide.

"Oh I get that. I had to work hard to open my training center." Tegan twists in her seat to face me, tucking a piece of sandy hair behind her ear. She reminds me of Tucker, and I love how close everyone is. It's refreshing as hell. "What are you gonna do after your contract is up? Gonna keep sculpting or do you have other passions?"

Well hell. That's a thoughtful question. I adjust my glasses nervously, my lips twitching, probably giving my indecision away. Still, I'm a conversationalist at heart so I clarify. "I like sketching. I don't know if I like it as much as I like sculpting but... I like sketching."

"I know," she sighs, shaking her head a little.

"You know?" I stutter, unsure of what her comment means. "You know that I sketch?"

She flips around in her seat, and Theo glances out the passenger window as he navigates the unending swarm of pedestrians in downtown San Francisco. Practically everyone walks.

"I mean, I always assume artists are multi-faceted." Tegan turns around again, grinning. "I trained a ferret once, so I get it."

Theo erupts in laughter, slapping the wheel as the navigation barks out his next move. "I don't think your ability to make multiple breeds of animals sit is the same as her being able to sculpt and sketch." He glances at me in the rearview with a smile, then over at Tegan, who is partially giggling. "But maybe."

"Maybe," I add, finding their laughter contagious. "So do you visit Tucker at the studio often?" I ask, because seeing them on set right after Tuck wrapped his scene and covered his nude junk, it was a surprise. To me at least.

"Oh yeah," Theo calls back to me as he rolls the window down, sticking his palm out, letting it ride the ripples of wind. "This is what, our fifth visit?" he questions, glancing at Tegan for validation. She volleys her head.

"I haven't kept count but something like that. Tripp was even here last time." She turns to face me again, and I'm starting to get comfortable with Tegan. Something about her open and honest personality makes it easy to converse and feel comfortable with. "Tripp's our other brother. He's older than me but younger than Tuck."

"I'm the oldest," Theo clarifies, letting me free from the mental burden of sorting out their family tree.

"It's pretty cool you two own your own businesses. Your

parents must be so proud," I reply, because my parents would likely shit themselves if I ever created my own successful business. I'd be their little braggable dream. Unless of course that business had anything to do with art or creation.

Theo lets the navigation take him down another street, and up ahead I spot the Waterfront 21 sign. I'm kind of sad to say goodbye to these private minutes I got with Tuck's siblings, but kind of happy too because I'm eager to see Tucker again.

Holy crap, I'm in a dangerous place. I'm Alice and Tucker is my rabbit hole and I'm moving full speed towards a smash and crash at the very bottom. One I doubt I'll be able to climb out of, something I definitely can't recover from.

"They're proud but they would be proud no matter what we did," Theo says matter of factly, and it's spoken so simply that I know it's true.

"I mean, Tripp's been working on a cruise ship for the last year and mom and dad tell anyone and everyone they can that their son sails the seven seas for a living."

Theo parks the rental and we all step out in the chilly bay area afternoon, sun warm on our shoulders as the sea air nips our noses. "Working on a cruise ship has to be fun," I think aloud as Tegan links her arm with mine, Theo in front of us leading the way around the corner where the side entry door is marked.

"We make whatever we do fun, because life is too short to have a stick up your ass and we learned to be proud of every job we have, no matter how big or small," Theo states plainly, wearing a prideful grin as he yanks open one of the doors, exposing the inside of the restaurant to the daylight.

"That's a great ethos," I smile, heading inside to find the rest of the crew already there. Tucker's green eyes capture mine, and my entire body melts beneath his gaze.

He steals me from his sister and with his hands beneath my

elbows, whispers down to me, "I drove so I could get here before you. No way I'm letting you sit next to someone else."

A moment later, the doors open again and a handful of actors and a sprinkling of crew members filter into the restaurant, immediately shaking hands with and greeting Tucker's family.

I hear a lot of 'again's' drifting about, and I realize that their support of Tucker isn't an act, or something they're forcing for the sake of equality between their children. They really do support him and his career as an adult film star.

Meanwhile, my dad won't acknowledge me to his coworkers because he's ashamed yet I am at a prestigious art institute.

"Good to see you again," I hear Aug say to Tim as they slap palms together in a hearty, genuine shake.

A moment later we're shuffling around a long table as two waiters push it tight to another, creating enough room for all fifteen of us here.

Tuck sits at my side with his hand draped over my thigh, both of us stealing glances at each other whenever we can. Tucker talks to his brother and Augustus about a gold Leica camera that came through the shop months ago.

Next to me, I'm engaged in conversation with Maxi. With her phone out, she scrolls through photos of her son, telling me all about his play she attended yesterday.

"And I don't like memorizing lines, so I figured he'd be the same way," she says, stroking her delicate fingers through her long, blonde hair. "He's like me in so many other ways," she beams, tapping her phone to find a photo of her son on a small stage, lots of other little kids around him. His little hand is out in a wave, and I notice how pridefully she beams at his image. "See, this was him. He remembered all three of his lines."

"He's adorable, Maxi. Really," I say, finding myself smiling at the photo of the little boy.

"I know, and look at him with his bike." She swipes again, this time the little boy is straddling a bike a bit too big for him wearing the largest grin I've ever seen. True happiness sparkles in his little eyes, fingers gripping the handle bars so tight his hands are white. "Tucker bought him that," she says almost thoughtfully, gaze fixed on the image of her boy.

I look down at the thick fingers mindlessly stroking my inner thigh, the sound of Tucker's conversation still at my side.

"He did?" I ask. His long fingers sweep the private flesh of my inner thigh, warmth shuddering down my spine.

She nods, taking a sip of her iced tea before putting her phone back into her clutch. "Yeah, see, I'm taking care of my dad and trying to get him out of medical debt." She rips the edge off a piece of buttery focaccia and pops it into her mouth, talking around the delicious chunk of carb. "I am making progress, but it's taken every single cent of my signing bonus and salary so far. So when my son had his birthday, Tucker said he wanted me to keep working on the debt, and that he'd get the gift. When a bike showed up, fully assembled, I cried. Because I could've done it, sure. But he understands how important my goal is, and supported it by showing up for my son. And that's... that's a testament to his character."

"But you two..." I start, hating how the question paints me with jealousy and insecurity because it's a gross misrepresentation of how I feel. I'm not jealous or insecure because of Maxi, but I am curious. I can't help it.

She shakes her head, snorting as she takes another ambitious bite of warm bread. "No way. That's not the type of relationship we have. Besides, the respect we have for each other and what Aug is trying to build at Crave... It's sacred."

"It would complicate work, I imagine," I say, understanding

what she means despite the fact that I'm not part of their team, not in that way.

"It totally would. And you know what, it's nice to come to work and know just what I'm doing and know that I'm safe with the people I'm doing it with. I don't know if everyone else at Crave knows how good they have it, but I didn't always work here. I know how rare and beautiful what we have is."

She dunks bread into oil and vinegar as Tucker's attention turns toward us, his knee driving into mine as he twists to face Maxi. She just made him orgasm not more than thirty minutes ago and yet, as I sit between them, not a single ounce of jealousy worms through me. In fact, I feel... safe and comfortable. Like Maxi is as much my friend as Tucker's, despite the fact I know that's not true. They've known each other much longer. Still, the energy is giving kindness, not exclusion, and it fills voids in me that I shouldn't still bear at my age. But better late than never.

"I'm just explaining to Vienna how no one signed to Crave starts a relationship because we love Aug and what he's built way too much," she says, not even meeting his eyes as she swipes yet another piece of bread through oil. It's not the energy of let's lock eyes and get our stories straight, but rather, it's the plain truth and they have no problem sharing it with me.

"Oh yeah, we respect Aug and are proud of what we have at Crave," Tucker says, watching Maxi as she folds the maroon napkin over the remaining piece of bread, passing the basket to him. He digs in, taking a lump of bread, too. "I never worked anywhere else but Otis and a few others have and the stories they've told have been... awful."

"Oh god, Vienna, did you know that at other companies, guys are usually taking shots in the dick so that they stay hard? And they're usually not allowed to come for like, two hours." She picks up her menu, spreading it open over her bread plate as she nods at me. "Wild, right? Not to mention dangerous. The long term risks with these practices are insane."

Tucker steals my attention, his hand traversing the gap between my legs, coming to rest on my opposite thigh. It's gentle but territorial, and it makes my heart go wild.

"Yeah, it's not good. Times like today, where I'm just..." He trails off a little, his green eyes stealing my breath as they settle on my lips, then find my eyes. "Preoccupied and way too horny for my own good, and I can't hold back. On another set, I'd likely face a financial penalty. But Aug... he rolled with it and even changed the scene for my *inability to hold back*, shall we say."

I find myself blinking up at him breathlessly, in a moment I never imagined myself to be in. What he's implying settles between my legs, my clit pulsing at his words.

"Come back to my place after lunch," he says privately, smoothing his palm over my knee before it drifts up my thigh. Looking down, I see my black dress nearly bunched around my waist, and wiggle urgently to pull it down.

I cover his hand with my dress, and the grin it earns me causes my chest to hollow a little. Pleasing Tucker is honestly quite the fucking aphrodisiac.

"Spend some time with me and my family," he says before adding a soft and sweet, "Please," bottom lip sticking out.

"Oh girl, go spend time with the Eliots. They're literally the best," Maxi adds, and I realize she's still part of our conversation. "I can only hope my future boyfriend's parents are as cool as Tuck's but honestly, I'm not sure it's possible."

I glance down at Tuck's hand stroking tenderly against my skin, and then up across the table, watching Tessa tip her face toward Lance's screen where he undoubtedly is showing her a new set design or something work related. That's Lance. He doesn't take a moment off, not even for Tuck's mom. But her face is bright with excitement and she pokes around on the screen as Lance presumably answers questions. Tim and Augustus are deep into a conversation, Aug's arms moving through the air as he undoubtedly details an on-set story. Tim's hands are on the tabletop, eyes wide with disbelief. Adjacent to them, Otis and Theo are both running curled fists to their eyes, wiping away tears of serious laughter, and Tegan is asking Cohen, the shy and quiet set designer, a million questions about the leftover supplies after set creation.

This is the kind of family I've always dreamed of.

And Tucker is the kind of man I've always wanted and assumed I'd never be lucky enough to have.

"Yeah," I reply to him finally, with a smile that holds so much more than happiness. "I'd love to come back to your place."

22

Tucker

I think I just got friend-zoned.

Dad and mom ask me a trillion questions about Vienna's presentation on the drive back to my apartment, despite the fact I already told them I don't have any details.

But that's what pride and excitement does.

"And you don't know which cast they preferred, huh?" Mom asks while her fingers fly around her phone screen, replying to a client email likely from memory.

Mom's been a photographer for so many years, I can't remember when she did anything else. Same with my dad and carrying letters and packages for the post office. Just about every memory I have of him from when I was five until now is him in that faded blue uniform, pinstriping down the length of his slacks.

There's comfort in thriving within the same space while

allowing yourself to adjust rather than striving to outgrow it. Many times Dad expressed his displeasure with his job, but he altered it to find joy, changing shift times and sometimes even mail routes. And when Mom has complained of a creative stalemate, she'd take her camera to the foothills and spend time under the sun. A palette cleansing, she called it.

As I explain to them one more time that I don't know any of the details, I wonder how long I can do this. Not answer my parents' questions—that I'll be doing forever, God willing—But working at Crave.

It's been a wild two years, from newbie to novice, and though I've already made a ton of money—yep, porn does that well and my investment guy is that good—I like my job. The same way dad likes his and mom likes hers. The same way Tegan thrives from what she does and Theo lives for his shop, too.

Am I like them? Can I do this for as long as I can without missing out on anything?

Mom and Dad find their joy in what they do, but they also have each other. Yes, I have my family but I also want a partner. Is it wrong to want it all?

Kicking out of my shoes, I set my wallet and keys down on my counter before popping open the fridge to grab drinks.

"Beer for Dad," I recite aloud, sifting through cans to find mom her drink. "And a La Croix for Mom."

"I'll have a La Croix, too," says Tegan, pushing through the door like she owns the place, Vienna on her heels, Theo on hers.

I stand there, feet rooted to the floor, a cold beer and chilled La Croix making my hands go numb, condensation from the cans falling in little heavy thuds around my bare feet.

Vienna is holding the door open for Theo as he carries in

three suitcases, and she's giggling so hard at whatever dumb shit he's saying to her that she nudges her glasses up her nose.

With everyone I love piled into my penthouse, I realize, as long as I have these people, I could give *anything* up in the blink of an eye.

I love working at Crave. Yes, it's made me wealthy, but more than that, it's given me a second family. That's how I think of Otis, Aug, hell, even Lance. They're all the blood of another, but my family. Maxi and the other actresses, too. When love and respect runs this deep, you become family, whether we all share DNA or not.

I could be Tucker Eliot, and only him. But I don't want to give up Tucker Deep. Not yet.

For this moment in my life though, I'm proud of my career and what I've achieved with the support of everyone around me. It's difficult for me to imagine abandoning all I've worked for right now, but that doesn't mean things will always be the same. I feel like I'm where I'm meant to be, where I've been led to. But who knows what the future holds. What destiny has in store for me.

"I don't know how," Theo announces as he walks across the space, clapping his hand along dad's back, "but this place seems bigger."

"I got a smaller couch," I reply as their heads swivel to the very large gray sectional centered in front of the big screen. The TV hangs on a small portion of exposed brick, the rest of the walls being composed of large, city-view windows. Perks of the penthouse.

"Is that it?" He asks, surveying the open floor plan, eyes veering past the open sliding doors to my bedroom, landing on my messy bed.

I say a little prayer hoping that he doesn't look straight at

Vienna, and promise to thank him later when his eyes come to mine, lips in a subtle smirk.

"Hey Mom, come show me the balcony. Last time I was here it was dusk. I never got to check the view in daylight," Theo says, attempting to give me a singular moment with Vienna.

"It's a wrap-around," my dad adds, as if anyone in the apartment couldn't see the entire balcony tracing out the apartment through the floor to ceiling windows. But that's a total dad move, stating the obvious as a first time discovery. And right now, his mission to prove to everyone that it is indeed a wrap-around is giving me a moment with V, so I egg him on.

"Show 'em, Dad."

"Tegan," Theo calls, whipping his head toward the door. "Get your ass up and enjoy this view."

Already plopped happily on the couch, Tegan pushes to her feet, her pony tail swaying behind her. "Fine," she says, running her hands down her thighs, clad in cut-off jeans. Her tank top, which features two dog faces strategically placed over her boobs, reads SHOW ME THE PITTIES, and makes me snort. I didn't notice it before because I never really pay attention to what my sister wears.

Vienna, catching sight of Tegan's top at the same time as I do, snorts, wagging a finger at the tank. "Cute," she giggles.

Tegan tugs at the ends of her tank, surveying the design. "Oh yeah, it is, huh? I got this from one of my friend's moms. She's got a printing press and makes shirts on Etsy."

"I think it's important," I clarify, loving to give my sister shit here and there. "That by friend you're referring to a dog, not a person."

She rolls her green eyes. "Duh. Dogs make better friends anyway."

I leave that statement alone, because as open as I am with

270

my family, and as much as that is reciprocated throughout, Tegan is the only Eliot to hold her cards close to the vest. Well, she confides endlessly in Mom, but otherwise, her woes are hers.

"Okay, I'll go let Dad show me the wrap-around like he was the architect of this place so that you guys can have like, two minutes alone together," she adds, winking at Vienna which of course makes her go flush. Once the slider seals us in privacy, I turn to face her.

"I want to know every damn detail of that presentation." The words rush out of me, demanding and urgent, because I've now gone two and half hours without knowing. I slide a hand around her waist and pull her toward me, not missing the opportunity to steal a kiss while the rest of my family peruses outdoors.

"It went so well, Tuck. Honestly, it went better than I could have ever imagined. And I'm so glad I saved all the failed proto-types at Crave because Dalton wants them. I think he said something about using one of the more average molds at one of his sister companies or something but either way, it went so well," she gushes, her entire body radiating happiness. "And Fuck Tuck, come on, that's... perfect."

"And true, you said it yourself while we–"

"Fucked," she finishes bluntly, though I was going to select a softer word better representative of how I feel.

I nod. "Yes, we did." Clearing my throat, I add, "Vienna, the other night, what we were talking about before we were interr–"

"I will never understand why one person needs all that space," Mom huffs as she runs slender fingers through her pale blonde, foofy hair. Dad comes in behind her, followed by Theo, who mouths the word sorry, and then Tegan, who just shakes her head.

"So Vienna," Dad muses as he settles into a place at the couch, patting for her to come join him. I smile seeing that she does, and seems to do so eagerly, not even casting me a nervous glance over her shoulder. "Tell us how it went with Debauchery today." He leans in using a stage whisper and adds, "We came a few days early hoping we'd catch you."

Now she glances back at me, her glasses on the end of her nose, vast dark eyes searching for answers in my gaze before smiling, making my pulse skyrocket.

With her focus back on Dad, and consequently my entire family now as they've all taken a seat around Vienna, she clears her throat. "Well, I was hired to make four prototypes and I've just presented the options for the phase one release. This will be their main toy, the hard launch item, with the other three being additives to the line later on, pending the launch success." She tugs the hemline of the black skirt that fits her so well. But looks just as good bunched around her waist, too.

"They let her name the line, too," I add but mom smacks me across the knee as I squeeze in between her and dad.

"Let her tell it, Tucker, this is *her* project."

"Well, *our* project, I guess," Vienna muses shyly. "I mean, without Tuck–" She stops herself, realizing that we're actively talking about dicks and dildos.

"So what's the name of the line?" Theo asks, popping an unwrapped Hershey Kiss into his mouth. Tegan, leaning forward to dig through the candy bowl, finds a Rolo and unwraps it, chewing aggressively with her focus on Vienna. "Yeah," she smacks caramel. "What's the name?"

Vienna looks at me, her smile faltering. I should bail her out right now, but then she sits up taller, letting her chin drift pridefully as she answers. "The line is called Fuck Tuck, because you will buy the toy and as literally as possible, fuck Tuck."

She holds Mom's gaze before moving to Dad's then to me. I feel like a sap, beaming at her proudly, but she held her ground on that and I really didn't expect her to. The thing is, she has nothing to prove and no one to overcome in this space, but I know what she did wasn't about my family as much as it was about herself, and overcoming the stigma behind what she's just created.

With my dick or not, Vienna is the one who created Fuck Tuck, and she deserves to reap the rewards of her hard work.

"That's perfect," Mom beams, "and a play on words." She clasps her hands together, driving them under her chin. "I love that, Vienna. You're so creative."

"That's brilliant," Dad adds, going for the candy bowl now. Mom smacks his hand as he reaches, but he perseveres.

"Funny, too," Theo chimes in while now fighting Dad to get to what appears to be the only Reese's in the bowl.

Tegan nods to the dish. "You don't even eat this, why do you have it?"

"Cast and crew party last night," I tell her, "I hosted."

"So Vienna," Mom continues, not giving a crap about chatting with me on this visit and I love it. And as much as I want to soak them up, Vienna is flourishing under their focus, in a way I've never seen her before. "Tell us about your plans for after your contract with Crave and Cure is up."

"Oh," she says, glancing at me, her brows lifted with genuine surprise. I can't tell if it's because I've clearly told them so much about her or if it's because I like her enough to tell my parents so much. Or maybe both.

My parents have always said I'm a romantic. I'm choosing to believe something in between those two, and that she's not weirded out.

"Well I'm graduating from the Art Institute here in the city in a few weeks. I have one piece left for grading." She wrings her hands in her lap, twisting a ring then running a finger over her nails.

"What is your last graded piece?"

She swallows nervously. I heard the story of Madeline's piece, but I don't know if Vienna ever shared what she was working toward.

"A sculpture of man in his weakest and most powerful moment."

Mom's eyebrows raise as her hands come to her cheeks, giving Kevin McCallister a run for his money about thirty years too late. "Weakest and most powerful, oh my god," she gushes, her head turning in a whoosh of white. "I love interpretive art. Oh, it's my absolute favorite," she promises, nodding her head fervently when she's through shaking it. Mom is emphatic about this because it's the truth. As a photographer who puts babies in loaves of bread and cut open pumpkins, she gets the whole art is anything you make it vibe.

I'm glad she has someone who understands. Even if it can't be her own mother.

"Oh Vienna. That's wonderful. Your parents must be so proud of you." My mom scoots to the edge of the cushion and reaches out, patting Vienna's knee.

She blinks down, taking in the kindness. After a few blinks she smiles up at my mom and nods. "They're not, actually. My dad is a banker and my mom cares a lot about the opinions of people who think the way their lawn looks is more important than who they are as human beings."

"Ahh," Mom nods, a smart smile curling her lips. "I know the kind."

"I love them for raising me, but I'm not here because of them." She sits taller, and Mom pats her knee again, and I can see the bond fuses between them before my eyes.

It's greater than what I'd hoped, but it also makes me

worried. If it's too much too soon, too intense a connection she may get overwhelmed.

We can be a lot.

"I don't want to sound ungrateful or rude," she continues, her shoulder slumping as indecision wracks her. She's thinking that my mom is going to judge her but she doesn't really know Tessa Eliot quite yet. She is the least judgmental and most supportive human ever. Next to Dad.

"No," Mom waves a comforting hand through the hair, casting away the possibility that Vienna bore any malice. She sits taller, watching my mom a little dreamily as she speaks to her with such kindness. "You support your child's dream, I won't hear anything from you on that," she says, mollifying Vienna's fears.

"Well, anyway," Vienna trudges on, glancing at me for a sweet but brief half second. "I don't know what I'm doing after my contract with Crave is up but at least I won't have my student loans hanging over me."

I hate that she is worrying about that when I could easily pay it off. What she doesn't know is that if Debauchery's projections are right, she'll be able to pay it off very soon, too. But I save that for another time, a time when she's mine and it doesn't seem like a tool or tactic.

Because it's not. What I had that lawyer do was fair and square in my eyes.

"That's great," Dad adds, snacking on a Twizzler. "No debt is a great canvas to be working with."

"What's your favorite TV show?" Tegan asks, knuckling my dad out of the bowl for what looks to be a mini box of Milk Duds.

Vienna pulls her finger through her hair, twisting the end. I've never seen her do that, but as she pushes her glasses up her nose with her other hand, my cock twitches. I'd love to see her do that naked. Maybe even while I fuck her with the other Tuck.

But I'm pulled from fantasy as my brother, sister and folks spend the next two hours tearing through my candy bowl while getting to know Vienna. She shares with them and I learn things I hadn't gotten to know yet. Like the fact that she loves living in San Francisco, she's never seen the entire Star Wars series, and that one day, when she has enough money saved, she wants to travel the world and see all the best man made sculptures, Pieta at Mount Golgotha being the top of her list.

It's a perfect afternoon and three o'clock rolls around and when Vienna has to get to her sculpting lab at the Institute, I swear my family is just as disappointed as I am.

"Start MarioKart without me. I have to get Vienna back to her car at Crave," I say, stuffing my wallet into my back pocket as Vienna gets to her feet, passing hugs out to my family.

"Yeah," Tegan says, pulling away from Vienna. "We did kind of kidnap you a little."

Vienna nods. "Kidnapped and fed Italian food with good company? I'll take it."

Dad and Mom laugh, taking their turns hugging her next, and after she says goodbye to Theo, we walk out of my place, waiting for the elevator to pick us up at the end of the hall. "Thanks for coming back to my place. It meant a lot to me to have you here, with my family." She stares up at me as the doors pull open, and I place my hand on her lower back, ushering her inside.

The doors seal us in and she's literally on top of me, fusing her mouth to mine, and I love it. We make out like teenagers before curfew, her tongue making messy swipes in my mouth. My back hits the bumper bar in the elevator as she fishes her fingers through my hair on either side of my head, pushing into me as if the world is burning down and these are our last moments.

The doors open, and she steps back, full lips swollen, her usual rosy hue comfortable in her cheeks. She nudges her glasses up her nose. "I wish I didn't have sculpting lab. I wish I could stay and hang out with you and your family."

"You're not far from not having classes at all anymore... ever again," I say, referencing her upcoming art school graduation. "Are you excited to be done?"

She collects her long, dark hair in her hands, twisting it in circles until she wraps an elastic from her wrist around the mass. The messy bun and glasses look has me completely bricked up as we exit the private parking garage, immediate sunshine rendering us both a little blind for a moment.

Blinking and laughing at how bright it is, we walk side by side to Crave, which is just a few blocks away. Walking with a hard-on is not my favorite thing, but walking with Vienna is definitely worth it.

"Debauchery signed off on the first release today, right in front of me. Units are going into production starting as early as next week," she says, glancing over at me as we walk. With the sun at her back, loose strands of wild hair falling across her lips, her nose wrinkled as she relays the good news—I have never felt so drawn to another person before. Truly. "The first round of market testing will be to Crave & Cure fans, and that's next month, as long as production has no hiccups." And with less than half a block between us and her car, I stop in my tracks.

"Vienna, I know we haven't had a chance to really talk about things and we only just slept together but... It makes me insane to think about going about my days being in this city with you, knowing that I didn't take my chance when I had it."

"Your chance?" she asks, looking genuinely confused. "I just mauled you in the elevator."

"I want more than mauling in the elevator but definitely, still mauling in confined places. Cars, alleys, closets, wherever you wanna maul me, I'm yours. But... I want you to be my girl-friend, Vienna. I want the real thing with you." I hold her eyes. "I want to finish that conversation from last night."

"Oh," she says, in the most underwhelming response to asking someone to be my girlfriend that I've ever received.

And that 'oh' hits like 'fuck off', because she steps away from me a little, an awkward smile twisting her lips.

"You want to be... *together*," she rephrases, "like a couple? Exclusive?"

Exclusive? "Yeah," I nod, "I do. An exclusive couple. Me and you. Because I like you a lot and I've never felt this pull to anyone else the way I'm drawn to you."

Well, I've officially played all my cards.

I stand and wait, my pulse jackhammering in my throat, my nerves making my asshole clench.

Her lips fall into a thin line. "Can I think about it?" she asks, glancing at the Crave building sitting securely behind a black iron fence.

Think about it?

I try to hide my disappointment and instead view her request for time as a positive thing. That she's taking me and us seriously, and therefore really thinking about her response. The fact that she's not taking the question lightly should make me happy.

But instead, for the first time in my life, I feel unsure about myself. Unsure of what I mean to her. This entire time I thought I was fighting to show her that my work is separate from who I am, and that I can work in this industry and have a woman I love, too. Now I think I've been worried about the wrong thing.

Maybe I've just been a fun experiment all around. Working

at Crave, fucking the porn star, then moving on. Maybe that's what her story has looked like all along, and it was me who backloaded an entire fated idea into us.

"Okay," I say, smiling, knowing lingering in the indecision won't do anything for either of us. "That's fair."

She smiles, but it's stunted and the day, which has been one of the best of my life in a long time, feels tainted. "I'll see you tomorrow at work," she says, instead of offering to text or call me later.

Space, I reassure myself, is what she needs right now. "Okay. Have a good class. Bye, Vienna."

"Bye, Tucker," she says, before turning and disappearing into the Crave property. I stand and wait until she pulls her car out and drives off, watching until her tail lights disappear on the horizon.

I think I just got friend-zoned.

Fuck.

23

Vienna

Holy crap. It's the trifecta.

"Thanks for coming over on such short notice," I breathe as I close the door quietly behind Darren, dragging him by the wrist to my kitchen.

There I have two shots poured and the only booze I have on hand is unfortunately cheap Vodka. We're talking less than seven dollars for a liter, cheap.

"I'm not taking that shot," Darren huffs, folding his arms over his chest in refusal.

"Fine, I'll take both," I huff, lifting the first tiny glass to my lips. The booze burns its way down like actual fire, but lightens the weight on my shoulders as it sears through my veins.

"Don't you have lab in like, forty minutes?" he asks, glancing down at the expensive gold watch glittering on his wrist. He's wearing his fancy clothes, which means he came from work.

"How's the museum? How's Dahlia?" I ask though the truth is, right now, I don't even care. "You know what, no offense, we can get to you later."

Darren's lips twitch. "Okay, so why am I being summoned here in the afternoon? To watch you get buzzed on off-brand booze or what?"

He swipes the other shot before I can take it, holding it over my head. "You aren't taking this. You have lab soon." He places it in the sink, and overfills the glass with water.

"Ugh," I huff, "Fine. But the next time you want to take a shot to drown your worries, I'm not going to let you!"

He rolls his eyes. "I'm assuming this is about Tucker and all those feelings you caught," he says, hopping up on the counter, plucking a shiny apple from the fruit bowl.

I point at it. "That's Madeline's."

He takes a juicy bite and around the crunching says, "Don't care. Now spill it before I have to go meet Samson and his parents for dinner."

"Tucker asked me to be his girlfriend," I spit out, hopping up onto the counter across from him.

"I don't get the problem," Darren says around the bite of an apple.

"He's a porn star, Darren. That's the problem." I push stray pieces of hair out of my face and reach for my water, feeling hot at the mention of him. "That means he would have sex with other women and men all day."

Darren strokes a finger along the worn label on the Vodka bottle. "Do you not believe him that he says work is just work?"

"It's not that," I add quickly. "I really do think work is just work, for all of the actors, actually."

"Then, if you aren't afraid he's going to catch feelings for another actor or actress, what's the problem?"

I twist my fingers in the hem of my black dress, the same dress that was shoved around my waist while Tucker fucked me with his toy cock.

I clear my throat and despite the fact that Darren has been known to give me a hard time, I find comfort in his eyes. "Everything is hot and great now but when my contract with Crave is up, and I'm not there... I may feel differently about what he does. Or if we argue, or hit a rough patch, and he goes to work and fucks other people... will I still find it hot? I mean, I'm just trying to be real with myself. So I don't commit to something I can't live up to. To prevent heartbreak." Though my heart is already so attached, I think even if we ended things now, I'd be destroyed.

Darren sits up a little straighter. "So you like watching him but when you aren't there, you're worried you'll be jealous?"

I shrug as the bedroom door down the hall squeals, Madeline and a gust of Ralph Lauren perfume filling the hall.

"Great. Your asses are where I make my salads. That's *wonderful*," she snarks, sauntering in to swipe a glass bottle of water from the fridge. Because Madeline buys bottled water in glass bottles, and trust me when I say it's not about the environment. Even her hydration is pretentious.

"Well hello Madeline," Darren smiles, sifting a hand through his shiny dark hair. She keeps her nose in the air as she drifts around the small kitchen, making a show of having to pull out drawers around us to get what she needs.

"Darren," she says drily as she pops ice out of her silicone tray from the freezer. She opens a probiotic sparkling soda and slowly fills her glass as her eyes come to me.

"Sausage, what's the occasion? You aren't in your overalls." She drops a metal straw in the glass with a tink, and stirs.

"I had a presentation at work," I say slowly, catching Darren's gaze to shoot him "don't fucking say anything" eyes.

"Fuck, how'd that go, by the way? That was this morning and I didn't hear from you until what, three?" Darren reaches over, collecting a can of warm Diet Coke from the box next to the fridge. He pops the can, and takes a sip.

"So good," I beam, tempering my voice so as to not gather too much attention from Madeline. "But that's another conversation. One thing at a time."

"And what's the thing bothering you right now, Vienna?" Madeline asks, wrapping her hand around her glass as she pinches the straw between two fingers, looking at me with so much condescension and hatred that I really start to believe that in another, past life I must have like, pissed in her quinoa or something.

Knowing she's such a butthole that she won't believe me, I tell her the honest to goodness truth. "I'm falling in love with a really, really handsome guy but the thing is, everyone else wants him too. And I'm wondering when I'm not around, can I handle it?"

She snorts with uproarious laughter and honestly if it was anyone else I'd be offended. But with Madeline, I expect her to be a snobby assclown. I mean, there's something to be said for getting just what I expect.

"And does this god know you exist?" Madeline asks, blinking her lash extensions at me while Darren's lip rolls with a snarl.

"Indeed he does," I add with a smile, because it's a total waste of time when it comes to Madeline.

I slide off the counter and head to my bedroom, eager to get changed and get to the lab. I want to escape Madeline, too, but unfortunately, we sit right next to one another in class.

Darren, hot on my trail, walks past Madeline and says, "And he's hung like a fuckin' horse, *Maddy.*"

He closes my bedroom door behind himself.

"Why did you tell her that?" I ask, annoyed because I don't want her knowing anything about Tuck. But then again... if she knew his name, he's just one Google search away. And there she can find out anything she wants, including the size of his dick.

Hell, she can fuck herself with his dick one day very soon if she wants to.

I flop down on my bed and drape an arm over my eyes. "When I said I like watching him, I mean, I get super turned on watching him. With men, with women, I don't know how to explain it. But there isn't even a single pinch of jealousy inside me."

Darren lies down next to me, and we both watch the blades of the ceiling fan turn lazy circles. "You kinda get off on it?"

"Definitely."

"So... you're a voyeur. You like watching for your own pleasure," Darren says simply, as if he didn't just put a name to the thing I'd been feeling and stressing over for the last few weeks.

"I mean. Yes?"

He sighs his annoyance, and I wonder for a second if he and Lance are the same person because holy irritability. Sitting up he looks back at me, still a puddle of confusion on the mattress. "You get horned up when you watch him fucking other people?"

I clap my hands to my eyes. "Horned up? Jesus, Darren, could you say it in a less embarrassing way?"

He peels my hands back. "It's true, isn't it? And honestly, Tucker Deep is hot as shit. I don't blame you."

I sit up and stare at our reflections in the mirror across from us. "It's true. It's just... I'm afraid that I'll agree to be his girlfriend and then, in like, three days, be totally and utterly in love because, if you can believe it or not, the inside is somehow better than the outside."

"Damn, even Samson is equal inside and out. But do not tell him I said that," he warns, smiling.

"Well, Tucker is amazing. I'm just terrified I'll fall for him only to realize that him being with other people isn't as sexy and hot as I think it is now. Then what? I have to say, *yes, I agreed to be with you under these terms but I actually can't stand it now so choose: me or your career?* I can't do that to him. I can't. Or his family. And oh my god, his family!" I drape a hand over my heart, feeling it rattle beneath my ribs at just the mention of some of the nicest people I've ever met. "They're amazing. They're so accepting and cool and I really honestly vibed so hard with them."

"Pump the brakes a little, Vienna. First of all, you don't know that one day it won't be hot anymore, or that he even plans to do porn forever. You're setting yourself up for a big no when you should just talk to him about all of this. See what he has to say."

"Yeah," I say, dragging my toe through the shag rug. "I do need to talk to him. Because there is some part of me that feels like we're... perfect together. I mean, I do like thinking of him on set with other people. Something about knowing he's doing the most erotic, intimate thing while people stand idle, transfixed by them, getting hard or wet, going back to their people and using what he made them feel to own their own pleasure... it's so hot."

I push out a long, heavy breath. "But will it always be? What if it wears off and it's no longer sexy voyeurism and fantasies but jealousy and angst?"

Darren rises from the bed, picking invisible lint from his black dress pants. "Talk to him. But don't build out a scenario and make a choice based on fear and things that haven't happened yet. That's not fair to Tucker."

I get to my feet and dig a pair of overalls from my drawer. "I know. You're right. Maybe I'll see if he wants to meet after his shoot tomorrow and talk."

"Good. Take my advice. Don't shoo away the hot guy because you're scared," Darren says, making his way to my door. Abruptly he turns, hand on the knob, and asks, "Hey, what's your final project in sculpting gonna be since the downfall of banking flopped?"

"It wasn't the downfall—nevermind," I reply, the sculpture no longer important. After all, not only did my dad not come to the mid-semester showing to see I made a piece of art as a middle finger to him, but I also lost to Madeline's sculpture of labia. So, yeah. "I'm actually... doing a bust. Of Tucker."

He arches an interested brow. "Is that right?"

Tucker's orgasmic face floods my mind, sending hot chills over my skin. "He makes this really sexy face when he orgasms, and the noises... Jesus, Darren, he's just... incredible. So I decided to sculpt his orgasm face. It's representative of both sides of control. Him losing it as he comes, but him also having it as he gives someone else release, too."

I dig out my phone and show him a picture I took last week. "It's almost done. Tonight is actually just smoothing. Then it sits until the final show and last grading ever."

Darren cups the phone with both hands, blinking at the screen with admiration in his eyes. "Vienna, this is amazing. This is absolutely incredible."

I peel the dress off overhead and step into the overalls, hooking them and tossing my hair up while Darren stands in the hall analyzing the photos of my bust. I slip into Crocs and close the door behind me, snatching my phone from his hand. Madeline is still in the kitchen, and looking off.

I ignore her because yeah, fuck her. I walk out with Darren and he opens my car door for me once I'm at it. "Good luck but honestly Vienna, that piece is gorgeous." He taps his chin. "Too bad you didn't submit that for the grant."

I had that thought already, but the truth is, if I would've won the grant, I would have said no to Lance the day he came to the museum. And I'd never have met Tuck. So maybe Madeline's shitty labia sculpture is a good thing.

We say our goodbyes, and I head to the lab to put the finishing touches on quite possibly the best piece I've ever sculpted. Even better than Fuck Tuck, which is saying something because that cock earned me a hundred thousand dollars.

I keep my work station covered, and Madeline does her very best job ignoring me completely, which is a relief for today.

I have enough on my mind. Like if I say yes, can I be the woman that Tuck deserves?

A fter lab, I head out of the corridor, into the early evening air, only to stop short just a few paces out.

"Tucker," I breathe, taking in his wind swept hair, gray sweats riding low on his hips, and his black hoodie. Even in the growing evening, his eyes twinkle and his teeth shine. God he's gorgeous. "What are you doing here?"

"Excuse me," Madeline huffs, pushing past me to take the steps two-by-two until she's at the bottom, standing right next to Tucker. "Oh, hello," she smiles up at him, her blonde hair gleaming.

He nods at her then looks back up at me. "I wanted to continue our talk. Do you have a few minutes?"

My classmates file out of the building around us, and any privacy we were going to have is gone. I chew my lip, deciding my options. If we go out for coffee or a meal, people will be around us and this isn't a topic I want to be overhead discussing. At my place, he will see my mess and chaos but with a closed door, we'll have privacy.

"Yeah. My place is really close. We can go there and talk?"

Before we can decide, the devil interrupts.

"Is this him?" Madeline interjects. I can't help it, I glare at her. Really fucking glare because this tiny moment is likely on the cusp of a really important, bigger moment, and I just want to get him to myself and talk.

And she's totally sticking her tits out and playing with her hair like the attention whore she is.

"Him who?" I shake my head and descend the stairs to come to stand by Tucker's side. Glancing down at me, he winks, and my insides stir from it.

"The bust you sculpted for your final project." She rocks to her toes and narrows her gaze, inspecting Tuck's brows and eyes. My stomach quickly souring as she smiles gleefully at me. "Oh yeah, that's the guy you're sculpting."

She sticks her hand out, and she's close enough that the tips of her fingers graze his sweatshirt. And I've never wanted to chokeslam anyone as much as I do now.

But violence isn't the answer, etcetera etcetera.

"Hi, I'm Madeline, Sausage's roommate." She blinks her full, dark lashes at him, fingers wiggling for a shake. "You must be Tucker. The guy Vienna's both sculpting and unsure about," she uses air quotes on the last bit, sending me into what can only be described as a murderous rage.

The rage seizes my nerves and transforms into palpable anger. "You were eavesdropping on me and Darren?"

Tucker looks down at me, deep grooves between his eyebrows. "Who's Darren?"

I wave him off because I see what Madeline is doing, and hell no. "My best friend, I've talked about him, I'm sure." I turn to Madeline, absolutely seething. She can call me Sausage at home all she fucking wants. Half the time, I'm not paying attention to her. But in front of the man I'm more or less obsessed with? Fuck that. And to ruin the surprise of my bust? I'd only shown Darren today. I wasn't even sure if I was going to show or tell Tucker. "Why were you spying on me, Madeline? I mean, it's not enough you're a raging bitch all the time but now you're spying on me?"

"So you said it, then?" Tucker asks, his voice light and disbelieving.

"I said what?"

"You said you were unsure about me," he recites. "You must've said it if you knew she was listening."

I push my glasses up my nose and take a deep breath, realizing my mistake. Madeline wants me to lash out, she wants me to look like a fool. And Tucker came here to sort things out with me. I took the bait foolishly, but I won't continue. Another deep breath, hands balled at my sides as I try now to focus only on Tucker.

"Tuck, listen, I was just telling Darren that I wasn't completely sure if I'd always enjoy watching you..." I widen my eyes in an effort to impart the subtext. "You know," I say, nudging him. "But that I like it now, I do, and it's not a negative to me at all. I just worry about the future, getting jealous and stuff." I roll my lips together and drop my volume. "This is kinda what I wanted to talk about at my place."

His eyes dart between mine and I think this is the first time in my life I've ever been truly scared.

I was nervous to pay my own way in the city, at the Institute, without my parents' help. But I wasn't scared. I've always been a hard worker, and I have always been able to support myself.

I got my tonsils out when I was fourteen and I was more concerned with missing the school dance than anything. I wasn't scared.

But as Tuck tries to make sense of the chaos Madeline has slingshotted our way, I realize he *could* walk away.

And I'm scared. I'm scared to walk away without him.

I wanted to have this talk in private. I wanted it to be slow and cautious, and pay respect to every corner of this discussion that begged for attention. But my fear is driving me, and not in the way that Darren warned.

It's driving me toward truth and risk.

Maybe real fear is all I needed to realize what I want.

"I'm scared. I'm scared of all of the beautiful, erotic, extremely artful things you do for your job... I'm afraid of them one day coming between us."

Shoulders deflating, his green eyes search mine, Adam's apple sliding down his throat with slow acceptance. "You had a man named Darren over?"

I press a hand between his pecs to stop his train of thought. "Darren is just a friend and I'm not done with my mini-speech."

With another lungful of air, pretending as best as I can that Madeline is not audience to my most private conversation, I forge ahead, the beat of his heart against my palm keeping me steady. "I was afraid of it coming between us, but I realized just now that... *anything* could come between us. It's up to us whether we let it." I stare up into his eyes and take a moment to steady the heavy thudding in my chest. "I love watching you, Tuck. I really do. And no matter how long you do what you do, I'd love to give it a go." I take a chance and grab his hand, weaving our fingers together. "Me and you."

His hands swallow mine, and it throws goosebumps up my forearm, and a flutter in my pulse. "I want to be with you, if you still want to be with me. Because I imagined not being with you, and I felt really, really scared."

Slowly, a grin spreads across his face. Using our linked hands, he tugs me into his chest, and wraps his arm around me. I suck in his scent, and feel my cunt pulse in return. His voice rumbles through his chest, quashing any remaining tension as he turns us to face Madeline.

"Did you call her Sausage?" The disgust in his voice makes me wonder how long I can hold my breath, and how good my gag reflex is.

"Vienna Sausage," she says, her tone clipped.

He snorts, and for a second she looks pleased as his grip closes on my shoulder. "Are you really so insecure that you feel the need to reduce such a beautiful name, one of the most beautiful cities in Austria to a canned weenie? " He shakes his head, and my eyes fill. "To call a beautiful woman *Sausage*." He shimmies his shoulders and mimics a chill rippling through his spine. "That gives me the ick for you. Big time."

He looks down at me, and my eyes are so fuzzy from tears that I swallow hard and just stand there like a complete fool.

A happy fool, and I think that's the best kind of fool you can be.

"I was going to see if you wanted to go back to my place and talk but–" We kind of just did it live.

"Let's go to Crave. I have an evening shoot but it doesn't start for another few hours. We can have some privacy there," he smiles against my lips before sweeping his tongue through my mouth, leaving a delicious moan for me to swallow up. "My family is at my place," he reminds me. But I remembered.

"Well... bye, Cookie was it? Oh no... Madeline..." Tucker retorts before tugging me away toward the parking lot. He loops his arms around my waist and hoists me up, my legs instinctively wrapping his hips. The real Fuck Tuck is hard and pressing to my core as he smiles at me, walking us to my car.

"I feel that," I whisper in reference to the steel pressing into me, then add, "and it's not fair that you're taller than me even now."

He kisses the tip of my nose as he nudges my glasses up, surprised they aren't freaking foggy from the heat whirring between us. "You fit me perfectly. And I'm so happy you're giving this a chance."

Without question, Tucker slides me into the driver's side, reaching across me, smothering me with his musky scent. I clutch his hoodie and suck him down, earning me a laugh.

"What? I love the way you smell," I reply, emboldened by my own honesty and the beautiful way the last few minutes have unfolded. He clips my seatbelt at the lap and closes the door, walking around the front of my car toward the passenger side. Tall and built solid with muscle, I'm made that much more feral by the fact that I know he can fuck. It's one thing to know a hot guy with a decent personality, but a ten on the inside, ten on the outside, and a ten in bed?

Holy crap. It's the trifecta.

He slides into the passenger seat and tells me immediately the quickest route to Crave, which I actually didn't know. And while taking the world's most narrow one-way alley behind the row of commercial buildings on the way, Tucker unclips his belt, leans over the console, and rests his big hand on my belly.

"I'm yours no matter who I'm with," he says, not whispering but keeping his voice calm and low. It rattles me to hear him rasp such sweet honesty to me, and with his fingertips exploring the side buttons on my overalls, I get a little dizzy and let off the gas. Nearly idling down the alley at eight miles an hour, my head falls against the seat as Tucker's hand slips beneath the denim bib, delving into my panties.

Thick, warm fingers spread my wet lips, and the guttural moan he lets free at the revelation of how ready I am for him has my foot to the pedal. He chuckles as he dusts his lips along my throat, feathering kisses along my pulse, his fingers slowly circling my electric bundle of nerves.

"All of this is for me, isn't it, Vienna?"

I nod, letting off the gas again, the car lulling through the narrow passage. I fight to keep my eyes focused, but as his fingers stroke my clit and tease my hole, it becomes a feat.

But before I can complain, he takes his hand out of my panties and proceeds to reach into his sweats and stroke himself with what I left on him.

The cock that I know so well, the one I've analyzed in photos and molded nearly fifty times, it's all I want. As I watch his hand beneath the gray sweats, up and down, leaving a dark spot of arousal against the fabric, all I know is *I want that fucking cock.*

I want to fuck Tuck. Now.

"I want you so bad," I rush out, the back of Crave coming into view after what feels like an unending alley drive. "So bad, Tucker."

"I know," he breathes, draping his arm along the back of my seat, fingertips stroking through my hair. "I want you too. And guess what? I'm yours. And you're mine."

I pull into a parking spot and find myself in his arms as he carries me to the rear entrance. "Are you sure it's okay for us to be here?" I whisper as he inputs his access code on the keypad outfront. "I mean, shooting isn't until what, nine?"

He nods, and I remember seeing the call sheet for tonight. They're filming a scene in the alley, and Augustus doesn't fake anything. He wants real moonlight, real shadows.

"It's fine. I call it showing up early. If anything, being here now makes me a better employee," he says, grinning at me as he throws his hip into the metal door, shoving it open. Darkness from the closed studio swallows us as he steps inside, lowering me to my feet. Weaving our hands together, I follow him in darkness until he stops, and I smack right into his back.

Flicking a switch, dim lights illuminate the small set in the middle of the studio. The last thing they shot was apparently a multi-cast member scene, as three twin beds sit spaced just a few feet apart.

"The three bears and Goldilocks," he says of the set. He pulls me to the middle bed, and we sit on the edge. I look up into the studio lights, which are off, and around the sleeping cameras. "So this is what it feels like," I whisper, kind of in awe of the feeling.

He presses his hand to the strap of my overall, and unclasps it. "Almost what it feels like." The other strap gets unclasped, and then the bib is down. "Stand up."

He drags the work clothes off my body, and takes off my panties and bra, too. Then I watch in breathless suspense as he reaches behind his head and yanks off his t-shirt and hoodie in one hard pull. Next, the sweats and briefs are gone, and then we're completely naked with each other on the dormant movie set.

It feels so brazen to be naked on set.

With the lights only partially on, the set so quiet you could hear a pin drop, Tucker lays me down in the center of the small bed, hooking his hand under my knee. Bending one leg, his beautiful steely erection disappears into the mattress as he settles between my legs, keeping one palm pressed to the back of my thigh, pushing my leg up.

His eyes hover on mine as he brings his mouth to my pussy, pressing a hot, electrifying kiss to my clit. "You like to watch me," he breathes, skimming his tongue though my lips, moaning at how wet he finds me. "But could you be watched?" We glance over at the dark camera, and he hops off the bed. Digging through his sweats, he retrieves his phone, turns the camera on, and balances it against the actual camera. "Can you be my co-star, Vienna?" He hits record and walks back to me and as much as I love his abs and mountainous shoulders, I can't keep my eyes off the hard rod swinging between his legs, and the full sack beneath. My lower half actually aches at the sight of it, desperate to be fucked and flooded.

"Let's make a movie for us to watch later," he whispers against my clit as he repositions himself between my open legs.

I nod. "Yes, I want to make a movie with you, Tuck. Please."

24

Tucker

The OG is mine.

I want nothing more than to slide inside of Vienna completely bare, to feel her soft walls pulsing all around me, to watch her take every bit of me with nothing between our writhing bodies. Nothing keeping her release from mine.

But I want her to see my results, see that I'm clean, and I want it to be outside of heated moments and panted breaths. I want it to be a decision she makes with the utmost clarity.

Burying my face in her pussy, I lick her sensitive clit in long, slow passes, making her spine roll and her hands come down in my hair, tugging in despair.

"Imagine sitting on my cock," I whisper, kissing her pussy as I work the tip of my finger inside her cunt. She's soft and so wet that I can't help but moan, which makes her tug my hair even harder.

"I love your moans," she admits breathlessly, her eyes hazy as she strains off the pillow to watch me feast.

"Imagine sitting on my cock, riding me as I suck your perfect tits. Imagine us on the TV screen, our noises all around us as I fill you up and make you fucking moan."

She whimpers, bearing down on my face and hand, seeking out more attention, more pressure, more friction. More of everything, and I'm eager to give it.

"Did you picture this when you watched me?" I ease my finger further into her, my cock fattening at how tightly her soft walls clench me, how her body seals around my digit. "Did you imagine me tasting you? Fingering your needy little pussy?" I drive another finger inside, curling them, letting my thumb fall to her swollen clit as I fan kisses along her groin.

"Tucker," she breathes, a healthy arch curling her back as I finger fuck her to the brink of explosion. Small passes of the pad of my thumb along her clit, my two fingers nudging deep inside her, I continue my steady rhythm of stroking and curling until her hands fall from my hair, gripping the comforter as her head thrashes against the pillow. Sweat glistens on her collarbone under the dim lights as I drag my tongue all along her groin, teasing her as I fuck her.

"Come for me, just like this, Vienna, and then you're gonna spread those legs and let me inside. Let me in this sweet, tight cunt. Let me fuck you until you can't do anything but writhe and whimper my name."

With the tip of my tongue, I flick her clit in swift, short strokes, pushing my fingers just a tiny bit deeper.

"Yes, Tucker, yes, yes, yes!" She screams, her palms smacking my shoulders and the mattress, her hips lifting off the bed as she comes in quick, rolling waves. Clenching around me, her tight pussy attempts to milk my fingers, and against the mattress my cock begs to play. Hard and dripping,

I keep him smothered as I use my mouth to finish her orgasm.

Dazy, eyes hooded, cheeks flush, dark hair a stormy mess, she lifts her head and blinks down at me. "Fuck me, Tuck."

I know the purpose of this is so we can watch ourselves later, letting Vienna explore her voyeuristic fantasy without having to watch me fuck other people. But as I get to my knees on the end of the bed, for the first time while in this studio, I forget a camera is rolling. I forget the lights on my back are studio lights. And I forget that I'm on set.

It's just Vienna and me, and our earth-shattering connection.

Reaching beneath the bed, I snag a prop tray full of rubbers, and snatch a square packet. She watches with confusion etching the corners of her eyes in slight lines as I open and begin to roll on the condom.

"Until you can read my tests, see that I'm clean and we have a conversation about this where we're not already naked, we use protection."

She runs her fingers through her messy hair, and her breasts at this angle have me salivating. Once the condom is on, I cage her to the mattress with my arms and suck her nipple into my mouth, moaning into her warm flesh.

"Yes Tuck," she breathes as I drag my stubble-laden chin through the valley between her breasts, only to suckle at her other nipple long enough to make her flood the set with moans. Fingers stroking my head as my sheathed cock rests on her thigh she whimpers, "Oh my god, that's so good."

My lips skim her throat and latch onto the side of her jaw where I feather kisses and gentle bites as I move toward her full, swollen lips. "I know you believe me, but I want us to start from a place of absolute trust." It's not that I think she needs to see them. It's me. I need to start from a place that honors communication and honesty. I've waited nearly three years for Vienna, I want to do this right. And I know, very soon, I need to show her the sketch, and explain why she feels so destined to be mine.

"I'm going to fuck you now," I tell her, and I don't know if I'm warning her, or preparing myself, because I have no idea how things will be once I'm inside her again. I'm overrun with the need to make her come again while simultaneously trying to take it slow and savor every morsel and moment. She looks over at the camera, then back at me.

"Thinking about watching this later?" I coax, wanting her to utter filthy words, because they sound so foreign and delicate on her tongue, like French spoken in a perfect accent.

She nods, succumbing to the comfort of the small show bed. With one knee still up, I lift the other, placing my palms on both. I hold her eyes as I push her apart, putting her pink, glossy cunt on display directly beneath the set light. She whimpers and resists a little, her knees pushing against my palms. But when my eyes fall to her slit, my lips physically ache to be there again, and my cock weeps within my sheath.

"Until recently, when I would get ready for a scene," I tell her, keeping my voice low as I position myself between her legs. "I would stroke until I got hard enough to roll a condom on, then we'd go." Angling my hips, I push inside of her, watching her eyes pinch and relax as the widest part of my cock breaches, then settles inside of her.

"Now just thinking about you can get me hard." Dipping down, I press a kiss to the corner of her mouth and work in a jagged line, placing kisses down her throat, along her collarbone. "I want you so bad, Vienna. I always do."

She nods, but hits me with a new expression as I settle more inches inside. "Did I hurt you before when we had sex at my house?" I ask, studying the crumple in her brow and the way she shrinks into the bed as I go deeper.

But she shakes her head, sending the question flying. "No, I'm not hurt, you're not hurting me. I just... I'm more excited to have you now that I know you're mine."

I blink down at her, trying to understand what she means, but the throbbing in my balls and the heat swallowing my cock is making it challenging. She reaches up, stroking a hand over my cheek, then through my hair and down my arm. "It feels so satisfying knowing *it's* mine."

Being hers feels better than anything I've ever experienced, and I've had a 7 way—twice. Feels better than landing a sex toy deal. Feels better than the penthouse, even.

"It's yours and so am I," I tell her, chest puffed with pride at being claimed so boldly by Vienna. I don't think she's territorial or controlling, so her desire to mark me as hers is that much hotter. And sweeter, too.

"It's about to be a million others' too," she breathes, smiling as I piston my hips, owning her pussy in slow, deliberate strokes. Our eyes idle together, breathing thick and hot between our faces. "But the OG is mine."

"Yours," I agree in a growl, picking up the pace. All this claiming is turning off the emotional part of me and soaking the feral part of me in lighter fluid. The moment she starts to orgasm, she'll drop the match.

"I'm yours, beautiful. And I can't wait to claim this pussy *bare*," I drop my lips to her earlobe, "and that tight little ass," I groan, slamming all the way inside, settling there.

Vienna moans, throwing her legs around my waist, driving her cunt upwards, seeking more thrust, more friction, more me.

"I'm gonna fuck you every which way from fucking Sunday, Vienna, and leave you so full that you'll be leaking my cum for days." I pant, a tickling drop of sweat sliding down my chest. "You're the only one who gets me bare. Ever."

She claws at my shoulders, rolling her head into the pillows as I saw with strength in and out of her, fucking her now hard and fast, driving her to the edge of insanity.

"Yes, Tucker, yes, yes," she cries, and holy shit is she loud and fucking hell is she sexy. At my place, we had to be quiet. But now, we're alone and she's free to react.

I love the way her body responds to mine, comes alive solely for me, me and no one else.

"How do you like taking this big thick cock? One you've been studying, learning every ridge of for months? How does it feel ravaging your slick pussy?" I growl down at her, keeping my eyes on her face, eager to watch her react to every filthy sentence. Each time she bites into her pillowy lip, every time her tongue makes a pass, and when she wrinkles her nose and goes motionless—I memorize how beautiful she looks while full of me. I know I'm going to carry those images with me through work every day from here on out.

She nods, craning up off the bed to stare down at where my sheathed cock ruts in and out of her.

"God, you feel so good. I pictured this, every time I cast you, I pictured this," she admits breathlessly as her cunt seizes up around me, her core knotted with pressure as she strains further up off the bed. "Oh god, Tucker, I'm gonna come," she pants, her body flailing, almost seizing, as another orgasm dismantles her from the inside out.

The moment those sweet walls swallow me up, straining and pumping around me as her eyes flutter closed behind her glasses, the match falls.

Scooping my arms beneath her torso, I lift her off the mattress, earning a breathy squeal. On my haunches, I hold her chest to mine, one hand wrapping the back of her neck, the other stroking up the crack of her ass. "Ride it out, beautiful, finish yourself and take me with you."

The slope of her neck is mouthwatering as her head falls back, her thighs growing tight around my hips as she thrusts toward me. She rides me in tiny, finishing strokes as her orgasm rails her, her tight cunt squeezing my thick, heavy cock.

Exploring the seam of her ass, I hold her neck tight, feeling her muscles give way to me as she rides out the rest of her orgasm, pulling mine from me inescapably.

"Vienna," I hiss, jerking her so close to me I can hardly breathe, but her body stills with my cock buried deep, and the final pulse of her cunt nearly causes me to black out. Forehead sweaty, I tip it down, smashing it to hers as my hips flex and my cock twitches. I seal my mouth to her naked shoulder and suck her, hard, hoping to brand her as I come in violent waves, flooding the rubber as animalistic roars of pleasure tear from my chest.

She wraps her arms around my back, dragging her nails up and down the length of my spine as I pump and pulse inside of her, her tight pussy milking every single drop out of me. She clenches again as I finish, then cups my face in her warm, delicate hands. "That felt amazing," she breathes before kissing me with a greedy mouth and roaming hands.

We part for air, and I stroke my fingers through her hair, grinning at the way her glasses sit a little crooked on her nose. "Good orgasm, huh?"

She looks stumped, straight puzzled for a moment, then says, "Yeah, my orgasms were fucking amazing but I mean you. Feeling you inside me, on set..." she blinks at me, crashing her lips to mine in a sudden and needy kiss. No wonder those adorable glasses are crooked. I adjust them for her once we part.

"It was amazing. You're magnificent Tucker," she finally finishes, staring sleepily into my eyes. "Inside and out."

I run my hands down her back, then her sides, resting my palms on the full globes of her ass. "You're fucking beautiful, Vienna."

"I don't think I can ever get tired of hearing that," she beams and then the mundane side of sex takes over.

Soft, too softened to stay lodged inside of her, my cock slips out and hits my thigh with a wet slap. We look down to see her arousal stringing between her cunt and my cock, and I reach beneath the bed and grab a cleanup towel. "The perks of being on the set of a film that is used to and actually expecting lots of fluids," I say with a grin as I begin wiping her gently, cautiously. The truth is, most of the aftercare I give is just a performance for the rolling camera. With Vienna, it's my first time truly giving it, and wanting to get it exactly right.

I take my time, wiping her gently, pressing kisses to the pink and tender places. Then I roll off the condom and dispose of it, and help her get dressed before I do the same.

As I watch her run her fingers through her hair, twisting and wrapping as she braids it in that magical way that women do, I realize I have to tell her that I was the one that requested her at Crave, and exactly why I did. How I knew her. I want her to know just how much of an impact she's had on me, even before Fuck Tuck.

We were going to talk about us, but just because we've established that doesn't mean there aren't things she needs to know. There are, and I need to tell her now.

I feed my fingers through hers and bring her to the phone where I stop recording and check the time. "I have over an hour before I have to film tonight. Come back to my place with me really quick? There's something I want to show you."

Her hand leaves mine to go to her head, brown eyes vast pools of concern. "Right now? We just had sex."

I straighten out her glasses for her. "It's not like they're gonna know that." I consider what I've said then take her hand in mine. "Actually, they'll know because I will definitely tell my dad at some point and, well, the trickle down effect. But they won't know like, *right* right now."

She steps back, amused. "You talk to your dad about your sex life?"

I hold up a finger, eager to clarify the important distinction. "I don't talk to him about my sex life as much as I just talk openly about my life. And I don't share details, I just share... connections."

Now she looks stumped, her lips pressing into a twitching line. "What does that mean?"

I sigh. "We're close. And when I hook up with someone, I tell my dad, and then I'll tell him if I felt a connection or if it was just good old fashioned intercourse."

She snorts, bringing the back of her wrist politely to her nose. "Intercourse?"

I nod. "And you should know, my family is the most important thing to me." I lick my lips, heart racing, the words lifting from my lips without a second thought. "And you are, too."

"I really like your family," she smiles, then smooths her hands down her dark hair one more time. "Okay, to your place."

A note on the counter tells us that my family went out to get Thai food down the street, that they're picking up enough for both Vienna and myself if we want, and they'll be right back.

It couldn't have possibly been the text I sent to Tegan and Theo telling them to kindly get lost for the next thirty minutes.

I wouldn't mind them here, in fact, I get kind of enthralled at the idea of them spending time with Vienna. But I don't have a lot of time tonight, and I just want to show her.

"Firstly, here are my results." I say as I hand her the folder I keep of my Crave monthly medical records. "The other thing I need to show you, it's in my closet," I say, awkwardly fishing a hand through my hair as my nerves intensify, bubbling beneath my skin.

Suddenly, I wonder if this *isn't* flattering and in fact supremely weird. I've been hanging onto a piece of her garbage for two years. What's next, a lock of hair? A baby tooth? Jesus, Tuck.

And what about timing, should I have told her earlier?

But here we are. There's no going back. I slide open the hanging door, and flip on the lights. I take in her profile, button nose and full lips, high cheek bones and sleek, full hair. She's absolutely stunning as she blinks with confusion in her brows at my closet full of clothes.

"Wow, that's a lot of shirts." She smiles, and it twitches a little. "Cool."

She unknowingly breaks the ice, making me laugh. I reach forward, shaking my head. "No, not the clothes." I push them all to the side, and reach above the framed art hung privately behind the clothes, and flip on the bar light.

The sketch comes to life before our eyes, and Vienna

pinches the edge of her frames, bringing them closer to her face in timid disbelief.

She analyzes the sketch, taking a tiny step forward. A pace behind her side, I tell her everything.

"Two and a half years ago, I took a job as a life class model. I was told I had to cover my face, they didn't want me to distract the artists with my looks." That's actually true, and as douchey as it sounds to admit it, it is exactly what the professor said. "I'd wanted to enroll in art school, but I didn't have a direction and my parents didn't have the money to let me fuck around in an expensive school. So I started modeling to get on campus and see if I could poke around a little, try and decide what I'd do if I could get my shit together and attend."

She swallows, but keeps her focus on the framed sketch.

"On my first night, there was this really beautiful girl wearing glasses, sitting in the front of the class." I swallow hard, remembering her mortification that I caught her checking out my cock. "She got my attention and I think I had hers, though not for reasons involving freeform sketch, or art."

Finally, she slowly turns to face me, eyes welled with tears.

"She was so gorgeous, I winked at her, and I remember knowing I messed up because she wouldn't look me in the eyes for the rest of class. Then she crumpled her paper, tossed it and left. And I just wanted to know her name, so after class, I took the paper out of the garbage."

We both look back to the sketch. Graphite etches the white, leaving behind my figure, ripe with muscle and erection. But there's another figure there, too. A woman with glasses, long hair splayed down her back, curled onto her knees in front of me, hands gripping my thighs. Three words in the same harmless black pencil are scrawled beneath the two figures. *You control me.* And in the bottom right hand corner, Vienna Carnegie is written in all capital letters.

"I was transfixed. I didn't know if it meant he controls her or she controls him but the way she's looking up at him, the way he's looking at her..." I grab the back of my neck and squeeze. "I'm still in awe. But that very night, another student in class came up to me after and he passed me a business card. You remember me telling you Aug did that? Well, the next day, I called the number on the card." I reach into my back pocket and retrieve my wallet, knowing the card is still inside. I pinch it and hand it to her, watching her eyes dance over the words.

"I can't believe Augustus was in free-form sketch."

I nod. "He was. As a hobby. And he spotted me and said he knew he could make me a successful adult film actor if I trusted him." I lift my hands in the air. "And here I am. But you know what made me do it? You know what made me go to my parents house and say 'I'm considering doing porn'?"

I look back at the art hidden away in my closet, just for me. "I thought, if that beautiful girl drew that, if she was fantasizing about me like that, well, I may have a shot. Because if I can turn a goddess like her on, I got this."

Her eyes go wide as she processes everything, and it is a lot. "You and I were in there together. Like... we were supposed to meet." She pinches her gaze as if remembering something she wanted to ask. "So wait, did you go back? Did you finish the free-form modeling or quit for Crave?"

I shake my head. "I finished the class. It was only two hours a night for a semester, so I stuck it out."

"Would you have called Augustus had you not found my sketch?" she asks, eyes wide, bottom lip trembling.

"I don't know for sure but... I don't think so. I never considered myself fantasy potential... until you fantasized about us, and drew it."

She swallows hard, blinking at me with fuzzy eyes as warmth spills down her cheeks. "Tucker," she breathes, shoving her fingers under her frames, wiping away the evidence of how much this has meant to her. But it's always meant that much to me.

"When the opportunity arose to maybe find you in a legit, non-stalkery way, I took it. I told Debauchery I wanted to use my own artist when they first pitched the idea. I gave your name to Lance and.... here we are."

"Tuck," she whispers. "I can't believe it was you. And I can't believe I caught your eye... and you kept this." She smooths her fingers over the frame before stepping back. "I can't believe how much we've impacted each other's lives. It feels unreal. It felt so imbalanced, this opportunity dropping in my lap out of nowhere. But it's like we've both turned each other's world upside down... just at different times."

"I really wish I didn't have to go to work, but I do. It's only one scene. Should only take an hour or so," I tell her, then, because it's the first time I've had someone to tell, I straighten and take her hands. "Tonight is with Chanel. It's a standing scene, which on the call sheet is written as F/M. Short for feet missionary, meaning, we stand and it's traditional sex. And for complete clarity she's been with her boyfriend for a few years—he's a good guy, you'll meet him at the work Crave cast parties."

She nods slowly, processing the subtext of this conversation. Processing the actual facts, too. She rolls her lips together, finger combing the ends of her hair as she edges around her thoughts aloud. "So you're fucking her against the wall," she hedges. "And it's out in the alley, for optimal nighttime lighting."

I nod. "That's it." I take a breath and study her, but I don't see the striations of anger in her throat, lines of worry in her forehead. There are no signs. But I know that resentment is a silent killer. "How do you feel about it?"

Her gaze holds mine, and her chin lifts with confidence

when she says, "I only wish I could watch." She steps close, her lips brushing mine, making my cock thicken as she whispers, "and I *fucking* mean that."

I let out a feral groan that tears through the tension and makes Vienna erupt in laughter, slamming her fists against my chest playfully. "But guess what? If I'm invited, I'd love to stay here. At your place. And have dinner with your family. I mean, if that's something you–"

I grab the base of her throat and yank her mouth into mine, kissing her recklessly, teeth and tongue, spit and groans. "Please stay, thank you," I gush, kissing her again, over and over. She grips my biceps, whimpering as my mouth crushes her, my chest pressing into hers.

The front door locks twist, and we step apart, both of us wiping our mouths, me with the sleeve of my hoodie, and her with the back of her hand. "Go," she says, winking. "And thank you for a wonderful night. Have fun at work."

I wink back and pad through my apartment, catching the door for my family, informing them that I'll be back but Vienna is staying. Tegan squeals, Theo claps, and my mom and dad proceed to talk over each other about who's going to give up what so that Vienna can try it all.

I ride the elevator down to the lobby, lightheaded and happy.

25

Vienna

Dripping his orgasm like his personal fucking twinkie

"Two days out!" Darren shimmies in his high-top chair, the Americano in front of him rippling as the table wobbles.

I wave a weary palm his way. "Okay, just chill out. I don't want to wear your coffee." I steady his cup while holding my own. "And yes, thank sweet baby Jesus, two more days and I'm officially done with school. No more classes. No more grant submissions. No more. Done." I wash my hands in the air and wave them out.

"I'm happy for you." His smile twitches as he drags his fingertip along the rim of his mug. "And I'm happy for me. I'm kind of over all your college drama stuff. Let's bitch about APRs and politics like actual adults."

I blink at him, and he sips his coffee, winking and smirking as he lowers his mug. "Kidding."

"Of course. No one wants to talk about those things." I rub my hands together and dig out my phone, opening it to the exact photo. It's my final bust for sculpting, my last piece of graded art.

And since Madeline spilled the damn beans the other day, I've since let Tucker look through the photos. He was speechless. And I have to say, it's my best work. Ever. No drawing, painting—nothing I've ever created with my heart and hands has ever held a candle to my bust of Tucker. He's mid orgasm, he's giving all of himself while also being drained of everything, literally and figuratively. It's perfect. Detailed, smooth, erotic. Utter perfection.

Darren shakes his head, palm draped over his chest. "I really can't believe you made this."

"Rude."

He looks up, undeniable awe resting in his dark eyes. "You're incredible. You know I love you."

"I know, I know," I smile, happiness radiating off me in sickening waves. He can feel it, I know he can, because even Darren smiles for a quick second. Then back to business.

"You guys are meeting us for dinner tonight, right? It's time we meet this Mr. Tucker Deep."

"Eliot," I correct. "His name is Tucker Eliot. And since he's going to be your best friend's boyfriend, I think you should call him by his actual name."

He smiles and nods, and those two things validate me in a strangely indescribable way. There is something uniquely beautiful about the acceptance of who you love from the people you love.

"If I'm supposed to be assessing him to give him my stamp of approval in true best friend style, does that mean you're sticking me with the check?"

"Of fucking course. I'm not missing a free meal," I grin, lifting my mug to my lips for a quick sip.

He wags a finger at me. "Bitch. You're the one who got paid a hundred grand to make dildos."

I shrug. "Most of that is going to pay down my debt. I'm far from rich." I consider the numbers in my head again, though I've thought of them a million times in the last few months. "I'm actually going to need to find a job pretty quickly. Within the first six months post graduation, at least."

I glance at my watch and push gently against the round table, freeing myself. "I gotta go. Finishing touches."

His eyes question me.

"Just polishing at this point. You know me. He was done two classes ago, as you can see from the photos." I shrug and he nods.

"That's what I thought. But good luck. Shine that cum-face up nice."

I kiss his cheek and wave over my shoulder as I head for the double doors. "See you tonight!"

I stand in front of my cubby, blinking, blinking, blinking. My mind is a tilt-a-wheel of sickening, disgusting thoughts, and my heart beats so hard that passing out is a very real possibility. Pain radiates down my arms, and I wonder if I can even hold my weight. My knees wobble.

"Oh my god," I whisper, the words weak and quiet, my voice wobbly, sadness warming my eyes. "No, no, no," I breathe out, my stomach rolling like mad waves breaking an angry shore. A fight in my gut, a battle of strength. Can I keep it together or will I vomit at the sight of the most beautiful thing I've ever created being destroyed?

I reach in and collect the pieces of what was my most sacred piece of art, the best thing I've ever formed, dug my hands into and made something from.

Broken. Into two pieces.

I wobble on my feet, my back crashing against the wall, knocking my feet from beneath me. I crash to the floor, splinters of pain soaring up my tailbone, but keeping the bust remnants steady in two hands. I sit on the floor and stare, blinking, tears wetting my cheeks, wrists, and ankles.

Madeline did this. I know she did. And yet, I can never prove it. And even if I could, even in some CSI enhanced footage fantasy scene, what would it even do? It can't fix the bust. Nothing would work. The way the pieces have deteriorated. This didn't tip over. It was thrown against the ground. Deliberately destroyed.

My bottom lip trembles but I suck it under my teeth and force my head up. Rising, I put the pieces of the bust into my open bag, hook it over my shoulder, and leave the lab.

It's polishing day and I have nothing to polish.

I pass Madeline on the way out and her smug smile tells me what I already knew.

I'm dialing Tucker's number as I take the steps two-by-two, eager to get into my car so I can fully fall to pieces .

"Hey beautiful." His deep voice somehow radiates through the ether, vibrating in my belly.

I sob into the phone, uncontrollably and ugly. Too many snorts to do in front of a person you want to view you as beautiful, but once the flood gates open, I can't be stopped. "My bust is broken."

"Our bust?" he asserts, "what happened? Are you okay?"

My voice wobbles as tears burn down my cheeks, searing

off my makeup, and taking a bit of happiness and self-worth, too. That bust was representative of my growth as an artist.

"No," I sniffle. "I don't know. I got here and opened my cubby and it was in two pieces." I sniffle again after choking on a deep, ugly sob. Hideous, really. "It's been thrown, I think," I croak.

"What the fuck?" His voice is rippling with anger and dominance, and my skin prickles with heat in reaction. I'm sad about the bust. But my nipples ache at his assertion. "I'm coming to get you. Stay exactly where you are."

So I do exactly that, and ten minutes later Tucker is there, plucking me from the bench by my arms, spinning me into his chest, kissing me in the washed up sunset for the world to see. For the whole world to know that broken bust or not, I will be just fucking fine.

I made this guy into a sex toy and paid off my debt. My self worth will not be determined by one singular incident. No way. I've come too fucking far. But it took being in his arms to realize that.

"What are you going to do?" Tuck asks as he helps me into the car. This time, he's driving and I'm fine with that. "We'll come back for my car," he insists, climbing into the driver's seat of my crap car.

"I'll just say it was broken while in the cubby. What else can I do? It's not like I've got anything else I can submit, and I'm pretty sure Madeline knew that." I breathe out my nose and slowly in through my mouth. There is no reason to get worked up about this. It's done.

"That's bullshit." His jaw flexes, striations of anger heavy down the length of his throat. It's incredibly sexy to see him so angry on my behalf. I've never had that.

I've never had a man stand up in my defense. I've never had a man validate and support me.

314

Oh my god.

I think I've just unlocked a new kink. Yes, I love watching him with other people but right now, he's nurturing and protective, things I've sadly not felt coming from a man in my life. And Tuck isn't just supporting me but caring for and protecting me. He makes me feel... *cherished.*

I turn to face him, eyes wide, heart racing... pussy clenched tight. "I wanna call you Daddy," I blurt out, "in a sexual way."

His eyes veer from the road to me and then back again, and god am I an asshole for dropping this on him while driving. But he steadies his focus ahead as he strangles the wheel in his grip. "Fuck yes, call me Daddy." He glances at me, eyes wild, making my belly ache for fullness only he can give me.

"Take me back to your place," I whisper, but catch myself because I know his family has their last day there today. "Oh my god, I'm cutting into your last day with your family." I shake my head, feeling like I completely overreacted.

Tucker shoots a concerned glance my way, a thick clump of sandy hair skirting across his forehead. A lump forms in my throat if I look at him for too long. "Nah, Theo actually left last night." He glances my way then out the windshield again, winding the wheel along the swiftly curving road. "He wanted to say goodbye but there was a work emergency," he says. "And my parents are tired of me. They miss their cats." He grins.

"I'm sorry, all the same." I sigh.

"Don't be." He flicks the blinker on, toward my apartment. "I'm going to fuck your brains out, then feed you an ice cream sundae with absolutely insane toppings and put on your all time favorite movie." He reaches out and runs his hand along my thigh. "Don't think about the bust."

I swallow. "I wasn't going to."

He pins me to the wall with a one-armed cage and strokes his cock along my back, his knuckles grazing me with each pass.

I wiggle my ass against him, the feeling of him fisting his fat cock and moaning at my back driving me wild. My pussy is so wet, my thighs are sticky. And I want him so bad, at this point, I think I'll swallow him up the second he slides into me.

A risk I'm willing to take, because *this man can fuck*. Each time he takes me, he pushes deeper, moans lower, makes me thrum longer. His lips are soft when I need a tender touch, and cruel and demanding when I demand to be ravaged. He ebbs and flows, becoming every single thing I could possibly need. Inside and out of the bedroom.

"Yes, Daddy," I pant, already loving the energy, loving how Tucker leans so easily into it. I get a sense of what it must be like to work with him, and my heart beats hard at the splash of proudness that overtakes me. He's so good at what he does, every time, all the time. That has to be hard. And *he's so good.* "Please," I whimper, and though it's a bit of reality mixed with roleplay, the words, the begging—all of it makes me ache. Yearn to be driven into deep and fast by Tucker's thick cock, to be filled to the brim and left dripping his orgasm like his personal fucking twinkie.

He nods, his eyes clutching mine with brutal intensity. "My beautiful girl," he groans, "you're so good. You're so deserving." He slides his cock inside of me, bare, throbbing and sticky, greased with need.

"Daddy," I moan, my voice light and stretched thin, practically transparent with vibrant need. "Daddy, yes, fuck me there. It feels so good," I moan, loving the way his thick cock sends glints of pain through me, his girth spreading me wide. But the pain melts, leaving behind a glowing pool of pleasure, so pure and fine it makes me light-headed.

Tucker does that to me. He does everything to me.

His teeth sear like a match as he sinks them into the flesh of my earlobe. "My ripe little pussy for filling," he growls, slapping a hard palm across my breast. "My cunt to flood. My hole to own."

My insides clench and my thighs burn as my orgasm sweeps through me, burning my vision with white hot light, sending my legs into a turbulent wobble. "Oh my god," I shake all around him, my cunt seizing, clutching him, causing him to grow rigid beneath my fingertips.

"Fuck!" he growls, stopping himself a moment as he slowly resumes stroking in and out of me, trying to walk himself back from the edge. His strokes are tempered and shallow, and I know he's close.

Still, I ride out my orgasm, rocking my hips toward his as he slams inside of me. His hips slow and he groans, then his cock swells, pulsing rhythmic waves of release inside me, leaving me warm and achy.

"Goddamn it," he curses, his cum rippling through me in waves as his cock continues to erupt deep inside, flooding me in places no one has. He's the first to take me bare.

I clench around him again in an orgasmic second coming, literally. He wraps his arms around me, holding me as tightly to him as possible as his hips hammer between my spread legs, making me come a trembling, lip-biting second time.

When my body unclenches and he slides out of me, he's promptly between my thighs, my clit between his lips. He sucks and he licks, his tongue teasing and drawing out yet another orgasm. My core exhausted from clenching and my cunt sore from the same, I find myself begging.

And holy shit is it hot.

"Please Daddy, no more," I moan, and he lifts off, pulling my panties up my hips.

"Only because we have somewhere to go," he says. Tonight, we're doing the *friends are my family and I met your family so here are my friends which are really my family* dinner and I really want it to go well.

He grins as he slides his belt beneath the loop. "But otherwise, there are no breaks for that pussy now that it's mine." He shakes his head at me once I'm fully dressed, adjusting his crotch crudely, because he knows I fucking love it.

"Goddamn, Vienna, you're so beautiful. Honestly. I can't even believe I tricked you into being my girl."

I wink. "You hypnotized me with your monster dick."

And as we discuss everything under the sun except my broken bust and the cunt of the century, Madeline, we head to dinner. Darren and Samson get to their feet as the waiter guides us to their table with an arm extended.

"You assholes don't get up for me," I say, plopping down into the booth next to Samson who holds his tie to his chest with one hand, extending the other over the table to Tucker.

"Samson, nice to meet you Tucker." Samson nods hello to me.

"Nice to meet you too, Samson." He turns to face Darren, and they exchange a friendly handshake. "You too, Darren. Great to put a face to a name. I've heard a lot about you."

Darren smiles. "We've heard the same." He presses the back of his hand to one side of his mouth, a faux attempt to block his words from me, pointing them instead to Tuck. "We will not talk about the bust but I heard and it's devastating. It was an absolute piece of art, no question."

I roll my eyes. "I can hear you. And there's nothing to talk about. I'll pass the class with nothing turned in. Because I guess, when you think about it, it's all meaningless anyway. Submit a piece to pass the class. Have nothing to submit and still pass the class. I could've been doing something else for a year. A degree from the Institute doesn't even earn me a job in my field," I seethe, overcome with frustration with my situation. With anger that my project got destroyed and no one outside this group will ever see something I was so proud of.

At the crux this is the battle I feel I have been having with myself for years. The endless quest to prove my talents to my professors, my peers, my parents and myself.

What was the point?

Is there one? I know that was my best piece. Tucker knows. Darren knows. Is that all that matters? Yes.

All the self realization under the sun doesn't stop me being raging mad about it though.

The waitress comes, and she moves in a square around our table, veering from person to person to collect orders. When she leaves, our conversation veers to films, and actors, favorite tourist spots along the coast, our various experiences with the Alcatraz tour, followed with music and hobbies.

Tucker drops his card for the check and Samson, after whiskeys, doesn't have it in him to argue. As we wait for the waitress to return, Darren makes a final toast in my honor. We raise what's left in our glasses, and they clatter together.

"To Vienna on becoming a millionaire!" Tucker chants, clinking his glass to Darren's, then Samson's and mine at the same time.

I take a sip and giggle, the alcohol making laughter easy. "Well, not really a millionaire. More like a *one hundred thousand-aire*, if that's a thing."

Samson's brow furrows and he casts a sideways glance at

Darren, who focuses on his drink. Tucker reaches across the table and takes my wrist in his palm, stroking his thumb along my throbbing pulse.

He watches his thumb a moment, collecting his thoughts before his green eyes meet mine, snatching my breath away. Stealing some of my rational thought, too. "Vienna, when I signed my contract, I set it up so that half of my royalties were to go directly to the artist and creator." His eye flick between mine as his words flutter through me, taking a long moment to fully settle. "It won't be immediate, but by the time the line is established with all models on the market, it will be true."

"What?"

His thumb runs soothing circles, and my pulse melts a little, the edge dropping off, the urgency waning. "A quarter of the profits the Fuck Tuck line earns, goes directly to you."

I swallow hard, my voice meek. "It's projected to make ten million in the next five years across the whole line."

He grins. "We'll both be millionaires then."

Obviously I crush my mouth to his, hands clutching his cheeks as if we don't have an audience of friends across from us. "I can't believe you did that for me."

He shrugs. "It's just money."

I roll my eyes. "Says the guy with money."

He tips his forehead into mine. "Hey, you have money now, too."

I shake my head in disbelief. "I cannot believe you."

He leans in. "You can thank me later."

I smile, and give him my very best *yes Daddy* eyes.

26

Tucker

But you're gonna stay quiet, so only I know, aren't you?

"Can you believe that?" I growl into the phone as at the other end of the line my dad struggles, dragging his and Mom's suitcase behind him through the airport while simultaneously suppressing his outrage.

"That's unreal," he echoes, mad because I'm mad, but also pissed for Vienna. In a span of just a few days, the Eliot clan has opened their hearts and arms to Vienna, and she's run into all of them willingly. "So what's going to happen to her?"

"Vienna or Madeline?" I ask, after having explained the entire broken bust situation to him. Vienna is sound asleep next to me, and I haven't been able to turn my mind off since the incredibly bullshit news yesterday.

After we spent the entire night together at her place, we woke up together. Her apartment is small and somehow, even her bed felt small despite the fact it's bigger than the bed we fucked on set in. The blinds in her room don't block the cruel morning sun, so we awoke groaning and blinking, too.

But I woke with Vienna nestled to my chest, the sight of her glasses neatly on the nightstand making my dick hard. Even though the night before was heartbreaking to endure—watching my beautiful girl crumble—I'm so glad I'm here for her.

I want to fix what happened, but aside from a tube of Gorilla Glue and some really bad pasting skills I acquired in first grade, I don't know what I can really do. The first thing I did was take her back to my house, away from Madeline. And now, she's taking a much needed nap. Which gave me time to ask for help with that situation.

That's why I called my dad. He's great with advice, and even if he doesn't have any of that for this situation, I know he'll make me feel better. And by proxy, when she wakes up, maybe I can make Vienna feel better, too.

"Vienna," he says after relaying the gate direction to my mom and sister on the other end.

I stroke a hand through my sleep-tousled hair, and quietly get to my feet, padding through the apartment until I'm clear on the other side. I didn't close the bedroom door; there's something gratifying about talking to my dad on the phone while I watch Vienna sleep in my bed. It feels a lot like having it all.

"I don't know, Dad. I want to help. I want to fix this for her but it's not something I can fix. It's not something I can pay to get her out of. I feel so fucking helpless," I admit.

"Tucker Eliot, you're in love," he says. And I can hear the grin on his face.

I watch Vienna stir beneath the sheets, twisting and groaning before clutching my pillow to her chest and promptly falling back asleep. "What makes you say that?"

"When her pain hurts you, that's love," Dad says easily. "And you, my son, are in love." He pauses. "You disagree?"

I let out a controlled chuckle. "No, I don't disagree."

"Son," he says, the single word marking the moment.

"I officially made her my girlfriend the day you guys left," I tell him, though I'm sure they expected this announcement. After all, Vienna is the first woman I've had meet my family. She's the first woman to spend time with my family without me there, too. "And hey, I showed her the sketch, the one I kept from that first art class."

Dad laughs. "I take it she didn't think it was weird."

I laugh, too. "Luckily not. I told her how I found that sketch and then was propositioned by Augustus and taking his offer felt like fate. Because of her."

He lets out a low whistle. "I still can't believe you got her to do the line for Debauchery."

"Hey," I say, sitting on the arm of my couch, staring into the foggy San Francisco morning hovering outside. "There's something I wanted to tell you. Well, you and mom but I'll tell you and you can relay."

"What's up?" He asks, and in the background, I can hear him sink into a seat. "Yeah, hon, I'll wait here, go ahead and check us in," he says to my mom who needs to check in immediately despite the fact they have a few hours before their flight leaves. Since they just came to visit me, they're now headed to see Tripp, my younger brother who works on a cruise ship. He's docked at Catalina Island, so there they go.

"The deal with Debauchery. They take fifty percent of all the sales, and I take the other fifty. From my end, I've signed half of my earnings over to Vienna, as the artist and creator. And it's not because I'm in love with her. It's because she earned it. She worked way harder on this project than I did.

323

And even if she dumps me tomorrow, I won't regret her getting her share, fair and square."

"I think that's an incredible thing you've done," Dad says immediately, his words validating my choice, despite the fact that I never second-guessed it. Vienna made the cock, all I did was stare at her to keep it hard. She deserves that money, and Lord knows she needs it.

"I just want it to be fair," I admit, because I get paid an unreasonable amount of money as it is, and if I can't share it, I often don't even want it.

"Oh, mom's coming back, she looks peeved, I better hop off the call before we both get in trouble," he says, then adds, "I think you did a great thing and I'm happy to hear about you and Vienna. I'll pass the word to mom. Love you son. We'll call you later."

"Love you guys, too. Talk soon. Fly safe."

"Are you sure Augustus won't mind me watching today?" Vienna says as her fingers work artfully, leaving her silken hair lumped in a braid. She clips the belt at her waist. I'm driving her car, since mine was left at the Institute and I've been so lost in Vienna that collecting it hasn't been an immediate need.

Nothing is an immediate need anymore. Just being with Vienna, making her smile and making her come.

"Aug won't mind." I clear my throat and turn the wheel, my foot tight on the break as a pack of pedestrians stream through the crosswalk, despite the flickering DO NOT WALK light. "He's seen your sketch, by the way. He knew that sketch was the driving force behind me saying yes to him."

She blinks at me. "Really?" I can see nerves brewing, because in the time she's been working with us, Vienna has come to respect Aug for what he's built with Crave, normalizing real sex in the adult film industry.

"He loved it, and he loved the ambiguity of it, too," I reply, putting her worries at ease. "Aug is the one who encouraged me to tell Dalton Fitzgerald that I wanted my own artist."

"That's honestly really flattering," she says, cheeks flushing as she directs her shy gaze to the street outside.

"You're talented, Vienna, and I feel like taking the life modeling gig changed my life. And not because Aug was there. But because you were."

She twists to face me, eyes wet. I lean over the console and place a soft kiss against her full lips, enjoying the tenderness between us until the car behind us lays on the horn, and I'm torn back to reality.

"Oops," she giggles, waving back to the car behind us.

A block from Crave, I motion to my backpack on the floorboard. I usually bring a change of clothes, a phone charger, a random assortment of shit when we're shooting ads. Craft services isn't always there, as ad shoots are lower staffed, so coming prepared is a must.

I brought something for Vienna, too.

"In my bag, there's a small black pouch. It's for you, for during the shoot."

With a skeptical glance my way, her hands disappear into my old backpack, searching for a moment as the end of her braid drags against the seat. Finally, she produces the black velvet bag with the large cursive D on the front.

"Debauchery?" she questions, her brow arching suspiciously. "This is too small to be Fuck Tuck related," she ponders, feeling around the bag, trying to identify the toy inside.

"It's not a Fuck Tuck," I tell her as I slide into a parking spot and throw the car into park. Slowly she tugs the gold trimmed bag open and into her lap falls the toy.

She pinches it, holding it up for us both to see.

"I see," she draws out, rotating the toy for us both to see. She looks to her lap where the matching remote rests. I snatch it from her and grin.

"It's supposed to massage your clit and g-spot," I tell her of the u-shaped toy, "Debauchery's current top seller for couples."

"I've always wanted one of these."

"Good. I want you to wear that while I film promos, and I want you right up on the edge of the set, watching." I grind my teeth, getting hard at the thought of Vienna with that toy vibrating inside her tight pussy, edging herself as she watches me with Dallas, Otis, Maxi and Maya.

Her mouth falls open, and she nudges her glasses up her nose as she blinks at me in a mix of trepidation and excitement. "Really?"

Goddamn I know I shouldn't but every time she nudges those frames up her nose, I get a dirty librarian fantasy going in my head. Fucking her while she reads me a naughty book in a tiny skirt, silky hair twisted into a bun.

I shrug. "Of course. You like watching. You're my girl. Let's make it fun."

She closes her palm around the toy, beaming at me. "Want me to sneak in and put it in, you know, in the restroom?"

I pull the keys out of the ignition and enjoy the soft graze of her calves against my forearm as I reach over and take my bag. Tossing the keys inside, I smile at her. "Baby girl, I'm eating your pussy in the bathroom and putting that toy in myself.

Then I'll be hard for the shoot. Two birds, one stone, you know."

And within two minutes, we've said quick good mornings to Cohen and Lance, who largely ignores us, and we're locked in the bathroom, a bottle of lube in her hands.

"It's kind of handy there's lube in the bathroom," Vienna notices aloud, making me grin.

"We are in a porn studio, so there's lube like every five feet."

She takes the velvet bag from her pocket and plucks the toy from inside. Holding it between us, she steps apart, and pins me with a sultry smile that has my lower half alive.

"Before you put it in, tell me about the promo scenes for Fuck Tuck." Her eyes flick between mine nervously and I notice she's chewing the inside of her cheek.

I drop to a crouch and slide my hands up her dress, her yellow and white sundress. I'm so used to getting hard for Vienna in work clothes with a messy bun that I'm not used to having access to her pussy this way. But I could get very fucking used to it.

Tugging her panties down at the hips, I leave them banded around her thighs as I lift the front of her dress, taking my first peek at everything that is mine.

I press a kiss to her lips before pulling back and taking the toy from her hand. Coated in lube, I slip the toy between her legs, sinking it in slowly. "First, it'll be Dallas and Otis and myself."

She blinks down at me, eyes fighting to stay on me as I sink more of the toy into her cunt. I hold my thumb on the sensor, bringing it to life as I settle it deep inside her. She shifts on her feet but does her best to hold still as the vibrator caresses her. I lick over her clit as I apply more pressure to the toy with my hand.

"Dallas and Otis will be playing with Fuck Tuck together,

and then I'll come in, and they'll have fun with us both. The real Tucker and the Fuck Tuck."

She bites her bottom lip, a tremble rippling through her legs as one hand splays against the tiled bathroom wall. "Do you like thinking of that? Do you like thinking of Daddy getting his cock sucked by two other big, burly guys?" I slide a fingertip through her lips, over the toy, and up to her clit, collecting her pleasure. "You feel like you like it, baby girl, so tell me, how much do you like it?"

"So much," she breathes as I reach into my pocket and retrieve the remote for the toy, kicking the vibration into a rhythm of fast, fast, slow. She jolts as the toy dances inside of her, then slumps as it finally slows. I kiss her inner thighs and then trace her clit with the tip of my tongue again, unable to hold back the growl that's been lodged in my throat since I took her panties down.

"After Dallas and Otis play with me, Maya and Maxi are going to share me, and Fuck Tuck." The toy veers into high speed territory, and Vienna's glasses slip to the end of her nose as she moans, lips a thin line of desperate restraint.

"*Ohmygod,*" she breathes, "Tucker, wait, wait, wait, wait," she warns, nipples poking through the linen sundress as she buckles forward, the toy too powerful to keep her on her feet.

I catch her and hold her close to me a second, letting her regroup as the toy downshifts. "Don't come yet, baby girl," I whisper into her ear before bending to pull her panties back up. A slap to her pussy over her panties and the toy has her hissing in a breath, gripping the bathroom walls.

"*Ohmygod,* this thing is powerful," she moans as I smooth my fingers down her braid. Placing a kiss on her lips, I pull back and slide the remote in my pocket.

"I'm scheduled to come with Maya and Maxi," I drive my mouth into hers, kissing her aggressively so I can take her with me into the scene. "Dallas and O are coming, but they want me coming last. In case you wanted to come with me?" I brush my lips over hers as I cup her pussy over her dress, getting hard from the residual vibrations moving through my fingers. "Come with me, baby girl? Hold that perfect orgasm deep in your belly," I run the backs of my knuckles along her belly. "And wait for me. Wait and come with me, baby. Can you do that? Can you wait and come with me?"

She nods and I pull away from her, and then we stand in front of one another, chests heaving. Her gaze sinks to my crotch, and a growl emerges from deep in my veins because Vienna wanting me is my breath, it's what's keeping me on the tracks; she is everything.

"Wait," she asks, reaching out a little as if to hold me there. I'd stand in here forever if she wanted to. "Will anyone know that I'm... you know," she trails off, but I know what she's asking.

"They'll know what you want them to know," I tell her, taking another step back because I have to. I have to go and film in mere minutes and being this close to her is too dangerous. One more minute and I'll be backing her into the wall, pulling that toy out with my teeth and fucking her just the way she wants.

"But you're gonna stay quiet, so only I know, aren't you?"

"Yes Daddy." She nods as she licks her lips, smoothing her palms down her sundress. Her gaze drops to her dirty white Vans, then back up to me. "I can't wait to watch," she rasps, her eyes cinching up as the toy teases her.

"Me too. See you in a minute."

With that, I head out of the bathroom and straight to the dressing room where Russ and Cam, the traditional fluffers, are sitting across from one another playing a noisy game of Yahtzee.

Russ's eyes drop to my cock then back to Cam as she shakes

out a cup of dice. "He doesn't need us, per the usual," Russ says as he keeps watch on Cam, making sure she doesn't cheat.

"Hi Tuck," Cam calls. "Makeup is coming right back. She popped out for water."

I flop into the chair, my dick angry beneath my pants, and wait to be blotted and plucked before the scene. I stay hard until Augustus smacks the slates, all from thinking about coming with Vienna.

Dallas and O stand toe to toe, stroking their dicks toward one another as the camera loops around them, snagging a full shot. When the camera returns, Aug points to camera two, where it's positioned on Fuck Tuck, my dildo sticking up proudly from the bed behind them.

Entering the set, I cast a quick glance at Vienna who's eyes narrowed on me through her glasses. I strut across the set completely naked, completely hard, and grab my toy, joining their circle. An aerial camera takes the next shot completely zoomed in, nothing but big cocks and big hands stroking them. And when the camera pans up, Otis has a hand wrapped around me, Dallas is jerking Otis and Fuck Tuck, and I'm gripping Dallas. We take long, slow strokes, the air heavy with masculine grunts and pleased groans. This particular shot is designed to show that the length and girth of Tuck is like the real Tuck, and after several minutes of stroking together, Aug calls cut on the shot.

Dallas lifts Fuck Tuck between us, shaking his head. "Damn man, this is gorgeous. They really made it just like you."

I smile, dipping my body to the side to give way to Vienna, visible ten feet behind me. "My girlfriend was the artist," I tell Dallas and Otis, and I watch them find her and smile. I love calling her my girlfriend, and my chest rumbles with pride when I look at her. It's an honor to be hers and I wear the badge proudly.

Otis waves. We stand there, holding our real cocks and Dallas the fake one with his, and we chat. Nearby, Aug sets up the next shot.

"She did a great job, man. This thing is solid." Dallas passes it to Otis, who strokes a closed palm down the shaft. "Feels just like you."

I nod. "Right? Debauchery is using a new silicone formula, I think that's why it feels so good."

"Yeah, but the size and shape," Otis says, bringing the massive dildo to his eyes. "Look, she even got that vein you have under here," he beams, tapping the bulging vein simulation on the dildo.

"I know, man, she's so talented. This toy is absolutely going to crush," I say, meaning it, and not from my ego but from my heart. This toy doing well does good things for us both. It may help her see that bust or cock, she's the talent.

Aug steps up, clapping a hand on my neck. "Okay, now we need to show it in use." He looks between O and Dallas, because the *who* of the scene wasn't scripted. Only the actions. Since it's promo, everything is interchangeable based on who wants to earn the promo bonus. Otis and Dallas signed up first, and since we work together often, I was glad to do it with them.

Dallas leans toward Otis. "Dude, am I bottoming for you tomorrow? If I am, you should take Tucker today."

Aug reaches back where Lance is, and passes him the iPad. Flipping through the calendar, Aug nods. "Tomorrow you bottom for O twice. We're shooting that hockey movie, remember?"

Otis and Dallas nod. "I am so excited about that one," Otis groans with pleasure. "I fucking love sports flicks.

"Same," Dallas says, the two of them knocking fists.

Aug takes Fuck Tuck from Otis and passes it to Dallas. "Use this, go slow, camera two is just a tight shot of you giving it to O with the toy."

"What about the real Tuck?" Otis asks as he grabs a bottle of lube off the ground, near the set, and fills his palms. He reaches behind him, and we all know exactly what he's doing, but it's the adult film business, so plans continue as Otis fills his ass with lube.

"I think we'll have him on a chair nearby, stroking. The camera will pan between the two shots, showing the real girth and length of Tucker jacking off, and the toy, filling Otis. A comparison of the real to the fake, showing how real it looks and how it feels as good as the real thing."

Otis looks at the cock in Aug's hands then lets out a low whistle. "That thing is fancy. I think it will feel as good as you, Tuck."

I glance at Vienna who is fanning herself with Lance's iPad while he fusses with the camera position on shot one.

"Just a sec, guys," I tell the group as I duck to the edge of the set, opposite Vienna, and dig through my pants pocket to find the remote. Adjusting it, I send Vienna into a tailspin, and when I look back, she can indeed tell I've adjusted the cadence of the toy inside of her.

Crossing her ankles, she hands the iPad to Lance as she drapes a hand along her belly, gripping the back of the director's chair for dear life. Her eyes close a moment before opening, finding me, a tiny, seductive smile twisting her lips. I smile back and drop the remote in my pocket, clambering to my feet to get back to the shoot.

The next time the slates clatter, Otis is bent over the foot of the bed and Dallas is on his knees behind him, slowly pushing Fuck Tuck inside of him. Both men growl something fierce as the large dildo sinks into his willing ass, and at my spot in the pillows, back to the headboard, I begin stroking as the camera rolls on me.

The two cameras work in tandem, getting the exact shots that Aug laid out. I try not to let the husky groans of the two handsome men send me over, because Dallas and Otis are built and gorgeous, and no matter where my heart is, watching them use my toy to play, it's hot as fuck.

Then I look up at Vienna, who's clutching Cohen's arm and I'm not even sure she's aware she's doing it. Cohen, the quiet gentleman that he is, pats her hand and whispers something to her. He scurries off, a moment later producing a chair for Vienna to sink into. With her ankles still crossed, her eyes flit between the toy sliding in and out of Otis's tight ring of muscle, then over to my fists stacked on my cock, twisting and pulling torturously slow.

I'm not supposed to come in this scene. I'm supposed to save it for the scene with the women. They'll film scenes of the stars using the toy without me tomorrow, but for now, I have one goal.

But my eyes keep magnetizing to Vienna, and the way her body writhes in the canvas chair, how she clenches and unclenches the wooden handles, swallowing hard as she takes her glasses off a moment, smoothing her fingers down her braid. Sliding them back on, our gazes lock.

I can't help myself. With the camera on my cock, I mouth 'you control me' and force myself to look away, because if I don't, we'll likely both come.

From the edge of the set, Aug calls cut, and sends Otis and Dallas to the dressing room. Everyone always wants to know if we finish off-set if we're not written to finish on-set, and the answer isn't as exciting as you'd think.

Otis and Dallas will not wander off set and have a crazy fuck session. Otis may excuse himself to the fluff room, and rub one out, and Dallas could do the same. But not together. We always respect the rules and boundaries of Crave. Always.

Lance calls for Maxi and Maya to come on set, and Cohen runs out to adjust pillows and spread a new blanket over the queen sized bed. A moment later, Lance is guiding me to the edge of the bed, yanking me to my feet. "Step," he commands, and I lift my legs one by one, stepping into the harness. Against my groin, the empty ring hangs and a moment later, he's slapping a Fuck Tuck in my hand. "Suit up, the ladies are stacking, you're doing them both."

Stacking is exactly what it sounds like. I roll on a condom then grip my cock and push it down to make room for the big fake cock as I tuck it into the holster with my free hand. Maxi will lay on top of Maya, and I'll fuck her with Fuck Tuck, and I'll fuck Maya with my cock.

We don't do this scene often, as it's not a sex act that comes up naturally. It's actually quite tricky, but not impossible, to get two women off this way at once, but it's meant to showcase the possibilities that come with your purchase of Fuck Tuck.

From the edge of the set, Cohen stands by with the purple VIN flag. I catch his eyes as he waits quietly, always so quiet and polite.

"Dude, I have like, two minutes in me. You won't even need that." My eyes dart to Vienna who is flush, loose pieces of hair free from her braid like she's been running her hands over her head. I smile at her and she returns it, as much as she can.

Hooded eyes, white knuckles, fingers dug into the arm of the chair, I know we're on the same page.

Close.

Goosebumps coat my skin, and I don't want to ruin this shot because if I do, we'll likely stay and redo it. They need at least two full minutes before I can come, this I know is the minimum action shot length. They need that much to be able to splice and make demos and reels.

I cannot look at Vienna again, not until it's orgasm time. Because if I do, I will definitely fuck up.

Lance directs us to our positions while Aug double checks with lighting that we're good to go, and a moment later, we're in the scene.

I push the head of Fuck Tuck into Maxi, and she whimpers at the intrusion. Once the crown is in, I thrust tentatively and find Maya wet and eager, so I steady myself at her opening, and push. Driving my hips forward and back, I fuck both women in very slow, cautious strokes.

Maya whimpers. Maxi moans. With Vienna's eyes searing into me, I try desperately to stave off orgasm, but goddamn. Knowing how she likes to watch me, being able to give her the thing that gets her going all while a toy fills her while she *imagines* me? Not to mention, my cock is in a very warm place and I'm using a replica of my cock to fuck another woman.

It's a high pressure situation.

"Oh god," Maya moans, her tone warning. "I'm gonna," she pants, her voice slipping off a cliff, dwindling in energy. Her head falls back, and her hips shudder before stilling.

My orgasm swells at the base of my spine, putting undeniable pressure on everything below my hips. I wonder if I can even look at her, or if that'll shove me over.

From nearby, Cohen's arm gathers my focus as he waves the purple flag, indicating that I need to orgasm, and so does

Maxi. Maya is currently grinding and wriggling in pleasure, coming in elongated, rhythmic waves. The promo shoot with me is coming to an end, and I'm only contracted a certain amount of on-camera minutes, per our union, so I get things rolling so I can look at Vienna before I blow.

"Come for me, ladies," I coax, knowing verbiage is all up to me. They'll likely dub music over the footage anyway, so what I say now is just for us. Just to take the three of us to the finish line, to push us over the black and white checkered tape.

Camera one pans in on the place where I enter both women, and I take my chances, glancing over at Vienna off set. Maxi moans and Maya reaches around, collecting her friend's ass in her palms, spreading her open. Maxi starts to orgasm, and I watch their shaved pussies clench and tighten around myself and the cock, Maya egging Maxi on. Once they're nothing but fading moans and post-orgasmic bliss, I pull out and take Fuck Tuck from the strap, holding his tip to mine, quickly rolling off and tossing the rubber aside.

Stroking myself, I imagine Vienna holding the toy. I imagine her waiting for me to cover it in cum so she can slide her panties down, position the suction cup on the ground beneath her, then sink down onto it, taking Fuck Tuck and my cum, every single fucking drop, all the way inside of her.

I wager a glance back at her, and I know she's right there, hooded eyes, thick lashes hardly moving behind her frames as she keeps her vision tamped on me.

Release flies over the toy, making Maxi and Maya encourage me in a series of breathy pleas and encouraging praise. And though I'm sharing my orgasm with them, I'm also sharing it with her.

There's a separation between work and life that has always been there, established, respected, and non-negotiable. But finding ways to include Vienna in scenes, even if just on the sideline of the set, feels like the best blurring of those lines. A way to include the woman I love with the thing I love—creating healthy art.

The actors and actresses I work with, they're good at their jobs, just like I am. And they bring me to orgasm. But Vienna.

Vienna makes me weak. Her beauty alters the chemistry in my brain, making me unreasonably selfish and unforgivably needy. And I know undoubtedly that a day on set will not stop me from wanting her with every fiber of my being when I return home to her.

Thinking of returning home to her has me aching and grunting and my orgasm spills out of me along the toy, leaving Fuck Tuck a white hot mess. That's when the slates clatter, and the scene ends. Maya collects a cum towel for me from a prop box nearby, and smiles. "Here you go, good scene. That was hot."

I smile at her, then glance at Vienna as I begin to wipe the cum from the tip of my cock, then the toy.

Deep breaths wrack her chest, making her shoulders sag and chin lift. She came, too, and though she looks sated and pleased, something low in my stomach twitches, and a heated twinge radiates through my arms and legs, making my neck hot and my fingers ache. Having her watch and coming together, it was... incredible.

Today's shoot for Fuck Tuck was great. But my heart was there because of her.

I cross the room toward Vienna, and lean in for a kiss. "I want to take your face in my hands and really plant one on you," I tell her, keeping my voice just for us. "But I haven't washed yet."

She rises from her seat and together we walk to the bathroom, locking the door behind us, I clean up. The fluorescent lights look different now, in post-coital reality. They're bright, and they clear any residual orgasmic high left in my brain. And I'm left with clarity. Clarity and Vienna.

Wrapping her fingers around the hem of her linen dress, she lifts, revealing her panties, complete with a dark strip of cotton over her cunt. "Take it out of me?" she asks, still breathing a little heavy.

With my eyes on her, I fall to a crouch and hook a finger in the crotch of her panties, tugging them aside to reveal the sticky toy. I place my fingers on the device and begin tugging, thoughts elsewhere.

I love my job and I always have. And yet the prospect of shooting tomorrow knowing she won't be on set has my mind working overtime.

Her cunt weeps her release as I hollow her, dropping the toy into her palm as she lowers it down for me.

"Hey," she says as I get to my feet and start the sink. "What's the matter, Tuck?"

I take the toy from her palm and begin washing it, meeting her eyes in the mirror reflection. "We timed that just right," I smile, alluding to the orgasm we shared, trying to veer from the topic in my heart. It's not that I don't want to share with her but this is my career, and so the choice has to be mine and mine alone.

Maybe she sees the hesitation in my eyes, and maybe she doesn't. But either way, she opens the velvet bag for me to drop the toy and remote into, then ties it up.

"Yeah, we really did." She licks her lips as she smooths her hands down my chest, making my arms prick with anticipatory bumps. "That was hot, watching you."

My eyes flick between hers, and I don't see denial of anything, not a single fleck that would leave me to believe she's just saying that for me.

She likes watching me. And that discovery is hot, but also...

terrifying. Because what if I am more sexually monogamous than even I realized, and find performing for Crave without her there to be too emotionally difficult? I'd give it up for her in a heartbeat. Absolutely I would. But... she loves watching, and I think she has no problems with what I do, even if she isn't there to play with me.

That leads me to the hardest question: will she still want me if I can't do it without her? What if I'm just Tucker Eliot, and not Tucker Deep? Vienna isn't shallow, nothing about her says materialistic or small. But she's just discovered her voyeuristic streak. I've had two years to live sexual fantasies through my work. It would be unfair of me to stop her from living hers now that she's aware of it, simply because I'm done exploring.

Am I done exploring? If I am, that must mean that Vienna's the one. I watch her smooth flyaways, double check the tie at the end of her braid, then adjust the fit of her dress.

Knowing I have to answer these questions myself, I pull her into me, letting my palms smooth up and down her back after tossing the toy bag into my open bag.

"Thank you for playing with me today," I whisper, kissing her head, pressing my cheek to her hairline. I've never wanted to hold someone this way, and now I can't imagine life without this kind of embrace.

"Thank you for including me. I know you won't always be able to, so it means a lot to me that you did." She pulls back, and my veins burn with unease. I don't want to talk about it, and I'm afraid she wants nothing but. Then she surprises me, pressing her hands to my chest, staring at her fingers splayed along my bare, tanned skin. "Thanks for indulging me in a little daddy kink, too." She buries her face in her hands against my chest. "I can't believe I like it, but I do."

"You sound like me the first time I was topped. I was so

blown away that I enjoyed it as much as I did," I admit, giving her some insight into the sexual discoveries that took place with me long before she was around. "I realized then that there are a lot of things I probably like, as long as I'm open to it."

She nods, tossing her head to the toy in the bag on the ground. "I know what you mean."

We fuse our hands together by the fingers, and I take Vienna down the hall, past the set, then outside into the cool morning. "Tomorrow's the big day," she says as I link my hands together at the small of her back.

I cock a brow. I know what day she's referencing. It's her final show day for the Institute. The day I've been trying to take her attention off of the last two days. "You know what you're gonna do?"

She shakes her head, sadness pulling her expression to the ground. "I'm going to go and just stand there, and explain to my professor that I showed up despite everything, and hope that earns me his respect at least."

"I fucking hate that for you, Vienna," I groan, wishing more than anything I could fix this for her. My dad's words rush over me, and I pull her tighter to me in response.

I am in love with Vienna, and therefore, I have two glaring issues to solve.

And not a lot of time to figure them out.

"I'm going to go by the museum and see Darren," she says, raising a palm to my cheek, stroking her thumb along my lips then down my chin. "I'm going to take the bust and see if Dahlia is there and what she recommends." She shrugs, and I can see in her eyes there's a massive shortage of hope, and that her expectations are none existent. "I've seen pieces that have been mishandled and inadvertently broken so I know not to expect much. But still. I'm gonna try."

"You should." I kiss her temple, then swipe my lips across

hers, suddenly eager to tend to my problems, anxious to move past them and be in the end phase.

The *happy with Vienna* portion of life.

"Call me when you're done," I say to her as she walks backward toward her car.

"I will," she smiles and watching her drive away leaves me feeling renewed.

I take my phone from my pocket and call my dad, an idea hitting me the moment she left. I just need help figuring out if the idea is indeed good or if my love goggles have me fucking confused, and I'm about to do something stupid and risky thinking it's brilliant, because love and all.

"Hey Dad, sorry to bug you on your route," I say as my dad answers with an out-of-breath hello.

"No worries, what's up?" he asks, and in the background I hear the metal door of a large mailbox seal shut, the undeniable twist of a copper key in the lock. "Everything okay? Did Vienna get her bust fixed?"

"That's why I'm calling. I had an idea, because she can't fix the bust. She's gonna try but it's pretty demolished. But I had an idea and I don't know if it's really dumb or actually brilliant. I was wondering if I could get your opinion?"

Then I pace the parking lot, giving my dad all the details of my plan.

27

Vienna

The most glorious, girthy, beautiful dick I've ever seen.

"How long will you stay at this place with Madeline?" Darren asks as he flops down on the edge of my bed.

I tuck my blouse into my black pencil skirt, turn sideways to analyze my profile, then untuck the blouse with a sigh. "I don't know. The lease is up a month from now, and I have no plans to renew with her after the bust incident."

"Not to play Devil's advocate-" Darren starts, but I stop him.

"Then don't. Because I don't need camera footage to know she did it, Darren, okay? So don't. Not today, on the day where I'm presenting nothing to my professor."

He stacks his fist under his head, a guilty twist in his lips. "You're right. I'm sorry. I guess I was trying to make you feel better if you did have to keep living with her."

"I'll find something," I assure him, though I've already started poking around listings in the city and unless I want to share a twin bed in a studio with six strangers, it's not looking good. "Or I can couch surf with you and Samson?" I tease.

He ducks his head to his shoulder with nonchalance. "You wouldn't have to couch surf. We have a two bedroom."

I twist my hair into a fancy thingy, having temporarily given up on the blouse. But even my hair won't do that fancy thing it usually does with ease.

"Just wear it down," Darren says as he watches me struggle with literally everything, "and take a breath." He reaches to the side of the bed and produces a bottle of Veuve Clicquot. "Better yet, take a drink."

I spin to face him, blinking in awe at the bottle. "You got me that?" I press my hands to my chest. "That's really expensive Darren."

He looks at the orange label then back to me with a grin. "You're worth it. You only graduate from a prestigious Art Institute once in your life, right?"

My eyes fill with warmth, and though Darren doesn't usually do sappy, sweet things, we both know exactly why he is now.

He knows *they* won't, and more than that, he's spot on in thinking my parents will not be here today to celebrate with me. And now that my bust is broken, it's probably a good thing.

"Thank you," I whisper as he pops the cork, making us both wince a little. With two red party cups, he pours champagne while holding my eyes.

"You deserve to celebrate, Vienna. Bust or not, you made it through. You wanted this and now it's yours. Under your belt. On your resume. Done."

I nod, wrapping my hand around one of the Solo cups, taking a long swig of over agitated champagne. It tastes glorious;

accomplishment and freedom. I'm done with school, soon I'll be done with Madeline, and thanks to Tucker I'm done with debt and have a steady income and financial freedom to pursue... something.

Life is finally a clean slate, perched on that slate with a toothy grin that stops my heart and a huge cock that makes me moan, is my gorgeous boyfriend.

What a transformative few months I've had.

As we press plastic cups together in toast, my phone rings. Darren snatches it from the center of the mattress and passes it to me. "Loverboy calling."

I roll my eyes, but my chest jolts at the teasing nickname. He is my loverboy, as Dirty Dancing as the title is, it's true.

"Hey Tuck," I answer, wanting to use a more affectionate term but feeling a bit self conscious with an audience.

"Hey, you almost ready?" He asks because that's right, my boyfriend is picking me up and taking me to my very last artless art show for school. There's no walking graduation ceremony at the Institute, so this is it. The sayonara to school night. And although my parents followed up with me to check the date, I never told them because I couldn't face the disappointment either way. Their disappointment in me and my dreams, or my disappointment in them for their savage indifference. So I planned to go alone.

Well that was the plan, if it weren't for Tuck.

I turn to face the mirror. My hair is straight and limp, my blouse is wrinkled from where I've struggled for a neat tuck, and my face is completely bare. "Are you downstairs?" I ask as I snatch my glasses, slide them on, pull my hair into a ponytail and toe into my nicest black pumps.

"Pulling up now. Can I come up and get you?" he asks, sweetness throttling his voice. "I can't wait to see you."

His compliment and sentiment make my cheeks tingle and my stomach light. "I'll be down in one minute, I promise."

I manage to retuck the blouse in a more presentable manner, and roll on some lipstick, giving my face a much needed pop of color. I wanted to look better but I realize as I order Darren around the room to fetch me my blazer and a pair of diamond studs from the box in my closet, that it's not my slightly unkempt look that's bothering me. It's the chaos in the back of my mind. The disappointment of the broken bust, the emptiness of being the parent-less student, the wave of purpose I felt when I started school finally coming to a crashing dissolution.

I don't know what to do or where to go with my life after this, and that feeling has me on edge. Checking my reflection one more time, I know that I look good. I've worn this outfit before, I've worn my hair and lipstick this way many times. I look fine.

But I feel so lost.

"Vienna, remember," Darren speaks softly, grabbing my attention, "If you needed it, you'd have it."

That helps. I take a deep calming breath.

Darren walks me down, waving to Tucker through the windshield, and it feels like my father giving me away at my wedding. Tucker pops out of his SUV, and when I see what he's wearing, I stop mid-sidewalk, frozen in my tracks.

A short-sleeved button up white shirt, the collar pressed and turned down, a few buttons free, exposing a bit of his bare chest. Below he wears fitted black slacks at rest just above his ankles, and some dress shoes that look both fancy and new. His hair is smoothed back, wet looking, without a single ripple of body. A gold chain loops his neck over the exposed skin, and when he smiles, I swear to god the sun picks up the green glint in his gaze, and his eyes fucking sparkle.

He looks down at his feet with humble insecurity, then back up to me, a shy grin on his gorgeous face. I notice now that his jaw is crisply shaven, and from his back he produces a bouquet of what has to be at least a dozen long-stemmed white roses.

"Happy last day of school," he says awkwardly, holding the florals to his chest. "But I'll put them in the backseat for now, so you don't have to run back up."

He comes to the front of the SUV, running his long fingers along the hood in a way that makes my lower half throb. I know what those fingers can do.

Standing in front of his car, he takes me in slowly, studying what feels like every molecule of me. "You look so beautiful, Vienna," he says, his voice low and raspy. Closing the space between us, he's on the sidewalk and I'm in his arms, soaking in the smell of his spicy amber cologne. "I have a surprise for you, too."

I swallow thickly as he leads me into the passenger seat, then leans over me to clip the belt at my hip. His lips find mine as he ducks out, pacing the back of the vehicle until he's in the driver's seat smiling at me over the console.

"I don't need a surprise. You coming with me is enough." I look out the window and pretend to look up at my apartment as some sort of double-check before we leave. I don't want him seeing the emotion already running over the surface. "I really appreciate you coming. I'm embarrassed I have nothing to show, but I know my professor realizes what I'm capable of."

He reaches over and weaves our fingers together, sending a pulsing squeeze through my hand. "Do you? Because the way I see it, bust or not, you're an incredible artist, and I think this last project is more about proving that to yourself before you're out in the world. Your professor is a smart man, he knows what you're capable of."

I look at our joined hands as his words dissolve in my thoughts. And when I think of the shattered bust, when I think of how hard I worked on it and how important it was to me, I come to the conclusion that Tuck is right.

"I thought I was working to impress my parents, to make them proud. But I think I let them get in my head so much over the years that I came here to prove to myself that I'm good, just so I can know for sure, once and for all, that they aren't right about me. That I'm not wasting my life with art."

"Oh Vienna," he murmurs, bringing our joined hands to his lips, dusting my knuckles with slow kisses. He brings our hands to his cheek and presses them there, his eyes holding mine. "You are doing exactly what you're meant to do."

"Thank you," I whisper huskily, trying desperately to stave off the tears. "But I have to admit, I'm feeling lost."

Concern dents his features. "Why?"

"Well," I say, loving how my hand looks fused with his, pressed to his handsome cheek. "I don't know what I'm going to do about my living situation in a month, I don't know what I'm going to do as a career, either. I know I have 3 more castings with Debauchery, but I don't have a plan beyond that." I shrug. "Those aren't small things."

I sigh, and let my head fall against the seat. He smiles and it brings a smile from me. He has that effect, like sunshine crawling over your skin after a chill. It just feels so good.

"We'll get through them," he says simply, kissing our fingers again. I just blink at him, because being *we'd* so casually by him, as if it's no question that from here on out it's me and Tuck against the world. "We can get through anything together," he says quietly, his voice drifting a little, his eyes going to the dash. "We should get over there, yeah?"

I nod, and try to shake off the vibe that maybe Tucker didn't want to talk about those things right now. He wasn't avoiding the hard talks about my life, rather, trying to get me to my show on time. That's all.

I watch the street whip by as he drives us there, telling me about the shoot today with Chanel as we go. It sounds hot, it sounds fun, but I can't get in the spirit because I'm so nervous about getting tonight over with.

Showing up to my final show without a piece is like the nightmare you have as a kid about showing up naked. It's just as humiliating, I swear. And to know I'll be standing next to Madeline and her stupid whatever sculpture, with her stupid supportive, overindulgent parents at her side. I look over at Tuck, and it's an instant and much needed reminder that I am lucky. That right now, I'm focusing on the negative when I should be staring down the positive. The positive right next to me in this fancy SUV.

He's brought me so much and I am extremely grateful. And lucky. And honored. I'm so many things.

And right now, all I want to do is add *Art Institute graduate* to the list.

Tucker walks me inside, his hand resting protectively on my lower back. Every woman we pass turns to check him out, and all he does is keep his eyes forward and his hand in mine, and I've never felt so good.

Inside the building, people are leaking from open doors, bleeding into hallways, and we find ourselves shimmying through. There are more people here than I anticipated, and it brings me even more sorrow now that my bust is broken.

Tucker stops me right outside the door to the part of the gallery where the pieces were transported. Not mine of course, but everyone else. "Do you remember that I said I had a surprise?"

I swallow hard, so nervous already that I'm not sure what I can handle at this point. "Yeah," I say, my voice a little wobbly. "We can wait until after," I offer, heat rising up my neck as my anxiety bubbles up in my lungs, seizing my breath. He rubs the hand not holding mine down my arm, then cups my cheek. "Relax, baby girl," he whispers, and those two words soothe me like warm tea or a strong hug. He has that way.

I nod, and fidget with my glasses. "You didn't have to get me anything."

"I didn't," he says, peering into the gallery a second then returning his gaze to me. "I just transported it here for a surprise, but what I brought isn't actually anything from me." He looks nervous, his green eyes darting between mine, pulse visibly thudding in his throat. "If you don't want to do this, we don't have to, but I brought something here for your show, if you want it."

I'm thoroughly confused as Tucker yanks open the door, drags me through the gallery to the back corner, and opens the private staging area in the gallery. "Tuck, we can't go in there," I tell him, knowing how museum and gallery curators are about their private spaces.

But he pulls me inside and flips on the light after the door is closed. "I have permission." He clears his throat. "Augustus pulled some strings."

"Aug? For what?" I look around the space, thoroughly confused. "What's going on?"

He steps toward a long rolling cart that is covered by a thin sheet. Turning back, one green eye on me, he says, "Let me walk you through my thought process."

With one strong tug, the sheet is drifting to the cement floor. Atop the cart are all the cocks I cast for Crave. Every single one. Even the first one that looks more like an oversized finger than anything else, as at that point I didn't realize the temperature in which the mixture was formed also had bearing on it's long term sustainability when subjected to chemicals, such as soaps and cleaners.

I've never seen them all side by side, together in this way, like a garden of cocks. But I step forward, toward them, and hover over the tops, letting myself recall the day I cast each one.

I point to one that is crooked, and how I dropped that casting on the floor when Tucker told me he doesn't like maple syrup. "That's the one I dropped the day you told me you're insane," I point at it, reaching forward to tap my fingertip on the misshapen head.

"Maple syrup is too sweet," he says from behind me, and I can hear the grin in his voice. I point at another cock, this one from the midpoint where the silicone was getting close but the details were underwhelming. "The Slick Dicks week," I recall of the virtually veinless toys.

From behind me, Tucker laughs. "Yeah, those are them."

I step back and take his hand, still staring at the tray of cocks. "It's fun seeing all of these now, because they remind me that the best thing ever happened, and that's that *you found me*." I turn and face him, and in the best movie moment ever, we share a long kiss. He fills my mouth with moans, and I swallow them eagerly, filling my belly with pleasure and comfort.

"I agree," he pants once he peels away, neither of us eager to let go. I've never had that feeling, either. "But the reason I brought them is because they also represent the evolution of understanding a medium in art."

He steps toward the tray of dicks and motions over the top of them, from the starting side all the way to the finished product, the one they based the first 50,000 Fuck Tucks on. "Even with a blueprint and gameplan, art requires focus and dedication." He lifts Fuck Tuck from the tray and turns it over in his hands. "Look at all this detail. This looks exactly like my cock,

Vienna." He sets it down. "And that's where the talent of being an artist comes in. It's all of those things to be a successful artist, and your evolution at Crave & Cure has proven that very thing."

He comes to me, taking my hands, holding my eyes with his. "This can be your final submission, if you want it to be. And if you don't, I'll have them sent back to Debauchery."

"I can't believe they let you take them," I whisper, surprised that Dalton Fitzgerald would part with his potential money farm. "Dalton wanted to use those for casting less high quality dildos for his sister company."

Tucker smiles, holding his lips together with intention. "So there's something else, too."

I genuinely have no idea. "What?"

He kisses me. "I think Dalton will want these back, at least until he talks to you himself on Monday."

"I don't have a meeting with Dalton on Monday," I reply, knowing I'd remember something of that magnitude. I have no meetings with anyone other than Netflix and hopefully Tuck's cock.

Maybe some Daddy kink.

He strokes the backs of his rough knuckles up my arms, sending a flood of chills down my spine, everything between my thighs growing warm.

"You do, Vienna. They want to bring you on. Make you the head of research and development, and the first project is a new line, based on the top grossing female film star." He blinks at me slowly, a thick strand of his product-coated hair falling across his forehead. He swipes it back and grins, a rush of excitement flooding my lower half.

"What?"

He nods. "Dalton loves you. He can't believe you made all these. He expected there to be like, five. And have the final product look like one of your mid-point cocks. He was literally blown away."

I sniffle. "It is a great cock."

He laughs, and strokes a thumb along my cheek, dipping his frame a bit to lock his eyes to mine, straight on. What chaos that once tumbled through my veins, nearly rendering me immobile, has evaporated. Simply disappeared. And I feel great. I feel lighter, like I've been freed.

"I can't believe it, they really liked what I did? I thought I was just following the brief, but I wanted so much to do it well. Get it right," I admit, still trying to process the fact that I'm about to be offered a job, right out of fucking art school, the way I always dreamed. "This is literally everything I've always wanted." I pause, and rephrase. "A job out of school was always the goal, I never anticipated it would be making what I assume are going to be pocket pussies–"

"Vienna," Tucker grins, stepping close, his energy brimming with masculinity as he dips his lips to the side of my throat. A hot shiver snakes down my spine and makes my hungry cunt throb. "I like you saying pocket pussy."

I wink. "If you're not bullshitting me, and if you are, by the way, that's super mean," I warn, wagging a finger. He grins, and points his palms my way in surrender.

"I would not joke about this." And I believe him.

"Well then, who do you think is my pocket pussy tester?" I watch his eyes follow my tongue as it slowly drags along my bottom lip. "You, Daddy?"

He groans as the door swings open and Augustus pokes his head in. "Is it a yes on the cocks or no? If I have to take them back now, I want to know." He looks at his watch then rakes his hand through his hair, peppering slightly along the sides. "I have dinner plans."

I consider asking him if it's a date, but I remember that

Tucker told me that Augustus doesn't talk about his personal life. He said it as a warning, and I choose to listen as he glares at me, emotionally tapping his foot.

I look up at Tuck, realizing that even though the metaphor of these cocks is absolutely beautiful and true, they are indeed a tray of cocks.

But my boyfriend, who I am so definitely in love with, is a porn star. Shaming him at this point would be so fucking cruel. So absolutely awful.

In the sliver of exposed galley behind Augustus and the open door, a couple walks by. A Carnegie couple.

"Holy shit," I breathe as my stomach free falls into my asshole, I swear to god it does. "My parents are here."

Tuck's head whips down to face me, surprise angling his eyebrows, his jaw slack. "What? Are you serious?" Next his jaw grows tight in a way that has me a little concerned. He looks protective, and though my pussy seizes and my temples heat, I can't get lost in that right now.

My fucking parents are here.

They came.

They came? Honestly, why?

I swallow hard, and find courage. "This changes nothing." I look at the cocks, then back at Tuck. "Let's show the dicks."

He raises a celebratory fist in the air. "To the dicks!"

Augustus steps in, barely holding back an eye roll, and takes the edge of the table. "Tuck, grab it."

Tucker takes the other side and I grab the door, following them to the exact spot next to Madeline. Her eyes are wide with horror, and I really exercise self control by not laughing hysterically.

First of all, she made a big labia for her first sculpt, then a bigger one for the second, so this 'Celestial Moon' bullshit she's randomly turned up with is utter bullshit.

"Oh look," she brims with happiness when she sees a few horrified faces in the crowd around me. "It's Sausage with her table of Sausages."

"Oh good one, Madeline," I say, smiling just to annoy her. "We thought they would be right at home next to your 'Vagina 2.0' submission but..." I look around theatrically, "I don't see it. You were working on it in the lab the other day — what happened?"

She grits her teeth and growls, "I realized my final piece deserved more *integrity*."

Tucker's smile is toothy and beautiful when he faces her. "But your first piece was, what again?" He drums his fingers over his lips in mock-thought. "Labia, right, babe?"

He blinks down at me, and I nod. God I love this man.

"Right, so I'm thinking you saw V's bust and realized your sculpture needed some more work in order to measure up?" He ponders out loud, shrugging casually. "I mean I'm just guessing, but I'd say that didn't work out for you... I mean, considering you're presenting this and not Labia: The Second Coming. Your moon is..." he tips his head to the side, blinking at her piece from across the room. "Fantastic for something you created in 48 hours. You must be so proud. And it's not like you don't love that moon, right Madeline? It's not like you destroyed Vienna's cast out of blinding jealousy when you were left with this moon thing to present next to it." He looks down at me then back up at Madeline. "You've got too much integrity for that, don't you?"

I place my hand to his chest and turn to Madeline. "I'm sure my bust being destroyed had nothing to do with her," I say to Tucker, looking straight at her. She blinks at me like a deer in the headlights. Integrity, my left tit.

Tucker's likely right. She probably did see the bust and

overwork her own piece to compete, then sculpt that moon instead to have something to present.

Madeline looks at Tuck, then back to me.

She knows I know, I know *she knows* I know. And you know... she's not worth a single extra second of my time anymore.

And that's freeing.

We turn our backs and proceed to arrange the cocks and Madeline stalks off with her tail between her legs. I can't keep the grin off my face as Tucker's elbow rubs mine.

"Vienna," my mother's voice is there, above us, and my smile wilts.

I raise my head, my glasses fogging slightly as my face immediately flashes hot and rosy. I am standing in front of a table of cocks. In front of my parents. With my porn star boyfriend.

But I've paid off my debt, I have a job and a potential career, and a boyfriend. One who has a wonderful family, too. Then there's that tiny detail about how hung he is, and how good he is at reading my body, and making me come. I have to rid myself of the weight of worry. They may disapprove but I disapprove of them. So there.

I mean, I approve of myself more than I need their validation. Something I've come to see in meeting Tucker's lovely family is that not all families are good, and that's okay. It's normal even. What's been wrong was my seeking their approval because I thought I should. I grew up in a world that told me my parents were right.

But the world hadn't met my parents.

They didn't know the Carnegie family.

I've learned through my friendship with Darren and my experience with Tucker... the people who show up for you are the ones that count. It doesn't matter if they have a title. Their love is their validity in your life. They don't need to prove themselves, because they do every day in their continual devotion to you.

It's okay if that's not your parents. You don't have to have a Leave It To Beaver family to be a happy, successful human. You can in fact parent yourself and become whatever you can dream.

On your own.

And you may even fall in love with a hot porn star along the way.

If you're very lucky.

"Hi Mom." Back to reality, and I'm just not prepared to take shit at this point. Madeline ruined my bust. I'm starting to come to terms with the fact I may never come to terms with it. But I have Tucker, and the evolution of art in cock form, and my professor is absolutely loving it. He can't stop whispering and shaking his head, and tugging on Tucker's arm with a sated grin melting across his face.

"Hello Dad."

There is no way this is going to turn into a "we've been wrong all along" moment, because my parents don't admit to being wrong, and for all intents and purposes, the truth is, they can't possibly understand this display that Tuck has put together.

They have no clue that I've been working with Crave, and they are not sex positive people. As it is, when I got my period the summer I turned thirteen, my mother literally told me to read the pamphlet in the tampon box and put a bottle of midol in my nightstand. I learned the rest from Seventeen magazine and my roommate at summer camp. And speaking about our bodies isn't something we ever did, nor do my parents do it either.

Yet here we are. The entire Carnegie family standing side

by side in front of a table of cocks, some misshaped and odd, the others thick and proud, with the head of the table being the most glorious, girthy, beautiful dick I've ever seen.

Or blown.

Or fucked.

And the man who made it happen stands near the table's edge, hands held behind his back, spine straight, waiting for my cue. His eyes hang on mine, moral support in the rafters, and I love him so much for it. For everything, really.

I wouldn't be here if it weren't for him. I might be here, in this physical spot, but I wouldn't have opportunity and love in my hands.

I may have a shitty sculpture of a rotted shopping cart with a man melting into the pavement next to it, money spilling out. And it may have earned me another C, maybe a B-, and my father would likely misunderstand, or even laugh at it.

He isn't laughing now, and the way he's struggling for his eyes not to bulge out of his head, and the way his fists are rage-clenching at his sides, has me smiling.

Because fuck him.

"The evolution of artist talent," I begin, stepping up to the table, my hand splayed out like the Vanna White of dicks.

"Is this why you quit the museum?" A voice drifts over my shoulder and I look into Tuck's eyes to discover him glaring at someone behind me.

Madeline.

But of course. I plaster on a smile and turn to her. She tried to embarrass me in front of Tucker before and it backfired, and what she doesn't know is I no longer worry what my parents will think or say. For Christ's sake, they didn't approve of me working at the museum, so I know I've got nothing to worry about here.

Guaranteed disapproval, so there's nothing Madeline can possibly make worse.

"Yes, Madeline, it is. I was offered the lead artist job with Debauchery to work on a project to create a model of the lead actor at Crave & Cure, an adult film company here in the city. I took the job and worked for months to turn their top performer into a sex toy for millions to enjoy. So yes, I quit sweeping floors at the museum to take a real job, in art, using my skills. And in the process, I paid off all my debt and lined myself up a new job."

"A new job in porn?" she asks, folding her arms over her chest as a satisfied twitch moves through her thin, flat lips.

"Nope," I smile, so glad to knock her down a peg. "Researching and developing more toys." I turn to my parents, completely disregarding Madeline's attempts to destroy me. "Sex toys are a lucrative industry, and high-end lines require skilled artists." I lift a hand in a motionless wave. "And they want me."

Madeline stands speechless, and my mom's mouth opens but words fail her, so she twists her neck to look up at my father, who still appears to be moments away from blowing a gasket.

I didn't think I'd be thinking the words, *why don't you blow then Daddy* in this context, but again, life is a wild ride.

"Everything okay, Dad?" I ask while turning to face Madeline, brightening my smile to creepy lengths.

My mother turns to Madeline. "Hello Madeline. How are you?" She smiles at my arch enemy, and somehow her kindness to Madeline hurts more than her disapproval of me. She may not know all of the things that Madeline has done to me, but over the last years, I've dropped enough hints.

Caring for my enemy and showing her kindness isn't because my parents practice being kind to everyone. There's no

Coexist sticker on the back of their BMW. It's just another way to hurt me, and quite frankly, as my art professor bobs his head and pulls another professor over to my table, I no longer care.

Caring about people that don't care about me is only holding me back.

"I'm doing well. Nice to finally meet you Mrs. Carnegie," she extends a hand to my mom and shakes, then turns to face my father. He glares at her and doesn't shake her hand, turning to me instead.

"What is this?" he hisses, tempering his voice in that way life-long assholes do, where only you can hear them, but somehow their tone is still frothy with anger and judgment. He's a master of that.

"My final presentation."

My mother leans toward me, and that's the closest we've been in years. "Is this a joke?" she questions, her phony smile still on her lips, eyes darting around the room, making sure she doesn't need to pacify any onlookers

Except with the exception of Madeline and a few others, most of the room is oblivious. Everyone has their own piece to show, with its own story and meaning. And the worries I had about presenting this seem to fall away, and I look across the table at Tucker, because he was right. This was a good idea.

"It's not a joke."

"This is why we didn't fund this venture. It's completely ridiculous. You are so disappointing, Vienna," my father says, letting his head swing in a judgment so heavy, it's meant to blow me back and make me think.

I'm on the cusp of defending myself, of maybe even lashing out, because who the fuck cares at this point. This is my last day here, and my last time seeing them for the foreseeable future.

But Tucker steps between us, weaving our fingers together.

With his palm to mine and our bodies staggered so that he faces them, he nods. "Mr. and Mrs. Carnegie." He doesn't try to shake hands but lifts his free palm in a quick hello. "I'm Tucker Eliot, I am Vienna's boyfriend, and I just want you to know, she's an incredible artist." He turns, opening his body to the room full of artists and hopeful students, professors and museum curators.

"This entire room is full of people who are passionate about art. Vienna is the only one to turn it into a joke," my dad asserts, standing taller, squaring off with Tuck.

Tucker nods. "As your daughter already stated, they are not a joke. They are an expression of evolution through a new medium. These are why Vienna secured a job as head of research and development and lead artist at the top performing adult toy company in the country." He looks at me, pride wafting off in palpable waves. My chest floods with heat, and so do my cheeks. "No one else in this room can say they're walking into a six-figure salary which is in addition to the six-figure contract they already have." He scratches his chest and looks around the room casually before his eyes come to settle on my father.

"Gee, Mr. Carnegie, she may even be making more than *you*, once royalty checks start coming in for her final pieces."

My dad bristles and my mom's eyes widen in horror, completely shocked that Tucker had the audacity to what? Speak the truth? Defend me? Call them on their shit? Give them a taste of their own medicine?

"We're leaving," my father announces, and without so much as another glance, he hooks his arm with my mother's and they leave.

And for once, them walking away from me *feels good*.

I hope one day they can learn to love me as I am, but I'm no longer holding my breath. I'm breathing now and Tucker is my oxygen.

"Your professor wants to have a word with you, but while he does, Aug and I are going to load the dicks up. He'll take them back to Debauchery downtown," Tucker says, rubbing our twined hands with his free one, pressing a kiss to the top of my palm. "Does that sound okay?"

I nod. "Thank you. I don't think you understand how much I value what you did for me here tonight." I rise to my toes and kiss his cheek, the adrenaline of this evening wearing off, leaving me feeling happy but tired.

Madeline still stands before me, smug grin on her face having witnessed my parents essentially disown me.

"Oh Sausage, you're alway good for entertainment," she sneers.

I turn to her with a dry smile. "You know, Madeline, I might owe you an apology. I thought your first piece was so... trashy." I glance at my casts. "But there's art in everything. And working on these was so creatively satisfying." And then in a whisper meant just for her, I say, "Not as satisfying as the real thing obviously. What did you think about the likeness?"

"What are you talking about, Sausage?"

"Well, you spent an entire semester in sketch class drooling over and drawing my boyfriend's dick. Gorgeous isn't it? And since you've seen the real thing, you know how close the toy is. What a good job I did." I barely keep a straight face when I add, "As well as I did, nothing is like being with the real Tuck. But you'll have to take my word for it."

Fire in her eyes, Madeline storms off.

I watch Tucker and Aug carry the table back into the private room then have a twenty minute conversation with my professor on all the processes around the cock casting. He wasn't as interested in the actual cock function at the prototype stage—understandably—but he was very interested in the tweaks I made along the way. About the growth and adapting I did while learning something new.

We shook hands, and I earned a top grade on the project, and left with a promise for a letter of recommendation, should I need one. He called me sharp, he told me I was brilliant, and said he appreciated the leap of faith I took in showing up without my original bust.

When I wander out into the hall and call Tucker, I hear his phone ringing somewhere around me. Turning, I find him at the very back of the corridor, next to the steps, arms behind his back, a smile on his face.

The people in the hall disappear around me as my eyes lock on him. Making my way toward him, my heels clicking against the tile floor, I want nothing more than to go back to his apartment with him and celebrate everything about tonight.

"Again, thank you," I whisper, falling into his open arms when I get to him.

He showed up for me big time tonight and all I want to do is make him feel as good as he makes me feel.

He holds me tight, and I feel his excitement to get home pressed against me. I pull back. "Let's go back to your place."

28

Tucker

You're my girl

I don't know what the hell we talk about on the trip back to my apartment. It's not that I'm not listening to Vienna because I am. It's just... tonight went so fucking well for her, and she's deserved it so much. It's hard to contain my excitement.

And also, I'm kinda lowkey dying to tell my dad how things went. Because he was well aware of my plan tonight, and if I know him, he's probably told the entire family and everyone likely has a vested interest in this.

That's what Vienna needs. And even though tonight was a lot—Madeline; her parents; the courage it took to put the cock farm on display—I want to give her one more thing.

"Vienna," I say as the elevator doors in the apartment open. I usher her in and tap the P for penthouse, and take her by the hips as the doors seal us inside. "Before we celebrate, I have a phone call to make. Okay?"

When the doors open again, we saunter into the apartment.

Kicking off her heels, she smiles, raising to her toes to kiss the corner of my mouth. "Sure. No problem." Glancing at the wall of windows, the moon and stars gaining visibility in the quickly darkening sky, she wanders toward the sliding door, holding the handle as she glances back at me. "I'll just wait on the balcony."

"No," I tell her, retrieving my phone from my pocket. "I want you to be part of the phone call."

And as she walks to me, leaning against the long bar in my kitchen, I hold the ringing phone out for her to see. Before she can even read the name, they answer.

Though I called Dad, Mom and Dad answer, both of their faces struggling for real estate on the screen.

"Vienna!" They shout, despite the fact she's technically in the background. I pass the phone to her, and notice that behind her frames, her eyes glisten with unshed tears. "Tell us how it went, sweetheart," my mom begs, her voice soft but pleading. And I know Vienna hears her genuine interest, I know she can distinguish between a person asking to *ask* and a person asking to *know*. My parents are wholeheartedly the latter.

"Did you go with Tuck's idea?" Dad adds before Vienna can answer.

She slips her glasses off, placing them on the counter, and doesn't hide that she uses her free hand to blot beneath her eyes.

"I did go with Tuck's idea and my professor was blown away at what I was able to create." She looks over at me, another stray tear slipping down her cheek.

"Oh Vienna, we're so proud of you," Mom continues,

stealing my beautiful girl's focus, which makes me so proud of my family. "Tucker told us what happened to the bust."

Dad takes over. "He texted us the pictures of it. It was absolutely gorgeous, Vienna."

"Better looking than our son!" Mom adds, laughing, then Dad cracks up, too. And their laughter makes Vienna laugh, and I don't think I knew what the warm and fuzzies were until this moment.

Seeing the woman I love being loved by my family.

"Did that witch ever apologize?" Tegan asks, earning a happy little squeal from Vienna. The way she's excited to see and speak with my sister again now has my ribs warm.

"Tegan! I didn't know you were there! How are you?" Vienna brings herself closer to the phone in an adorable attempt to get closer to them. I take a can of LaCroix from the fridge and take the phone from her hand, propping it up so we can stand together and talk to them.

"Good, got bit by a teacup terrier today. Let me tell you, those small cute ones are always the worst behaved. You can't treat a small dog like a baby, it's not good for them!" she rants, squeezing in between our parents at the kitchen table. "How'd it go V? I heard the full story. First, fuck Madeline, what kind of pretentious name is that anyway?"

Vienna snaps her fingers, leaping up and down in my arms, laughing. "Yes! Thank you! I tried to tell Darren that before but he said I was being dumb!"

Tegan shakes her head as she tears into an orange on the other side of the screen. "No, that girl was totally pretentious. We're American, of course a French girl who adventures with other girls is the dream! You don't have to rub it in our faces so much," she leans forward, exacerbated. "Madeline."

Vienna looks at me, eyes brimming over with love. We share a moment, a smile, a look, an exchange of emotion, and I put my hand on the small of her back as she faces my sister again. "Totally. But alas, Madeline didn't have to pay for what she did."

"She pays everyday, just by being herself. She's miserable for disliking someone as lovely as you," my mom says, shoving Tegan out of the way to claim the screen.

The best part of this call is that I didn't put them up to this. I didn't bloat them with ideas that Vienna needs this.

Vienna does need this.

She does deserve it, too.

But they knew that on their own.

"But once in a while," Dad adds, shoving his way back into the screen. "A good dose of karma is nice."

Tegan nods. "I agree."

"Well, so," mom moves on, striving for more positive ground. And I'm glad to be done talking about Madeline anyway. "How do you feel it went?"

Fuck, I didn't even ask her that. Not yet at least.

Vienna smooths her fingers through her dark hair, and my cock twitches. "I am very pleased to be done with school, and I am beyond grateful for what Tucker did for me tonight." She looks up at me in a moment made for a movie, only, not like the kind I make. More like the kind where the wind is always blowing, the weather's always cool, embraces are long, tips of noses are pink, and love is always in the air.

But I fucking love how she looks at me. With sincerity and gratitude, and it makes me proud in ways I've yet to feel.

I know what it's like to be a good son. A good friend. A good actor. The guy who picks up the tab. The guy who loans his car. The guy who hosts the party.

But to be a man who genuinely makes a beautiful, smart, incredible woman better off than she was before? I've never done that. Not truly. Not in this deeply fulfilled way Vienna looks at me.

She looks back to my family. "I'm so glad I got stuck with Tuck. My life is a million times better."

Thankfully Tegan spotted the eyes Vienna sent my way, and with that last comment, she's reaching for the phone. "We're happy, V. So happy. And hopefully Tuck brings you this way soon so we can hang out again. But we should let you go."

Dad leans over and winks. "Have fun celebrating." Very sly Dad, thanks.

Mom waves, Vienna says her goodbyes, and then we proceed to tear the clothes off one another like crazed animals.

My belt tumbles onto the ground with a clink, I kick off my slacks, and my shirt's buttons are skittering off the counter as I tear my shirt open. When I glance up, I realize Vienna is quicker than me.

Completely naked, fingers working through her hair to leave a loose braid behind, she smiles at me. "Take off my glasses," she whispers. And with my cock semi hard between us, I reach out and lift the frames from her face, folding the arms in before gently placing them on the counter.

"Do you like me better with my glasses off?" she asks, finishing the braid as she steps toward me, my cock pressing to her lower belly. She's warm and soft, and all I want to do is lie her down and spread her open. Lose myself in this incredibly gifted woman who showed an entire class of contemporaries a tray of my cocks, because she trusted and believed in me enough.

"No," I tell her honestly. "But you're my beautiful, perfect girl, no matter what you do."

The tip of her tongue peeks out as she wets her lips. "I want you to do whatever you want to me tonight." My hand slides along the soft curve of her hip, skating over her ribcage, my palm cupping her breast. With my thumb, I move over her nipple, back and forth, watching the nub grow tight and needy. "Have me anyway you want me, Tucker," she breathes as I drop my face to her chest, and suck her little breast into my mouth.

She moans, sifting a hand through the air on the back of my head. Her touching is dizzyingly intimate, and so is sucking on her nipple like this. The lights are on. We are sober. Taking her this way after such a momentous night is grounding.

She's who I want.

Forever.

There are so many goddamn things I want from Vienna and her sweet little pussy, but tonight, I don't want to take her body in those ways.

Tonight is still about her, for her.

"Stay here," I say and walk past her through the apartment to my bedroom. A few days ago, Debauchery sent me a promotional box with the first edition Fuck Tuck, and some accessories.

One of those was a strap and holster.

While I'm grabbing the box, I also snag a large bottle of lube.

Returning to her, I groan and reach for myself, giving the OG a tug at the stunning sight before my eyes. Vienna's nipples, stiff peaks of peanut butter, melted perfectly into the best handfuls of breasts I've ever touched or seen. I love that she doesn't shave herself bare, or wax herself into a tiny strip. She trims, and everything about the way she carries herself drives me goddamn insane.

I set the box on the counter between us, and shimmy the lid off, my other hand still parked right on my cock. I stroke, and her eyes follow before drifting lazily over my knotted belly and resting on my eyes.

"You have one?" she asks, her eyes hazy as if she knows we're about to get up to some delightful, freaky shit.

I nod. "I do. And I want you to fuck me with it."

Her mouth falls open and she looks at Tuck, then back to me. "That'll hurt you," she says, her voice practically shaking.

I smile as I stroke myself, taking Tuck from the box. I set him on the counter and run a fist down him. Her eyes hang on the gap between my fingertips and thumb.

"You can take him just fine," I rasp.

"But you're taking him..." she tips her head to the side, and something in my belly tickles me at her adorable response. In a whisper she finishes, "you know, *back there*. I've haven't even taken you there yet!"

With the hand that stroked Tuck, I cup her cheek and lower my lips to hers, taking my time as I sweep my tongue along her lips before diving inside her mouth. "I want you to understand me better," I whisper before stepping back to the box. Collecting the strap, I pass it to her and watch as she steps into it far more easily than I would have imagined.

"Have you done this before?" I ask as I get Tuck ready, squirting lube on his head and shaft. My own cock is heavy and hot, my orgasm already deep in my veins, waiting to be unleashed.

She shakes her head. "No, but I zip line a lot. Same concept for the harness."

Goddamn do I like that answer, too.

Once she's comfortable, I step to her with Tuck in my hands. "Kiss me," I tell her, and she wraps her hands around my neck, breathing a happy sigh against my lips.

"Gladly," she smiles, bringing her mouth to mine in the slowest pleasure possible. Letting a hand roam low between us,

I find her pussy beneath the harness and use my pointer and middle fingers to spread her open. Our kiss falters as she cries out in pleasure, praising my touch.

"Oh god, Tuck, your fingers," she pants before our mouths collide again. I touch her again, making her rock to her toes and tremble against me. And then, I take Tuck and slip him through the ring, using a little muscle to make it happen.

With our foreheads touching, I kiss her and say, "Put your hands on my hips, turn me around, and bend me over the barstools. You can do this baby girl, trust me."

She swallows hard, so hard that my cock throbs from it, and I let free a noise of need. Raw, starved, feral need. A feeling so intense that I'm driven to share things I've never shared.

I have to give these things to her—these peeks into how I work, because I want us to understand each other. And getting close to her feels like the only thing that will sate me.

That and pumping my cum deep inside her perfect cunt, of course.

"Please let me share this with you, Vienna?"

Her slender hands come to my hips and then I'm spun around, a grin on my face as her palm comes down on my lower back.

I peer back at her over my shoulder, loving and hating that I can only see her slightly. "When I have sex with a man, I use my fingers to get him ready," I tell her, my voice husky and low.

Her hand falls from my waist and then her fingers are crawling up the globes of my ass, kneading me softly. I can no longer distinguish what is meant to help her understand me and what is foreplay. Explaining to her how I feel during scenes, how I feel as a bisexual man... those feel imperative. And I want to do it right. I want her to really know me.

"I use two fingers, and I make circles, you know?" I drop the words down my back over my shoulder, as her fingers move in, toward my cinched hole. "Then I slowly start to finger him, to loosen him up and sometimes play with his prostate," I husk, my voice unrecognizably deep. Between my thighs, my cock aches with how hard and heavy it is.

Two fingertips come to my ass and slowly, she works them inside, and at the extremely personal intrusion, I can't help but moan.

Loudly.

And in response, she moans. Breathy and sweet, her moan causes my cock to pulse, arousal dripping from the tip. "Tucker," she breathes, sounding as turned on as I am. Or maybe more.

"Curl your fingers baby girl, that's how you find the prostate," I advise, and then lurch forward letting a wild groan fly from deep in my belly as she strokes over my prostate.

Fuck.

"Okay," I breathe, surprised that she's already making me feel so goddamn good. Ass play usually requires a learning curve, and it's not to say we won't have that. But right now, it just feels like we fit.

"I like to grip the base of my cock and move my head up and down his ass. I tease him a little. I love the contrast of feeling this strong masculine body yielding for me. How does it make you feel, baby girl?"

"Like a fucking queen, Tuck," she gasps, sweeping her other hand down my ass to the tops of my legs, stopping at my thighs that tremble as a result of her probing fingers.

I wait, heart pounding and cock dripping, and then Fuck Tuck is knocking on my door, Vienna's hands gripping my hips tightly. "I push in more assertively when I'm topping a man, because they usually like it."

She starts to ease in slowly, her breaths short, her hesitance not to hurt me thick in the moment. "Vienna, faster," I tell her, and then she sinks Tuck into me all the way, and my own size nearly makes me cough.

"Are you okay?" she asks, stretching her arms out along my back, grabbing at my shoulders.

"Good," I tell her, giving myself a moment to adjust to the massive intrusion. Poor Otis and Dallas. My rings of muscle spasm all around the cock as my body struggles to accept it, but when Vienna pressed a finger to the cock and my ass, tracing where we meet, I open for her. My stomach unclenches and my ass releases, and she begins stroking in and out of me slowly.

"Just like I would, Vienna. Take my cock in your hand. Feel how much you claiming me *ruins* me. And I like to dirty talk; talk dirty to me, baby girl." I share everything I'm thinking, everything I'm feeling. Wanting her to take me, to experience how I feel and how I fuck. I don't think I've ever felt closer to someone.

Her tits press to my back and then she's got my cock in her hand, her little horny moans flanking the back of my ear as she pumps her hips and fist.

"Anyone who gets to have you this way," she breathes, her voice dripping with desire, "is an extremely lucky person." Fuck Tuck still sliding in and out of me as her hips maintain a perfect cadence, Vienna slaps one of my ass cheeks before her hand returns to my cock.

"Do you come for them, Tuck? When you're the top, do you breed them and fill them, the way you fuck and fill me?"

Jesus Christ.

"Vienna," I breathe, the stitching along the leather barstool definitely imprinted on my face at this point. But fucking worth it. My baby girl has a filthy fucking mouth and I can't wait until it's in my ass and all over my cock.

"I come on their backs," I groan as she swipes her finger

over the slit of my cock, smoothing thick precum down my shaft.

"And when you're the bottom," she says, slowing her tight passes of fist over my dick. Her fingernails tease my balls and my spine wobbles. "Do you let him come on your back?"

I consider the question, though thought is getting challenging, the tightening in my stomach getting harder to ignore. "I like to be fucked on my back, and then they come with me on my stomach and chest."

And then it's time to show her what else I like.

"My turn," I whisper, collecting myself so I don't come in her hand.

Understanding, she steps back, and Fuck Tuck slips out of me, and I stand up. I work on the harness, freeing it so she can step out. With our fingers linked, I take her into the bedroom where I lie her on her back in the center of my bed.

The city bleeds into our space, casting shadows into our light, pops of color gliding down the walls as cars drive past. The space feels like us, exciting and beautiful, unique and special.

"When I'm with someone, I usually only have one goal. And that's to make them come." My head swings down and my lips crash into hers. "On set I focus on how it feels. I don't see eyes or make up or clothes. I work through the mechanics of what makes each person come, and I focus on the swell of my cock inside of them. And that's how I come, zoned in on the gripping pulses all around me."

She coasts her palms over my biceps, wrapping her arms over my shoulders. "You think with your cock," she says.

I nod. "That's right." I swallow thickly, find my mouth dry but the words are unstoppably powerful. They forge ahead, despite the fact my stomach has reserves, twisting madly inside me. "And with the person I love, I like to first fuck really slowly, and make sure my mouth has been all over their naked body before we even get to anything else." I lower my mouth to her ear lobe, my voice a husky whisper as I say, "but I'm not sure what my style is yet. You're my first."

I nip her neck, making slow circles along her musky skin with the pad of my tongue. She rakes her fingers through my hair, her legs spreading wide open beneath me.

My mouth maps out a route in sloppy kisses, making Vienna writhe and moan beneath me, making my cock ache. When I reach her nipple, I suck it into my mouth like a greedy, starved man, groaning all around her breast as I suckle and nip. She likes it when I nip, clutching my head closer to her chest as I do.

But I keep moving, staking a new claim on her belly as I suck her velvet skin into my mouth and suck her so hard I leave her purple.

Then I'm at her pussy, sucking her lips onto my tongue, loving her sweet, tangy flavor. She thrusts her cunt into my mouth, her hips jerking up off the bed. Hands deep in my hair, digging into my scalp, she calls out my name.

"Tuck!"

The sweetest thing I've ever fucking heard. I get to my knees between her open thighs and stare down at her wet and ravaged body, her chest heaving, nipples perky from being tongued.

"You look goddamn beautiful."

A wanton smile lifts her lips as thick lashes come together in a sensual gaze. "Show me how you fuck the woman you love," she says, and my skin prickles in waves, leaving sweat sliding down my spine.

I lower my mouth to hers, my energy suddenly growing serious. Guiding my cock to her open pussy, I tip my hips forward and slide inside, growing achingly hard to the hiss of approval she gives when I'm fully seated.

"Oh god, Tuck, I'm so full." She reaches between us and presses a hand to her flat lower belly. "I can feel you up here," she moans, wiggling her cunt against my cock, begging for more.

That's my girl.

"You like how Daddy fills you up, don't you?" I growl, giving her a taste of my job, a taste of what she likes, in more ways than one.

She nods, eyes rolling back in her head. Ecstasy drips from her limbs as I hammer my cock deeper into her cunt, faster.

"You like that big, fat, deep cock, don't you? Because you're such a good girl." I clench my ass and flex my abs in an attempt to stave off the rolling pressure in my groin.

"Oh god, yes, yes, Daddy," she squirms against me then all of the sudden, her body goes rigid, eyes fluttering as they roll back into her head. "Yes!" she pants, her exhale so loud that my ears ring.

And it's a goddamn rite of passage I'm proud to earn.

Her cunt milks me as she comes in thrashing, wild waves. Her spine rolls, she claws at my arms, pulls at my hair, seals her mouth to my throat. She does everything as she comes on my cock. The most beautiful, intense orgasm I've ever felt.

And I lose it inside of her, buried so deep that I don't even feel the first pump. But I still, clutching her hips, groaning her name, coming violently, erupting deep inside her cunt. Seemingly endless pumps of hot cum filling her slick pussy.

Her hands come to my face, and she brings our mouths together in a dizzying, slow kiss. Her tongue strokes mine slowly, artfully, as her fingertips explore my cheekbones. When she pulls back, her lips are swollen and puffy and the most beautiful thing I've ever seen.

"Thank you," she whispers, her lips tickling mine. "Thank you for helping me understand. Thank you for letting me be part of you," she adds, stroking my cheek in a way that makes my eyes burn. I blink, because I don't want my eyes to burn like this. Not right now.

Because I've been thinking. And that was the best sex I've ever had, hands down. But Vienna and I need to talk.

I swallow thickly around the fear and nerves stuck in my throat. Fanning my fingers along my thighs, I force out a quick exhale, and set my eyes on hers, through the darkness.

After making love, I cleaned her up and got her dressed in one of my t-shirts, and now we're sitting beneath a blanket on the balcony, the starry sky a gorgeous backdrop to what may be a difficult talk. Not the way to end a wonderful night, but this can't wait any longer.

The moon drips gold along the slope of her nose, spilling down her lips. When she faces me, concern alters her features, filling her forehead with wrinkles and her eyes with worry. I take one of her hands in mine, noticing we fit so well together.

"Vienna, I want to talk to you about us. In the long term."

"Those are the words every girl likes to hear her boyfriend say," she says, a trace of a smile on her lips.

"Well, I know we've only been dating a few weeks but..." I stroke my free hand through my hair then down my neck, squeezing. We've tiptoed around it, but now it's time for no uncertain terms.

"I'm in love with you, and I have to be honest. The last few days at work... with you not there... I've been feeling weird.

And I just... I want to talk about it because if you think you see a future with me, then what I do now isn't just a *me* decision, but something I want to talk about *with you.*"

Finally, with my heart thundering against my ribs, I hazard a glance at her, tearing my eyes from our linked hands.

"You love me," she shudders, like it's a wild surprise or unbelievable feat, and I just want to pull her against me and prove it. She blinks back tears.

I stroke my thumb along the top of her hand slowly and gaze into her wide eyes, like if I wished on every single star up in that sky above, I still couldn't get as lucky as I am now. "I love you so much," I tell her, letting the words curl my lips into a meaningful smile. "That's why I want to talk."

Her lips twitch, her happiness sliding away, shattering silently. "Oh no."

"No," I stop her thought process. "Not an *oh no.* Just... a realistic talk about us. Because I need to know how you feel about us being together while I'm still performing." Our gazes hold, and the noises of the still stirring city fall away, my heart battering in my ears as I wait for her to speak.

"I understand you're not in love with anyone you work with, or even romantically interested, and I also understand that you and everyone else respects Crave and Aug so much that it won't ever be anything but professional performance." She strokes my hand with her thumb now. I need the small, comforting gesture.

"How are you feeling about it?" she inquires, her tone soft, reminding me of being wrapped in a warm blanket when you're shivering. Instant comfort and immediate warmth, and it has me edging nearer to her, shifting us closer beneath the blanket.

With my free hand, I rake a hand up the back of my head, searching for words to explain how I'm feeling.

"I'm confused because... I've done this for two years and I love it. I really do. And I know despite the fact I've been single, a lot of the actors aren't. Some of them are even married. So I know doing what I do while maintaining a healthy relationship can be done. But I have to admit... I'm concerned. I'm concerned that if I quit, regular me wouldn't be enough or that if I don't quit, the novelty of what I do will wear off and one day you'll be resentful that we're in this weird, one-sided open relationship and—"

She raises a palm. "We *aren't* in an open relationship. I'm not allowing you to have other relationships, emotional or physical. You understand that, don't you?"

I nod. "Fuck, of course I do, I wonder if I were in your shoes, would I feel like it's a one-sided open relationship, even though I know logically that it isn't." I squeeze her hand and she squeezes back, her generous smile easing my nerves. "I don't ever want you to resent me for what I do, and I want you to know that I *would* quit Crave for us, if that's what we need."

"If you were unemployed, I'd still feel the same way about you, Tucker. But Crave & Cure loves you, and you love them. This is your deserved, beautiful, fulfilling career, Tuck." She pauses, her head tilting, long dark hair curling beneath her breast. "I want you to do what makes you happy, because that's what I think love is about. But do *you* want to quit Crave? Do *you* want to stop being in adult films?"

Our eyes idle together, thick silence drifting between us, the air heavy with indecision. My answer here matters for me, for us, and for the future.

"I love what I do, but I love you more."

Her lips twist to the side and as she adjusts her frames. "Tucker, do you *want* to work at Crave?"

"Yes."

"Then will you trust and believe me when I say that I fully support that? Will you give me credit and have faith that if I, at any time, start to trend toward disliking it or being uncomfortable with it, that we will have a conversation?"

"Yes."

"And know that I trust you, Tuck. One of the things I love about you is your loyalty and honesty. I see you with your family, I see you with the other actors. And I know *you with me*. You're a good guy. I know that you would never breach my trust at work or anywhere else. I know that's not something I even have to worry about."

"You don't," I say, needing to verbalize what Vienna clearly already realizes. I'd never hurt her, and I'd especially never cheat on her, and I'd never ever muddy waters at work. Separately, all of those things mean too much to me.

"We can do things to feel connected during the day, if you feel like you need to connect to me more," she adds softly, taking my other hand with hers, waffling our fingers together over our knees. "Is that... something you'd like?"

I look at our joined hands again, and in a split second see our lives stretched out before us.

Pieces of unfinished art scattered across a long wooden table being kissed by the sun. The sun that falls through an open window, because our house is all windows, all sunshine, all light. Feet pitter patter up and down the halls, laughter and love vibrating off the walls. There are unwashed dishes stacked in the sink basin and loads of laundry waiting to be folded, much like my house growing up.

But there is so much love. Vienna reaches into a crib, lifting a smiling baby from the bed, clutching him and his wild, dark hair to her chest as she twists to face me in the doorway. I see our entire lives with her hand in mine, and I feel our story with certainty. Our wild past of me acting in adult films, and the storied, colorful circumstances in which we met.

In that perfect, beautiful life, I don't see myself as a porn star. I see myself as a husband, a father and... I don't know what else, but that's the beauty.

Then I look up and see her. *Really* see her, this beautiful artist, this gorgeous human being inside and out, one who has evolved from self-proclaimed close-mindedness, a person who worried about what people thought, to a woman comfortable being loved by a man who makes his living giving his orgasms to other people.

It's incredible. *She's* incredible and her growth is goddamn inspiring.

"I would like it," I say, choosing not to sink in the vulnerability pooling at my feet. Instead, I'm comfortable in it, because it brings me closer to the one person I want to spend forever with. "I would like to include you, feel connected to you throughout my work day, and sometimes that can be just a FaceTime or text. But other times, I want you to play with me. I want to play with you. I want to *include* you."

"I'd like that, too. And I promise to always tell you where I'm at with things. Okay?" She nods encouragingly, and her smile radiates warmth, and the hinges of my jaw ache and my fingers throb. All I want to do is grab her face and kiss her, because how can I be so lucky to find someone to do life with that supports me? I didn't think I could, and I never thought anyone could support me as much as my family.

But Vienna does.

"And," she says, tracing the hem of her sleeve with one finger thoughtfully. It's almost like she can sense that my desires to be at Crave have an expiration date. "We keep talking like this. We need to communicate about us *and* about work. We can't expect things to stay the same forever."

"You're right," I nod, stroking her cheek. "I'm happy right now but I don't see me in porn forever. I never did. And it's amazing right now that you get to start a career and learn an entire industry with the support of Crave. You're just starting out. Things are always evolving. But right now, we're both so damn lucky."

She wiggles her eyebrows suggestively and says, "Maybe down the road we could start our own toy company. For men only."

My head falls to the side. My beautiful girl and her brilliant mind. Why is this not something I've considered? That could be perfect, a blend of both our talents.

Though my brother and sister each own their own businesses, it's never been a thought or dream of mine. In fact, I always felt like if I scored anything outside of the 9 to 5 that let me be even one fucking iota creative then I'd take it.

"I could be research and development, and you could be testing and modeling." She traces the hem of her top. My heart picks up pace. It's clear to me that she's really thought about this. Finally she looks up at me, and I know exactly what I want.

"Whatever we do, that should be our goal. Working together to create something we're proud of creatively." I know I can't stay at Crave forever, and more than that, I believe Vienna and I could easily work together. We already *know* we can. "We can pursue our careers for as long as it feels right, but we communicate how we're feeling, and when we are ready for a change, we'll do it together. There's a lot still to achieve and learn and enjoy. Especially with *your* new job."

The way her whole body smiles at my words has shit fluttering in my chest. She's proud of herself, and that makes me feel tingly things.

We'll be together while we both work hard at jobs we love. Careers that fulfill, that we're good at, working with wonderful people. In my marrow, nothing has felt more right. Working as-is and merging our talents into something new in the future—a slow dance, a beautiful transition of individual lives to coupled.

"I love you, too. I love that you can talk to me about... everything." She smiles, tracing the crown of my cock through my sweats, tapping the head with the blunt tip of her finger. I let out a smoky groan, take her by the wrist, leaving the blanket on the ground of the deck as I drag her back in.

Inside, I feel the overwhelming need to hear her say all the things I'm so excited about, to prove to me they're real. *We're real.* Because, despite the fact I'm a porn star, this feels too good to be true.

"You're my girl," I whisper. She grins, and I'm tingly again.

"I'm your girl."

"We're gonna work to make us both happy with me at Crave, and my babygirl is going to be the naughty little voyeur that she is, right?"

She bites her bottom lip and rocks to her feet, grabbing my fattening cock again. "Yes, Daddy. I'll be your dirty voyeur and your playmate as much as I can."

"And when you can't?" I question, because she sounds like she has a plan.

She squeezes my shaft, earning a moan from me. "Then you'll come home and connect with me, whatever way that manifests."

She reaches inside my sweats, her bare hand hot against my aching dick, making my spine straighten as she clutches and pumps me. Her lips graze my chin.

I pull back. "I don't know what my dreams look like, Vienna. Fate brought me you, it convinced me to say yes to Aug, which brought you back to me. Now that I have you, I can't wait to see what comes next."

"I may have been fated to find you but you brought me my destiny, Tuck. Opened up a whole world to me. Whatever that future is, I'm so happy that I have someone to do it with. I've never really had that until you."

I arch a brow and try to focus on her words, not the way she softly jerks my cock. But it's impossible. "Right now, I want to watch you take me, as much of me as you can for as long as you can."

I press my hand to hers, applying pressure to my cock. "You ready to get on your knees and be a good girl for Daddy?"

She hums through her smile, and then I take her to my room and feed her every inch of my dick. She traces my veins with her fingers, licking them after, pressing kisses of worship to my head. She tongues my precum, stroking while she sucks, and then when I'm leaking and growling with need, she fits her mouth on my cock and swallows as much as she can.

Her throat tightens around me, her gag reflex fighting to push me out. My fingers tangle in her silky hair, and as much as I want to empty myself down her throat and watch her as I do, I can't come without her.

"Tuck," I groan, sliding my hand beneath her chin to tip her face up. With my cock filling her spread mouth, I groan down at the sight, fiery need zipping down my spine, flooding my groin. "Get Tuck and sit on it while you take me."

She pops off, a thick strand of saliva threading from my head to her mouth. She pulls her finger through it, dropping it on her tongue. "Whatever you say, Daddy."

Goddamn. I've done daddy kink in the studio and it's been fine. But roleplaying with Vienna is insanely fucking hot. I never thought I'd be a daddy guy but if it scratches an itch for her, then fuck yes. Call me Daddy.

She brings the toy back to the room, and suctions it to the ground between her feet. "Did you bring lube?" I ask, conditioned to the question because we use lube at work for everything. It's not always even about lubrication as it is *on-screen sparkle*. Everybody likes glistening cock.

Reaching down, she parts her lips with her fingers, exposing her clit and cunt to me. Shades of pink, arousal swelling her, I moan her name as she sinks down the wide head of the toy. "I'm so wet for you, Tuck, I don't need the lube."

Well, fuck me. "Jesus, Vienna, you're so sexy," I rasp as I slide my hands around her head again, this time using her ears to bring her back to my cock. "You want me to use your mouth?" I ask her, my voice husky and low. Spit pools beneath my dick along the floor as she struggles to deepthroat me. My gaze moves between her wet, pink lips sucking up my cock between her thighs, and her mouth sealed tight around my erection, my veiny shaft moving in and out in hypnotizing strokes.

Glancing over at the windows, I focus not on the glow in the sky outside but in our reflection dancing in the glass.

"Look at what a good girl you are, getting fucked hard in two holes," I growl down to her before I take her off my cock and twist her head. The spit coated crown of my cock smears against her cheek as she turns, and the gasp that echoes between us when she catches sight of us makes me grip the base of my cock.

She turns to face me. "We look so good together."

"We are good together," I tell her before pushing her back down on my dick. When she starts to moan and mewl around my cock, making my balls ache, I know she's close, so I talk her through an explosive orgasm.

"That's right, you were a good girl for me all night. Letting me help you so much. Fucking Daddy so well, then taking all of my cum so deep. You deserve a reward, baby girl. So ride until you come, and I'll fill your mouth till you're overflowing, and make sure to tuck you in *nice and full* tonight."

Her head falls back slightly as her tight fist pumps my base, her mouth suckling at my head as she moans. The vibrations melt down my shaft, tickling my groin, my lower half seizing in urgent need.

She bounces and moans as she sucks and comes, and I find watching her and holding back to be impossible to do together. I keep watching.

"Take every drop Daddy gives you," I howl, the final restraint severs as she reaches down to stroke where Fuck Tuck spreads and fills her.

Urgently I come, blasting in thick, long waves, filling her mouth so much that cum dribbles down her chin, painting her bare breasts in a few ambitious drops. She swallows three times and gets to her feet, still moving her hand up and down my shaft, this time in lazy, sated strokes.

"Before you, I thought doggy-style was wild," she laughs, still fondling my cock. As if she didn't notice until now, she looks down at her hand and my sticky, softening dick.

"Doggy-style can be wild, especially if you're getting double penetrated," I smile, wiggling my eyebrows.

"Two Tucks in the same hole? I don't think that's physically possible," she grins.

We spend the rest of the evening in bed, naked, touching and talking, whispering in the late hours of night, letting our dreams and future marinate in the glow of the city moon.

And I officially feel like the wealthiest human alive, and it has nothing to do with money.

29

Vienna

These are my people.

Though Tuck hadn't intended to ruin any big surprises, when Dalton Fitzgerald contacted me a week after my art show, I knew exactly why.

In an out of body experience, I sat and listened to the CEO of Debauchery Sex Toys offer me a position they created just for me, telling me that they're partnering with Crave & Cure yet again, this time to source the top female adult film actress and turn her into a toy. At that point in the meeting, I learned Augustus had secured Lucy Lovegood in a contract, and that she'd be coming to Crave under special terms. Debauchery wanted her turned into a pocket pussy right away.

It was learning Debauchery's plans that had my mind running off the cuff. I'd explained to Dalton that I'd very much like to have the job, and that I was actually honored.

After much deliberation, a call to the Crave lawyers and a call to Samson to double check, I signed on the dotted line. Then I called Tuck to squeal with delight that I was leading R&D at the leading toy manufacturer in the country.

I'd negotiated that I needed a year at minimum of training before creating anymore designs. Fuck Tuck turned out great, but a pocket pussy is a completely different type of toy and I wanted to get it just right. Mr. Fitzgerald said they are having a lab built at Crave as part of the partnership to make the research process more efficient.

Everybody was able to get on the same page—sign me and promise me lots of research and lab time before having to create, Lucy was fine with the delay and Debauchery and Crave were fine with it.

Something I didn't expect from this industry, and I guess that's the Carnegie judgment still rearing its head—is just how much everyone wants to work and succeed together. Listening to Dalton and Augustus work through potential issues left me blissfully aware of what a fun career lies ahead of me.

And having a lab onsite at Crave meant access to watch Tuck fuck and get fucked at my leisure. What other post-grad career has perks like that?

Debauchery also got me up to speed with the Fuck Tuck progress. The prototypes are doing so well in the test market, it looks like Tuck's cock is going to put us all in a very comfortable position.

Tonight, we're having a family dinner to celebrate.

The Eliot family, Darren and Samson, and me and Tuck.

I stand in front of my bedroom mirror, knowing it's one of the last times. The lease is up in just a few days, and I've already begun tossing my stuff back into the same plastic totes I used years back. I don't have much. Records, clothes, some gems and stones, books. My life before Tucker could fit into less than five totes, and it makes me happier than ever that I'm leaving that life behind.

I sweep my hands down my hips, turning sideways to analyze my profile, hoping that leggings and an oversized turtleneck are appropriate for the restaurant. I have to hide the trail of love bites he left on my skin, purple and knotted. I graze my fingertips over one of the bites and smile at the memory of his mouth latched to my neck, my legs spread wide with his hips sawing in and out of me as he called me his good girl, his beautiful girl, his everything.

I like these love marks.

I love being in love with Tucker. I love being loved by Tucker.

And I can't wait to have our worlds come together at dinner tonight, and to share our good news.

"There she is." Tuck's mom grins, her arms open wide. Tim and Tessa Eliot have flown here twice in the span of two months, and while I'm so glad they are here, I feel bad they're spending their weekend traveling, only to be here with us for a day and a half.

When I express my guilt in Tessa's arms, she puts a splinter of distance between us, beaming at me with green eyes that she gave Tuck. "Tucker paid for the flight—he always does—and anyway, he said you have news to celebrate, so we *had* to be here for you." She strokes her fingers through my hair, and suddenly I feel so... sad.

This is what I've always wanted with my mom. This

tenderness, this eagerness to explore my life and celebrate my achievements together.

I press my hand to hers and fight my wobbling bottom lip to tell her how much she means to me.

"I know we're still new to each other, but I just want you to know that you feel so comfortable and safe to me, and it means so much to me to be supported by you and Tim, Tegan and Theo. Honestly."

She rubs my arm in a way that mother's do, and holds my eyes with earnest sincerity. "It doesn't matter that we're new. Tucker loves you, and you're the first. And we think you'll be the last." She weaves our hands together while grinning. "So we love you, too. We're your family, too."

Tim approaches, saving me from ugly crying at just how touching the moment is. "I can't lie to you, Vienna, but Tuck did send us a text message and fill us in." He opens his arms wide, taking Tessa and myself straight to his chest. He smells like Brut aftershave and warm coffee, and Tessa's perfume clings to my hair, matronly and soothing, and I've never felt more loved.

Tucker's hand wedges between us as he takes my wrist, reclaiming me into his arms. "We're so proud of you," he whispers, dropping the words into my ears for just me. "I love you, baby."

The Eliots are rustling around, looking for purses and shoes as we get ready to head downtown for a nice dinner, and Tucker takes the opportunity to yank me into his room, sliding one of the hanging barn doors closed for a moment of privacy.

"Movers are picking your stuff up tomorrow," he says slowly, memorizing every bit of my eyes as his hands sweep down my hips, warming everything below my waist. I don't have much stuff, but Tucker said he'd hire movers so we can both avoid Madeline. Why taint our happy day if we don't have to? "Are you excited to live together?"

Looping his hands behind my back, he tugs me toward him, and our chests move together as our breathing syncs. "I'm excited to do everything with you," I tell him, because my excitement and happiness dips and dives into every single crevice inside me. Getting groceries, paying bills, being sick, sleeping in, cleaning house—everything seems exciting at the prospect of doing it with Tuck. Life just feels different.

"I'm excited for the mundane, and that's because of you."

He wiggles his brows as he smears his groin into mine. "I'm excited for everything, and that's because of you."

"Are we insanely corny right now?" I grin at him, knowing the answer is yes but happy that it is. Happy, period. And I never realized I wasn't happy before. It's strange how complacency works. It's not like I ever believed I had a great support system, but I never realized I was missing out on so much living. Focused on art and finding success as an artist—I was so tangled in the idea of what it should look like that I closed myself off to opportunities around me.

But not anymore.

At dinner, Samson and Tegan go deep into a legal conversation regarding care of dogs at overnight kennels and whether or not the owner is required to disclose long-term illness to the business owner. I get the feeling, the more I get to know Tegan, that she can strike up a conversation with anyone at anytime.

But I get that vibe from the entire Eliot crew.

They weave seamlessly into conversation with both Darren and Samson, and while dessert is being ordered, they show me yet again where their allegiance is as Darren delivers some tasty news.

"Okay so I have some dessert for you and you better believe me when I say I've been saving this information for right now because it is so damn sweet," he beams, shimmying his shoulders a little to bask in the moment.

Samson's eyes take mine from his spot next to Darren. "I'm gonna second him on this. It's very..." he looks over at his partner, who chooses much more colorful words than himself, and winces as he says, "sweet."

Darren glows and their arms move together beneath the table, likely linking hands. Tegan is grinning as she focuses on Darren, and Tucker's palm is skating and up down my thigh, fingertips applying soft pressure. Theo is next to Tim, and they've both got jovial expressions on their faces, and Tessa has her head propped up with two fists beneath her chin, smile wide.

These are my people.

Darren clears his throat. "Dahlia replaced you," he announces, his eyes scanning the room like he's telling a ghost story.

"A new dust sweeper?" Tuck asks, knowing full well what I left behind. Not much when you look at my horizon.

Darren's lips twitch, the juicy gossip wracking his body, core wobbly as he tempers his voice, exercising slow control as he says, "Yes, a new floor sweeper. And it's Madeline."

"No way," Tegan coos. "Well," she leans back, folding her arms across her chest with supreme satisfaction that floods my belly with warmth. "Karma."

"That girl may need to sweep floors for a while to get her head right," Tessa adds in a motherly tone. "It could do her good."

Tucker presses a kiss to the bottom of my earlobe. "Is it ironic to you?" he asks, sweeping hair off my shoulder as he gazes tenderly at the slope of my neck. I know that look in his eye.

He wants to pound me into the mattress, and as much as I

want that, I think we both know that's not going to happen for another day until his family flies out.

"What?" I reply, a bit breathy from the way he's eating me up with his eyes.

"That *Cookie* is getting her sweet karma," he smiles, eyes flitting between mine. "That the garden of cocks she mocked has earned you a career while she is stuck taking your after school job." He shrugs.

Theo, listening to our conversation, reaches over with a curled up fist which I bump with mine as he says, "That's the way the cookie crumbles."

Tim erupts in laughter and gathers his wine glass, encouraging the rest of us to do the same. He raises his glass, and everyone follows suit. "To Vienna, and her garden of..."—he searches for a restaurant appropriate word—"phallic items!"

We clink to praise Tuck's cock, all of us laughing so hard that our eyes and cheeks are wet from hysterics.

The waiters begin bringing out plates of cheesecakes and mousses as we grab at our composure, and when everyone is quiet and nibbling, oohing and ahhing around the Michelin-award winning dessert, Darren clears his throat.

"I actually didn't get to the best part." He casts a sideways glance at Samson, whose expression confirms there is indeed more tasty tea on the way.

"Dahlia doesn't like Madeline. And she has said to her no less than fifty times already... I wish I had the last girl back. She was so much better than you."

Imagining Madeline being told I am better than her is so sweet, but the happiness that fills me watching the table full of people I love enjoy themselves is so much more filling.

And tomorrow, I'll be moving in with Tuck, and his family will be there to help me unpack and get situated.

All of this because I said yes to casting a cock and being *stuck with Tuck*.

30

Tucker

And I can hardly wait.

...TWELVE MONTHS LATER

We're finishing a scene today. Yesterday was the first part, and today is the second. It's my first scene with the new star, Lucy Lovegood.

The top billing female porn star and the top billing male porn star in a scene together. It's supposed to be big, but it's very different than anything I've done.

Lucy came from a terrible film company called Jizzabelle Studios. They'd somehow roped her into a three-year contract, and did everything they could to make her as miserable as possible along the way. Rumors are that her ex is the head of Jizzabelle, but Lucy is tight-lipped about her personal life.

When Augustus told me he'd signed her months back but that we had to wait for her contract to be up, he'd put a hand on my shoulder and held my eyes for impact, saying, "We have to show her what the good side of this industry is about. Because she's been caged on the bad side too long."

While I didn't do porn before Crave, I do know from the other actors that we have it good. We're treated like actors, not porn stars, and that humanity unfortunately doesn't extend beyond Crave. At places like Jizzabelle, actors are expected to take performance enhancing drugs, not orgasm for hours, and are often even shot up with things to keep them alert and active. It's insane.

Because films from those companies are a thousand times worse than our films. It's like they're doing all those things because that's the old school porn way, but the truth is, sex work is evolving. People want real, they want kink, they want genuine orgasms from real humans.

But Jizzabelle and other studios haven't got the message.

I'm happy for Lucy that she's out of that space. I'm very fucking happy for her.

And today I'm extra happy because Vienna is on set, waiting to speak with Lucy after the shoot. She's been working with Lucy to create the best pocket pussy ever and today Lucy is seeing the first generic prototype.

Until then, she and I have a scene together.

I glance to the edge of the set where Vienna stands, wearing her trademark stained overalls, a white tank top beneath, her long dark hair knotted into braids. She pushes her glasses up the bridge of her nose as she waves excitedly at me, smile so wide that it makes me chuckle. Lucy follows my gaze and sees Vienna, and they exchange a greeting.

"I love your girl," Lucy says to me as she positions herself on the bed, legs spread wide. I hold her eyes and nod as I stroke my fist down my cock, fattening from knowing Vienna is here.

Though Vienna is still hard at work in the lab, learning new techniques and improving her casting skills, she says she's not ready to cast Lucy yet. Still, they've stuck up a friendship on-set. While Lucy has walls up, I'll admit, she seems to lower them a millimeter for my girl.

"Me too," I laugh. "And she is so excited to work with you." Then, because Aug's words always resonate, I add, "We're glad you're here."

"Thanks," she says, shirking off the nicety uncomfortably. "So you plan to stay here? Now that you're in a forever relationship?" she asks, switching gears as she pulls open her silk robe, dropping it on the floor. A crew member scoops it up and disappears. She lotions her chest as I glance back at Vienna, giving her a wink.

She blows me a kiss, and heat crawls up my neck.

"Not forever. But for now, we're both happy. She's loving Debauchery. She really can't wait to cast you, Lucy."

She sighs with traces of hope in her eyes. "That's... awesome. I'm happy for you guys." She looks at her bare body, making sure she's positioned right. "And I can't wait to be cast."

Augustus likely under-embellished Lucy's treatment at Jizzabelle the last three years, because that's the kind of guy he is. He doesn't air your trauma in the wind. In the last six months, I've learned that Lucy is a woman who has been hurt and used; it lingers in every word she speaks. But she's here now at Crave, where we have benefits, mandatory mental health care, mandatory monthly nights together to bond, and so much more.

Crave will help her, I know we will.

"I'd quit if she wanted me to, but it's just not who she is. She understands what we do is work," I say, remembering Vienna's crumpled piece of art in the trash and how I felt when I spread it open. "I know how lucky I am."

Lucy smiles, but it's tempered with sadness. "You really are. That kind of love isn't written in all of our stories."

Interrupting, Aug approaches with Lance at his side. "Mutual masturbation scene, I'd like you both to orgasm, but Lucy I'd like you to come first, Tucker you after."

Lucy swung a deal with Aug that she would be a solo star moving forward, never being penetrated by a man on camera again. She agreed to scenes with men and sex with women, but no more male penetration.

Aug easily agreed and now she's in her third month here, and her videos are more popular than ever.

But like I said, today is our first together.

"Everyone know what to do?" Lance asks as Aug talks to Cohen quietly.

Lucy takes in Cohen, the quietest, kindest guy I've ever met. I think in all the years I've been here, I've never heard or seen Cohen be anything but docile and kind. He's cute as hell, too. Tall, broad shoulders, slim but fit frame, wavy sun-kissed hair.

He's got fucking style to boot, and because I usually slop in here with basketball shorts and a hoodie, I always take note of how well dressed he is.

But the man is quiet and reserved.

He's also damn good at his job. He's here all hours, almost like he's avoiding real life. But the set is always fucking perfect. Everything he's in control of is always immaculately done.

Lucy leans my way, her smoky voice low. "Who's that?"

I've noticed her eyeing him here and there, so she likely knows who he is and what he does. She's asking beyond that.

"Cohen. He's great. I don't know him well but he's extremely kind and great at his job. Keeps to himself."

She nods and a moment later, Lance is motioning for us to

take positions, lights change shades, the slates slam, and we're rolling.

As the first two cameras hover over Lucy's naked body, I look back at Vienna whose cheeks are flushed and lips are held tightly together.

With a wink in my pocket, I turn back to Lucy just as the cameras come my way.

"I love watching you come," I tell her, the scene following two alleged virgins, their fear of premarital sex leading them to a life of mutual masturbation and voyeuristic jerk off sessions. I kind of dig it.

"I can't wait until you're putting that inside of me," she moans, slipping her fingers to her cunt, spreading herself open. She's pink, wet and wide as the camera takes a shot of her rubbing her clit, and I stroke my hand through my hair, giving Vienna our cue.

When she's here, and we've decided we're going to play, she has a cue. A simple stroke of my hand through my hair, and it means turn on your toy.

I won't be able to look back much more, as this part of the scene only lasts a whopping six minutes. But it's enough to get her there, because she always gets there when she watches me on set. Every single time.

Speaking to Lucy but in truth, delivering words I'd predetermined with Vienna off-set, I duck my chin to my chest and drop my voice to a gut-scraping timbre. "I can't wait to bury myself inside you," I groan, tightening my fist at the base, using my other hand to reach beneath myself and tug my full sac.

Vienna edged me last night. Sucked my crown, licked my balls, buried her tongue in my ass as she reached around and stroked me. Teased my nipples too, with her tongue, her teeth, and our set of clamps because she knows they're my Achilles heel.

And she didn't let me come.

We're coming together today, in a scene, and I can hardly wait.

"Show me how you touch yourself when you think of me," Lucy breathes, her arm driving back and forth as she touches herself. But my eyes don't notice the friction between her legs. My eyes drop to my own cock as my thumb strokes along one of the bulging veins, tracing the ridged edge of my crown, then smoothing the pad of my thumb over the slit. I touch myself slowly and deliberately, the way Vienna likes it.

We do this, too, because in the last six months, I'm not sure there's a single stone we haven't *flipped the fuck over.*

Vienna discovering she's a voyeur and that her boyfriend is bisexual had her kicking in sexual exploration doors, Lara Croft style.

Mutual masturbation is just one of the many things that have made it into our normal rotation.

When she jills off for me, she uses the prototype of Fuck Tuck 2 that Debauchery has been working on—with her input. How hot is that? FT2 is prefilled with a fluid mimicking semen in terms of color and consistency, but is formulated with the same ingredients as lube for safety. She drives me wild fucking herself with that thing then making it explode all over her bare body as she wriggles and moans my name. I love when it gets on her glasses, too. *Fuck me.*

In this scene, I'm following Lucy, and Lucy has her own vibe. She puts a toy inside of herself that is imperceptible to the rest of us, and that's what gets her off so quickly. And I can tell by the way she outstretches her bare feet in the satin sheets—that's her *tell*—that she's close.

Tugging my sac and stroking my thick cock, I lick my lips and say the words we've planned. Words that are right for both scenes I'm in.

"Show me how much you want me. Prove to me that you're tortured without this cock. Come with a beg and my name falling off your lips," I grit, dropping my balls to stack my fists on my shaft. Desire coasts down my spine as my knees grow weak, sweat pebbling up on my pecs.

From behind me, I swear I hear Vienna's soft exhales as the toy brings her to her metaphorical knees, her orgasm taking control. But at the same time, Lucy's toes collect the sheet as she moans out my character's name, her cunt seizing closed with the first violent wave of orgasm.

She moans and thrashes and I pump as hard as I can as Cohen, off set, waves the flag, the purple color sending my mind into the "finish" headspace.

"Look at everything I'm gonna pump inside you. Look at all this cum I'm gonna paint your pussy with. I'm gonna empty myself and put a baby in you, just watch," I groan as I twist my hand around my crown several times, bringing my orgasm to the surface. I look at Lucy and see Vienna on my bed, her legs inviting me home.

Lucy moans and I tip my cock up, shooting the first rope up to my shoulder. The next cascades across my pecs and abs, and after a few more strokes, I'm covered in cum, and that's my cue to find Lucy's eyes.

"Yes," she pleads, preparing the viewers for the end of scene, her voice the perfect blend of enticing and raw.

Then, it's over.

A simple scene made so much hotter by having Vienna there. Lucy passes me a towel as I go to reach for one, and I clean up right away.

Vienna's hands come around my waist, her nails tickling me, the contact making my heart pound. "That was so hot," she sighs, her words tickling the back of my ear.

I place my hands on top of hers and sink into our reverse

hug as Lucy slips her robe on and approaches us.

"Hey Vienna." Her smile is wide, giving Vienna more friendliness and sunshine than most of the other men on set.

Vienna weaves our fingers together, stepping to my side, lifting her hand to say hello in return. "Hi Lucy, you were so good up there. I loved it." Her voice ripples with honesty and sincerity.

"Yeah," she says, smiling at my girl as she stacks her hair on top of her head with some claw contraption. "It was fun. You wanna show me the lab here? So I know for the future?"

Vienna practically bounces on her feet with excitement. "Yes! I'd love to!" She rolls to her toes and kisses me on the cheek, next to my ear. "See you later," she offers sweetly, in a tone that has me wishing I were going into a private casting room with her. Over her shoulder, she winks after letting my hand go and I watch Lucy and Vienna disappear down the hallway, the way she and I used to.

After getting dressed, I duck into Augustus's office for a private meeting. Lance is there, collecting sheets of paper from the printer tray, his back to me. With Aug at his desk, I close and lock the door, knowing Lance is likely already aware of what's about to take place.

"I had his help," Aug announces as I take a seat in front of his desk, knees grazing the wood as I lean forward eagerly. Augustus turns his computer screen and begins scrolling through a highly detailed itemized list, color coded.

"I couldn't remember if you wanted to work your way through the United States, or just overseas, so I plotted out the best of both," Aug says, using the tip of his pen to point toward the first item on the list.

"He only had three on his list," Lance says to Aug, speaking of me like I'm not there. But even Lance's offbeat personality cannot steal the wind from my fuckin' sails right now.

Aug ignores Lance and nods to me. "I included the three you wanted in both plans. Did you want to travel outside the United States?"

I make him a face that says *get fucking serious.* "Of course I do. It's an *important* trip. I want to do it big."

He nods. "That's what I thought." He drags his pen to the top of the other list, scrolling once to align it with the screen. Then he proceeds to read me off a list of places both Augustus and Architectural Digest approved, taking me across the United States, around Brazil and the United Kingdom. Oh and France, but of course.

Augustus explains to me why the Ayrton Senna statue in Barcelona is crucial for us to see, and as he does, Lance slides the printer paper my way.

"Facts about all of the places, so you can learn together as you go."

Augustus twists to look at Lance, his face softening. "That was nice of you," he says, and for a second, my gaze flicks between them.

Their relationship is not for me to understand, and that's lucky, because I really don't.

"Thanks, Lancelot," I grin. "I appreciate that."

For the next twenty minutes, Aug walks me through the places we should visit, telling me that when he and Lance traveled for work years back, they saw some of these places. And the whole time, I try to picture Vienna seeing all of these sculptures, visiting all of these places with me.

After securing the time off for both of us, I take all the information given from Aug and Lance, and head out. I stop by the workroom and say goodbye to Vienna, telling her I'll meet her at home.

When I'm home, I call my family, making sure they're still down for the greatest proposal of all time.

Epilogue

Tucker

Marinate, beautiful girl

She cried when I surprised her with the trip. She stared at the plane tickets for a full minute before she realized it wasn't a joke.

And for two whole weeks, we traveled to see some of the biggest, most intense sculptures out there. For Vienna to fill her soul with things that make her feel passionate about art, to remind her of all the different kinds of beauty out there.

She wept with all of her heart when we traveled to Budapest and saw The Shoes on the Danube.

She clung to my shirt, eyes wide in horror when we stood outside the Guggenheim in Bilbao, Spain and took in Maman, the huge spider sculpture that represents both strength and fragility of a mother's role.

We saw Franz Kafka in Prague, Czech Republic, and traveled to France to see Les Voyageurs in Marseille-Fos Port.

And from there, we went to the Eiffel tower. Where we are right now.

In her Converse and jeans, a large puffy coat keeping her upper body snuggly and warm, the gentle wind lifting her dark hair, tossing it around like a kite in a wild sky, she looks more beautiful than ever. Her head tips back as she takes in the tower, the glow twinkling against her glasses.

"Tucker," she breathes, her exhale hovering in a white cloud in front of her as she gazes up in utter amazement. When she finally levels her gaze with mine, I find appreciation in her eyes. "Thank you so much for this. Truly."

She doesn't have to say thank you, but I press a kiss to her temple. "You're welcome, beautiful. You deserve the world." A corny line, but now I know why corny lines exist. Sometimes you're just so in love, you turn into a corny fool. And I'm good with that.

We take photos, and snag some galettes from a street vendor, before slowly making our way back to the hotel. The trip ends in Paris, but what she doesn't know is that I'm taking her to Oakcreek. The annual Christmas tree lighting is going on, and I have something planned.

Better than Paris.

Vienna, groggy from sleeping on the plane, slides into the passenger seat of the car as I load the back with our luggage.

"You care if we make a little pitstop?" I ask, starting the car to get the heat on. Wrapped in my hoodie, sleeves pulled up over her hands, she shakes her head sleepily at me across the cab.

"No problem," she offers through a yawn. She's jet-lagged and honestly, I am too. But right now, adrenaline has me feeling well fucking rested.

"You can go back to sleep, baby girl, I'll wake you up when we're back at our place." *Our place.* That still makes my dick hard.

She curls up in the seat, tipping her head toward the window as her eyes fall closed. I'm totally taking full advantage of her exhaustion because if she stopped to think about it, we're at SFO—San Francisco International airport. Our place is a mere twenty minutes from here, forty tops if we're fighting commuters.

But she's asleep before we even pull out of the parking lot, and for that, I'm grateful. Because I want this to be a surprise. Bigger than the trip. Bigger than Paris.

I get my phone out, glancing her way to make sure her eyes are still closed, then text my Dad.

> Be there in an hour. Did you get all the roses I sent?

> Son, I can't even see your mother in the living room because there are so many long-stemmed red roses.

> Drive carefully, we'll head downtown to Main Street now.

> Thanks. See you soon.

I stash my phone away and head to Oakcreek, the quaint, dreamy little town I grew up in. The very same type of town

405

Vienna said she always dreamed of seeing. She grew up watching romance movies on cable, and my hometown easily embodies all of the things she said she loves.

Forty-six minutes later (I guess my nerves gave me a lead foot), I nudge Vienna awake then traipse through the light layer of snow on the sidewalk to get to her side of the car. She grins, and even though she's exhausted, she looks as beautiful as ever.

"Where are we?" she asks through a yawn, her breath hanging in the air, white and thick. I loop my arm around her, and we walk down the sidewalk. I parked a street away, where it's dark, so the entire Main Street would be part of the surprise.

"Somewhere you always wanted to go," I whisper to her, placing a kiss on her temple as my chest tightens with anticipation. We turn the corner, and Vienna stops in the slushy snow, her eyes wide behind her frames.

"Oh my god," she faces me, the tip of her nose already pink from the chill. "We're in Oakcreek?"

I grin and she squeals, her eyes sweeping over the shops before they hang on the thirty-foot fir in the center of the road. It's strung up with thousands of lights, kids all around, some clinging to their mothers' hands, as people take photos in front of it and make magical Christmas wishes. It's only November, but we do it early in Oakcreek. Tonight is the first night the tree went up. It's a night to remember in our small town. Everyone comes out, helps with the lights, eats sugary treats from street vendors and has a good time.

"I can't believe we're here!" she sighs as she takes it all in.

"Well in my defense we would have visited sooner if I could have dragged you away from the lab or if my family would have stopped descending on us unannounced to abuse the free room and board with Penthouse views." I chuckle. "But I couldn't finish this world tour without visiting the place that feeds *my* soul. And I hope it feeds yours, too."

Tonight won't be just a night to remember. It will be one we never forget.

"Look up at the star. Check out the whole tree. Isn't it fucking awesome?" I ask, urging her forward. She steps toward it like she's walking into a dream and goddamn do I like that she already loves Oakcreek and gets to experience it at its best. With her gazing up at the tree in awe, I turn and give the signal to no one, knowing *they're* watching.

My family and her friends, who have waited around the area inside little soap shops and quaint coffee houses for the last hour, crowd in behind me as I fall to my knee, waiting for her to turn around after taking in the beauty of the large fir.

And when she finally turns around, her eyes drop to me at her feet, hand dropping across her chest. Lips trembling, she lifts a hand to yank hair away from her face, and that's when she notices.

Darren and Samson arm in arm, Tegan and Tripp, my folks, and Theo on the other side. They're each holding a dozen red roses and her eyes fill with tears as she takes in the moment, centered in the heart of my perfect smalltown. We are surrounded by *our family*. I wish her parents had said yes when I invited them, but what I know in my bones is that it's their loss, not ours. I will spend a lifetime protecting and supporting my wife, and so will every other person that is here for us now

"Vienna Carnegie," I start, my voice shakier than ever before. Dad presses his hand to my shoulder, and I have the courage to continue. I don't know why I'm so nervous. I know Vienna loves me; I know she'll say yes. But still, energy sweeps through me, my hands trembling around the little blue velvet box. "That freeform sketch class changed my life. And you were part of the reason for that, so when I had the opportunity to see you again, I took it. And for some reason, the universe is on my side. Because you came to Crave. You took the job. And you let your walls down to let me in. And dammit, Vienna, being with you is the only place I ever want to be. Forever."

She tips her glasses up, fog from her heated tears making it hard to see. Smiling, she wipes away tears, and rubs beneath her nose as she inhales a shaky breath.

"Marry me," I whisper. "Marry me and make me the luckiest man in the entire world."

Her eyes scan my family members, ending on Darren and Samson. When she brings her gaze back to me, a tear slips through her lashes, and she drops to her knees at my level, letting me wipe it away.

"Yes," she whispers.

Everyone erupts into cheers around us, and when I say everyone, I mean all of Oakcreek. People have gathered— Delilah, the deli owner, and her brother Mars and his husband Dave, Mrs. Dawson, the seamstress, even the ninety-five-year-old George Wilson who owns the watch repair shop. Everyone comes out, crowding the sidewalks, wearing smiles, some even tearing up. Their phones are out and clapping ensues. We get to our feet and I take the ring from the box, turning it to show her.

She wiggles her ring finger at me as I slide it on. Holding it up to the giant Oakcreek Christmas tree, she beams up at it, smiling and crying.

"The trip was so amazing, but being back here in your

hometown, you proposing here," she shakes her head, still looking at the rock, still processing.

"I thought about proposing in Paris," I tell her softly as the tree lights twinkle against her glasses. "But I remembered what you said about wanting to find a town that resembles Hallmark movies." We both look around us, taking it in. I think I know everyone around us by name, and our annual Christmas tree-lighting always brings everyone out. The Edison lights strung from building to building, cast a romantic glow on our moment.

"And I wanted to come here. I wanted to see where you grew up. And..." she looks around at all the smiles, all the happiness that exists for her. "This is perfect. It's better than anything I could have ever dreamed of, more than I ever could have expected."

At her words, I almost cry. Giving someone exactly what they want just hits different. Especially when you'd end the world for them, but don't have to. Because all they want is love.

"I can't believe I'm getting married to you, Tucker," she breathes, turning to fall into my open arms. I hold her tight to me, our loved ones snapping pictures quietly.

"It's an honor to marry you, Vienna," I admit, sealing the engagement with a kiss. She takes my face in both hands, holding me like her prize, the way I've longed to be held. Nothing has ever felt so right.

"Vienna Eliot," she tries out as we hug beneath the platinum glow. "Sounds good, doesn't it?"

I kiss the tip of her nose. "Nothing has ever sounded better." And I mean it.

Vienna

...TWO YEARS LATER

"And is that what you're interested in, or are you looking to launch a predesigned line?" I hold my smile in place as I watch the man churn through the decisions I've set forth for him.

He scans the price sheet again, and looks over at the starlet he's brought in with him. "What are your thoughts? Are you set on having a line specific to your body, or could we buy a premade line and just rebrand it?"

She reaches for one of the prototypes in the center of the table, and slips her fingers inside the opening. Fingering the pocket pussy with a curious expression on her face, she looks at me. Still knuckle deep, she asks, "Can we change anything about what's currently produced or is it this?"

"Pre-existing stock would be as is. After our first line, Fuck Tuck, took off a few years ago, we mass produced the safety net and second-in-line prototypes for our sister company, but they were sold and since we hold the patent and rights, the stock returned to us. It can't be altered. All packaging of course can be tailored to you and we have options for you to include additional accessories. Those would be customizable." I lift the spec sheet from the table and slide it to them. "These are the test market reports. Everything in this line performed very well."

"A minute?" The man asks, and I nod. I get to my feet and move around the table, stepping into the hall. Outside, my husband waits with a cardboard cup of coffee, and a gorgeous smile.

"Mrs. Eliot," he growls, pulling me into a coffee-flavored kiss. "How's it going in there?"

I teeter a hand between us as we separate, taking the coffee from his hand. "Okay. They're not sure so they're taking their time."

"Are they thinking about another company or?" Tucker asks, letting his sentence die on the vine because there is no company better.

I started with Debauchery and I'm still here. With a few years under my belt, I'm now credited with Fuck Tuck and Love, Lucy, the pocket pussy that outsells all others. I'm the thriving head of artistry and R&D here, and I'm loving it.

Though recently. Tuck and I were offered a buy-in by Dalton. He'd said, with my creative skills, and Tuck as a spokesperson, the company felt good about partnering with us to make a sister company, letting the Eliots spearhead. It's still a trip that *Tuck and I are the Eliots.*

Debauchery wanted to launch us as real partners, and give us our own outlet. With our own company being dangled in front of us, I have to admit, I'm excited.

I love it here, and I think we've got what it takes to launch a new line. And being with Debauchery and Crave while we do it makes it that much sweeter.

"No, I think the guy's just trying to please his actress but keep the bottom line in mind," I tell him, rubbing the tip of my nose to his. "Are you thinking about Dalton's offer?"

The offer is new, made to us just a month ago, and we've been talking about it randomly off and on ever since. Truthfully, we can say no. But neither of us want to. And I've seen the deep in thought dips between Tuck's brows lately.

He's not just thinking about Dalton's pitch. He's brewing a pitch of his own.

"I am. I'm thinking it's perfect time for me to go half time at Crave. Maybe even less."

I cock a brow. "Really? You feel ready for that? You won't get bored? I mean, while we're in the R&D phases on any new line, there won't be a lot for you to do."

The smile that washes over his face makes my belly burn

with excitement. "I was thinking of other ways I could stay busy."

"Yeah?" I smile, because I know. I know though we've yet to discuss it. I feel his answer in my veins, because my husband is a family man at his core. In his heart.

"I'll be at home with the baby. A stay at home dad."

I grin. "Oh yeah? You got it figured out, huh? And I'm not even pregnant."

He grabs my ass. "I can solve that easily. And yeah, I have thought of it." He finds my mouth with his, and the kiss he delivers is full of emotion and depth, reflecting the thought he's put into the topic at hand. My chest tightens with all the love he puts in, so much that sometimes I think I'll explode into heart confetti. "You keep working on that career of yours, you beautiful little badass," he grins, filling me with pride. "And I'll go into Crave for whatever Aug really wants me on, but otherwise, I'll stay home with the baby..." he trails off, his smile widening. "*Kids*, I'll stay home with the kids. And if the new line we launch together at Debauchery is a huge hit, who knows, maybe I just moonlight as a creative at Crave and hang up the name Tucker Deep."

"Tucker," I breathe, tears stinging my eyes.

He wants a family with me more than he cares to continue as a star, and that has me ready to go to bed right this second. "I love that," I whisper, kissing him to seal his words, to turn them into promises. Because I've only known the plan for a minute, but it's so perfect, I have to have it.

"We can tell Dalton after our board meeting later." Placing my hand on his chest, I lean in and kiss him.

With the first big check from Fuck Tuck royalties, Tucker suggested we make a big investment, in both real estate and business.

We bought the museum that Dahlia ran. We made the

owner an offer—double the worth—and they greedily accepted. Then I fired Dahlia and made Darren the curator. I let Darren decide about Madeline and last I heard, she's still sweeping floors. It makes no difference to me how her fate plays out. I'm just happy Darren finally has the job he's always dreamed of having. And that we could help him with it.

We're on the museum society board now, ensuring better practices are in play when it comes to getting new, young artists into formal show settings. We host artist showcases and invite companies from all industries to inspire artists to consider non traditional career pathways. Obviously we don't just invite porn companies. In fact our latest success was an Aquarium who hired a grad student to design a living coral reef art installation. It's pretty cool.

It means a lot to me that all artists have that opportunity, and therefore, it means the world to Tucker, too.

"You still coming to the board meeting?" I ask, dancing my eyebrows playfully. He reaches around and swats my ass over my black pencil skirt.

"Of fucking course."

SIX MONTHS
We attend a Debauchery/Eliot toy line meeting then retreat to Crave to finish up loose ends, but end up closing and locking the door to my office.

The *soundproof* door. Because on an adult film company set, there are many distractions.

With Fuck Tuck stuck to the office door, my saliva dripping

from it as I bob on it, Tucker's fingers grip my hips as he fucks me hard from behind.

"Fill me up, Daddy," I moan before sucking the slobbery toy back into my mouth. The soft silicone fills my throat, and I gag around it, refusing to come off. He loves to come deep inside me when I'm deepthroating Fuck Tuck. It makes him come so hard. Gasoline to a match, I swear.

"Oh my beautiful fucking girl," he growls, his timbre sharp and jagged as his orgasm lurks around the corner. "Daddy's gonna breed you so good. Gonna fill this sweet little pussy full of cum. And I'm gonna use that toy to keep it in you all night. I'm gonna put a baby in you tonight."

He thrusts his hips, the head of his cock putting pressure on my g-spot, making me writhe. I suck more of the cock on the wall, my pussy tightening as he drops a heavy palm across my ass.

"That's right, suck me and fuck me, let me stuff your cunt full, baby girl," he growls, egging on my orgasm. But it doesn't take much. With my full mouth and pussy burning from the way he tunnels me in unrelenting, powerful strokes, my belly tightens and my breath seizes.

"Tuck!" I shout before I'm taken down by seismic waves of pleasure, my cunt throbbing and spasming all around his length, milking him, drinking him down, needing his cum.

As soon as I come, he follows, grabbing my hip with one hand and shoulder with the other as he shoves his cock as deep inside me as he can. His balls assault me as he thrusts in tiny, hard pumps, fucking me through his release.

My insides warm as he fills me with cum, and knowing what I'm supposed to do, I pull Fuck Tuck off the door and hand it back to him.

When he's done thrusting three days of cum inside of me, he slides out with a groan. The first hot dribble down my inner thigh is collected with the head of the toy, and then I'm full again as he pushes the toy as far inside me as he just was.

"Marinate, beautiful girl," he whispers, smoothing his palms over the bare globes of my ass. Then, with a hand on the dildo, he takes my hand and leads me to the couch.

He guides me to lie down, taking a seat on the edge of the couch next to me. "This could be it," he smiles, looking like an actual god written about in text books as sweat glides over his disciplined chest and belly.

"I think it is," I say, crossing my fingers with a grin.

Tucker is a natural caring partner. And through the relationship I've built with his family, I've learned that I'm nurturing and patient. And together, I believe we will be exceptional parents.

"I'm going to go get you some snacks and water. Don't get up. Soak me up," he teases, and I dreamily watch his perfect body disappear beneath jeans and t-shirt. He leaves the office, closing the door behind him, and I lie there, in my office, at the company I own and create art at, with a belly full of what I hope to be a baby with the man I love.

I smile, thinking how fucking lucky I am that I got stuck with Tuck in the first place.

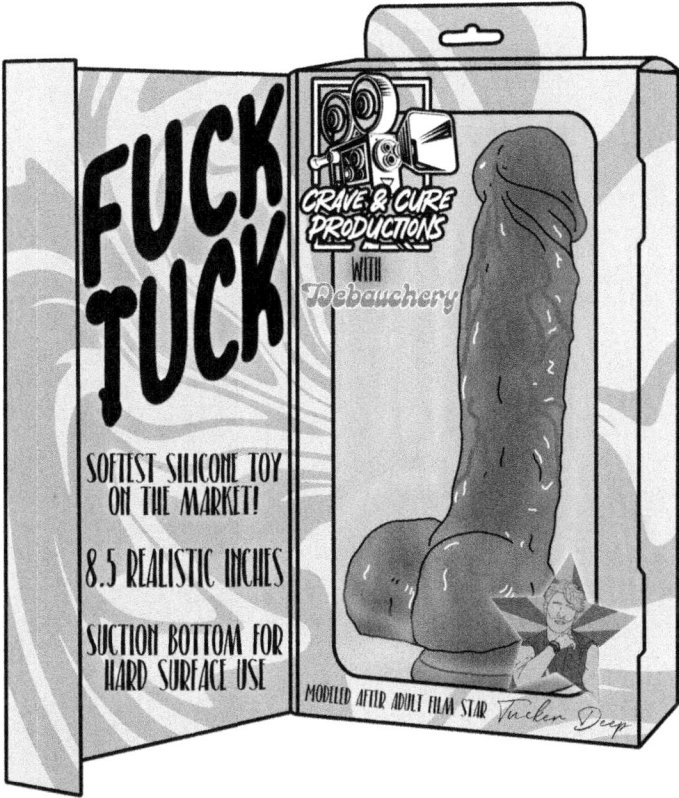

FUCK TUCK

SOFTEST SILICONE TOY
ON THE MARKET!

8.5 REALISTIC INCHES

SUCTION BOTTOM FOR
HARD SURFACE USE

CRAVE & CURE PRODUCTIONS
WITH
Debauchery

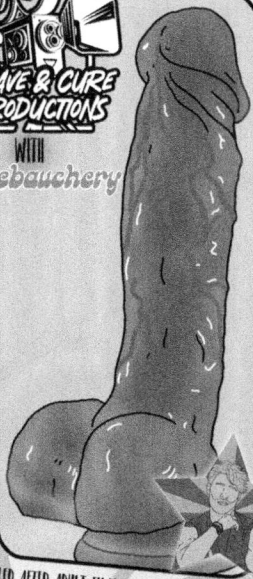

MODELED AFTER ADULT FILM STAR *Tucker Deep*

Acknowledgments

Laura, my editor, my friend, one of my very favorite people. Thank you for another wonderful experience.

Randi and Jes. My missing pieces, my main squeezes, my favorite humans, my girlfriends. Thank you both for literally every single thing you say and do. I love you both so much.

To my husband, for everything.

About the Author

Daisy Jane pens everyday people with exceptional sex lives. Her books are exclusive to Amazon. This is her 24th novel.

She lives in California with her husband of 15 years and their two daughters.

When she's not writing contemporary romance with kink, she enjoys true crime, hiking, the outdoors, coffee, pottery, reading, and music.

Follow Daisy everywhere for bonus content, teasers, freebies, and more.

Also by Daisy Jane

CRAVE & CURE PRODUCTIONS

Stuck With Tuck (friends-to-lovers romance)

Patreon

I write erotic novellas over on my Patreon. So if you like my writing style but want something shorter in length, I release a new chapter every week.

Also, as a Patron, you'll receive eArcs of my new release up to one week before the ARC team.

You'll also have access to commissioned NSFW art featuring your favorite heroes and heroines from my books, Men of Paradise and Wrench Kings included.

You'll get access to everything in my one and only tier.

Come on, hold my hand.

Patreon.com/DaisyJane

(Content 18+)

Printed in Great Britain
by Amazon

25243149R00249